P9-DHN-636
PINO

RAVE REVIEWS FOR ELAINE BARBIERI'S PREVIOUS BESTSELLERS:

DANCE OF THE FLAME

"Readers will find themselves captivated!"

—*Romantic Times*

TATTERED SILK

"A powerful story that evokes every human emotion possible...pure reading pleasure...a must read."

—*Rendezvous*

WINGS OF A DOVE

"A magnificent love story." —*Rave Reviews*

DEFIANT MISTRESS

"Ms. Barbieri's wonderful writing is a marvelous mingling of sensuality, passion, and adventure."

—*Romantic Times*

UNTAMED CAPTIVE

"A five-star read! Elaine Barbieri has proven that romance is well and alive!"

—*Affaire de Coeur*

Other *Leisure Books* by Elaine Barbieri:
DANCE OF THE FLAME

"Elaine Barbieri is an absolute master of her craft!"
—Romantic Times

THE QUEEN OF HEARTS

"You knew I saw you on the street this mornin', and you knew I've been watchin' you since I came in tonight. I didn't miss the performance you gave for my benefit. You enjoy dealin' cards...and you cheat. You also enjoy playin' with the emotions of men. Do you cheat there, too?"

Drawing back spontaneously, furious when she was unable to escape, Honesty spat out, "You are a cold bastard—just like everybody says you are!"

"You're wrong, Honesty. I'm anythin' but cold when it comes to you."

Realizing that the situation was rapidly slipping out of her control, Honesty grated, "Let me go." Wes ignored her. Not wishing to betray the bent of their conversation, Honesty forced a smile, repeating, "I said, let me go."

"What's the matter? Things aren't goin' the way you thought they would?" Wes drew her closer. "Tell me what you really want from me, Honesty." His voice deepened. "Tell me, because I know what I want from you."

ELAINE BARBIERI

DANGEROUS

VIRTUES

LEISURE BOOKS  NEW YORK CITY

A LEISURE BOOK®

October 1996

Published by

Dorchester Publishing Co., Inc.
276 Fifth Avenue
New York, NY 10001

Printed in the United States of America.

To Evelyn Favati.
You were my mother and my dearest friend, Mom.
You'll be with me always.

Honesty

Part One
The Beginning
1867

. . . all the past is but the beginning
of a beginning . . .
—H. G. Wells

Chapter One

A spring storm howled, battering the canvas walls of the wagon that rocked and swayed along the isolated Texas trail. The cumbersome vehicle groaned and shuddered under the assault of the pounding rain, dropping into a cavernous rut to tilt precariously for endless moments before rocking upright once more.

Inside the wagon, Justine Buchanan's genteel features tightened with anxiety as the fevered moans of her children became frightened shrieks. Her tension did not abate when their wails subsided at last and the wagon resumed its slow progress onward.

Justine scrutinized her daughters' flushed faces. Honesty . . . Purity . . . Chastity . . . her three beautiful little girls. She had named them after three of many virtues she hoped they would exemplify when they grew to maturity. At ages four, five, and six, however, they were her rambunctious angels, as different in temperament as they were in appearance—unique unto themselves, despite their youth and closeness in age. Yes, angels who were too young to be displaced from the only home they had ever known, only to be cast into this uncertain hell which now enveloped them.

Justine brushed aside tears. She glanced upward nervously at the canvas roof shielding them from the elements as another fierce gust shook the wagon and raised the children's cries once more.

"There, there . . . Don't be frightened, girls." Speaking softly in an attempt at comfort, Justine stroked each of her daughters' cheeks in turn, her own fear mounting at the acute heat she felt there.

"I'm hot, Mama . . ." Eyes that were intensely blue met Justine's as Honesty croaked, "I'm thirsty. My stomach hurts."

"I'm thirsty, too."

"Me, too."

Justine almost smiled. Two little echoes—so typical. Her daughters were extremely close despite the childish squabbling that often prevailed between them. They were so close that she had sometimes been at a loss to ascertain if the duplication of physical complaints, often occurring when one of them was sick, was caused by sibling empathy or true illness.

Justine's inclination to smile faded. This time, however, there was no doubt. Her daughters were sick—all three of them. They were *very* sick.

A slow panic invaded Justine's senses. She dared not allow herself to think how high her girls' temperatures had risen, and what the result would be if they did not reach a doctor soon. Their playmate, little Sarah Ann Payne, had died of a similar fever shortly before they left home three weeks earlier.

Sarah Ann had been only five.

"Mama, my throat—"

"I know, Honesty." Justine interrupted her daughter's hoarse whisper in an effort to forestall the inevitable echoes to follow. "Your Papa's doing his best to get you to a doctor. The storm is slowing us up, but we'll reach a town soon. Just a little longer, dear."

"My throat hurts too, Mama."

"Mine, too."

"Hush, girls." Justine admonished the children gently as she pressed a cup to their lips, each in turn. Their coughing and sputtering as they attempted to drink caused her own throat to tighten. It was useless. Her daughters hadn't been able to swallow any more than a sip of water in days.

Another violent gust and the wagon lurched unexpectedly. In the confusion of frightened cries and fevered moans, Justine did not realize that the wagon had come to a halt until a damp blast of air swept over her, snapping her gaze up toward the rear, where the separated flaps revealed Clayton Buchanan's rain-soaked figure outlined against the fury of the storm. Water ran in rivulets from the broad brim of her husband's hat onto his oilskin-clad shoulders as he scrutinized their children with obvious concern. When he looked up at her at last, his weathered, unshaven face was haggard and touched with an element that set her heart to an accelerated pounding.

Her emotions in tenuous control, Justine raised her voice over the unrelenting din of the storm.

"What's wrong, Clay?"

No response.

"Clay?"

* * *

Numbed from the day-long misery of rain-soaked clothing and exhaustion, Clay assessed his daughters' conditions more closely. They were sick, dangerously so. And he was powerless to help them. This was not the way it was supposed to be.

Frustration flashed vivid pictures across Clay's mind, conjuring up the day eight years earlier when he had slipped his ring onto Justine's finger. He remembered the love that had shone in the incredible blue of her eyes. He recalled that the future had appeared wonderfully bright, despite the rumblings of war, and that his hopes and dreams had seemed to merge into reality in that sacred moment when they became man and wife. A second-generation Texan, he had wanted nothing more than to raise the children Justine would bear him on the beloved Texas soil his father had so proudly bequeathed him.

Then the war . . . Justine had shared his patriotic fervor, and he had not hesitated when the call had come for him to fight for Texas and the rights of the Confederacy. He had seen Justine occasionally during the interminable, difficult years that ensued—only long enough, it seemed, to produce two sisters for his beloved first-born daughter, Honesty. The strain of separation and the pain of war had been made bearable only by his unshakable faith in the righteousness of the cause for which he fought—and by his unyielding certainty that the Confederacy would emerge victorious.

Clay's dark eyes grew briefly moist. He was certain of very little now. He had returned home at war's end still suffering the effects of grievous wounds that had refused to heal, only to find that his home and his land were his no longer.

Carpetbaggers.

It had been more than he could bear to see the land

he loved in the hands of those unscrupulous vultures.

Fully recovered at last, he had been determined to put the anguish of the past behind him by seeking his fortune in the gold fields and starting anew. Equally determined never to be separated from his wife and daughters again, he had packed up everything he had left in the world and started out. Life had held promise again, until—

"Clay, please, tell me what's wrong."

Justine's question resounded in Clay's mind. With one storm after another impeding their progress almost from the beginning of the journey, *everything* was wrong. Unable to withstand the stress of badly deteriorated trails, the wagon had broken down the second week out. Shortly afterward, the lead horse in his team had become sick, delaying them further. Then his daughters had come down with a fever.

"Clay . . ."

"The girls are worse, aren't they?"

"They're . . . They need a doctor . . . soon."

A moment's silence passed between them as Justine stared at Clay. Her eyes were brimming. Justine's eyes were beautiful—great, round orbs with dark lashes that contrasted vividly with her fair hair. They were mirrors of her soul that glowed with the love and simple decency within.

Many said his eldest daughter, Honesty, had inherited her mother's eyes because of their similarity of color, but he knew that wasn't so. Although as large and brilliant as her mother's, Honesty's eyes were provocatively slanted, with incredibly thick black lashes emphasizing a sparkle that revealed her dauntless personality. He saw in Honesty's coloring and delicacy of feature the image of a beloved Irish ancestor, a grandmother he had never met but of whom his mother had spoken so often and so lovingly in his youth that he had grown to love her as well. He remembered his mother's lilting brogue as she described her mother as being "comely beyond compare, with hair as black as the devil's heart and eyes as blue as the heavens."

He had repeated his mother's words often to Honesty, tugging playfully at her silky black braids. He knew she felt somehow special when he did that, and he was glad . . . because she was special.

Honesty had fulfilled his expectations by growing more beautiful every day and by the quick-wittedness and fearlessness of her irrepressible spirit. She would be a woman to reckon with when she was grown, he was sure. And if she was strong-willed almost to a fault, a trait she had also inherited from the great-grandmother his mother had described with such warmth, he could not help feeling that same, unyielding tenacity would serve her well one day.

It had never ceased to amaze him how different his daughters were, in so many ways. In direct contrast with Honesty's vibrant coloring, his second daughter, Purity, was pale-haired and light-eyed, like her mother's side of the family. Aside from the strip of freckles that covered the bridge of her pert nose, Purity was almost angelic of countenance, an appearance that was vastly misleading, since she was the most mischievous of the three—a little imp who was both a trial and a joy to her mother and him.

And then there was Chastity, his youngest, whose resemblance to him, with her red hair, hazel eyes, and sometimes overly sober expression, was so keen that it was obvious, even to himself. She was a cuddler, a little lap-dog who had trailed lovingly at his heels from the moment she could walk, and he cherished her.

But to his mind it was Honesty who shone most brightly in his trio of stars. Her quick, dazzling smile lit up his heart. It pained him that he had not seen that smile for many days, since fever had dimmed her eyes and—

"Clay, you're frightening me. Please answer me!"

The anxiety in Justine's tone snapped Clay back to the present at the same moment that a crack of lightning lit up the stormy sky behind him. The clap of thunder that followed delayed his response a moment longer, allowing him respite from speaking the words he dreaded to utter. When he could delay no longer, Clay responded over the roar of the tempest surrounding them.

"We've reached a crossing but it's flooded. It isn't safe. We have to find a better one or . . ."

"Or what?"

"Or we'll have to wait until the river goes down."

"Until it goes down?" A thread of desperation entered Justine's voice. "It's still raining! How long will that take?"

"It could be another few days, maybe three or four—"

"But the girls need a doctor now!"

"It isn't safe to cross, Justine."

"Clay . . ."

"There's nothing I can do."

If he lived to be one hundred, Clay knew he would never forget the weight of those words, or the pain that struck his heart at the sight of the single tear that slipped from his wife's brimming eyes to trail down her pale cheek.

In that moment he knew that he would find a way to cross the river—somewhere, somehow.

* * *

Deafening booms of thunder resounded, shaking the earth. Lightning followed, cracking across the darkening sky, releasing another deluge to pelt the battered earth below.

No relief from the storm . . .

At the reins as the wagon lumbered onward and afternoon rolled into night, Clay ignored the chill that had begun to set into his bones. He chose not to think of the saturated clothing beneath his oilskins, or the hands that had become so numb, he could no longer feel the reins. Instead, he squinted, staring at the riverbank along which he drove.

A whimpering cry from the wagon behind him, almost indiscernible over the fury of the storm, turned Clay briefly in its direction. It had been several hours since he had left the flooded crossing behind, but the moment was still clear in his mind. Also undeniably clear, although Justine had not said the words, was the truth that if they did not find a doctor soon, his daughters might not survive.

Damn . . . damn . . . he should have known! He should have been forewarned when they entered country where rain was more frequent and he had seen the swollen condition of the several small streams they had passed. He knew those streams had their headwaters in the Staked Plains and that their condition was an intimation of recent rains to the west of their route. He should have realized that flooded conditions might prevail!

But then, he had not expected that his daughters would become so ill and that an immediate crossing might become a matter of life or death.

Realizing that his trembling had no relation to the weather's chill, Clay struggled for control. This uncharted river, probably an insignificant stream under normal conditions, was an impediment he had not anticipated several days earlier when he had mapped a new route toward a town several miles to the west where he had been certain they would find a doctor. There was no ferry crossing because there would ordinarily be no need for one. He had made a mistake with his attempted shortcut, and the mistake was a bad one, for which his daughters were now paying.

Abruptly aware that his lingering self-reproach served no constructive purpose, Clay resolutely forced it aside. He had made mistakes before, but he had always found a way to correct them. He was determined that this time would be no exception. He would find a way to get them across the river—soon.

But determination aside, the storm continued.

And the flooded river raged.

Justine stirred. She was uncomfortable, her body stiff and aching as she opened her eyes to see the first gray light of dawn penetrating the dark interior of the wagon. Clay, his stubbled face weary beyond measure even in sleep, lay motionless beside her. She remembered that he had pushed onward the previous evening until it had grown too dark to continue any longer. He had then entered the wagon too exhausted to speak and had moved directly to his daughters' side to stare silently at their wan faces as they slept. Too tired to eat, he had stripped off his wet clothing and collapsed into an exhausted sleep minutes later. She had lain down beside him then, needing the comfort of his strong body warm against her. She had needed it because she had never loved him more than at that moment, and because she had been uncertain what the next day would bring.

Her sleep-drugged mind slowly clearing, Justine

glanced toward her daughters where they lay side by side in the limited space afforded them. They were so still, so devoid of movement . . .

Fear suddenly stealing her breath, Justine sat up abruptly—just as Purity twitched in her sleep. Her other daughters' moans were the most welcome sounds she had ever heard, and she closed her eyes briefly with a silent prayer of thanksgiving. Her girls had made it through another night.

"Justine." Justine turned at the sound of Clay's voice. She was about to speak when he raised his finger to his lips with a single word. "Listen."

Justine listened.

Silence.

Sudden realization.

The rain had stopped!

Almost unwilling to trust her ears, Justine slipped to the rear of the wagon and looked out.

It was true! The storm *had* stopped! The river would go down now, and they'd be able to cross! They'd find a doctor then, and all would be well, she knew it!

Turning back to her husband with a sob, Justine threw herself into his arms.

It had taken most of the morning, but he had found a spot where the flooded river narrowed and the water appeared less turbulent.

Clay looked up again to assess the brilliant blue of the cloudless sky. As if in recompense for its failure to appear for countless days, the sun had baked the muddied landscape with unrelenting heat since early morning, and its drying effect was already obvious.

A bell of caution rang in Clay's mind, tempering the hope rapidly rising there. It reminded him that a clear sky overhead did not mean that the rain had stopped to the west of them, where sudden, excessive downpours were not uncommon at that time of year. He knew that flash floods were occasionally the result, and that in a matter of seconds the river could again become a maelstrom of churning waters which would prevent crossing.

Clay considered that thought. His decision made, he turned toward Justine where she stood on the riverbank a short distance away. She was staring at the water in a familiar pose of silent contemplation, her hand tightened into a fist around the locket she wore. The locket was gold, heart-shaped, and inscribed with her name. He had given it to her on the day he asked her to be his wife. He knew she cherished it as a symbol of his love and that she somehow gained comfort from holding it in times of stress. Each of his daughters wore a similar locket inscribed with her name—a gift of love from him on the day of her birth. His girls were particularly proud of their lockets because they were copies of the one their mother wore, and because they were from him.

Justine turned toward him as he started to speak.

"This is the best spot we've passed all day. The water level has dropped a bit, but we can't be sure how long that will last, so we'd better take our chance now. I want you to wait here with the wagon while I ride across and check things out."

"Are you sure you should? The current looks so strong. Maybe we should just . . ."

Justine's voice trailed away as she held his gaze. Her pale hair was windblown, her refined features drawn and tight with concern; her eyes were darkly ringed, and she looked exhausted beyond words, but her gaze completed her thoughts in silent eloquence. She loved him, and she was worried about him. To his mind, she had never looked more beautiful than at that moment.

"Justine . . . darlin' . . ." Clay slipped his arm around his wife and drew her close. "I'm not sure of anything right now except that we have to get across. Don't worry. Big Blue's a powerful swimmer, and I'm going to let him do all the work. If it looks like things are getting out of hand, I'll turn him around and come back."

Justine pressed closer. "I . . . if the girls weren't so sick, I wouldn't let you take the chance, no matter what you said."

"If the girls weren't so sick, you wouldn't get an argument out of me. I'd stay right here with you." Clay smiled reassuringly. "Don't worry, darlin'."

Releasing her, Clay mounted and urged his horse into the river. Big Blue balked unexpectedly upon entering the water. Nervous tremors shook the powerful animal's frame before he finally moved forward. Clay spurred him on, sensing the gelding's mounting fear as the animal shuddered and snorted, struggling to maintain forward momentum when he sank to mid-chest in the rapids. He felt the horse's panic and held his breath for an endless moment before the stalwart beast surged forward with a supreme effort and began making progress against the current.

Emerging on the sandy soil of the opposite bank minutes later, Clay turned to wave triumphantly at Justine. Her smile flashed as she waved in return and elation surged. He had beaten this river, and he would beat the odds against him! He would deliver his wife and daughters to a new life where all the hardships they had suffered would be put forever behind them. Life would be good again! He was certain of it!

Confidence renewed, Clay gave his mount a nudge, and started back into the water.

Justine looked up at her husband as he stood on the wagon beside her and placed the reins in her hands. She knew he was as tense as she as he repeated, "Remember, keep the team moving forward once you get into the river. I'll stay in front to guide you across. The current gets strong midway, but there shouldn't be any problem as long as I'm leading the team."

Justine nodded. Her husband had risked his life for his daughters and her when he had gone into the river minutes earlier. There could be no greater proof of his love. He would not let them cross if he wasn't sure it was safe.

Resolution rang in Justine's soft response.

"Don't worry. I'll keep them moving."

Pride, love, and unfaltering respect swelled within Clay as he stared for a silent moment at the brave, uncomplaining woman who was his wife. When he spoke at last, his whispered words were husky with emotion.

"I love you, Justine Bates Buchanan. You know that, don't you?"

Not waiting for her response, he covered her mouth with a kiss that was all the sweeter for its reluctant brevity; then he stepped down and walked to the rear of the wagon.

"Honesty . . . can you hear me, sugar?"

Papa's voice.

Honesty struggled to awaken. She was hot, and her throat and stomach hurt. She forced her eyes open and saw his face. Papa was smiling. He always smiled for her.

"Papa?"

Her father's cool hand stroked her cheek as he whispered, "No, don't talk. Just listen. Mama and I are going to take the wagon across the river now. It's going to be a rocky ride, so if your sisters get frightened, I want you to tell them it'll be all right."

"But Mama—"

"Mama is going to drive the wagon. She won't be able to sit with you. You're the oldest, so it will be up to you to take care of your sisters. Can I depend on you, sweetheart?"

"Yes, Papa."

Papa kissed her cheek. His hair brushed her face. It was cool to the touch despite its fiery color. She loved the color of Papa's hair. She had told him countless times that she wished her hair was the same color as his, just like Chastity's. But Papa always said he liked her just the way she was. He said her hair was as black as the devil's heart and her eyes as blue as the heavens—just like her great-grandmama's.

"I love you, Papa."

"I love you, too, sugar. Take care of your sisters. Promise?"

"I promise."

"I promise, too, Papa."

"Me, too."

Papa's smile broadened when Purity and Chastity squeaked their unsolicited responses. He whispered, "I know my girls love each other just like I love them, and I know they'll always look out for each other."

Papa kissed Purity and Chastity's cheeks in turn, but Honesty knew that his special wink was just for her as he closed the wagon flaps behind him.

"Where's Papa goin', Honesty?"

Honesty turned toward Purity, rasping in response, "He's takin' us across the river . . . to the doctor."

"Good, 'cause I'm sick."

"Me, too."

"Go to sleep." Honesty closed her eyes. Her throat hurt and she didn't want to talk anymore. But she'd be well soon. Purity and Chastity would be well soon, too. Papa was taking them to the doctor, just like Mama said he would.

Remembering her promise, Honesty opened her eyes again and whispered dutifully, "Don't be afraid, you hear? Papa will take care of us."

The wagon jerked forward.

Justine's throat was dry and her hands were trembling. She was unconscious of the pale strand of hair that had worked loose from its binding to flay her face, and of the perspiration that beaded her ashen brow as they reached the mid-point of the river.

She had never been so frightened! The current was so strong. It was dragging at the wagon with increasing force, and the horses were beginning to resist her rein. Their lead horse still hadn't recovered full strength after his illness and he seemed to be weakening. The opposite bank looked so far away. . . .

"Keep them going, Justine!" Clay's voice broke into his wife's panic, startling her as he encouraged her from his forward position in the river astride Big Blue. "Don't let up now, darlin'! The worst is over. It's only a little farther."

Justine took a tighter grip on the reins, love surging at the sound of Clay's voice. What was the matter with her? Clay had never let them down and he never would. He'd die before he'd do that.

Taking heart as the horses abruptly began making stronger progress, Justine felt her confidence begin to soar. Clay was right. The current lessened just past the middle of the river and the horses were struggling less. They would make it.

But . . . what was that sound?

Justine glanced around her at the sound that she could not identify. It was a muted roar that was growing rapidly louder. She had never heard anything like it before and she—

Struck by a moment of soul-shaking terror, Justine froze at her first sight of a great wall of water sweeping down the river toward them!

A glance at Clay's expression of horrified incredulity confirmed Justine's fear. The sound became deafening as she dropped the reins and turned toward the rear of the wagon. She thought she heard Clay call her name as she scrambled toward her daughters. His voice echoed in her mind as she reached frantically toward them. She heard it still as the wall of water crashed over them, tumbling them into a watery eternity that drowned her husband's cries and silenced her children's wails, sweeping them away.

The sunlight of late afternoon shone with golden warmth on the river. It glinted on the rapids caused by the recent rains, transforming its surface into a sheet of rippling jewels. The wreckage of a wagon that bobbed and dipped with the current was inconsistent with the pristine beauty of the scene, as was the tragic spectacle of the battered male body caught on debris at the river's edge, and the slender female form floating lifelessly on its way downriver.

The mournful sight bespoke the story of a journey brought to premature end for two who had started out with hope, for two whose last words had been spoken with love . . .

. . . as the river flowed on.

Chapter Two

Jewel LaRue wrinkled her short, straight nose with a derisive snort as the wagon bumped along the rough trail. She glanced sideward toward the sour-faced driver seated beside her as she raised her hand to the upward sweep of her outlandishly red hair and straightened proud shoulders covered with a garish gold dress. She was intensely aware that some would derive great pleasure at seeing her there, traveling under such primitive conditions in a common prairie schooner packed to the brim with all her worldly possessions. A tawdry queen seated on a crude throne . . . They would crow at how far the mighty seemed to have fallen.

To a certain extent, she supposed they were right.

Jewel LaRue, the most popular saloon girl and dealer at the Lonesome Steer Saloon, would not have chosen such an unsophisticated manner of departure from the south Texas town where she had spent the last two years of her life if the choice had been hers. Nor would she have chosen a surly, grimy, bewhiskered old man like Sam Potts to drive her and her possessions to Abilene if any other option had been open to her. Unfortunately, the unanticipated appearance of a fifth ace in the deck of cards she had been dealing had turned several important men against her when it had revealed too clearly for denial the reason for her uncanny luck of late. A committee of irate and jealous wives had then taken the opportunity to descend upon her, further emphasizing the need for her swift departure.

Just as unfortunately, Sam Potts had been the only man available to drive her wagon when she made her hasty exit.

Jewel's heavily rouged lips twisted into an unconscious sneer. She had already struck from her mind the traitorous fellow who had sworn undying allegiance to her in more intimate moments, only to turn his back on her when his angry wife appeared at the saloon doors, leading the committee against her. He had reenforced a lesson she had learned long ago—that the only person she could truly rely on was herself. Retaining that thought, she had shrugged him off just as easily as she had brushed the dust of that town from her high-heeled satin shoes.

As for Sam Potts, she supposed she should be grateful to have him. He was an excellent driver, and he had proved himself to be honest and trustworthy.

Jewel sniffed uncomfortably. The trouble was that he *stank*.

Reaching toward the carpetbag lying behind the seat, Jewel retrieved a small bottle of perfume and doused herself liberally. Lilacs . . . She loved that fragrance. She had loved it since her childhood. It was *her* scent because it put her in mind of the only time in her eventful life when she had been completely happy—the years before her pa died and her ma got sick and ended up depending on Willis Cotter to take care of things.

Willis Cotter . . . the slimy lecher.

Jewel's unconscious sneer returned. She had borne Cotter's pawing in silence, knowing that her ma was too sick for another problem to be added to her burden. But when her ma died, she had hardly waited for the last shovelful of earth to settle on the coffin before running off with only the clothes on her back and the determination that she'd never be at the mercy of a man like Cotter again.

Uncharacteristic moistness briefly touched Jewel's brown eyes before she determinedly shrugged her sorrow away. She had learned a lot since then. She had learned that a woman had only herself to blame if she let herself be taken advantage of; that a pretty woman had the edge over a plain one in almost every situation; and that the prettier a woman was, the more she could get away with in her dealings with men—and the more generous men would be. She had made a good living on that precept, and she wasn't ashamed to admit it. Of course, starting out as plain and pale as she had been, it hadn't been easy.

Jewel adjusted her daintily fringed shawl over her shoulders, careful to shield the firm, white flesh exposed at her neckline from the sun's burning rays. She smiled. She had worked hard at becoming pretty enough to turn men's heads. Her mousey brown hair had been blazing red for more years than she cared to count now, and she had made it a practice never to start the day without applying enough color to her face to compensate for nature's lapse. She dressed flamboyantly in clothes that emphasized her feminine attributes, generously exposing her ample bosom, which was the only positive natural attribute she possessed. She had made all the adjustments necessary to ease her way in the world—and she had never again allowed a man to use her without using him in return.

Yes, she'd done all right on her own and she had no complaints about her life . . .

A sudden gust assaulted her anew with her companion's odor and Jewel grimaced.

. . . until now.

Determined to put her present difficulties aside as she had done so successfully many times before, Jewel patted the carpetbag behind her. That carpetbag had allowed her to leave that south Texas town behind her without any true fears for the future. She had been planning to leave there within a year's time to pursue her dream in any case. After ten years on her own, she had sufficient funds stored in that bag and enough equipment piled in the wagon behind her to open her own saloon in Abilene.

Oh, yes, she had heard about Abilene. That trail town was a gold mine for those in her profession. All she would have to do there would be to sit back and rake in the profits once she got herself a few good girls to work the bar. As for the tables, she'd manage them herself. After a few years, her future would be totally secure.

Jewel's smile faded. Yes, she had left her pa's ranch and little Jenny Larson behind forever the day her ma died. She was Jewel LaRue now, heart and soul. And if somewhere deep inside she occasionally mourned the woman she might have been if the lilac time of her life had not come to a bitter end, she had thrust those thoughts firmly to the back of her mind. She had just as firmly resisted allowing anyone to enter her life who might possibly get in the way of the future toward which she had worked so relentlessly.

Jewel turned toward Sam Potts as the leather-faced fellow clucked at the lagging team, slapping the reins against their backs to urge them to a faster pacc. She then glanced up at the clear sky above, which was painted with the red and gold of the setting sun. She was relieved that the rain had stopped. Sam had kept to the winding river trail northward since the early morning hours. The sun had efficiently baked the trail since then, improving conditions to such an extent that they had made the best progress since the inception of their journey. They would reach Abilene soon.

The wagon dipped into another rut in the road, and Jewel wiggled uncomfortably. Her immediate problem was of a personal nature, and it was rapidly becoming urgent. She addressed Sam directly.

"Sam . . ."

Sam's eyes remained focused forward.

Damned if the man wasn't hard of hearing, too!

"Sam!"

Sam turned with an annoyed squint. "Ain't no need to shout! I heared you."

"You didn't answer me."

"I'm answerin' you now, ain't I?"

Jewel gritted her teeth. "I need to stop for a few minutes."

"Again?"

"Just do what I say!"

Ignoring Sam's grumbling as he drew the team to a halt and glared, Jewel climbed down from the wagon and walked toward the river, cursing softly. The man had a bladder of iron, damn him! She was sick and tired of his foul disposition. She was paying him good money to drive her to Abilene and she was going to make sure that she set him straight when she got back to the wagon.

But in the meantime . . .

Grateful that the riverbank dropped at the side of the trail, providing a natural shelter from prying eyes, Jewel descended carefully to the edge. She had not given Sam the satisfaction of telling him that she was pleased he had followed the river trail for most of the day, but she was. Cast with the colors of the setting sun, the river flowed a molten amber-gold that stirred bittersweet memories of the lilac time of her life. Its beauty, however, was not now her primary concern.

Thrusting sentiment aside, Jewel continued her unsteady progress toward a group of bushes on the sandy bank. After attending to necessities, she was determined to wash. Contrary to Sam's obvious aversion to water, she had suffered from the lack of bathing opportunity since their journey began. She also knew that a little water on her face and arms would do wonders for her disposition, even if the refreshing effects would be temporary.

Jewel frowned. The last thing she needed was to enter Abilene smelling as bad as Sam!

Jewel made a mental note. When she reached Abilene, she would get herself a room and go immediately in search of a bathtub. Then, when she was clean and herself again, she would put on her best red dress and her highest-heeled satin shoes, and she'd step out in all her glory to show Abilene what Jewel LaRue was really made of!

Her thoughts were interrupted as her attention was caught by a cluster of debris snagged on bushes at the river's edge. Jewel slowed her step. She walked closer, noting that the wheel and jagged pieces of wood did not seem to have been in the water long. Farther on she saw pieces of torn clothing and assorted supplies that appeared to have come from a settler's wagon which had not made it across the flooded river.

Jewel unconsciously shook her head. Too bad. She was not unfamiliar with that kind of luck. She walked closer and picked up what appeared to be a woman's calico dress. She squinted at its narrow proportions, then dropped it back on the ground. She had outgrown that size years ago.

Jewel glanced warily around her as she started toward a row of bushes close to the water. Sam had shown no inclination to intrude when privacy was demanded, but she had learned the danger of forsaking caution the hard way. For that reason, she never traveled without a little derringer strapped to the garter on her thigh. Neither did she—

A sound from the bushes ahead struck Jewel stock still. Her heart began a rapid pounding as she slid her hand toward the open pocket in her skirt that allowed free access to her concealed weapon. The noise sounded again just as her hand closed around the handle of the derringer.

Confident as her finger curled around the trigger of the small pistol, Jewel walked toward the sound. She rounded the fringe of bushes boldly, only to stop short.

A little girl.

The child was lying on the ground, motionless. Her long, dark hair was twisted and tangled, and the white nightdress that was plastered against her thin body was covered with sandy residue from the river.

The girl whimpered and Jewel kneeled beside her. She touched the child's cheek and frowned. It didn't take much experience to know that she was burning up with fever. The thought crossed Jewel's mind that if the girl had been in a wagon that had overturned while crossing the river, someone was probably looking for her. She glanced up and looked around, seeing no one.

The child mumbled incoherently, and Jewel felt the nudge of panic. What was she supposed to do until the girl's parents showed up to claim her? She didn't know anything about taking care of children, and the girl needed a doctor. She needed one soon, dammit!

Standing up abruptly, Jewel took a deep breath and called out at the top of her lungs.

"Sam! Get down here—now!"

Jewel waited a few minutes, then shouted again.

"Sam, dammit! Where are you?"

An irritable shout came in return. "Hold your horses, I'm comin!"

It took only a moment for Sam's cantankerous frown to turn concerned as he kneeled beside the unconscious child a few minutes later. When he turned toward Jewel, no trace of his former sullenness remained as he said gravely, "This little gal is damned sick. Looks like we got our work cut out for us."

Sam did not wait for Jewel's reply before sweeping the child up into his arms and starting back to the wagon. Following silently behind, Jewel realized that for the first time since she had left Jenny Larson behind her, she was glad she was not alone.

"Mama . . . Papa . . ."

Honesty fought to focus as fragmented sights and sounds assaulted her mind . . .

A loud noise like thunder, growing ever louder.

Mama's frightened face.

Chastity's screams.

Water . . . so much water!

The water filled her nose and mouth, choking her. It turned the world into a terror of darkness as everything tumbled around and around. . . .

"Mama! Papa!"

Where were they?

She was hot. Her throat hurt and her body ached so bad. But someone was bathing her face and forehead with cool water.

"Mama?"

"Your mama's not here."

Straining to see through the haze blocking her vision, Honesty saw a lady. Her hair was brighter than Papa's—so bright that the color almost hurt her eyes.

Honesty glanced around her. She was lying in a wagon, but it wasn't Papa's wagon.

"I . . . I want Mama."

"Don't you start wailin' now!" The red-haired lady's expression hardened. "It won't do you any good. Your mother and father are probably out lookin' for you now, and I don't intend listenin' to you cry until they find you!"

"Papa . . . Mama . . ."

"They aren't here, I said, and we're doin' the best we can for you."

"That ain't no way to handle a sick little gal, dammit! Don't you know nothin'?"

The male voice that sounded out of nowhere abruptly took on the face of a bewhiskered old man, who leaned over Honesty to continue with surprising gentleness, "You ain't feelin' so good, are you, little darlin'? Well, don't you worry about a thing. I had a little girl like you once and when she was sick, I was real good at makin' her feel better again. Your folks will probably be catchin' up with us soon, so don't you worry about nothin', you hear?"

Honesty stared at the wrinkled face above her. It was a homely face, but it was kind. She managed a grating whisper. "Where's Purity . . . Chastity . . . ?"

The woman's face suddenly reappeared. It drew closer as the woman laid another cool cloth on her forehead. Honesty was struck with the thought that despite her harshness, the woman appeared concerned.

Honesty rasped through the pain in her throat. "Purity . . . Chastity . . . ?"

The woman blinked, then responded with a slightly raised brow, "Purity and Chastity, huh? They're nowhere to be found inside this wagon, that's for sure."

"Dammit!" The old man spoke again. "What are you tellin' that little gal?"

"Only the truth, old man!"

The truth . . .

Darkness hovered as the woman's words reverberated in Honesty's mind.

The truth . . .

Mama said truth was important over all. That was why Mama had named her Honesty.

A warmth unrelated to physical heat relieved Honesty's fear. Mama would like the red-haired lady because the lady told the truth. And Mama would like the old man, too.

Mama and Papa would come to find her soon.

Honesty closed her eyes.

Jewel swallowed against the thickness that formed in her throat as the little girl's eyes slowly closed. So young and helpless . . . She remembered another girl who had not been as young as this one, but who had been just as helpless. It was not a pleasant memory.

Jewel drew back, suddenly angry at the direction

her thoughts were taking. She had no room in her life for maudlin memories *or* for this child who had taken such an inopportune time to appear. Damn. If only Sam had stopped the wagon a little farther down the river, she wouldn't have to be bothered now, and she—

The little girl twitched violently in her sleep and Jewel's thoughts abruptly halted. She turned toward the man beside her. "I'm tellin' you now, Sam Potts—all that talk about your knowin' how to make this little girl well again had better not be nothin' but a lot of hot air!"

"Don't you worry about that! I didn't spend all that time livin' with the Injuns for nothin', you know! We'll camp here tonight, and I'll go lookin' for some Injun plants."

"Injun plants?"

"Then I'll boil 'em up."

"Boil them up?"

"You ain't no parrot, so stop repeatin' me, dammit!"

Sam shook his head with a few mumbled curses, then continued, "I'll tell you what to do, then you'll stay in back and care for the little darlin' while I make it to Abilene as fast as them two old nags up front will take us."

"Now, wait a minute!" Jewel's blood began a slow boil. "This is *my* wagon and *I* give the orders around here, not you!"

"That so?"

"Yes, that's so!"

"You know how to make this little gal well again, do you?"

Jewel gritted her teeth.

"Well, do you?"

Damn him . . .

"Do you?"

"No!"

"I don't need to say no more, do I?"

Cursing under her breath as Sam turned abruptly and jumped down from the wagon, Jewel was aware that Sam was cursing as well. A shudder passed over her womanly frame. She didn't like this. She had no time for outside problems at this crucial point in her life, when her entire future depended upon the impressions and contacts she would make when she reached Abilene.

At a sound from the pallet beside her, Jewel looked at the child who twisted and turned restlessly there. Nor did she have the time or the inclination to nurse a sick child!

Damn!

Jewel took up the cloth and again bathed the girl's fevered skin.

Damn . . .

"I don't like it . . ."

"Drink it anyway."

"No." Honesty twisted her head to avoid the cup of bitter medicine. "I don't want it."

"Look at me, Honesty."

Honesty squeezed her eyes shut as the wagon rattled relentlessly onward. She had no idea how many days it had been since she had been found beside the river, but it seemed like forever. During that forever, that same female voice had penetrated her restless dreams countless times, urging her to drink that terrible stuff. She had drunk it because she hadn't been able to refuse it, but she was feeling better now and she wasn't going to drink anymore.

"I said, look at me."

Silence.

"Look at me!"

Honesty popped her eyes abruptly open.

The red-haired woman Honesty had come to know as Jewel stared at her, her expression tight. Jewel had taken care of her and Honesty was grateful. She knew Jewel wasn't really a bad lady. It was just that Jewel was bossy, and she didn't like bossy people. Mama always said that she was too bossy herself for her to like others who acted that way. But somehow there was no anger in Mama's eyes when she said that. Mama also told her that although it was her duty to be courteous, she should remember that the only people who had the right to tell her what to do were Papa and Mama.

Honesty forced away the tears that momentarily threatened. She missed Mama and Papa so bad, but she would be back with them and her sisters soon, she was sure. Jewel said her mama and papa would probably go to Abilene to look for her because it was the biggest town around. She had already decided that if Mama and Papa weren't in Abilene when they arrived, she would wait there for them, no matter what Jewel said.

Honesty sniffed. She would take care of herself in Abilene until Mama and Papa came to get her. She was the oldest of her sisters, after all.

Jewel's pointed stare grew more intense. "You are goin' to drink this medicine that Sam made for you because it will make you better."

"I *am* better."

"No, you're not."

"Yes, I am."

"I'll tell you when you're better!"

Honesty's delicate lips tightened into a firm, straight line. "Mama said nobody has the right to tell me what to do but Papa and her."

"Do you want to see your mama and papa again?"

"Yes."

"And your sisters?"

"Yes . . ."

"Then you'd better drink this medicine right now or you won't be well enough to look for them when we get to Abilene."

"I'm well enough now."

"Honesty . . ." Jewel's voice dropped to a warning hiss that Honesty had come to know well. "If you don't take this medicine now, I'll tell Sam you don't want to take any more of his medicine. His feelings will be very hurt."

"No!" Honesty frowned. She didn't want to hurt Sam's feelings. She liked him better than she liked Jewel. Sam smiled and he had never lost his temper with her, no matter how cranky she had been when she was sick. She liked Sam . . . even if he did smell bad.

"I'm losin' my patience, Honesty. I'm goin' to call Sam in a minute."

Honesty's fine lips twitched. "All right, I'll drink it."

Forcing herself to ignore Jewel's brief, victorious smile, Honesty swallowed obediently. She grimaced when she was done, and then closed her eyes. It occurred to her that she might be sicker than she thought because she was still so tired all the time. It also occurred to her just before sleep claimed her that if she was, Jewel was right and she was wrong. She didn't like that idea. She didn't like that idea at all.

Honesty sighed. Mama . . . Papa . . . where are you?

Honesty choked back a sob.

* * *

Jewel sat back on her heels, the empty cup still in her hand as she stared at her young patient's countenance, angelic in sleep.

The little brat . . .

Surprising herself, Jewel stifled the inclination to smile. How very much Honesty Buchanan reminded her of another strong-willed child she had known so long ago . . . a girl named Jenny Larson.

Jewel paused at that thought. She had never realized how annoying a child she must have been until she came up against the formidable young Honesty Buchanan. But the truth was, she could not help admiring the little twerp for her spunk—and for the soft heart she hid that would not allow her to hurt the feelings of a smelly old man who obviously was totally smitten with her.

Her thoughts springing ahead to Abilene, Jewel felt a familiar knot tighten within. She was not the only person whose future hung on what she would find waiting when she arrived in that infamous trail town. She only hoped that Honesty would find—

Jewel drew her thoughts up short. What did she care what happened to this little girl? No one had cared what happened to her when her mother died, and she had been the better for having been forced to make her own way. She was now on her way to total financial independence, and she owed her success to no one but herself. Honesty Buchanan could learn a thing or two from her . . .

. . . if she had the need.

The thought of Abilene loomed more darkly.

Oblivious to the raucous sounds of Abilene echoing hollowly in the street beyond the office door, Jewel stared at the short, grey-haired doctor in disbelief. The odoriferous Sam, her mulish young patient, and she had arrived a short time earlier in the notorious trail town of saloons, brothels, gambling houses, and wildly spending cowboys just waiting for the right woman to empty their pockets. Their entrance, however, had borne not the slightest resemblance to the one she had envisioned making for herself.

Jewel winced at the memory. She had entered town leaning out of her mud-caked wagon and shouting like a veteran mule skinner so she might be heard above the chaos of music from competing dancehalls along the street, pounding hammers from buildings under construction on all sides, and the angry bellows of man and beast that comprised the turmoil of midday in the bawdiest town on the Chisholm Trail. She had queried one cowboy after another for the location of the nearest doctor with complete disregard for the havoc long weeks on the trail had wreaked on her appearance. Her answer obtained, she had then spurred Sam on to the doctor's door without delay.

Jewel's heavily rouged lip twitched. No one had to tell her that her young, reluctant patient had not recuperated as well as expected on the trail. That reality had concerned her to the point of sleeplessness during the past few nights.

And how she resented being sleepless! She resented it almost as much as she resented her youthful charge's infringement on her life!

Determined to eliminate the cause for her sleeplessness so she might step boldly into her future without distraction, she had resolved to seek out the nearest doctor—*any* doctor—where her sick charge might stay until her family could be found. She had steadfastly put from her mind the possibility that she might hear exactly what the doctor was telling her right now.

Realizing that the frowning doctor was awaiting her response, Jewel began hoarsely, "You . . . you're tellin' me that Honesty's mother and father are dead—that their bodies were found in the river?"

"You said the little girl told you her name was Buchanan, that her mother's name was Justine and her father's was Clayton."

"That's right."

"The man was wearin' a moneybelt with his name on it—Clayton Buchanan. He was a big fella with reddish hair."

Red hair. Jewel inwardly shuddered. That was him, all right—Honesty had mentioned the color of her papa's hair. She pressed, "And the woman? How can you be sure who she was?"

"Considerin' that the wreckage of the wagon was found, who else could she be?"

"Honesty said her mother is small and thin, with blond hair and blue eyes."

The doctor's expression eliminated the need for response.

"It *was* her, then . . ."

"I told you it was."

"What about her sisters?"

"We haven't found their bodies, yet, but I'm thinkin' we will, sooner or later."

Assessing her in silence for long moments, the doctor offered, "Do you want me to tell the girl? I don't mind."

"No."

"All right. Anythin' you say." The doctor's bloodshot eyes softened. "In any case, you don't have to worry about her. I'll take care of her until she's well, and somebody will take her in, especially as pretty as she is. We have a fire-and-brimstone preacher who came to town with his wife a couple of months ago. He'll do his duty by the girl, I'm sure."

Duty . . . Jewel restrained a sneer. Willis Cotter had promised to do his duty by Jenny Larson, too.

"Ain't no fire-and-brimstone preacher goin' to take that spunky little gal! He'd squeeze the life out of her!"

Sam's unexpected interjection turned Jewel toward the old man with a start. She had almost forgotten that he was standing behind her.

His wrinkled face flushed an almost apoplectic hue, Sam pinned her with his gaze. "You ain't goin' to let that happen, are you?"

Jewel remained silent.

Well, was she?

"They aren't dead! They aren't!"

Doc Lang's office rang with the echo of Honesty's spontaneous response as she covered her eyes with her hands, ashamed of the tears that were falling. She never cried. Only babies cried. It wasn't true, anyway! Mama and Papa, and Purity and Chastity, weren't dead!

"Listen to me." Allowing Jewel to pull her hands from her face, Honesty looked up as Jewel whispered, "It's true."

Honesty yanked her hands from Jewel's grasp. "No, it's a mistake!"

"It isn't a mistake. The doctor described your papa. He was a big man with reddish-brown hair and a scar on his chin."

A painful lump rose in Honesty's throat. "It wasn't a big scar. . . ."

"Your mama had blond hair, and she was wearin' a locket."

Honesty clutched her locket. "Was it shaped like a heart?"

"The name engraved on it was almost worn off, but it was . . . Justine."

A slow shuddering began inside Honesty. "But Purity and Chastity aren't dead! Somebody will bring them here just like you brought me. You'll see!"

"I don't think so. Doc Lang said they probably—"

"They're not dead!" Shouting over the sobbing that had begun deep within, Honesty declared, "They're not dead, and I'm goin' to wait here for them to come, no matter what you say!"

"Honesty . . ."

"They're not dead!"

"Come on now, little darlin', that ain't no way to be."

Honesty turned toward Sam as he spoke. Her anger melted into a fervent plea as she rasped, "Tell her, Sam. Tell her Purity and Chastity aren't dead."

Taking her small hands between his callused palms, Sam held them tightly. His response as fervent as hers, he whispered, "I can't tell her no such thing, little darlin', but I wish with all my heart I could."

Unable to restrain sobs that came from a heart that was breaking, Honesty was uncertain of the moment when Sam relinquished her hands to slip his scrawny arms around her . . . just as she was uncertain, when she looked up briefly from the circle of Sam's comforting embrace, if she had truly seen Jewel wipe away a tear.

"You did the right thing in calling me, Dr. Lang."

Reverend Hutton's nasal tone reverberated in the doctor's small office as his cold-eyed gaze moved appraisingly toward the cot where Honesty lay.

Honesty sensed his gaze upon her, and she felt strangely alone. Jewel and Sam had left her in the doctor's care earlier and she had dozed off, only to awaken to the sight of the reverend standing over her. A tall, thin man dressed entirely in black, he had looked like an oversized raven with his peculiarly piercing stare. His smile had been as cold as his eyes, a smile that did not warm as he proceeded somberly in his conversation with the doctor.

"Abilene is Satan's lair. An innocent child needs strict guidance under such circumstances. This child's prolonged exposure to the soiled dove who brought her into town has doubtless already contaminated her. But you need not fear. I will purge the evil from her."

Honesty frowned. Evil? She wasn't evil. She didn't like this man at all. He wasn't like Reverend Bretton back home. Reverend Bretton's smile had made her feel good inside, and he had made Mama and Papa smile, too.

Mama and Papa . . . who wouldn't be smiling at her anymore . . .

Honesty forced back the heat of tears as Doc Lang responded, "I don't think you have to worry about that, Reverend. I'd say any mother who named her three daughters after important virtues probably gave them a good Christian start in life, wouldn't you?"

The reverend's narrow face darkened. "Evil is insidious, doctor. It sprouts from seeds which are sown in the most covert of ways—seeds that bear bitter fruit. But you need not distress yourself with the state of this child's soul. I will purify her."

A great sadness welled inside Honesty. She was tired and she didn't feel good. And she was lonely.

Mama and Papa were gone, and Purity and Chastity were lost.

But they weren't dead. She knew they weren't.

The increasing vehemence of the preacher's voice broke into Honesty's thoughts.

"I will call the power of the Lord down to strike the evil from this child's soul."

Anger touched Honesty's mind. Mama always said that God smiled when He looked down on her three girls. God wouldn't smile if she was evil, would He? Mama wouldn't like that preacher saying those things about her.

And neither did she.

Honesty's youthful voice rang with conviction as she addressed the solemn-faced preacher.

"I'm not evil."

The preacher snapped toward her. Unexpected fury smoldered in his deep-set eyes.

"You have no part in this conversation, child."

"I'm *not* evil."

The preacher's pale face reddened. " *'Foolishness is bound in the heart of a child; but the rod of correction shall drive it far from him.'* "

"Come now, reverend." Red color infused Doc's face as well. "There's no need to talk of usin' the rod when this child's still recuperatin' from a serious illness."

"You may tend to the child's body, doctor, but it is my duty to tend to her soul. And it appears I must not delay. I'll be back with my wagon tomorrow to pick her up."

"It would probably be best if she stayed here for another few days."

"I'll be back *tomorrow.*"

Tomorrow.

Honesty's eyelids grew heavy . . . too heavy to hold

up. The preacher's footsteps faded from the room as she closed her eyes. But the thought remained that the preacher wasn't a nice man, and she didn't like him at all.

Jewel surveyed her reflection in the hotel bedroom mirror as she touched the scent of lilacs to her throat. She liked what she saw. Red hair piled high atop her head, plain features skillfully enhanced with bold color, the scarlet satin that outlined her lush curves contrasting vividly with the creamy flesh of her generous bosom, and the black net stockings that she had saved for this particular occasion covering long, shapely legs that she would flash at the most opportune of times—all finished off with high-heeled red satin shoes that drove most men wild.

Oh, yes, Jewel LaRue would set Abilene on its ear tonight!

Snatching up her shawl, her heart pounding with excitement, Jewel turned toward the door. Sounds of evening revelry rang on the street below. The time had come to face her future—the future toward which she had planned since the day she had bid the sad, abused Jenny Larson good-bye forever. Within a week she would have picked the best site for the grandest saloon Abilene would ever see, and she would have spirited enough workers away from other saloons, both with her charm and with the backing of the considerable sum she had deposited in the bank that afternoon, to enable her to make her dreams a reality. Her skill, both with men and with cards, would take over from there. She had no doubt that her future was bright! No doubt at all!

In the hotel lobby moments later, Jewel was aware of interested glances from every quarter. A flutter of heavily kohled lashes, low, throaty replies to masculine inquiry, a twist of the hips and a dip of her bosom—she was drunk on her power!

Out on the street, Jewel laughed aloud as the glaring lights of the Alamo Saloon appeared in the distance. Her bold spirit had been confined too long, and now she was free to—

"Harlot! Adventuress! Jezebel!"

Startled as a tall man dressed in black stepped out to block her path, Jewel remained motionless. The man's thin white face was distorted with the passion of his words as he shouted, "Bride of Satan! You thought to take the soul of an innocent child and damn it to perdition, but you will not succeed! I will stand in your way, just as I stand in your way now, as an emissary of the Lord!"

A crowd quickly gathered as Jewel responded, "I don't know what you're talkin' about!"

"A child—an innocent child—sullied by the shadow of your sins!"

Her patience expired, Jewel ordered, "Get out of my way! You're crazy!"

"You call me a crazy? I, the Lord's witness here on earth?"

Jewel's responsive laughter was sharp and quick. "The good Lord I know wouldn't be desperate enough to have a lunatic like you speakin' up for him! Now, get out of my way!"

"No, you'll not escape so fast!" Grasping her arm, the threatening stranger held Jewel immobile as he spat, "I warn you, tomorrow the child is mine. Do not try to see her or talk to her ever again. If you do, both you and she will suffer the consequences!"

Releasing her so abruptly that she staggered backward, Jewel's unknown accuser turned and disappeared into the shadows of the evening.

Crazy . . . the man was crazy!

Trembling, Jewel struggled to regain her composure. Still unsteady as she continued down the street at a brisk pace calculated to disguise her distress, Jewel gasped aloud as a hand grasped her arm once more.

"Jewel, you all right?"

She was still battling to catch her breath when Sam stepped out into the light, demanding with unexpected concern, "I asked you a question, dammit, and you ain't answerin' me! Are you all right? What did that crazy fella say?"

Annoyed at the sudden thickness in her throat at Sam's concern, Jewel shook off his hand and raised her chin. "No, he didn't hurt me. And what makes you think I need an old man like you to watch out for me, anyway?"

Sam's low snort restored the last of Jewel's composure as he responded, "Well, I should've knowed that you wouldn't be needin' nobody's help—most of all mine! But everybody ain't like you, and that's a damned shame!"

"What are you talkin' about?"

"It don't all stop here, you know!"

Driven beyond the limits of her patience, Jewel snapped, "I'm startin' to think you're as crazy as that fella back there, and if you don't tell me what you're talkin' about right now, I'm goin' to leave you flat, standin' right where you are!"

"I'm talkin' about Honesty!"

Jewel's painted face stiffened.

"That fella back there is the preacher who's goin' to take Honesty to live with him tomorrow! Him and his crazy notions—he's talkin' about *purgin' the evil* from that darlin' child's soul!"

"The evil?"

"The evil that you and me put there, contaminatin' her."

"Contaminatin' her?"

"There you go repeatin' me again, dammit! Ain't you gettin' a word I'm sayin'?"

Jewel shook her head. "I hear you, but I don't understand. . . ."

"That fire-and-brimstone preacher the doc was talkin' about—that was him!"

The stranger's bizarre behavior suddenly slipped into place.

"And he's takin' Honesty off to live with him tomorrow."

Jewel stood stock still. The sounds of Abilene dimmed around her as all thought of red satin and black mesh vanished from her mind. Rising in its stead, so powerfully that she was almost overwhelmed, was the fragrance of lilacs.

Suddenly freed from her immobile state, Jewel turned abruptly on her heel and started back in the direction from which she had come.

Honesty heard it again—the frightening roar of a wall of water sweeping toward them! Caught fast in a hazy world she did not recognize, she felt her heart pounding in her chest, hammering so hard that she could scarcely breathe as the sound faded and a kaleidoscope of fragmented pictures flashed before her.

She saw Chastity! The long, red strands of Chastity's hair were darkened by the water in which they floated as she lay at the river's edge. Chastity's nightdress was soaked and stained, and the small foot protruding from its hem was cut and bleeding. She was lying . . . *so still.*

Somehow unable to call out, Honesty felt the rise

of panic. Chastity needed her! Papa had asked her to take care of her sisters, but she couldn't reach Chastity. She couldn't move!

Someone was coming. She saw two ladies with big, feathered straw hats walking along the riverbank. She saw one lady, then the other, run toward Chastity. They turned Chastity toward them and brushed her hair from her face. And then . . . then she saw Chastity open her eyes.

Tears she somehow could not shed filled Honesty's eyes. Chastity was still alive! Someone had found her!

Honesty gasped aloud as the scene suddenly changed. The sun was setting and the dust was thick, despite the rains recently fallen. But that was because there were so many cattle—a herd that stretched as far as her eye could see! She saw two drovers riding alongside it. She saw the big man turn his horse in the direction of a calf that stumbled out of sight over the edge of the high riverbank. She saw him again on the river's edge, urging the bawling calf back toward the herd. Then she saw the drover stop to stare out at the surface of the river. She saw his face stiffen with surprise the moment before he spurred his horse into the water.

And then Honesty saw *her.*

A sob escaped Honesty's throat as the big man snatched a small body clothed in a nightdress from the river. He held the motionless child close as he urged his mount back toward shore. She saw that the man was almost beside himself with concern until the girl's body jerked unexpectedly into movement and she began coughing. She saw his relief when the girl gave a loud wail.

And then she saw the girl's face.

Purity!

Tears of elation stained Honesty's cheeks. She had known it all along! Purity and Chastity had been found! They were alive, and she would see them again soon! She could let no one deter her from believing what she knew was true—just as her mama and papa had taught her. She *would* see her sisters again.

The swirling mists faded as abruptly as they had appeared, and the pain of bleak emptiness returned.

Oh, Mama . . . Papa . . . She missed them so.

Honesty could not seem to control her tears.

"Honesty . . . wake up, little darlin'. You're havin' a bad dream."

Sam's familiar voice was unexpected. It drew her back, forcing her to open her eyes to the night shadows of Doc's office as Sam continued, "Wake up . . . that's it. Jewel and me are here 'cause we got somethin' to talk to you about."

Doc Lang raised the flame on the lamp, and Honesty saw Jewel standing behind Sam—Jewel looking as bright and shiny in her red dress as the flame in the lamp behind her. Honesty brushed away her tears under Jewel's unsmiling scrutiny. She raised her chin, her mind still foggy as she waited for Sam to continue.

"Well, it's like this, little darlin'. The doc says . . . I mean, Jewel has agreed . . . What I'm tryin' to say—"

Jewel's grunt of disgust halted Sam abruptly as she pushed him out of the way to assume his place at Honesty's bedside. Jewel held Honesty's gaze intently with her own as she spoke.

"This preacher the doc was talkin' about isn't exactly what we were expectin' him to be. Doc's agreed, so it's up to you. Do you want to stay with me for the time bein'?"

Honesty raised her chin a notch higher. "When my sisters come, I'll be going with them. Papa said I should take care of them."

Jewel did not respond.

"They'll be here soon."

Silence.

"They're alive. I saw them."

Silence. Then, "Do you want to stay with me until they do?"

Honesty considered Jewel's offer. She studied Jewel's sober expression.

Maintaining Jewel's serious stare, Honesty nodded abruptly.

Jewel nodded in return.

The agreement was struck.

His gap-toothed smile flashing, Sam pushed past Jewel, wrapped the blanket around Honesty, and scooped her up into his arms. He winked down at Honesty, whispering in a tone that carried easily in the silent room, "I knew you was goin' to come with us, 'cause that's where you belong now."

Comfortable in Sam's familiar arms, it occurred to Honesty as Sam turned toward the door and Jewel fell in behind them that she had been somehow certain that this was the way it was going to be . . .

. . . at least until her sisters arrived.

Following behind as a grinning Sam carried Honesty toward the door, it occurred to Jewel that she wasn't at all certain how she, Honesty, and Sam had become *us*. But she was somehow certain that however it had happened, this was the way it was going to be.

And she wondered if she would regret it.

Part Two
All That Is
1882

"... all that is and has been is but
the twilight of the dawn."
—H. G. Wells

Chapter One

1882
Caldwell, Kansas

Bright lights and raucous music . . . female laughter and hearty male guffaws . . . the clatter of clinking glasses, jingling spurs, and dancing feet as the steady call of keno numbers from the balcony added yet another measure to the mirthful chaos of the scene . . .

There was no doubt about it. The Texas Jewel was the liveliest saloon on the Chisholm Trail.

Honesty laughed aloud with the sheer pleasure that thought evoked, her fingers moving nimbly as she shuffled and dealt the cards with the aid of long practice. Nor was there any doubt in her mind about the effect of her smile on the men seated beside her at the green gaming table, or on the ring of cowpokes who stood observing with drinks in hand. Fluttering long black lashes that had no need of artifice, she glanced at each player in turn, her startlingly blue eyes raising a flush even on the most weathered of faces as she whispered huskily, "All right, gentlemen, what will it be?"

Honesty laughed again at the grunts and restrained mumbles that sounded in response. She was well aware of her impact on men. She knew she was the best-looking woman many of them had ever seen. Only a fool would deny the truth of black hair so lustrous that it seemed to glow with a light of its own . . . blue eyes so clear as to stop men in their tracks . . . smooth white skin and features so delicately drawn as to draw comparisons to the fine porcelain figurine on display in the only jewelry store in town. And then there were the graceful lines of a perfect female body.

But Honesty accepted that truth without a trace of conceit.

. . . Hair as black as the devil's heart and eyes as blue as the heavens . . .

She remembered little of the child she had been before that fateful day in the river, but she remembered the pride in Papa's smile as he said those words, comparing her to the beautiful Irish grandmother she had never known. She was silently grateful for the gift of beauty that was a physical link to the family she had lost so long ago.

Honesty's smile broadened. She had no doubt that same Irish ancestor described to her in such loving detail would approve of the way she now employed her legacy to such advantage.

Looking up from the table, Honesty caught Jeremy Stark's eye where he stood at the bar a short distance away. She winked, noting that his youthful face flushed at the open attention she showed him before she returned to the game and the cards being checked and discarded all around.

Honesty dealt again, setting the hands. Only then did she pick up her own cards and glance at them briefly. The patrons of the Texas Jewel were a trail-hardened lot who were quick to anger and slow to forget. It amused her that although caustic remarks were occasionally passed about her incredible luck, not a one of those patrons had ever accused her of cheating.

Because . . . *she did.*

Honesty's eyes glowed in silent enjoyment of her thoughts. Of course, she only cheated occasionally, when necessary to offset a particularly disastrous turn of the cards . . . or when the notion struck her. That was the fun of it—the danger of her daring when playing cards with cowmen who left neither their spurs nor their guns at the door.

Honesty turned over her cards.

Three queens.

Sweeping the chips from the table amid a chorus of groans that had sounded over and again during the past hour, Honesty swept the faces around the table with her gaze as well. She halted at Jake Winters' florid rise of color.

"Jake, darlin' . . . looks like I've made you unhappy." Leaning toward the leather-faced trail boss in a way that dipped the neckline of her bodice appealingly, Honesty feigned a thoughtful frown as she continued in a throaty whisper, "I'm going to be leaving this table for a little while, but I sure do hate leaving a man frowning." She paused, fingering a black curl that spilled down from the artful cluster atop her head as she continued, "Since I've won so much of your money, seems like I should be giving you something in return. Maybe you'd like a lock of my hair for a keepsake. Or . . . would something more personal do?"

She smiled, her voice dropping an intimate note lower. "You think about it, you hear?"

Pushing herself away from the table as snickers sounded all around, Honesty directed a momentary lift of her brow to the grinning male dealer who assumed her seat. She turned toward the bar, knowing it was established policy that a female dealer never replaced her when she quit a table. The reason was simple. There wasn't a woman in the place *capable* of replacing her.

With one exception.

Jewel, who had made The Texas Jewel everything she had ever hoped it would be.

Jewel, who now only dealt cards when it struck her fancy.

Jewel, who often had other priorities now.

As for that sun-baked, frowning cowman she had left behind her and all the others like him, Honesty didn't have a moment's concern. After all, who would ever accuse a woman named "Honesty" of cheating? Most especially when that woman was she?

Honesty neared the bar, the heart-shaped locket that was as much a part of her as her smile glinting at her throat. She ran her hand over the bodice of her dress, smoothing the blue satin that lay against the well-rounded swell beneath like a second skin, her inner smile growing at the knowledge that every man within view wished that hand were his. It amused her to leave men panting in her wake. It was a game that never palled . . . and it was a game she *never* lost.

"All right, Honesty, that's enough! I'm tellin' you now, that ain't no way for a lady to act!"

Honesty turned toward the sound of the familiar,

gravel-voiced rebuke, responding, "You know me long enough to realize that I've never tried to be a lady."

"And that's the problem, ain't it?"

"Oh, Sam . . ."

A loving warmth reserved for Sam Potts alone rose inside Honesty. Sam—who had always been at her side when she needed him, whose devotion had not failed her since that day when Jewel and he first found her bedside the river. She hadn't seen him for a week while he had been chasing down some fellow who owed him money. She hadn't expected to miss him so.

Suddenly more grateful to see Sam than she ever imagined she could be, Honesty planted a kiss on his unshaven cheek. She winced, pursing her lips at the sharpness of his wiry beard as she slipped her arm through his and drew him along with her toward the bar. She scolded him teasingly.

"The least you could've done was shave, since you knew you'd be seeing me tonight."

Sam's small eyes narrowed. "Oh, no, you don't. When you was little you got me into changin' my clothes once a week 'cause your mama always told you a person should. Then you got me to takin' a bath, even in winter when I near to froze my tail off, 'cause you mama told you that cleanliness is next to godliness. Now you're tryin' to get me to shave off my beard, just when I'm gettin' the damned thing where I want it! Well, I ain't goin' to do it! Nobody said you had to kiss me, you know. An old man like me don't need none of that silly stuff, nohow."

"But, Sam . . ." Honesty sighed. "You know I can't resist you."

"There you go again! Flirtin'! You mind what I say. You're not always goin' to get away with leadin' all them fellas on like you do! You're goin' to get yourself in a heap of trouble one of these days, and I just might not be here to help you. I ain't goin' to live forever, you know."

"Don't say that!" Good humor momentarily deserting her, Honesty fought to regain her smile. "You know I don't like it when you talk that way."

"And I don't like it when you go actin' like one of them women in Maude's House of Pleasure up the street!" Sam shook his head. "I thought I raised you better than that!"

"Oh, leave her alone, Sam. If you don't want her flirtin' with you, she can flirt with me instead, 'cause I don't mind."

Turning, Sam gave a low snort as Jeremy Sills appeared beside them. His glance was disapproving. "Oh, it's you. Don't you say nothin', 'cause you're as bad as she is, both of you headin' for trouble if you don't watch out."

Noting the spark of anger that flashed in Jeremy's eyes, Honesty linked her other arm with his in a companionable gesture calculated to temper his response. Jeremy had walked through the door of Jewel's saloon looking for work ten years earlier, an eleven-year-old boy with an ailing mother and a drunken father who was the joke of the town. She had been eleven years old, too, and something about the lost look in his anxious brown eyes when they first met hers had struck a chord of affinity that touched her heart. Jeremy's father was killed in a fall from a horse shortly after she met him, and when Jeremy's mother died years later, it was almost as if she had lost her own mother all over again. She knew she would find her sisters again someday—no matter what anybody said. She reaffirmed that secret conviction every day of her life, but during those endless years of questions without answers, she had almost despaired . . . until Jeremy. Somehow, he had been the only one who really understood.

Without being truly of her blood, Jeremy was her brother. She knew he had somehow been sent to help her fill the void in her heart. She would always love him—no matter what he did.

But Jeremy wasn't easy to love. He was hot-headed and restless. He was impatient. He had been in and out of trouble ever since she could remember, and he was looking for respect in all the wrong places—with all the wrong people—and Tom Bitters was at the head of the list.

Jeremy stared at Sam, his lip curling with resentment. "I don't like what you're sayin', old man."

"The truth hurts, don't it? And if you was really Honesty's friend, like you make out you are, you'd realize you're only goin' to bring trouble down on her if you don't change your ways!"

Aware that the situation was getting out of hand as it so often did between the two men, Honesty interrupted firmly, "Now look here, you two!" Reluctantly surrendering each other's angry gazes, the two adversaries turned toward her as she continued more softly, "You're two of my favorite men in the world. You know that, both of you. You know it makes me feel bad to see you arguing, especially when you're arguing because of me, so I want you to stop right now. Do you hear?"

Sam's response was immediate. "Ain't nobody goin' to make me stop lookin' out for your welfare, no matter how mad it gets you!"

"And no old man's goin' to tell me what to do!"

"That's because you're either too damned stupid or too damned stubborn to see I'm right!"

"You take that back, old man!"

"Stop it!" Her eyes glinting with anger, Honesty took a deep breath, then turned toward the bartender, who eyed the trio cautiously. "Bring a bottle and three glasses, Henry. It looks like my friends need to calm their nerves tonight."

"Yes, ma'am!"

Waiting only until the three glasses placed before them were filled to the brim, Honesty picked up hers and raised it to the two men standing on either side of her.

"To two of my favorite fellas—and the peace they're going to make with each other, at least for tonight."

Honesty raised her drink to her lips . . . and waited.

Sam snorted, then picked up his drink.

Jeremy's brown eyes snapped with anger as he took up his drink with obvious reluctance.

The two men downed their drinks in a simultaneous gulp.

Honesty poured them another, grateful the crisis was temporarily over.

"That's not the end of it—you know that, don't you, Jewel?"

Turning toward the handsome man seated at the saloon table beside her, Jewel raised her carefully darkened brows. She saw true concern in the downward lines of Charles Webster's face as he stared a moment longer in the direction of the bar, where Honesty and her two companions maintained an uneasy peace.

It occurred to Jewel that if any other man had made that comment while staring at Honesty so intently, she might have believed he was as infatuated with Honesty as most other men were. But she knew that wasn't the case. She also knew that the reason for her confidence was not the fact that Charles had been *her* man for seven years, or because she knew that her appeal to the opposite sex had not eroded during that time. For the truth was that there wasn't a woman in all of Caldwell—on either side of the bright saloon lights—who could hold a candle to Honesty. She had acknowledged that fact with a pride that was just short of motherly the first day that Honesty had put up her hair.

Motherly pride. Jewel almost shuddered. She couldn't make herself believe that the state of embattled coexistence that had reigned between Honesty and her since that first day beside the river had finally boiled down to that. She was too passionate a woman for motherly feelings!

She was passionate about The Texas Jewel, the saloon that was both her life's work and her life's dream. She had worked tirelessly and without reservation to make it the talk of the Chisholm Trail. It was now successful beyond her wildest imaginings, and the security and total independence she had sought was her reward.

Yet, her triumph had begun to fall flat . . . until Charles.

And, yes . . . she was passionate about Charles Webster. How could she not be? He was everything a woman wanted in a man. He was a gentleman, as befitted his position as manager of Caldwell's largest bank. He was handsome. Neither the streaks of gray in his dark hair nor the lines of maturity that marked his even features had altered that fact. He was a fine figure of a man and his grooming was impeccable, the superior cut of his clothes and his fine, dark mustache setting him apart in a territory of shaggily bearded, unkempt men.

But most important of all, Charles was the only man she had ever known whose passion was a match for her own. His touch set her on fire, and when they lay flesh to flesh, there was no one else in the world but them.

Perfect.

Almost.

The tarnish on that perfection lay in one small detail. Charles was married to another woman. He had been for as long as she had known him.

And then there were those sudden, unexplained trips out of town that Charles avoided discussing, and the woman who—

Refusing to complete that last thought, Jewel raised her chin in an unconscious gesture of defiance. Whatever doubts nagged, she knew that Charles's need for her was as great as hers was for him, and that his passion was hers alone.

She also knew that Charles's affection for Honesty was sincere. Admittedly, she had been jealous at first, recognizing an immediate bond between the young Honesty and Charles that did not exist between Honesty and herself. But she had come to recognize that Honesty's curious mind had seen in Charles a glimpse of a world totally foreign to her, and that they had somehow sensed in each other a kindred soul.

As for the whispers about "Honesty's three men," Jewel ignored them. She knew full well what inspired those whispers. She also knew that the men who voiced them would gladly give the last drop of their blood to be one of Honesty's "three."

When all was said and done, the truth was that Honesty—the stubborn little brat who had given her no peace—had turned out to be a damned impressive woman!

Not that Jewel would ever admit it aloud.

Nor would she allow herself to admit her concern at Honesty's recklessness, the part of Honesty that seemed somehow driven to push things to the limit, both with cards and with men—almost as if she were tempting fate.

Few knew the vulnerable side of Honesty that was hidden by her gay, teasing exterior—the part of Honesty haunted by recurring dreams she had suffered since childhood and by a belief she refused to surrender. Jewel knew it was that hidden side of Honesty, revealed to her three men alone, which inspired their devotion.

Acknowledged only in the darkness of the night when Jewel could no longer avoid it, however, was the chilling certainty that because of their devotion, there was not a one of Honesty's three men who would hesitate to die for her.

Jewel struggled against the familiar knot tightening deep inside her. Damn Charles for again forcing her to face her concerns!

"Jewel, did you hear what I said?"

"I heard you."

"Well?"

"What do you want me to say?" Jewel's response was terse. "You know Honesty never listens to a word I say. She heeds you more than she does me."

"No. Honesty tolerates my advice. She doesn't take it."

"So?" Jewel brushed a strand of flamboyantly red hair from a cheek remarkably unlined by time. Her heavily kohled eyes snapped with anger. "I'm not Honesty's mother. I never tried to be. The relationship between Honesty and me was temporary from the start, and as far as I'm concerned, it still is." Jewel took a steadying breath, her next words difficult.

"She confides in you, so I don't have to tell you how she feels. She won't let go of that promise she made to her father about takin' care of her sisters. She can't seem to get it into her head that they're gone forever. She stopped talkin' about findin' them years ago, but she's still certain the day will come when they're goin' to walk through those saloon doors and back into her life. She's just bidin' her time until then. As far as she's concerned, *they're* her family, not me."

The sudden shards of ice in Charles's eyes cut deeply as he grated, "So you're telling me that you're going to sit idly by, knowing Honesty's heading for trouble by standing between those two men?"

"I'm not Honesty's keeper. She's a woman now. She handles her men the way she chooses."

"Jewel . . ."

"Just like I handle mine."

Jewel saw the flicker in Charles's dark eyes the moment before she pushed her chair back and drew herself to her full height. The white swells of her breasts heaved with restrained agitation, bulging against the gold satin of her bodice as she spat, "I've said as much as I have to say about it. I'm of a mood to take over one of the tables tonight. Unless you'll be playin', I'll be sayin' good night."

Not waiting for his response, Jewel turned away. She felt Charles's eyes on her back as she walked toward the farthest table and signaled the dealer to rise, but she felt no regret for her abruptness. She loved the man, and it had taken all the strength she could muster to pick herself up from that chair and turn her back on him, but the days were gone when she'd conduct her life according to anyone's views but her own.

Glancing up briefly as she assumed her seat and picked up the cards, Jewel saw that Honesty still stood between the glowering Sam and the hot-tempered Jeremy.

The knot within Jewel tightened.

Honesty, wise in so many ways, was too blind to see that Jeremy loved her in a way she didn't love him.

But Sam saw it all too clearly, and he was determined to do anything he must do to keep Honesty clear of the trouble Jeremy was heading for.

No, a wink of the eye and a sultry whisper wouldn't get Honesty out of the kind of trouble in store for her if she didn't—

Jewel again halted her thoughts. Damn that Charles! None of this was her business! Honesty had made it clear a long time ago that she could handle her own affairs without any help from her.

Besides, she had problems of her own.

Her smile strained, Jewel dealt the cards.

The escalating sounds of revelry dimming around him, Charles stared at Jewel as she assumed her seat at the card table, treating every man there to a flash of her sultry smile as she did. Pangs of momentary jealousy twisted his stomach into knots as he picked up the bottle in front of him and poured himself another drink.

He should have known better.

Tossing the drink down in a gulp, Charles waited for the heat of it to fade before taking a stabilizing breath. No, it wouldn't do for the president of Caldwell's largest bank, a man who was highly respected in *most* quarters, to indulge himself in the bottle.

Appearances . . .

Charles gave a short, self-deprecating laugh. Appearances had at one time been so important to him. He had been a pompous ass then, as only the sole progeny of wealthy parents could be. He had been puffed up with his own sense of importance until the family bank failed after being tainted with scandal. Forced to go West in order to earn a living for himself and his ailing wife, he had struggled for his livelihood for the first time, spending every penny he earned in attempting to make Emily well again. His eventual need to finance Emily's transportation back East, and her stay in a sanitarium where she would spend the rest of her days, had then forced him into debt so deep that he believed he would never surface again.

His emotional and financial devastation had been complete. He had known Emily since childhood. She had loved him and supported him without reservation through all his difficulties, and she had never stopped believing in him. She had been too sick to function intimately as his wife for years before her illness forced their separation, but he had never stopped loving her. The truth was that he loved her still. Each winter trip back East to visit her was a torment greater than the last.

But Emily, once beautiful and full of life and now only a skeletal shadow of herself, still remained one of the most loving women he had ever known. She had continued to offer him his freedom until he had demanded she never speak the words again. For another truth was that Emily would remain his wife, both in his mind and in his heart, until the day she drew her last breath.

He had met Jewel shortly after Emily had been institutionalized, when his life was beginning to regain an even keel. Jewel had reawakened the joy in him with her straightforward approach to existence, and with her undisguised passion. She had made his life worth living again. At one time, the choices Jewel had made in order to survive would have bothered him, but that was no longer true. He admired her courage. He respected her determination. And even if she did make him damned angry at times, he loved her in a way he had never loved Emily. He didn't care what the "good people" of town whispered behind his back. Not a one of those tight-lipped matrons who looked down on Jewel from their lofty perches of self-righteousness was fit to shine Jewel's shoes.

He wanted never to lose Jewel.

But he was afraid he might.

Because no matter the passion between them, no matter how well she understood his feelings for Emily, or how many times he said the words, Jewel didn't trust his love. He wasn't certain she ever would.

And although he knew Jewel loved him, he was not certain that she loved him, *enough*.

Charles poured himself another drink.

And then there was the constant friction between them about Honesty. Actually, he was at a loss to define in his own mind what had drawn him to the youthful Honesty the first moment he met her. He only knew that despite her smile, he had sensed a crying ache inside the beautiful child Honesty had been that was similar to his own. He had been unable to ignore it. Honesty and he had grown close as she matured, and he had somehow come to feel responsible for her safety and happiness. He knew Jewel understood his feelings for Honesty.

The problem was that he could not understand *hers*.

And last, but not least, there was the silent threat hanging over his head, one that Jewel would not ever—

A round of raucous laughter sounded from Jewel's

gaming table, returning Charles's attention there. A mustached wrangler leaned close to Jewel and whispered into her ear. Jewel's husky response sent a hot flush of jealousy again surging through him.

Tossing down his drink, Charles stood abruptly. He turned toward the bar, grateful to see that Honesty was making her way back to her table.

Beside her moments later, Charles leaned down and whispered, "You'd better give those two fellows of yours some cooling off time, Honesty. Sam looks like he's about to bust a blood vessel, and Jeremy doesn't look much better."

Honesty's incredibly blue eyes looked up into his. She glanced toward the card table where Jewel laughed companionably with the men there. "I've taken them to task. They'll behave themselves for a while. Don't worry, Charles."

Don't worry, Charles. . . .

The irony of those words still ringing, Charles pressed a light kiss to Honesty's cheek and turned toward the door—unaware of the intense gaze that followed him out of sight.

Staring venomously at Charles Webster's well-tailored back until the saloon doors closed behind it, Jeremy turned back abruptly to the bar. Nobody had to tell him what Webster had whispered into Honesty's ear.

Stay away from Jeremy Sills. He's trouble. You can do better than him.

They were all against him. Everybody but Honesty.

Jeremy's reaction to that thought was a curt, "Pour me another drink, Henry."

A voice from beside Jeremy interjected warningly, "I'm thinkin' you've had enough already."

Jeremy turned toward Sam with a snarl. "I didn't ask your advice, old man!"

"Old man . . ." Sam's faced creased into the myriad lines of a mirthless smile. "Yeah, I'm an old man. But I'm thinkin' I must've done somethin' right to have lived so long. On the other hand, you ain't goin' to live—"

"Get this through your head," Jeremy grated, "I'm not interested in anything you've got to say! Keep your nose out of Honesty's and my business."

"*Honesty's and my business* . . . ain't that a joke!" But Sam was not laughing. "You're right, I ain't got no right to offer you advice, especially since you're too damned dumb to take it, but I'm feelin' you got a right to know exactly where I stand, once and for all. You was a nice enough kid a while back, before your mama died and before you went hell-bent-for-leather in the wrong direction. Well, you're hangin' out with the wrong kind now—them that ain't the kind to do neither you nor Honesty no good. But Honesty feels responsible for you and she—"

"I told you—"

"—and she's not the kind to back off when a friend needs her. So I figure the situation is this. Either you straighten yourself out, or I'll make it my business to see that *you* back off!"

Slow rage inched Jeremy's hand toward the gun at his hip as he rasped, "Who do you think you're talkin' to, old man?"

"I'm talkin' to a wet-nosed kid who ain't goin' to live long enough to see his first gray hairs if he moves his hand one inch closer to that gun on his belt."

The lifelessness of Sam's tone dropped Jeremy's hand to his side as the old cowpoke continued, "Just so's you understand me—there ain't no way I'm goin' to let you ruin Honesty's life, just 'cause she feels sorry for you. That's my final warnin' . . . and that's all I got to say."

Allowing his squint-eyed gaze to linger a few silent moments longer, Sam turned toward the door.

A driving urge to finish what he had started minutes earlier raised Jeremy's hand to the gun at his hip. He rested it there, his fingers twitching toward the trigger. If it wasn't for Honesty . . .

Jeremy darted a glance at Honesty, suddenly sick with fear that she might have seen his reaction after the volatile exchange that had just passed between Sam and him. The last thing he wanted was for Honesty to get mad at him again. The last thing he wanted was to make her unhappy. Hell, he loved her so damned much . . .

Jeremy's throat tightened with unexpected emotion. Honesty was everything to him. She had been his friend when he had none, and she was the only person who had never let him down. It didn't really matter to him that Honesty was beautiful. It wasn't the brilliant blue color of her eyes that touched his heart. It was what he saw in them. Honesty loved him. She had loved him when he was a ragged kid scratching for a living for his mother and him. She had never stopped loving him through all the dark and heavy years in between. He knew she never would.

Jeremy briefly closed his eyes. The only trouble was that he wanted *more.* He wanted Honesty to love him the way he loved her—with a heart so full and with so much yearning that there wasn't an hour that passed when he didn't see her face. He wanted her to share his hunger to hold her close the way he had never held her. He wanted her to long for the touch of his lips on hers. He wanted her to crave the stroke of his hands against her skin. He wanted to lie close to her, their naked flesh hot against each other, so close that he could feel each breath she breathed and each sigh she sighed—the way he did with Maude's girls when he pretended they were Honesty.

Damn it all, he was tired of pretending! He wanted Honesty for his own, once and for all, so he would never lose her.

Taking a moment to steady his emotions, Jeremy reached for his drink and swallowed it in a gulp. The trouble was that when Honesty looked at him, she saw a boy, not a man who loved her.

Jeremy tapped the bar in a silent signal for another drink and waited impatiently for it to be poured. He tossed it down and tapped the bar again, grateful for the stinging burn in his stomach that steadied him as his mind raged.

He knew what the trouble was! How could Honesty see him as a man when all he owned in the world was a silver-studded saddle he had won in a poker game and the twelve-year-old mare he put it on? He'd never earn enough money at his job in the holding pens outside town to do more than just get by. He was twenty-one years old, damn it, and so was Honesty! One day real soon she would realize that she was never going to find her sisters and that it was never going to be just the three of them again, the way she had always dreamed. She would decide to go on with her life, then. She'd start looking for a man.

And she wouldn't look his way.

'Cause the truth was that although Honesty loved him, she didn't *respect* him.

Damn . . . damn it all!

Emotions held tightly in check, Jeremy tapped the bar again. He waited, then barked, "What's the matter, Henry, are you deaf? Pour me another drink!"

Henry's smile did not reach his eyes. "You've got a few under your belt already, but I don't mind pourin' you more . . . as long as you show me your cash."

Gritting his teeth, Jeremy reached into his pocket and slapped his coin onto the bar.

"That only covers what you already drank."

A hot flush suffused Jeremy's face. "What's the matter? You know I'm good for it!"

"No more credit. Jewel's orders."

Jewel's orders . . .

They were all against him, damn it!

It all came down to money! He had never had any, and nobody thought he ever would. Money made people look at a man differently, like he *was* somebody. Money earned *respect!* If he had money, he would laugh in all their faces. Then he would tell Honesty how much he loved her, and he'd take her away someplace where he'd spoil her until she forgot everybody but him.

Henry raised his bushy gray brows. "Well, you goin' to put up the coin or not?"

Bastard . . .

Jeremy's hand twitched again toward his gun, only to be halted by a grip on his arm as a voice droned into his ear, "Let me buy that drink for you, partner."

Jeremy turned unsteadily toward his voice. A smile slowly spread across his lips as Tom Bitters withdrew a few bills from the roll he held so casually in his hand and slapped them onto the bar. Bitters' voice conveyed a touch of menace as he spoke again to the silent bartender. "And keep them comin'."

Jeremy ran his hand through his hair and straightened his shoulders. Then he reached for his drink.

The incessant pounding of the piano in the corner of the crowded saloon . . . the steady screech of the fiddle . . . bursts of drunken laughter and slurred voices raised in song . . . the unsteady sway of be-whiskered cowboys and their satin-clad partners dancing around the floor . . . stifling clouds of blue tobacco smoke encompassing all . . .

When had the merriment of the evening taken such a garish turn?

Honesty raised a hand to her pounding head. She was unaware of the knowing glances she received from the men around the table as she glanced again toward the long mahogany bar where swaying drovers and smiling saloon girls stood three deep. Her thoughts were for one person alone.

Jeremy.

He was drunk again.

A familiar sadness close to despair tightened Honesty's throat. She didn't have to look at the card table nearby to know that Jewel was as conscious of Jeremy's drunken condition as she. Jewel didn't miss much. Jewel knew how she felt about Jeremy's drinking. It seemed she always knew. There was a time, when Honesty was younger, when Jewel had seemed to know what she was thinking even before she did. She had resented that. Perhaps that was the reason that the conflict between them had not lessened over the years.

Not that she wasn't truly fond of Jewel, because she was. She was proud of all Jewel had accomplished. She was proud of the part she now played in Jewel's success. She was proud of Jewel. It was just that . . . well, Jewel was still bossy. And Mama was right. She had never liked being told what to do. She supposed she never would.

The strangest part of it all, however, was that without it ever being discussed between them, Honesty knew Jewel had never expected nor desired more from her than she gave. She supposed mutual acceptance of each other just as they were was the true basis of their relationship. Whatever it was, they both knew with unerring certainty that they could depend upon each other. Jewel's order not to extend Jeremy further credit at the bar was proof of that.

Jeremy, who lost the ability for rational thought when he drank.

Jeremy, whose wild streak grew wilder when he held a glass of red-eye in his hand.

Jeremy, who was beginning to resemble his father more and more each day . . .

As Honesty watched, Jeremy hoisted another glass and downed the contents with a hand so unsteady that the liquor spilled down the front of his shirt. His loud laughter was echoed by Tom Bitters's hardy guffaw. It galled Honesty to realize that although Bitters encouraged Jeremy to drink, Bitters himself was as sober as a judge.

Oh, Jeremy . . .

The ache inside Honesty deepened.

No matter how many times she told him that Bitters was making a fool of him, Jeremy refused to listen! He had worked hard to ingratiate himself with Bitters and his shady partners after they'd arrived a month earlier flashing a lot of money around town. She knew the prospect of easy money was what attracted Jeremy to Bitters. Jeremy had been looking for the easy way all his life. What she did not comprehend was what Bitters wanted with him.

Sensing someone's gaze, Honesty glanced at the nearby table to see Jewel looking her way. Charles had left early. Jewel and he had argued again. She could always tell. She was uncomfortable when they did because she somehow knew that although their feelings for each other ran deep, more than Charles's sick wife stood between them.

She also feared that there would come a time when Charles would not return.

Jeremy's sudden burst of laughter caught Honesty's ear the moment before he staggered backward against a nearby table and fell to the floor amidst the sounds of shattering glass and angry shouts. He was still laughing when Bitters dragged him to his feet.

Her pounding head close to bursting, Honesty stood up abruptly and signaled a nearby dealer to her table. Jewel's professional smile did not falter as Honesty approached her and announced flatly, "I've had enough for tonight. I'm going to bed."

So heavily was Honesty's head pounding as she walked up the staircase to the second floor and turned the corner toward her room, that she was unconscious of the curious eyes and lustful stares that followed her.

The door to her room loomed like an oasis in the desert as Honesty reached for the knob with a trembling hand. She closed the door quickly behind her and leaned back, breathing deeply of the dark silence before lighting the lamp.

The lamp's soft glow revealed a satin-draped bedroom that reflected Honesty's bold, vivacious spirit—a spirit that was now sadly lagging. Opening her wardrobe, Honesty ignored her usual preference for satin robes and reached for the cotton nightgown pushed into the corner. She stripped off her clothes, dropping them on the floor in her haste to discard them, and drew the nightgown down over her bare skin. She smoothed the wash-worn fabric with her fingers and hugged it close around her for long moments before raising her hand to her neckline to grasp her locket.

The locket's familiar shape was the reassurance

she sought. It brought her back to her youth, when she had felt truly whole, before a part of her had been wrenched away so cruelly by the river's flooding waters. Its warmth in her palm was her only real consolation at times like this, when the vivacity of her adult personality slipped away, leaving her with the strange, undiminished loneliness lying beneath the surface. She could not explain her deep conviction that her sisters still lived. Nor could she explain the longing to find them that was an unrelenting ache inside her, or her certainty that until they were reunited, neither her sisters nor she would ever feel truly complete.

She was the oldest. It was her obligation to find her sisters—an obligation she had accepted with her last words to her father.

A shiver rolled down Honesty's spine despite the warmth of the room, and she clutched her nightgown closer. She had taken comfort in the belief that Jeremy truly understood this driving need within her . . . but at times like this, it was more pain than she could bear knowing that he was as lost as she.

Leaving her clothes where they lay, Honesty climbed into bed, pulled the coverlet up over her, and closed her eyes.

Clutching her locket with a desperate grip, she whispered into the shadows of the room, "Oh, Papa, sometimes I feel so alone."

Swaying, his vision unclear, Jeremy stared at the staircase to the second floor where Honesty had disappeared from sight minutes earlier. Honesty had left, and she hadn't even said good night.

Jeremy suddenly laughed out loud. Honesty wasn't as smart as she thought she was! She didn't realize how hard he hard been working on the future he had planned for them! Bitters and he were now getting along so well that he had even managed to get Bitters to promise to include him in the next "business venture" he had planned.

Business venture—hah! Jeremy knew exactly what Bitters meant. Bitters and his two partners did all their business with their guns. He'd be happy to do his business the same way if it would get him the same kind of roll that Bitters flashed each night. He wasn't going to be like his father, ending up lying in the street, a destitute town drunk with a broken neck. Not him.

"Hey, partner, how about another drink?"

Jeremy turned back to the bar. Bitters's face was starting to blur, which meant he was probably getting drunk. Honesty wouldn't like that.

Bitters took his glass and refilled it again. He held it out to Jeremy. "Come on. I'm not ready to quit for the night yet."

Jeremy smiled. He'd make his excuses to Honesty tomorrow. She'd forgive him. She always did.

He accepted the glass.

Honesty twisted restlessly in her sleep as fragmented sights and sounds assaulted her mind. She heard a loud noise like thunder, growing ever closer. She saw Mama's frightened face. She heard Chastity's scream. She saw it, then, a towering wall of water sweeping toward them! It crashed over them, tumbling her around and around . . . filling her nose and mouth . . . choking her . . . turning the world into a terror of dark emptiness that would not end!

No. She saw a light in the distance, growing brighter. It was the sun. Day was dawning fresh and clear, and there was no water in sight. Someone was approaching. A woman. She was tall and slender.

The sun at her back held the woman's outline in dark relief, but there was something about the way she walked, a long-limbed stride that struck a chord of familiarity. The woman's hair was unbound. It streamed out behind her on the warm breeze as the sun gradually rose, illuminating . . .

Honesty caught her breath. The woman's hair was blond, a sweet, golden blond that she recognized so well! The woman lifted her hand to her neck as a ray of the rising sun touched a necklace there. The flash of glittering gold was momentarily blinding, even as it sent a jolt of joy straight to her heart!

She knew who that woman was! It was Purity! Purity was coming!

Honesty held out her arms as the image grew closer. Tears streamed down her face as she waited . . . waited . . .

Purity slowed her advance. She stopped still.

Honesty wanted to shout. She wanted to call Purity's name. She wanted to tell her it was all right, that she had been waiting for her and for Chastity for so many years!

But she could not.

The image gradually faded and a slow sobbing began inside Honesty. Her tears were so heavy, her anguish so intense, that she was momentarily uncertain of the other feminine outline she saw in the distance.

A flash of red hair.

Honesty gasped! Chastity!

She was gone.

Another figure appeared in its stead, but this time Honesty did not smile. . . .

The revelry in the saloon reached a riotous pitch as Tom Bitters again refilled Jeremy's glass. Bitters smiled, the downward lines of his unshaven face making his expression more like a sneer as he urged, "Drink up, partner. There's plenty more where that came from."

Jeremy emptied his glass with a lopsided grin, and Bitters laughed. "That's it! I like to see a man who isn't afraid to tilt his glass."

Jeremy swayed. Spittle leaked from the corner of his mouth, and Bitters barely managed to conceal his disgust. It was all he could do not to wipe that stupid smile from Sills's face with the power of his naked fist. Instead, Bitters refilled his glass again and waited. The bastard had a constitution like an ox, but it wouldn't be much longer.

Noting the sudden drooping of Sills's eyes, Bitters signaled Riggs and Gant where they stood at the bar a few feet away. They were ready when Sills's knees began to give and he started slipping to the floor. Laughing and slapping Sills companionably on the back as he pretended a degree of intoxication he did not feel, Bitters led the way in an unsteady path toward the door. He acknowledged the nods of several familiar faces, his pose wearing thin at some of the snide remarks he heard in passing.

Maintaining his facade with sheer strength of will, Bitters pushed his way through the chaos of midnight revelry as he emerged onto Caldwell's main street. He hardly reacted as drunken cowboys raced their ponies down the crowded thoroughfare with complete disregard for pedestrian and observer alike, and others shouted encouragement, firing their guns wildly into the air. He pushed aside the brightly painted women soliciting for Maude's House of Pleasure up the street. He allowed his mask to slip only when he turned out of general sight toward the shack that Sills called home.

Kicking the door open minutes later, he stepped inside. He ignored the dirt and disarray within as he grated, "Throw him on the bed and let him sleep it off."

Standing over Sills's unconscious form minutes later, Bitters muttered, "The stupid bastard actually thinks I've taken a liking to him."

Riggs's jowled face twitched. He responded with open resentment. "I don't mind tellin' you that I'm tired of babysittin' a drunk who ain't worth nothin' to nobody. I don't know why you're wastin' time on him. We ain't never had trouble takin' a bank before, and Caldwell ain't any different."

"Oh, yes, it is!" Bitters' expression grew tight. "Sometimes I think you're as stupid as he is. How many times do I have to tell you that there's goin' to be big money comin' through Caldwell soon. *Big* money."

"You don't know that for sure." Speaking for the first time, Gant was openly skeptical, even as he remained watchful for the hair-trigger temper that others had fallen victim to before. "Just because you heard somebody talkin' in a saloon—"

"It was the telegraph clerk I heard talkin', the one who took the first message from back East."

"Well, that don't mean he knew what he was talkin' about. I don't like hangin' around like we've been doin'. It's askin' for trouble. There's enough money in that bank right now to satisfy me."

"Well, there ain't enough for me! I told you what that clerk said. He said the Eastern syndicate is goin' to be sendin' through the financing for some special projects in a couple of weeks. That money's goin' to be goin' through Caldwell's main bank—that Webster fella's bank. Sills is all but beggin' me to let him in on our next job. He's got a real hunger for some cash so he can impress his girlfriend. And you know how close his girlfriend is with Webster. Sills don't like that one bit, and once I put the burr under his saddle, he'll make sure he gets all the information we need out of her about when that money's goin' to start comin' in."

"What if Webster don't tell her nothin'?

Bitters gave a short laugh. "There ain't nothin' them three fellas hold back from that Honesty Buchanan. She wraps them around her little finger with no trouble at all. And I'm tellin' you now, Sills will get us what we need, one way or the other. He's that hot to have some real foldin' money in his pocket."

"Yeah, if his brain ain't too pickled by then for him to do any thinkin' at all."

"He'll serve his purpose."

Riggs shook his head. "I ain't so sure. I'm thinkin' he ain't smart enough to handle it. I'm thinkin' we'd be better off without him."

"And I'm tellin' you he'll do. I'm also tellin' you that you can back out right now if you ain't got the stomach for what's comin' up." Bitters' swarthy complexion darkened with anger. "You and Gant both, if you got a mind!"

Riggs's jowled face stiffened. "Don't go gettin' mad. I was just tellin' you what I think, and what I think is that this kid ain't dependable."

"And I'm tellin' you that I ain't interested in what you're thinkin'! What's it goin' to be? Are you in or not?"

Bitters's expression had turned savage. Riggs knew that look. Bitters was like a bull dog. Once he got his teeth into something, he never let go. He'd get that information any way he needed to—and he'd pull off that holdup, whatever it took. Besides, Bitters didn't like being challenged, and Riggs wasn't about to be on the receiving end when Bitters got mad.

He nodded. "I'm in, whatever it takes."

Bitters turned toward Gant, his expression tight. "What about you? Either you're in or you're out."

Gant nodded. "I'm in."

"All right." His eyes black pinpoints of menace, Bitters rasped, "Then listen good. *I'm* the boss, and what *I* say goes. When this fool wakes up in the mornin', all he's goin' to hear is how his 'friends' carried him out of that saloon and brought him home. He's goin' to feel beholden, and he's goin' to think he's got to prove to me what a man he is so I'll let him in on what we're plannin'. He'll be ripe for the pickin' when I ask him to get that information for me."

Bitters paused, responding in a lower tone to the unvoiced question he read in the eyes of both men. "We won't need him after that, and if he gets in the way . . ."

Bitters's harsh laugh finished his thought more eloquently than words.

Reading satisfaction where he had read uncertainty only moments earlier, Bitters turned a contemptuous glance toward the bed where Sills lay unmoving, then ordered, "Let's go."

The three men stepped back out onto the street.

Another figure appeared in its stead, but this time Honesty did not smile. . . .

Mesmerized, Honesty stared. The new figure that had replaced the feminine outline and the flash of red hair she had seen so fleetingly was clearly defined. It was tall and masculine, its shoulders broad. It did not need encouragement as it approached with an instinctive male grace—walking steadily, without hesitation.

She sensed determination in its advance.

She sensed anger.

And she sensed . . . danger.

The figure strode closer. Honesty strained her eyes as the distant light of the sun brightened, lifting the shadows. She could almost see—

A loud burst of sound from the saloon below awakened Honesty with a jolt, shattering the images holding her in their thrall. Not ready to surrender them, she searched the shadows of her room, even while knowing she would find no trace of them there.

Honesty's eyes closed with acceptance. Another dream, like the many that had haunted her before . . .

Yet, it was not. For instead of hope, a sense of danger remained.

Unable to dispel it, unwilling to submit to its pall, Honesty closed her eyes. She locked her jaw tight, willing her mind clear of thought. She would not dream again tonight because she would not allow it.

Chapter Two

Early dawn lightened a summer sky still bright with stars as Wes Howell rode slowly down Caldwell's main street. In an unconscious gesture, he pulled the brim of his hat down lower on his forehead, deeply shadowing the tight planes of his face. An intimidating figure, he was tall, with an unusual breadth of shoulders and powerful build. Uncompromising coloring—midnight black hair and brows, sun-shaded skin, and eyes that were unrelievedly dark—merged with sober, equally imposing features and a strong jaw.

Allowing his mount a leisurely pace that belied his close scrutiny, Wes observed the rutted thoroughfare lined with hitching racks and posts, where board sidewalks more often than not yielded to dirt paths. He recalled the stockyards at the edge of town, obviously newly improved to accommodate increased trade while homes, stables, and corrals remained carelessly built. He saw occasional stone and brick buildings mixed with frame structures, noting the abundance of saloons with their gaudy false fronts. All was conspicuously silent in the advent of the new day, while debris from the previous night's revelry littered the street, sharing space with snoring drovers sleeping off their drunkenness. He recognized in the scene an honesty exclusive to dawn, which faded quickly after the sun rose.

He had caught the town unawares. He was good at catching people and places unawares. It was his specialty.

Holding his mount to a steady pace, Wes continued his surveillance, reviewing in his mind the information provided him before he had left south Texas a few weeks earlier.

Caldwell, Kansas, had sat astride the Chisholm Trail since the original village took root eleven years earlier, and it had been an enterprising town from the first. Its businessmen had been eager to get their share of the tremendous profits generated by the country's insatiable desire for beef following the Civil War. They had competed openly for traffic generated by the great drives northward from the cattle-rich state of Texas. Like other trail towns of its ilk, Caldwell had willingly supplied fun-starved drovers with every manner of diversion desired. It was only when the Santa Fe finally extended rail service to Caldwell a few years earlier, however, that the town was in a position to compete for business that had formerly gone to Abilene and other larger trail towns before the quarantine against Texas cattle in some quarters, and the censure of local citizens in others, had taken their toll.

But with new profits had come new problems. Always a rough-and-tumble town, Caldwell was now dangerous, with drunken rowdies lining the streets in the late hours and shootings an everyday occurrence that had resulted in many deaths, including the town marshal's a month earlier.

But the trail herds continued to come. That had been evident during his approach through the sun-drenched grazing land outside town where a herd of thirty thousand or more lingered prior to being driven into the stockyards to await transportation. The new trail broken through to Caldwell in the early spring had raised speculation that Caldwell would probably see 1882 as its peak year.

Wes stiffened his back, his gaze going cold. He was determined that 1882 would be his peak year, too.

A flash of light in a darkened stone structure ahead suddenly caught his attention, and Wes snapped his gaze toward the sign in front. The Caldwell Bank. His reaction instinctive, he dug his heels into his mount's sides at the exact moment that an explosion rocked the early morning silence. Gun in hand, he jumped from the saddle within a few yards of the bank entrance just as the door burst open and two men carrying heavy money bags broke out onto the board sidewalk.

Standing fast, Wes shouted, "Stop where you are!"

The men turned sharply toward him. Their hands snaked toward the guns at their hips.

Wes fired, once . . . twice!

There was no need for a third shot.

Scanning the street as startled townsfolk began spilling from nearby doorways, Wes approached the fallen men with caution. He kicked the money bags aside and kneeled briefly beside them, confirming his belief that no doctor would be needed.

Standing again, Wes jammed his gun back into his

holster, only then realizing that his hands were shaking. He addressed a heavily mustached fellow standing in his nightclothes nearby.

"Where's the marshal's office?"

"I . . . it's on the corner, over there."

Money bags securely tied to his saddle moments later, Wes mounted as townsfolk continued to emerge onto the street. He swung his horse in the direction the fellow had pointed, turning back in afterthought to address the mustached fellow who stood frozen to the spot.

"I suggest you call the undertaker."

Riding down the street at a cautious pace, Wes sensed speculative gazes following him. He felt no need for explanation. The curiosity of the town would be satisfied soon enough. He did not expect to remain a stranger.

Movement in the doorway of a shack some distance back from the street caught Wes's attention as he rode by. He perused the young couple standing there more closely. The fellow was young and blond. He was standing barechested, wearing only his trousers, as if he had just awakened. The young woman beside him appeared hastily clothed, the blue fabric of her dress clinging to the curves of her body revealingly. Her dark hair hung midway down her back, catching the rays of the rising sun as she turned to whisper something into the young fellow's ear. She looked back at Wes abruptly as she drew the fellow back inside, startling him with a flash of eyes that were incredibly blue, and with a glance of pure loathing.

Loathing . . .

Irritated to realize that he had been more affected by the unexpected hostility in the young woman's astounding blue eyes than he had been by the sight of the two men he had left lying lifeless on the street behind him, Wes cursed under his breath.

And with that same breath he dismissed them—both the men who had forced his hand and the woman who had judged him.

Stepping into the unlit marshal's office a moment later, he sat down and waited.

"Bounty hunter."

Honesty grimaced as she pushed Jeremy's cabin door shut behind her. Her expression remained grim. Alarmed by the sound of the explosion minutes earlier, she had rushed to the doorway of Jeremy's cabin and looked out into the street in time to see the big stranger fire his gun. She saw the two men drop on the spot, and she saw the casual way the big fellow had kneeled briefly beside them before picking up the money bags and leaving the dead men where they lay. She had known immediately that he had not happened on the spot by coincidence. His reaction had been too cold-blooded for him not to have done that type of thing many times before.

Oh, yes, she had seen his kind before. Bounty hunters were no novelty in Caldwell. Nor were shootings uncommon on the streets. She despised the senseless slaughter fostered by liquor and the heat of the moment, but she *abhorred* the cold-hearted contempt for life evinced by any man who would track down and kill another human being for a reward.

The big stranger was trash. He was less than nothing in her eyes. She dismissed him from her mind.

Suddenly aware that Jeremy was waiting for her to speak, Honesty felt a familiar frustration. Her head was pounding. Her disturbing dreams aside, her concerns for Jeremy had left her sleepless most of the previous night, even as she had reminded herself that she had resolved not to fall into the same trap again. She had told herself that Jeremy was a grown man who was responsible for his own actions. Somewhere during the silence of the night hours that had followed, however, she had recalled the boy she had known so long ago—a boy still very much present behind the soft brown eyes of the man Jeremy had grown to be. She had waited only until the first crack of dawn before throwing a dress over her bare flesh and heading for the door.

She hadn't bothered to knock. She had known what she would find inside Jeremy's shack, and she had not been mistaken. Sprawled on the bed, his hand pressed to his forehead and an expression of abject pain on his face, Jeremy had attempted a grin. But the grin had failed, and with it had gone her anger.

She had pulled Jeremy to his feet and forced him to strip to the waist so he might bathe away the stench of his previous night's mistakes. She had been waiting for the look in his eye that said he was ready to listen to what she had to say when she heard the boom of the explosion.

The bounty hunter's cold-eyed gaze returned again to her mind, sending a chill down Honesty's spine. Yes, she had seen men like him before. Perhaps that was the reason for the fleeting feeling of familiarity she had experienced on seeing him.

"I'm sorry, Honesty."

Jeremy's hoarse voice interrupted Honesty's thoughts, bringing her back to the present. But her head was still aching, and she was in no mood for words of repentance she had heard many times before.

"You don't have to apologize to me." Honesty

shrugged. "I'm not the one you're hurting. You're hurting yourself."

"I'm hurting you, too. I know I am . . . and I'm sorry."

The true remorse in Jeremy's tone tightened Honesty's throat to the point of pain. Jeremy was right. His face was blotchy and his eyes deeply ringed. He stood with the stance of a man three times his age because he felt too damned sick to straighten up. He was killing himself, going down the same road that his father had traveled, and he was too blind to see it! It hurt her terribly to see him this way.

Speaking the words before she realized they had left her lips, Honesty whispered, "Apologies . . . it's always the same! You say all the right things, and then forget you ever said them. Jeremy, if you know it pains me to see you this way, why don't you stop?"

"Things got a little out of hand last night, but it wasn't supposed to go that way. Bitters and I were gettin' along just fine. I was talkin' to him, and I think I finally convinced him to take me in with him on his next business deal."

"*Business* deal?" Honesty was incredulous. "What *is* his business, Jeremy?"

"He . . . he's a cattle broker."

"A cattle broker."

"He's been lookin' for the right herd to buy so he can run it up to the Blackfoot Agency in Montana. The government is payin' a good price for steers up there."

"And even if that were true, what does he need *you* for?"

Honesty knew she had made a mistake the moment Jeremy's jaw stiffened. She had demeaned him . . . hurt his pride. Jeremy's moods were erratic when his pride was hurt.

"I'm as good a wrangler as any of the damned trail herders that come through this town, and you know it! The only reason I haven't joined up with an outfit before this is because joinin' up would take me away from Caldwell for eight or nine months at a time, and . . . and . . ." Honesty waited through the tense, extended silence until Jeremy's smile flashed unexpectedly. ". . . and I figured you would miss me too much."

"Jeremy . . ." Honesty shook her head.

He whispered hopefully, "Well, you would, wouldn't you?"

Honesty did not respond.

Jeremy's voice took on the tone of a plea. "Wouldn't you?"

How could she deny it? "Yes, I would."

"So, you forgive me, because you know I'm only tryin' to make somethin' of myself for you . . ."

"*Do* I know that, Jeremy?"

"Yes."

"Then stay away from Bitters."

"Just because I drank a little too much last night—"

"I don't trust him."

"Honesty . . ."

"He isn't good for you, Jeremy!"

Jeremy sighed. "I don't want to argue with you anymore, Honesty. Hell, I've got a headache that won't quit."

"It serves you right."

"You don't mean that."

This time it was Honesty's turn to sigh. "No, I didn't mean it . . . not that I want to see you suffer, anyway. I suppose that's the reason I'm here. I brought you something."

Reaching into her pocket, Honesty withdrew a paper packet. "Doc Ward gave me these powders for those headaches I get. You know, after—"

"—after you have those dreams."

"Yes."

The knot in Honesty's throat tightened. Jeremy was the only person who didn't try to tell her to forget her dreams because they would never come true, that she would never see her sisters again. So why did she think she had the right to tell him to forget his?

Suddenly grateful for all the good things Jeremy was, Honesty hugged him with all her might. She felt him shudder the moment before she stepped back and put the packet in his hand. "Take this and you'll feel better. We'll talk later, all right?"

"All right."

Her hand on the door, Honesty was about to leave when she felt Jeremy's touch on her arm.

"Honesty . . ." Jeremy's pale face was sober as he whispered, "You know I love you, don't you?"

Too filled with emotion to speak, Honesty nodded. Still unable to respond, she pressed a kiss to his cheek and stepped out onto the street. She kept her eyes directly forward as she walked quickly back in the direction from which she had come.

"I don't like the idea of this." Marshal Carr's tone was stiff. "Those eastern bankers had no need to hire you to guard their shipments after they reach Caldwell. That's the job of the marshal's office."

"Slater Enterprises doesn't seem to feel that way."

Marshal Carr's wiry mustache twitched with suppressed anger. He had arrived at the scene of the aborted bank robbery only minutes after the unknown stranger had loaded the money bags on his horse and ridden away in full view of half the town.

And no one had tried to stop him.

His gaze narrowing into an assessing squint, Carr shrugged. He supposed he couldn't blame them. Hell, he couldn't remember when he had last seen a bigger or tougher looking fella than this one. And the way he had brought those bank robbers down with one shot each . . .

Marshal Carr mentally shook himself. That was neither here nor there. *He* was the marshal, and he didn't want anybody edging in on his territory. It didn't make any difference to him that the fella's name was Wes Howell, a name that struck fear in the heart of every outlaw in Texas. Hell, Howell wasn't a Texas Ranger anymore! And even if he was, this wasn't Texas!

Carr sniffed and rubbed his stubbled cheek. He had hotfooted it down the street in the direction that old Barney Knickerbocker indicated the stranger had gone. He wasn't sure whether he had been more surprised or relieved to find Howell waiting for him in his office with the money bags on the floor beside his feet. But relief had quickly changed to a resentment that still rankled as he addressed the hard-eyed Howell again.

"You stopped that robbery and that's fine, but I don't expect to give you any special treatment while you're workin' in this town. If you get in my way, I'm goin' to push you out of it."

Howell drew himself slowly to his feet. "I'm not in the habit of gettin' in the way of the law."

"And if you overstep your bounds, you'll end up in jail like anybody else."

"Nor do I make it a habit of findin' myself on the wrong side of iron bars."

Carr stretched his wiry frame up to a height that was still a head and a half shorter than his visitor's as he glared at Howell. "Well, you just remember what I said."

His expression unchanged, Howell responded in a softer tone than before, "I want you to remember somethin', too, marshal. I'm here to do a job. I'm goin' to do it. And if you get in *my* way, *I'll* step on *you.*"

Watching minutes later as Howell strode onto the street and mounted his horse, Carr muttered a low epithet. He didn't like that fella one bit.

And why did he have the feeling that there was more to this whole situation than met the eye?

His jaw tight as he rode back down Caldwell's main street, Wes allowed his mount a relaxed pace that masked his inner agitation. He had left Marshal Carr fuming in the wake of his warning. The exchange between them had not gone the way he had hoped. He had been counting on obtaining information that would save him valuable time, but it appeared the marshal would not be the one to provide it.

The damned fool . . .

The hard lines of Wes' face tightened. The man was too full of pride to let him help with a job that could get dangerous. He had no doubt that the arrival of the oversized shipments of cash Slater Enterprises had authorized in anticipation of Caldwell's increased traffic would soon be general knowledge. News like that had a way of getting around. The Caldwell Bank was to be the temporary depository for that cash, and every outlaw in the territory would soon be drawn there. It would take a lot more than one man to handle that situation.

A spontaneous pride stirred. It would take a lot more than one man to handle the situation—unless that one man was a Texas Ranger.

Wes felt no inclination to smile. Texas Rangers had earned every ounce of recognition given them with their sweat and with their blood. He had taken a leave of absence and slipped his badge into his pocket for the duration when he had been contacted for this job, and he had not done that easily. But the opportunity had been too good to be true, providing him the cover he badly needed for his more important, personal agenda.

His composure under tight rein, Wes unconsciously scanned the early morning street. He had waited seven years for the opportunity now presenting itself. He had lived those years with one thought in mind, and he—

A flicker at the corner of his eye interrupted Wes's thoughts, drawing his attention to the shack he had noticed earlier. The couple was again in the doorway. The woman paused there, looking up at the blond fellow as he whispered something to her. She responded by raising her lips to his.

Wes glanced away, annoyed with himself as he looked back a moment later to see the young woman walking quickly back down the street. Surprised when she turned unexpectedly toward the bank, he drew his mount to a halt. When she went inside and disappeared from sight, he waited. Time stretched on immeasurably until she emerged again and crossed the street, continuing until she reached the elaborate front entrance of the saloon there.

Wes was momentarily disconcerted. It was not uncommon to see a saloon girl slipping along the streets in the early morning hours as she returned from a night in her lover's arms, but he had never seen one go directly from her lover's arms to a bank that had just been robbed.

Wes spurred his mount into motion. Dismounting outside the Caldwell Bank moments later, he dropped his reins over the hitching post, noting that the crowd that had gathered after the blast had dispersed. The bodies of the two bank robbers had already been removed. The undertaker had obviously spared no time in collecting his charges, but the truth be known, it would not have bothered Wes in the least if the men still lay where they had fallen. They had made the mistake of breaking the law and had suffered the consequences. He had come to terms with those consequences a long time ago.

Standing in the doorway of the bank, Wes surveyed the damage within. The smell of gunpowder still hung over the room, but the damage appeared to be minimal. A large safe in the corner stood open, its door sagging on its hinges. The area in close proximity was covered with the residue of the explosion, but the remainder of the room appeared to be intact. The two teller's cages were none the worse for wear, and the mahogany desks and chairs nearby were not damaged. The dark-haired fellow at work gathering up the few papers and books that were strewn on the floor was the only person inside. He looked up as Wes entered.

"Can I help you with something?" The man hesitated, then added, "Or have you already helped me? You're the fellow who stopped the robbery, aren't you?"

Wes nodded.

"I recognized you from your description. My name's Charles Webster." He extended his hand. "I manage the bank here, and I want to thank you for what you did."

Wes accepted his hand. "My name's Wes Howell."

"Oh . . ." Webster straightened up, his smile momentarily faltering. "I'm surprised. I wasn't expecting you until next week."

"I'm ahead of schedule." Not in the mood for amenities, Wes looked at the safe, frowning. "Slater Enterprises will be dispatching the first of the money shipments soon. Will you be able to handle them without a safe?"

"We have another one." At Wes's raised brow, Webster added, "We keep a smaller safe in the back room. It's the one we previously used, before business increased. It'll do until we can get a new one shipped in. That's the least of our problems."

Wes's eyes narrowed. "And what's the worst?"

"I think you got a taste of it about an hour ago. This isn't a particularly peace-loving town."

"It wasn't much of a problem for me." Wes did not bother to smile. "What else do you have to tell me?"

Webster straightened up slowly and placed the papers he had been collecting on the desk nearby. His tone correspondingly cold, he motioned Wes toward the office in the rear. "I think we should get comfortable. This is going to take a while."

"There you are!"

Her hand on her bedroom doorknob, Honesty looked back at Jewel as the older woman, obviously agitated, emerged from her room at the end of the hallway. Her extravagant pink satin wrapper was carelessly donned over a matching nightgown that protruded from the hem. Her overly bright hair hung limply, unbound and uncombed. She was wearing none of the carefully applied makeup without which she was seldom seen, and it occurred to Honesty as she approached that Jewel was a truly plain woman. It was strange. She had never thought of Jewel that way before.

Jewel halted beside her, her lips tight. "Where were you?"

Honesty raised her brows.

"Don't look at me like that! Damn it, Honesty! I heard an explosion, and when I knocked on your door, your room was empty. You could at least have had the courtesy to let me know you were going out to see what was goin' on!"

"I wasn't in my room when the bank safe was blown."

"You weren't."

"No."

Jewel paused, drawing herself up stiffly. "I don't have to ask where you were, do I?"

No response.

"You're wastin' your time, Honesty."

Jewel's familiar expression turned Honesty back toward her bedroom door. She pushed it open and stepped inside, but Jewel followed boldly.

Jewel's expression was adamant. "You're not goin' to shut me out like you usually do. You're goin' to hear me out, because I'm not leavin' before I say what I've got to say."

"Jewel . . ."

"You're wastin' your time tryin' to straighten Jeremy Sills out, because he's past straightenin'!"

"You don't know what you're talking about!"

"Oh, yes . . . I do." Jewel gave a hard laugh. "I've been on my own most of my life, and I didn't get where I am today by bein' a nun! I know men. I've used them and they've used me, and I have no complaints about that because I knew what I was givin' and what I was gettin' in return. But that doesn't mean that I don't have some regrets."

Jewel took a steadying breath before continuing, more softly than before, "What I regret most is the time I spent foolin' myself about those few fellas I took to my heart who were destined to let me down. Jeremy's one of that same breed, Honesty. He'll take all you can give and he'll tell you everythin' you want to hear, all the while believin' he's goin' to follow through. But he won't. 'Cause he can't. Jeremy is his father all over again, whether you want to believe it or not."

"No, he isn't!"

"You know he is."

"He isn't!" Sudden rage choked Honesty's throat. "You can believe what you want, but I know the truth! Jeremy is having a hard time, but he's going to pull himself out of it. He promised me. . . ."

"He promised you."

"That's right! And Jeremy will do anything for me! Anything!"

"You think so."

"I know he will, and nothing you can say will make me believe otherwise. Just like nothing you could ever say would make me believe that I won't find my sisters again when I know I will!"

"That's all a part of it, isn't it?" Jewel's eyes grew cold. "You resent me for tellin' you the truth—that you'll never see your sisters again—and you think Jeremy's your only real friend because he hasn't got the nerve to tell you the same thing."

"Jeremy knows my sisters are alive, just as I do!"

"They aren't alive! They were killed just like your parents were killed. Their bodies were never reported found, but that doesn't mean that they aren't buried somewhere downriver where they finally came to the surface. If they were alive, we would have found out somehow by now."

"They're alive. I know it."

"You're never goin' to let this thing go, are you?

You're holdin' your whole life off, waitin' for somethin' that's never goin' to happen."

"It'll happen. I'll find them."

"They're dead."

"They aren't, I tell you! I saw Purity last night."

"Those dreams again."

"Yes, *those dreams!*"

"Listen to me, Honesty. You're never goin' to see your sisters again, just like Jeremy will go his own way, no matter what he promises you."

"He won't! And I *will* see my sisters again."

"Your sisters are dead."

"I told you—"

"They're dead."

"Get out."

"Honesty—"

"Get out of my room!"

Trembling, shuddering so hard that she could no longer speak, Honesty watched as Jewel's eyes flared wide in anger, but she felt no regret. Damn her! She was no longer a child, and she would allow no one—no one—to tell her what to think or do!

Silent, Honesty remained rigidly still as Jewel turned stiffly away. She did not move at all as Jewel pulled the door closed behind her.

Wes emerged onto the street, the Caldwell Bank behind him. He had had a brief, unsatisfactory interview with Charles Webster. For all the talking they had done, Webster had told him nothing that he didn't already know. He had learned only one thing—that Webster was somehow wary of him.

Wes paused to digest that thought, unconsciously squaring the broad width of his shoulders and flexing powerful muscles still stiff from his long journey. He glanced up the street toward the brilliant sun that had relieved the shadows of dawn. The town was coming to life. It was going to be another hot day, and he was hungry.

A flash of incredibly blue eyes returned unexpectedly to mind, and Wes frowned. He gave a low snort at the responsive tugging in his groin, silently acknowledging that another hunger had been stirred inside him that morning as well. Whoever the blue-eyed witch who had looked at him so scathingly was, she was not easy to forget.

Wes gave a scornful laugh. Women of that kind rarely were.

Must you go away again, Wes?

Memory tugged at his mind.

I miss you so much when you're gone. I get so lonesome.

Lonesome . . .

Other words echoed, returning a different memory to slice at Wes's innards as his father's sober, bearded face appeared before his mind.

A man among men.

Those words had resounded in the stillness of the graveyard where Captain William Bennett Howell had been laid to rest, consigned there by an outlaw's bullet. In truth, Wes knew his father and all other Texas Rangers were prepared for that eventuality. A bullet in the back, however, had been too treacherous a way for a man of such principle to die.

His own badge had been new, then. He had been working with his father in tracking down the members of a gang who had robbed a bank in San Antonio and killed two passersby. One of those passersby had been a young woman pregnant with her first child. He could still remember the outrage on his father's face as he had recounted the tale to him. Sharing that emotion, he had joined with his father in swearing to track down the gang responsible.

Within weeks, his father and he had been successful in catching two of the men who had robbed that San Antonio bank. The trail of the others, five in all, was still fresh when his father and he reached Austin. They had been there only a few hours when a shot rang out in the darkness, and Captain William Bennett Howell fell to the ground, mortally wounded.

It was strange. He could still feel the warmth of his father's blood on his hands as he held him on that darkened street.

He remembered the sound of his father's labored breathing.

And he knew he would never forget the hoarse rattle of his father's final breath.

In the seven years since, he had continued to wear his badge while singlemindedly pursuing the members of the gang connected with his father's death. He had successfully tracked down every member of the gang . . .

. . . except one.

It seemed to have been the hand of fate when an unexpected lead pointed in the direction of Caldwell at almost the same time he received a communication from Slater Enterprises. He had not realized that his reputation was so widespread as to have attracted the attention of an Eastern syndicate, but the circumstance had been opportune. He had agreed to protect Slater's interests in Caldwell until winter again halted the arrival of trail herds for another season.

And he had known instinctively, with an intuition that had never failed him, that his long quest to find the last man connected to his father's death would soon come to an end.

"Say, you're Wes Howell, ain't you?"

Wes turned toward the short, smiling fellow at his elbow who addressed him. The fellow was wearing a badge. He extended his hand as Wes nodded in response.

"My name's John Henry Brown. I'm Marshal Carr's assistant. I'm from Houston myself, and I'm mighty glad to see another Texan, most especially you." When Wes did not immediately respond, the cordial fellow added with unexpected candor, "I hear you already talked to the marshal. He ain't too friendly a cuss, but he's all right. He just thinks he can handle everythin' himself, no matter what happened to the previous marshal. But the truth is that the other marshal is lyin' in his grave, and I ain't too hard-nosed to admit that I ain't in a rush to follow him just because of somebody's stiff-necked pride. So, whatever I can do to help, you let me know."

A Texan and a honest man . . . yes . . . Wes read it in his eyes.

Accepting Brown's hand, Wes shook it firmly. "Pleased to meet you. I was just goin' for some breakfast."

"Birdie Cotter's place is the best in town. I was goin' there myself."

Wes nodded again and followed the deputy's lead. The sound of their booted heels echoed hollowly against the board sidewalk as Wes casually inquired, "What do you think of Charles Webster?"

You should have known better, damn it!

Still shaking from her exchange with Honesty a short time earlier, Jewel stood before her washstand mirror. The sun was up and the heat of day was beginning. She was perspiring, her lips were tight, and her skin looked pale. In the unforgiving light of morning, her hair was too bright and the lines around her eyes and mouth were too pronounced to provide her reassurance.

Reaching for the jar nearby, Jewel applied cream to her face. She massaged it in gently, even as the voice in her mind continued its fierce rebuke.

What made you think you had the right to tell Honesty what to do when you've never heeded a word of advice in your life?

Right . . . she knew the voice was right . . . but that hadn't changed the way she had felt when the explosion had awakened her from a sound sleep and she had gone to Honesty's room, only to find her gone.

She should have known better than to be frightened for Honesty's safety. Honesty could take care of herself.

She should have forced herself to calm down as she waited for Honesty to return . . . or not to return.

But she hadn't.

Strangely, she had not spared a thought for the two outlaws clearly visible from her window where they had lain dead in the street. Nor had she been concerned about Charles's bank.

You made all your own mistakes. Honesty has to make her own, too!

Yes, she knew that was the way it was, but *why* did it have to be that way? And why did Honesty have to suffer for the mistakes of others? Why did she have to suffer the danger? Because the truth was, when she heard the explosion, when she realized that someone had broken into the bank and that two men lay dead on the street, her first thought was that one of those men was Jeremy. What would Honesty have done if she had lost the man she loved as a brother? She still had not been able to accept the reality of her sisters' deaths so many years ago.

When are you going to learn? Honesty doesn't be-

lieve her sisters are dead! Maybe she never will.

But she has to!

No, she doesn't. Leave her alone!

Yes, leave her alone.

Jewel brushed her hair. Impatient, she threw down her brush and darkened her brows and eyelashes, then applied color to her cheeks.

Yes, leave her alone.

Jewel was painting a bright slash of color on her lips when she heard the soft knock at the door. She lowered her hand slowly to the stand in front of her, her reply curt.

"Who is it?"

"It's me."

Jewel turned rigidly toward the door. "Come in."

Honesty entered, her dark, unbound hair framing a faultlessly lovely face that was intensely sober. Jewel knew that if she lived to be as old as Methuselah, she would never become inured to Honesty's natural, unaffected beauty. It was a point of silent amazement to her that despite all the many times that she had been furious with Honesty, her pride in her had never faltered.

Honesty's brilliant gaze was as direct as her words. "I'm sorry, Jewel."

Jewel raised her chin. "You should be."

Honesty's chin rose a notch higher as well. "I shouldn't have lost my temper."

"No, you shouldn't."

Honesty's penitence was beginning to slip. "But it's none of your concern where I am, or whether my bed is empty in the morning."

"If I had thought you were sleeping with Jeremy, it would be different."

"Would you have preferred that?"

"In some ways. At least then I would be able to

believe you were seeing him as a man, not as a boy who needs your guidance—because he isn't a boy, and he's past guidance, yours or anybody else's."

"I don't want to go into this again, Jewel."

Jewel stared at Honesty for silent moments. Honesty was pale. She was emotionally drained. She had had enough.

So had Jewel.

"I don't want to go into it again, either. I accept your apology."

Honesty's gaze remained steady. Only the slightest hint of challenge remained.

"Thank you."

"You're welcome."

The door closed behind Honesty, and Jewel turned back to the washstand mirror.

Damn it!

Jewel was slipping the pins into her upswept hair when another knock sounded at the door. This knock was heavier, a man's knock. There were few men who would come knocking at her door at such an early hour.

"Who is it?"

"It's Charles, Jewel."

Curiously, Charles and she had argued the previous night because she had refused to voice her concern for Honesty—a concern they shared. The years had bound Charles and her together in so many ways, even though they weren't truly bound . . . even though there were so many obstacles between them.

But she didn't want to consider the obstacles between them now.

"Come in."

Charles was casually dressed, without a jacket, his shirt unbuttoned to mid chest. With the broad column of his neck and the fine sprinkling of dark hair on his chest exposed in his gaping shirtfront, he looked less the Eastern banker and man of wealthy upbringing and far more the inherently virile man who had stirred so rare a passion within her. The sight of him was both balm to the ache within and a torment like no other as she waited for him to speak.

"I'm sorry, Jewel."

A short laugh escaped Jewel's tight throat. "You're the second person to say that to me within the last fifteen minutes."

Charles did not ask the question that was reflected in his eyes. Instead, he walked toward her until they were standing so close that she could feel the heat emanating from his body as he said, "I love you, Jewel."

Jewel did not respond.

"I was sharp with you last night without cause."

"You were."

A smile twitched at Charles's lips. "That's what I love about you. You always make things so easy for me."

Jewel drew her wrapper tight around her. The lines of stress under Charles' eyes were obvious. He was worried about something. The attempted robbery. She had been too caught up in her own concerns to ask. She didn't like that about herself.

"I'm sorry, too, Charles. I heard the blast this morning. How is everything at the bank?"

"All right." Charles avoided her eyes and took a step back. He shrugged. "I had a visit from the fellow who stopped the robbery."

"The one who shot the two men?"

"Yes. He's a former Texas Ranger—the one Slater Enterprises hired to protect their money."

"Oh."

His expression suddenly tight, Charles closed the

final distance between them and grasped her arms. His gaze bore hotly into hers as he rasped, "I'm not much in the mood for small talk this morning, Jewel. The truth is that I had a miserable night thinking about you and wishing you were beside me. I told myself I would come straight over here this morning and say all the things I'm saying to you now. Then when this morning came and—" Charles hesitated, a frown touching his brow. "This morning reminded me only too clearly what is really important in my life. What's important is you, Jewel. I love you."

So intense was her response to Charles's impassioned words that Jewel could not reply. There were so many times when she questioned Charles's feelings for her, but not at times like this when she could see his need for her was great. The reality of his need tore at her heart, debilitating her, leaving her helpless against him.

"Jewel . . . why is it so hard for you to say you love me?"

Why? Because she didn't like feeling helpless in any way.

"Talk to me, Jewel."

Oh, how she longed to say the words he wanted to hear! They surged to her throat from a heart brimming with love, only to lodge there in the morass of doubts she could not quite dispel.

The pain in Charles's eyes deepened. "The truth is, I don't have the right to ask, do I?"

Still no response.

"Jewel . . . darling . . . if you can't say the words, show me. Please show me, because I need you this morning more than you can ever imagine."

Emotion so keen that it was almost overwhelming swept Jewel in a great torrent. The words were beyond her, but the rest . . . oh, no, the rest was not.

Softening in Charles's arms as they slid around her, Jewel gave herself up to his kiss. She opened her mouth under his, reveling in the taste of him. She gasped as his hands slid under her wrapper, as they pushed it away, then disposed of the slim gown beneath. She clung to him as he stripped away his clothes as well, as he grunted his impatience until their naked flesh met. And she heard his breath catch with the explosion of heat evoked.

Oh, how the heat soared within her as well!

Unable to speak the words he wanted to hear, Jewel whispered words from the heart in their stead.

"Make love to me, Charles . . . please make love to me."

Lips . . . tongues . . . moist flesh . . . searching, caressing hands . . . Charles's hard flesh seared hers as he lay atop her. His passion stoked the fire within as he sank inside her. He was loving her as no man had ever before loved her—with his mind, with his body, with his heart—and she was loving him in return.

There were no words, only flesh and fervor, building to a cataclysm so right . . . so strong . . . so powerful . . . so . . .

Charles's ardor erupted abruptly within her, in a blinding flash that ignited Jewel as well.

The glory was profound . . . matchless in scope.

Silent in the afterglow of their passionate exchange, Jewel felt Charles's caressing touch against her cheek.

"You're beautiful, Jewel."

The words jarred Jewel from her loving lethargy. "No, I'm not."

"You are."

About to protest again, Jewel paused, staring up at Charles. A smile lingered on his lips, and sincerity and love glowed in his eyes. And tenderness . . . she saw *tenderness*. . . .

The remembered scent of lilacs rose to permeate Jewel's mind.

Suddenly wanting that moment to last forever, Jewel drew Charles's mouth again down to hers. The words she longed to say still unspoken, the magic began once more.

Chapter Three

"He doesn't look like much to me."

The raucous music of evening in the Texas Jewel swelled around Honesty, but she was unconscious of its din as she stood amidst the brightly dressed saloon women who gathered in the corner of the crowded gilt and mirrored room. The day that had begun so disturbingly with the attempted robbery of Charles's bank, her painful talk with Jeremy, and Jewel's candid rebuke did not improve as the girls responded to her comment with a round of knowing laughter.

"Well, maybe he don't look like much to you, but he looks like plenty to me." Ginger's pale eyes narrowed with an assessing smile as she glanced back toward the crowded bar where the big Texan stood. A natural redhead with unremarkable features and freckles that no amount of face paint could conceal,

Ginger was popular with the patrons of the Texas Jewel for her good humor, her remarkable feminine curves, and her willingness.

Indicating the three women beside her, she continued, "Well . . . Anita, Julia, Lottie, and me have already tried gettin' next to that big fella, and he's still standin' alone. Who's goin' to be the next to try?"

"Does it really matter?" Honesty scanned the room. Jewel was not at her usual table, which accounted for the fact that the girls were neglecting their duties to chatter. Her annoyance increased. She was sick and tired of all the fuss that had been made about the notorious Wesley H. Howell, formerly of the Texas Rangers, since he had walked through the saloon doors an hour earlier. So he wasn't a bounty hunter after all! As far as she was concerned, he wasn't much better. She was sick of the way the crowded room had all but parted to allow him passage toward the bar, and the way Henry had all but tripped in his rush to pour the fellow a drink. And she was even more annoyed with herself for the strange sense of familiarity she had experienced again on seeing him, as well as for the fact that she could not seem to dismiss that inexplicable feeling.

Irritating Honesty even more was her realization that the infamous Wes Howell had been watching her covertly. Not that she wasn't accustomed to the admiration of men, but this was different. He appeared almost to be studying her . . . assessing her . . . and she didn't like it. So annoyed had she become that she had flaunted her illicit skill at cards, knowing his reputation as a lawman and deliberately provoking him. But he had not reacted . . . damn him!

Irked by her failure to heat the cold appraisal in Wes Howell's eyes in any way, even as she had somehow found it more and more difficult to keep her gaze from his broad back, she had left the gaming table for a breath of fresh air a few minutes earlier. To her further exasperation, she had been engulfed on her return by the gaggle of silly geese now standing around her who could not seem to get Wes Howell's name off their lips.

"I'd say it matters." Ginger laughed again, looking across the room to sweep the tall Texan's lean form so hungrily that it was almost nauseating. "I'd rather be spending my time with that fella's arm draped around me than I would with any one of them whiskey-soaked cowboys hangin' at that bar."

"Really?" Honesty shrugged. "I can't understand what you're all so excited about. So he stopped a bank robbery this morning! He killed two men in doing it and didn't bat an eye. I hardly think that makes him the hero you all seem to think he is."

"It ain't the bank robbery he stopped that's got us all to pantin', Honesty, and you know it."

Honesty turned toward Lottie, aware that the buxom blonde would never quite forget that a man she loved had found Honesty more desirable than she. The fact that Honesty had turned Lottie's man down had seemed to make little difference. With that thought in mind, Honesty responded casually, "It isn't?"

"Oh, come on! You're talkin' to Lottie Walsh now, and Lottie knows . . ."

"She does, huh? What does Lottie know?"

"Lottie knows that you've been staring at that big Texan from the minute he walked through the door. You ain't been able to take your eyes off him no more than we have!"

"You think so?"

"You don't want to admit it because he didn't come

sniffin' around you like the other fellas do."

Honesty managed a smile. "And why would I be afraid to admit it, if it were true? Nobody ever accused me of being shy about going after what I want."

"Nobody ever accused you of nothin' . . . even though there was times when they could have if they'd a mind to." Latent jealousy flashed in Lottie's smile. "But this big fella's different, and you know it. One look at them cold eyes of his, and you knew you couldn't twist him around your little finger like you do all the others, so you're stayin' away from him."

"He doesn't appeal to me."

"There ain't a man alive who don't appeal to you!"

The growing animosity in the exchange had the other girls taking a step backward as Honesty retorted, "I could break his heart with a glance."

"You think you're so great!" Lottie hissed. "You try to make everybody think you can get any man you want to sit up and beg for you, but I saw the way you've been lookin' at him, and you can't fool me. You're steerin' clear of him because you heard what they say in Texas, that Wes Howell's made of ice, that he don't know nothin' but the law and all a woman ever gets out of him is a quick tip of the hat and a short, 'Thank you, ma'am,' when he's done with her. And you know it's true! You know he wouldn't treat you no different!"

"Is that so?"

"Yeah, that's so!"

Honesty's annoyance turned to true anger. The blond witch had gone too far this time with her jealous taunting! There was *no* man she couldn't handle. There never had been! If her experiences with men in the past had all stopped short of a certain mark, it was because *she* had stopped them! Keeping herself free of any long-term intimate commitments had been her own *personal* choice, for her own *personal* reasons. She had half a mind to make Lottie eat her words!

Honesty stared into the seething saloon girl's eyes. "Wes Howell's a man, isn't he? Once he got a good look at what I have to offer, all I'd have to do is crook a finger, and he'd come running."

"Big talk!"

"You think so?"

"I *know* you're wrong!"

"Prove it!"

Her control finally snapping, Honesty held Lottie's heated gaze for long, tense moments. Speaking at last, she grated three distinct words.

"Just watch me."

Wes frowned as the piano player struck up another boisterous tune and the shuffling of dancing feet again joined the growing pandemonium of sound surrounding him. It was obvious that the Texas Jewel Saloon worked hard to provide every manner of entertainment for its customers. More pretentious than most, it sported a long bar with highly polished brass fixtures and a mirrored back wall that reflected invitingly the brightly labeled bottles of red eye awaiting its customers. Green gaming tables took up most of the floor space that wasn't devoted to dancing, while several other walls assaulted the eye with paintings of nudes in the style of the European masters, pictures that were said to be a special attraction of the Texas Jewel.

But he had no doubt what the special attraction of the Texas Jewel truly was.

Maintaining a noncommittal facade, Wes discarded that last thought, his mind returning to his entrance into the saloon an hour earlier. All heads had turned toward him as he walked through the doorway, but he supposed he shouldn't have expected otherwise. News traveled fast in towns like Caldwell. He had known that. He had relied on it. He had wanted to stir the speculation that was now abounding in whispers about his reason for coming to Caldwell. The unexpected excitement that had accompanied his arrival had only served to further his plan and lend credence to the talk about the cash shipments soon to begin. His talk with Deputy Brown earlier in the day had assured him that the Texas Jewel was one of the best places for that speculation to flourish.

Wes signaled the bartender for a refill and turned to lean back against the bar. He was unconscious of the frown that tightened his strong features into a formidable mask as he struggled to keep his gaze from straying back to the gaming table where Honesty Buchanan had formerly been holding court.

Honesty Buchanan . . . the young woman he had seen on the street early that morning, the one who had walked straight from her lover's arms into Charles Webster's bank, the one who had stirred an interest that had begun in a far more base portion of his anatomy than his mind.

It hadn't been difficult to learn her name.

Wes controlled the sardonic twist that pulled at his lips. The beauteous witch had surely adopted her name as some kind of private joke. He had been watching her deal cards for the past hour, and even a child could see that she was anything but honest. Even a child . . . but apparently not the men seated around her, who obviously could not see past the brilliant blue of her eyes and the calculated dip of her tempting bosom. It appeared that everything

Deputy Brown had told him about her was true. Honesty Buchanan made a practice of manipulating men as well as cards—important men like Charles Webster included—men who would do anything for her.

Wes sipped cautiously at his glass. Even more unbelievable was his certainty that Honesty Buchanan had known he was watching her cheat. It was almost as if she were taunting him with the strange immunity she enjoyed.

Taunting him . . .

A familiar tightening in his groin signaled that his body was responding all too predictably to her taunt. Wes muffled a curse. Tossing back his head, he swallowed the contents of his glass with a gulp, his expression unchanging despite the fire that burned all the way down to his stomach. He took a deep breath, welcoming the heat, grateful for its stabilizing effect.

Aware that he could not afford to surrender to the inclination to fight one nagging heat with another, Wes hesitated a moment before signaling the bartender to refill his glass. He was unprepared for the female voice that sounded at his elbow, a husky voice he somehow recognized without ever having heard it before.

"This big Texan here would like to buy me a drink, too, Henry."

Damn it all . . . it was Honesty.

Damn it all . . . how had she gotten herself into this?

That thought resounded in Honesty's mind as Wes Howell turned slowly toward her and eyes as black as ebony caught and held hers. Honesty unconsciously caught her breath. Oh, he was something, all right. She felt the aura of power and ruthlessness he exuded. She sensed the subtle savagery he concealed so well behind his controlled demeanor as he assessed her openly.

Using those moments to assess him in return, Honesty confirmed her original thought. No, he wasn't really handsome . . . not in the way Lottie and the girls seemed to think. His thick, roughly cut hair was dark, almost too dark. His features were too hard, his gaze too intense. And he was too big, even taller and broader than he had appeared to be from a distance. With every damned inch of him working muscle, he was too overwhelming. She was tall for a woman, but her head didn't reach any farther than his chin—a chin that was marked with a small, jagged scar that remained a strip of white against his sun-darkened skin.

Honesty stared at the scar. It was somehow mesmerizing. She wondered how he had gotten it—who had managed to mark a man like him. Suddenly possessed of a desire to touch it, she mused about what it would be like to stroke it, to touch it with her lips. She wondered what it would be like to taste the spot where this man's blood had once flowed, and she—

"Excuse me, ma'am, did I offer to buy you a drink?"

Momentarily shocked at the wandering path her own mind had taken, Honesty silently cursed the tinge of arrogance in Wes Howell's softly drawled question. She could feel Lottie's intense gaze digging into her back as she forced herself to slide a notch closer to him and reply, "Well, if you didn't, you surely should have." Her stability slowly returning, she cocked her head, allowing him the full impact of the smile she slanted up at him as she purred, "And don't call me ma'am. I know that you know my name."

Surprising her, the Texan replied without denial, "That's right, I do. And you know mine."

Honesty gave a short laugh. "There isn't anybody in Caldwell who doesn't. What you did this morning is the talk of the town."

His dark eyes pinned her. "You disapprove . . ."

Surprised by his perception, Honesty shrugged. "Maybe I do."

"But you're makin' it a point to personally welcome me to the Texas Jewel anyway."

"Is that what you think I am . . . a welcoming committee?"

Wes Howell's scrutiny tightened. "What are you then?"

"I thought you knew." Honesty paused for effect, adding with a huskiness that was not entirely feigned, "I'm the woman you've been waiting for all your life."

A quick, unidentifiable emotion flashed briefly in Wes Howell's eyes the moment before he slipped his arm around her waist with a grip that effectively imprisoned her, despite its deceivingly casual appearance. The innate power of him encompassed her, setting her heart to pounding as he whispered, "So, you're the woman I've been waitin' for all my life. Maybe you are . . ." His gaze intensified. ". . . but I doubt it."

Wes Howell's response startled Honesty from her intended reply.

"Nothin' to say? Well, I guess it's my turn." Wes's voice grew unexpectedly frigid. "You know I saw you on the street this mornin', and you know I've been watchin' you since I came in tonight. I didn't miss the performance you gave for my benefit. You enjoy dealin' cards . . . and you cheat. You also enjoy playin' with the emotions of men. Do you cheat there, too?"

Drawing back spontaneously, furious when she was unable to escape his grasp, Honesty spat, "You *are* a cold bastard—just like everybody says you are!"

"You're wrong, Honesty. I'm anythin' but cold when it comes to you."

Realizing that the situation was rapidly slipping out of her control, Honesty grated, "Let me go." He ignored her. Not wishing to betray the bent of their conversation, Honesty forced a smile, repeating, "I said, let me go. . . ."

"What's the matter? Things aren't goin' the way you thought they would?" Wes drew her closer. "Tell me what you really want from me, Honesty." His voice deepened. "Tell me, because I know what I want from you."

The heat emanating from Wes Howell's body and the taste of his breath on her lips were a heady combination she fought to ignore. Honesty rasped, "Bastard . . . what you want from me and what you're going to get are two entirely different things!"

"Is that a challenge?"

"Take it any way you wish!"

Wes drew her closer. "I accept your challenge. Do you accept mine?"

Recognizing that he was as intensely aware of the heavy pounding of her heart as she, a pounding that echoed his own, Honesty hissed, "I'm not interested in your challenge!"

"Liar."

"I told you—"

"You're afraid that you won't be able to wrap me around your finger like you do other men, aren't you?"

Honesty refused to respond.

"So, you are afraid . . ."

Afraid . . .

"I didn't think you were a coward, Honesty."

A coward!

The white heat of anger flared inside her. Honesty slowly raised her gaze, boldly linking it with his. She moved her body subtly, the motion deliberately sensual. Satisfaction soared at his revealing intake of breath, and she purred, "You don't really believe that, do you, Wes?"

Wes' jaw stiffened. "Witch . . ."

Slowly dropping her gaze to his lips, aware of the rapidly accelerated breathing he could not hide, Honesty felt the tide rapidly turning in her favor as she whispered, "Men have called me far worse names than that before, but the truth is . . . sooner or later, they usually end up calling me *darlin'*."

A slow flush of victory surged through her as Honesty raised her gaze to meet black eyes that were no longer icy. She revelled as Wes cursed again. She remained silent, enjoying his discomfiture as his body swelled hard and firm against her. She waited another long moment before whispering, "It seems you aren't as cold as I thought you were . . . at least, not too cold for me to handle."

Her smile abruptly fading, Honesty demanded, "So, I'll tell you once more, let me go . . . *now!* You wouldn't want me to call attention to your present embarrassing condition, would you? Not after the impressive entrance you made into town this morning, and with everybody thinking you're invincible."

"Do you really think I'd care?"

Enjoying the intimate tightening he could not deny as she raised her lips calculatingly to his, Honesty taunted, "Wouldn't you?"

The intense silence between them lengthened interminably, and Honesty felt the heat within Wes surge. She sensed a sudden danger in the tight lines of his face, in the powerful muscles locking her close, in her sudden realization that this was a man unlike any she had met before.

A movement at her elbow caught her attention. Honesty turned abruptly in its direction at the same moment that a familiar voice shattered the tension of the moment with a soft, "I've been lookin' for you, Honesty."

Damn! It was her lover.

A sharp, angry emotion surged within Wes as Honesty turned toward the blond young man who had suddenly appeared beside them at the crowded bar. The frivolity around them continued unabated, signifying that the intensity of the previous few moments between Honesty and him had gone unnoticed by the other patrons—

—with one exception.

Forcing an unaffected demeanor he did not feel, Wes assessed Jeremy Sills with a quick, professional eye. Honesty's lover was younger than he had appeared at a distance. Surprisingly, the fellow seemed more stricken than angry at finding Honesty and him in such an intimate posture. Observing him more closely, Wes saw that Sills's face had paled to an unnatural color and that he was struggling to hold his emotions under control. It occurred to Wes that this was probably not the first time Sills had found Honesty with another man.

I love you, Wes, please believe me! It's just that I was so lonesome. . . .

Wes forced the nagging memory from his mind as Honesty spoke.

"What are you doing here so early, Jeremy?" The

hint of annoyance in her voice was clear as she continued, "I wasn't expecting you. I didn't think you'd be up to it."

The young man shook his head, his reply almost childlike. "I felt better, so I came to see you."

The young fool . . .

His contempt not for Sills alone, Wes tightened his arm around Honesty's waist, determined to finish the business that Honesty and he had begun. He did not bother to smile as he interjected, "You're a little late, friend. Honesty's made other plans for tonight."

He did not expect the look of devastated acceptance that flashed across the young fellow's flushed face, nor Honesty's sudden attempt to escape his grip as Sills surprised him by turning away without argument.

"Jeremy, wait!" Honesty looked back up at Wes, glaring. "Let me go, damn you!"

"Tired of the game so soon, Honesty?"

"Tired?" Honesty shook her head, her smile hard. "No, *bored* would be a better word. You see, you're really no challenge at all."

Honesty's stinging words succeeded where all others had failed. Wes muttered a low epithet, releasing her so abruptly that she stumbled a step forward. He saw the incredible blue of her eyes flash with fury as she steadied herself, then turned back toward him. He remained motionless as she retraced the step. Then she startled him by leaning forward to slide her lush warmth up tight against him as she wrapped her arms around his neck and pressed her mouth to his.

A profound hunger shook Wes as Honesty's lips parted and her tongue brushed his with a taste so incredibly sweet that he was momentarily immobile. A groan sounded in his mind as her kiss pressed deeper, stirring a response within him that he could not restrain, a heat rapidly building to a fire so intense that he—

Honesty drew back abruptly, ending the intimate exchange as suddenly as it had begun. Wes saw the victory in her smile—a smile that dripped ice as she whispered, "That's just to let you know what you'll be missing, Mr. Wesley H. Howell, formerly of the Texas Rangers. You think about it . . . you hear?"

Watching as Honesty moved through the crowd toward the doorway to the street where her lover had slipped from sight, Wes waited only a moment longer before turning back to the bar. It occurred to him as he reached for the glass in front of him that the intense few moments just past had transpired without attracting the attention of those absorbed in their own diversions around him. For all intents and purposes, nothing had happened at all.

Wes raised his glass to his lips and swallowed the contents in a gulp.

Nothing at all.

"Jeremy . . ."

Concealed in the shadows of the alley nearby, Jeremy watched as Honesty stood outside the entrance of the Texas Jewel calling his name. The bright saloon lights behind her silhouetted her slender form, holding her face in dark relief, but Jeremy knew what was reflected there.

Impatience.

Disgust.

Pity.

Jeremy drew back farther into the shadows as Honesty advanced a few steps to scan the crowded street. She turned, searching the street in the opposite direction. He recognized the futility in her gesture as she raised her hand to her temple, then dropped it limply back to her side. He saw the almost indefinable slump of her delicate shoulders as she walked slowly back through the swinging doors into the brightly lit saloon beyond.

With her went his heart.

Leaning back against the building behind him, Jeremy closed his eyes. A silent sob tore at the lump in his chest. He had watched Honesty and Wes Howell together for long minutes before approaching them, and each moment was a torment beyond any he had suffered before. He had seen them whispering intimately, their lips so close that they almost touched. He had never seen Honesty look at a man the way she looked at Howell, and in a moment of startling revelation, he had known he was losing her.

A sudden rush of fury overwhelming him, Jeremy snapped his eyes open. How could Honesty be impressed by a man like Howell! Couldn't she see that Howell wasn't the kind of man she needed? She needed a man who could love her the way *he* loved her, so much that nothing else in the world mattered more! Everybody knew Wesley Howell's reputation. His only true love was the law. When he was done with the job he had come to Caldwell to do, he'd be done with her as well. He'd use her and leave her behind!

Or worse, he might take her with him. . . .

That thought was more than he could bear. Jeremy fought to control his panic. No, Honesty loved *him* . . . he knew she did. She had left Howell and had come running after him, hadn't she? She cared about him in a way she cared about no one else. He needed to make her realize that the friendship she thought she felt for him was truly love.

Jeremy fought to subdue the heavy pounding of

his heart as panic again soared. But time was growing short! He was penniless. He had nothing to offer Honesty. He needed to prove so much. He needed to prove he was a *man.*

How?

There was only one way.

Suddenly realizing that he was trembling, Jeremy took a deep breath. He needed a drink to steady him.

No, a drink wasn't the answer. Tom Bitters was.

Forcing his emotions under control, Jeremy squared his shoulders and glanced out into the street. Stepping onto the board sidewalk moments later, he started back in the direction of his shack. He didn't want to talk to Honesty now . . . not yet. Bitters came to town almost every night. He'd go back to his shack and watch for him. He'd settle things once and for all with Bitters, and then everything would fall into place.

As for Wes Howell . . .

Jeremy fought to dismiss the image of Honesty standing tight in the circle of the ex-ranger's embrace. Honesty had flirted before, and she had even allowed a few fellas to get closer than the rest, but no man had ever taken *his* place in her heart. He was determined that no man ever would.

Jeremy's step quickened as the outline of his shack came into view. He'd pour himself a drink—just one—and wait for Bitters. Honesty loved him. He knew she did. Everything would soon be well.

The clamor of wild celebration so typical of Caldwell's evening scene rebounded loudly in the night, echoing through Charles's bedroom window, despite his modest cabin's distance from the main street. Unconscious of the sounds as he stood in his shirtsleeves, his patrician features drawn into lines of strain, Charles stared at the sheets of paper lying on the desk in front of him. He glanced up abruptly as the wall clock struck the hour, aware that the time of his usual appearance at the Texas Jewel was long past. Jewel would conceal her concern behind an indifferent facade, but he knew she would be wondering where he was. He disliked causing her discomfort in any way, but he was somehow powerless against the sense of inertia holding him so firmly in its grasp.

Frowning, Charles ran an anxious hand through his hair. The passionate morning Jewel and he had spent in each other's arms had meant more to him than she could ever realize. He loved her, but the sheet lying on the desk in front of him, written so carefully in a neat, feminine script, called out to him as it had so many times in recent hours. It caused his hand to reach out and pick it up again, seemingly of its own volition, so he might reread the simple words transcribed.

"My dear husband, Charles,

I apologize for not writing this letter myself, but I have been too unsteady of late to accomplish a legible hand. I am fortunate that this lovely place, where you have so generously arranged for me to spend my remaining years, has as a part of its staff a charming young woman who has offered to pen this missive for me.

I am well, Charles. I spend my days much as I did when you visited me last year. I am comfortable and I am at peace with God and myself. I spend my time reading or having someone read to me, but the hours I cherish most are those that I pass in reminiscence, recalling our youth and the years we spent together. They were beautiful years, my darling, in spite of the hardships we later endured. They were beautiful because of your love, which never failed me. I thank you for that love from the bottom of my heart.

You have expressed your feelings for me many times and have told me that they will never change. I believe that to be true. I have never doubted your love. But love has many facets. I have learned that truth with great difficulty through the years. It is for that reason that now, more than ever before, I am compelled to put on paper the thoughts which fill my heart and clamor to be expressed. Please indulge me as I write them.

Be happy, Charles. Although we are legally bound and you will not suffer that bond to be severed, I wish you love. I wish you happiness that matches in scope that which we shared and that which you have brought me despite the distance and years that have separated us. Please know that the greatest regret of my life would be if I were to believe that you had suffered its lack because of an illness against which both you and I are helpless.

My darling, I hope you will always remember that whatever brings you joy, brings me joy as well. And whatever affords you consolation, affords me peace. We are one in heart and soul. We always have been. We always will be. That truth is as real and as everlasting as the air we breathe, the sun that warms us, and the God that watches over us all.

Charles, my dearest, I will always love you.

Emily."

Charles covered his face with his hand, removing it moments later to brush the dampness from his cheeks. Emily was failing. This letter, so lovingly sent, had been dispatched because she was afraid she might not have the chance to say good-bye.

Charles could barely restrain himself from making his way directly to the railroad station to purchase a ticket. But he knew he dared not.

The meeting with Wes Howell that morning had not gone well. The blemish that the Webster name still bore in Eastern banking circles could easily stain his present reputation if all did not go well with the enormous shipments of cash that had been entrusted to his bank by Slater Enterprises. The arrival of Wes Howell had brought his dilemma too clearly into focus for him to ignore it. If all did not transpire smoothly this summer, the negative effects would color the course of the rest of his life. It was the worst of all times for him to receive Emily's letter. Most difficult of all for him to bear, however, was his certainty that Emily would be understanding of his circumstances, as she had always been, and that her love would be undiminished.

His gaze moved slowly toward another sheet lying near Emily's letter; Charles felt tension of another kind swell within him. Written in a feminine hand as well, it stated simply:

Dear Charles,

We are waiting for you to come by. If you don't come to see us, the children and I will come to see you. The decision is yours.

Mary

Charles stared at the second letter until the scrawled words blurred before his eyes. Pulled in so many directions at once that he felt he could bear no more, he snatched it up in his hand, crushed it into a ball, and threw it across the room.

Emily, endlessly loving . . .

Mary, endlessly demanding . . .

Jewel . . .

Stepping back from his desk, Charles looked around him, seeing the neatness and order of the room that contrasted so sharply with the silent chaos of his life. He strove consciously and diligently to achieve that outward orderliness, while knowing that there were things that no amount of effort could rectify.

The errors of his life haunted him, ever threatening. They had already cost him so much. Would they cost him all he had accomplished, and the woman he loved as well?

His handsome face suddenly crumpling, Charles sat abruptly and buried his face in his hands.

Jewel walked swiftly along the narrow side street. The large basket covered in gingham that swung from her arm contrasted sharply with the gay, striking appearance she presented with her outlandishly red hair piled high on her head and a daring gown of pink silk embellished with gold braid tightly molding her generous, feminine proportions. Her gaze intent on the house midway down the street, she hardly noticed the unsteady wrangler standing nearby whose bloodshot eyes gazed in her direction as he addressed her.

"Good evenin', Jewel! Goin' somewhere special?"

Turning with a smile, Jewel quipped, "You wouldn't go askin' a lady personal questions, would you, Bill?"

A few steps more and the taller of two passing

drovers stopped in mid-stride to greet her warmly.

"Say now, if it ain't Texas Jewel herself! What're you doin' so far from home, and what've you got in that basket, darlin'?" A handsome fellow several years her junior, he pressed, "If you're lookin' for a picnic, I sure would be happy to oblige. As a matter of fact, I'd be happy to oblige you with just about anythin' you have in mind."

"Butch, honey," Jewel purred, "you're sure man enough to tempt me with your offer, but it comes just a little too late tonight. You ask me again, sometime. I just might surprise you."

Butch's youthful face creased into a hopeful grin. "Is that a promise?"

Her only response a flirtatious wink, Jewel was aware that the young fellow's gaze followed her for long moments as she walked on. Her spirits high, Jewel raised her chin, straightened her spine, and raised a hand to the upward sweep of her hair. She was wearing Charles's favorite dress. She had worn it just for him. She was looking forward to surprising Charles with the quiet supper they would share.

A niggling feeling within—like the touch of a butterfly's wings in the pit of her stomach—sent a sudden flush to Jewel's face as she drew closer to Charles's door. Charles was the only man who affected her that way. Her usual reluctance to acknowledge that fact did not temper her reaction as she climbed the three short steps to his front door and shifted the weight of her basket.

Pausing to allow the flush to fade, Jewel took a steadying breath. The loving hours Charles and she had spent in each other's arms that morning were still fresh in her mind, but no amount of loving had been able to erase the tension she had sensed within him. The robbery had awakened him at dawn. Howell's arrival under such negative circumstances had increased Charles's sensitivity to the old stain on the Webster name, causing him great stress. She knew Charles had probably worked hard all day to repair the damage caused by the blast that morning, that he was most likely exhausted, and that he probably hadn't taken the time to eat. It had occurred to her when Charles was late in appearing at the Texas Jewel that she needed some time away from her own duties as well.

A rare evening alone with Charles. She would like that . . . just Charles and her. It would be flirting again . . . with a dream that she doubted would ever become reality.

Suddenly annoyed with herself, Jewel forced that notion from her mind. The present, no matter how limited, was good enough as long as Charles was a part of it.

Encouraged by her thoughts, Jewel knocked lightly. Puzzled when there was no response, she glanced again at the bedroom window where the light flickered brightly. She knocked again, concerned when she heard no movement within. Charles's abode was a modest and immaculate two rooms within which her knock could easily be heard.

Unwilling to wait any longer, Jewel pushed the door open and walked directly to the bedroom. Charles was seated at his desk when she entered. He pushed himself to his feet, attempting a smile.

"I'm sorry, Jewel. I was engrossed in something. I wasn't sure I heard a knock."

"Is somethin' wrong, Charles? Are you sick?"

"No . . ." His smile faded. "Just tired." He shrugged. "I don't think I'll be very good company this evening."

Charles's hand dropped to the surface of the desk,

calling her attention to a sheet lying there covered with a neat, feminine script that bore no resemblance to Emily's flowery hand.

So . . . it was a woman.

Jewel took a spontaneous step backward.

"Jewel . . ."

Jewel forced a smile. "You *rest* then, Charles. I'll find some way to entertain myself for the evenin'. I don't think it'll be too difficult."

"It's not what you're thinking, Jewel."

"I'm not thinkin' anythin'."

Jewel sensed more than heard Charles's soft sigh as he whispered, "The letter's from Emily. She was too weak to write it herself. I think she's . . . dying."

Jewel knew she would never forget the hoarse break in Charles's voice as he forced himself to speak that last word. She did not recall closing the distance between them. She did not remember what she said as she slid her arms around Charles and clutched him close.

Nor was she certain of the moment when Charles's heartbroken sobs became her own.

It had been the longest evening of her life.

The blue cloud of tobacco smoke that hung in a misty haze over the patrons of the Texas Jewel seemed suddenly oppressive as Honesty glanced up at the clock on the far wall. Midnight had come and gone. She had had enough.

Signaling for a replacement dealer, Honesty forced a smile as groans sounded around the table.

"You ain't leavin'!" Joel Nigh's pale eyes swept her appreciatively as she stood up. "I thought you was goin' to give me a chance to get even."

"Come on, Honesty . . ." Frank Deitz's bearded faced turned glum. "Don't tell me you're goin' to sic old Sykes on us for the rest of the night."

"Honesty, you're breakin' my heart!"

Honesty cocked a brow as she shifted to give her frowning replacement her seat. "Now look what you've done, boys! You've hurt Sykes's feelings."

"Who cares about Sykes?"

"I never thought you'd quit on us."

Placing her palms flat on the table, Honesty leaned over, aware that the neckline of her crimson gown gapped generously as she whispered, "I owe you, fellas. You just make sure you're here tomorrow night, waitin' for me, and we'll go on where we left off. I just might have somethin' special for each one of you, if you do."

"Somethin' special, huh?"

"Honesty, honey, you're makin' my mouth water. . . ."

"I don't know about these other fellas, but I'll be waitin'."

"Why don't you all just shut up so Sykes can deal!"

The growling interjection from the unkempt drover seated to Joel's right snapped all heads toward him. Honesty was tempted to laugh at the expressions on the faces of the other three men as they responded without hesitation.

"You watch what you say, friend. That ain't no way to talk to a lady."

"I apologize for this fella, Honesty."

"Yeah, me, too."

Honesty managed a professional smile. "See you tomorrow, boys."

Climbing the stairs to the second floor minutes later, Honesty struggled to control the agitation that had been with her since her encounter with the infamous Wes Howell earlier that evening. Damn him! She was certain that if she examined her tender flesh, she'd find it was actually bruised from the weight of his unrelenting stare! Wes Howell had proved that he was all he was said to be. But she had proved something as well—that she was much more than he had expected, in every way.

The strange, indefinable discomfort that had plagued her since her volatile exchange with the former ranger returned, fixing a frown between Honesty's delicate brows. It mattered little to her that in proving to Wes Howell that she would be more difficult to forget than he anticipated, she had managed to prove the same about him. She knew she would eventually still the persistent tremor that moved down her spine when she recalled the hard heat of his body tight against hers. She would have no problem dismissing the breathlessness assaulting her each time she remembered wrapping her arms so boldly around his neck and drawing his mouth down to hers. As for the memory of his lips against hers . . . too brief . . . too lingering . . .

Honesty halted her thoughts abruptly. What was wrong with her?

Reaching the top of the staircase, Honesty turned down the hallway toward her room. She had met men like Wes Howell before. Her education had started young, and she had learned to recognize the type of man who held himself superior to women like Jewel and herself while attempting to avail themselves of all or more than was offered them.

Women like Jewel and herself . . . Honesty unconsciously raised her chin a defensive notch higher. Jewel had earned the respect with which she was treated in the Texas Jewel. As for herself, she had earned respect, too—the kind that had been shown to her at the table that night.

And she'd be damned before she'd accept anything

less from Wes Howell, or any man!

But she was learning that it wasn't going to be easy. It had been a matter of pride to deal the cards with a steady hand, refusing to allow Wes Howell to drive her from the table with his stare. He had finally left a half hour earlier, and she had waited only long enough to allow herself the personal victory of assuring herself that he did not intend to return before retiring.

Honesty briefly closed her eyes. She must have been crazy to let Lottie's jealousy force her into such a situation. She supposed there was a lesson to be learned somewhere there, but at present she was too tired to figure it out.

Well, at least she had seen the last of Wes Howell.

Refusing to examine her full reaction to that thought, Honesty reached into her upswept hair. She pulled out the pins, one after another, sighing as the heavy mass slipped down onto her shoulders, lock by lock. She reached to the back of her bodice, slowly unfastening the buttons there. She did not intend to waste any time getting into bed tonight. She wanted to talk to Jeremy early tomorrow morning . . . to explain. The look on his face when Wes Howell had spoken to him so contemptuously had frightened her. She had experienced the feeling that Jeremy was standing on the edge of a precipice, and that the slightest movement in the wrong direction might push him over.

Honesty's anger flared anew. She would not suffer Wes Howell, with his inflated opinion of himself and of his life's mission, to treat Jeremy that way!

Suddenly exhausted by her own inner turmoil, Honesty sighed again. As if all that agitation hadn't been enough, she had been intensely aware all evening long that Jewel had not made an appearance.

That wasn't like her. Had it not been for the fact that Charles had been conspicuously absent also, she would have been more concerned, but she recognized a pattern that had been established in their relationship. It seemed that each time Jewel and Charles argued, an intense reconciliation followed. They drew closer, if only for a little while. When she was younger, she had actually believed that the time would come when one of those periods of warm reconciliation would result in a permanent arrangement, but that had not happened. Over the years she had begun to doubt that it ever would.

A flash of latent memory abruptly assaulted her, halting Honesty in her step. She saw the simple interior of a covered wagon. So vivid was the scene that she could almost feel the warmth of the quilt stitched by her mother's hand that covered her and her younger sisters. She could hear Purity's labored breathing. She could feel the beating of Chastity's heart. She could almost—

The images disappeared as quickly as they had come, and Honesty's sense of loss was overwhelming. The fragmented scenes that flashed across her mind, returning when least expected, were so real. They had become an integral part of her life, renewing her conviction that neither her sisters' lives nor hers would be complete until they were together again.

But how? So many years had passed since that day on the river. The visions that badgered her, alternating between memories of the past and quick glimpses of the women her sisters had become, left everything so unclear. Yet, with all her uncertainties, she knew her sisters were waiting.

Her sisters needed her.

Jeremy needed her.

Wes Howell's heated stare intruded abruptly into her thoughts, snapping Honesty back to the present. Wes Howell was an outsider. He had no place in her life, and she was determined to oust him from it.

Struggling to loosen the third button on the back of her gown, Honesty pushed open her bedroom door, then kicked it closed behind her. The lamp flickered low, enshrouding the room in shadows as she slipped off a shoe, still struggling with her button. She looked up at a sound in the darkness, freezing into motionlessness as the shadows in the corner of the room coalesced into a male form. The wild pounding of her heart overwhelmed her other senses as the figure advanced toward her.

The figure was tall and masculine, its shoulders broad. It did not need encouragement as it approached with an instinctive male grace, walking steadily, without hesitation.

She sensed determination in its advance.

She sensed anger.

She sensed . . . danger.

The figure came closer. Honesty strained her eyes. . . .

Honesty strove to speak, but the words would not emerge. She had seen this image before. . . .

A pale rim of light illuminated the man's face as he walked closer, and Honesty saw that the anger and the danger she had sensed were real.

Wes heard Honesty's gasp. Her eyes widened as he approached, and satisfaction stirred within him. She hadn't been expecting him. He hadn't been certain if she would or not—if the entire episode downstairs had been staged in a deliberate attempt to taunt him into doing exactly what he was doing now.

Conflicting emotions assailed him as he stared

down at Honesty's flawless countenance. She knew how beautiful she was. She knew how a man felt when she looked at him the way she did. She knew that every inch of smooth white flesh so artfully exposed, every curve so clearly defined in the gowns she wore, tormented men. She knew that the closer a man got to her, the closer he wanted to be. And she knew that in that way, he was no different than any other man.

She knew he wanted her.

But she did not know what *he* knew.

Wes strained for control. He knew that Honesty had approached him earlier with some hidden purpose in mind. Her manner had been too deliberate, too enticing for a woman accustomed to being pursued. He also knew that a young woman who made her living by cheating at cards, one who went straight from her lover's arms to visit another man, was not likely to be attracted to an ex-Texas Ranger.

Instinct told him that there was something more to the situation than met the eye, and he was determined to find out. He had underestimated Honesty in their first contact, as well as his own susceptibility to her charms. He never would again. He was adept at playing the cards that were dealt him. With so much at stake this time, he did not intend to lose.

Those thoughts lingering, Wes halted his steps, perusing Honesty more closely. Brilliant eyes where traces of shock remained . . . black, lustrous hair streaming over narrow shoulders . . . faultless, creamy skin startled an even paler hue . . . Her full lips were parted, her gown partially unfastened, as if inviting his hand.

Steeling himself, Wes broke the silence between them.

"I've been waitin' for you. I knew you wouldn't

budge from that card table tonight until you were sure I was gone."

"How dare you come into my room uninvited?" The tremor in Honesty's voice was unexpected. She steadied it with obvious effort as she continued, "I want you to leave."

"Do you?"

"I think that's clear."

"Not to me."

"Then I'll make it clearer. Get out of my room."

"No." Wes took a deliberate step forward, bringing his body into contact with Honesty's. Reacting spontaneously as she took a step in retreat, he grasped her shoulders, holding her fast. "You're not goin' to run away again."

"Run away?" Honesty shook her head, her gaze sparking with anger. "It's amazing how you've managed to distort what happened downstairs to your liking. Let me clarify it for you. I didn't run away. Running away infers that I was afraid, and the truth is that you don't scare me, Wes Howell."

"I wasn't tryin' to scare you." Wes paused. "There may be a lot of things I'd like to make you feel, but fear isn't one of them."

"Bastard! I want you to leave."

"Not yet." Aware of the tremor that shook Honesty as he drew her closer, conscious that his own control was more tenuous than he cared to admit, Wes whispered, "We have some unfinished business to settle."

"No, we don't."

"That's where you're wrong, Honesty. Or would you prefer I call you *darlin'*?"

"Get out!" Honesty was trembling visibly, her eyes blazing as she hissed, "Get out . . . now . . . before I have you thrown out!"

As angry as she, Wes rasped, "Let's get this

straight, *darlin'* . . ." Wes paused as a white-hot heat gradually spread through his veins at the feel of Honesty's breasts heaving against his chest. Then he whispered, "You chose this spot for our little talk, whether you'll admit it or not. I'm merely obligin' you—just like I'll oblige you with anythin' else you might have in mind after you answer my question."

Honesty's eyes spat fire. "I didn't ask you to come to my room. And I don't answer questions—yours or anybody else's!"

"You'll answer mine."

"Never!"

"What do you want from me, Honesty?"

Honesty's short bark of laughter was harsh. "You're right, the answer to that question is too easy to refuse. Because the answer is *nothing!*"

"I watched you tonight. You draw men like a magnet. You don't have to go after any one of them. So why did you go out of your way to meet me?"

"Because I was a fool!"

"I don't believe that."

"Believe what you like!"

"Tell me the truth!"

"That is the truth!"

"I said—"

"All right!" Honesty's fury was barely controlled. "I came up to you at the bar because the girls were talking. They said you had turned them all down, and that you'd turn me down, too, if you had a chance. I told them that you weren't any different from any other man and that once you got a look at what I had to offer, you wouldn't want to let me go." Honesty laughed again. "Looks like I was right, wasn't I?"

Was she?

The frustration that had festered within Wes the whole evening long soared past control. He didn't like the way he was feeling. He didn't like having his concentration impaired by a cheating little witch who could bring him nothing but trouble. The shot in the dark that had brought his father down had rebounded too many times in his dreams for him to allow the tease now standing in the circle of his embrace to interfere, especially when he was so close to finding the man he was searching for. It was all a game to her, one that she played as deftly as she dealt her cards. Well, two could play that game.

Throwing caution to the wind, Wes slid his hand into the thick, dark waves at Honesty's temple. He barely withheld the grunt of pleasure that rose in his throat as the glittering silk slipped through his fingers. He cupped her head with his palm, the sweet, bodily scent of her sending his pulse hammering as he drew her mouth up toward his.

"So you think you were right, that I wouldn't want to let you go. Maybe so . . ." Wes' raspy tone deepened. "Maybe I do want you, darlin'. Maybe I've been thinkin' about a moment like this since the first time I saw you on the street. Maybe I haven't been able to get the taste of you out of my mouth, and maybe I've been thinkin' I need to prove to myself that I was wrong in thinkin' that nothin' ever tasted better or sweeter than you."

"Let me go, I warn you . . ."

Easily subduing Honesty's struggle to break free, Wes whispered, "And maybe I know that all your talkin' aside, you've been thinkin' the same."

Barely controlling the surging heat within, Wes pressed, "Do you want me to kiss you, Honesty?"

Honesty averted her face.

"Look at me, darlin'." Wes caught her chin, turning her back toward him. Their gazes locked and he felt the force of the connection right down to his toes.

"You want it as much as I do, don't you? You want to feel again the way you felt before. You want to know if I can make your blood sing. You want to know if I can make you feel like I'm the only man in the world."

"I don't!"

"You do. I know you do. Let me prove it to you, darlin'."

Wes brushed Honesty's mouth with his. Holding her still when she attempted to avoid him, he kissed her lightly, once, twice. His third kiss lingered, slowly deepening as a languorous heat spread through his veins. He heard her gasp as his tongue met and caressed hers. He felt the struggle that waged within her, even as he felt her resistance melting to join the rapturous flood of emotions rapidly sweeping them away. He heard the last, faltering protest within her fading with her breathless whisper, "I'm warning you . . ."

He swallowed her words in his kiss. Her protest silenced, he felt the first, subtle change as her lips gradually softened, clinging to his, as her body leaned into his embrace to indulge his kiss.

She was trembling as he was trembling. She was aching as he was aching. She was wanting as he was wanting.

Tearing his mouth from hers at last, Wes swept Honesty's forehead with his lips. He touched the wildly throbbing pulse in her temple with his kiss. He bathed her cheek and the hollows of her ear with whispered endearments that flowed from an unknown font within, following the slender column of her neck and shoulders with his lips to dip finally into the warm, white swells below.

More . . .

He needed more.

He sought her mouth once again.

Gentle lips, caressing hands . . .

Honesty's bemusement was complete as Wes's seductive ministrations continued. Her heart pounded thunderously as she separated her lips under his kiss, allowing him the pleasure he sought, knowing it would be her own. Her lids fluttered weakly as he caressed her face with his lips, his hands splaying wide to roam across her back before he withdrew to look down at her once more. Scorched by the black heat of eyes that had once been frigid, she came to the sudden realization that the cold-hearted lawman had disappeared from view. In his stead was the man within, the man she had sensed from the first, whose familiarity she could not define.

She recognized him now. *He was the man in her dream.*

And in that moment of startling recognition, Honesty knew something else as well.

She knew that she was his.

Wes heard Honesty's rapturous gasp. He recognized her moment of surrender, and exaltation flared hot and deep within him. Her hair, her trembling lids, her cheek, her lips . . . he tasted them anew as his hunger grew. Her sweet flesh was warm and damp with promise, the neckline of her bodice an impediment he could not endure as he slid it to her waist to expose the perfection of her breasts. Dropping to his knee, he worshiped one burgeoning crest with his lips. The taste of her jolted him with yearning as he devoured the firm, white swell, kissing, bathing, drawing, while Honesty's soft cries of pleasure stirred a driving need for more.

Honesty's gown formed a crimson pool at her feet as Wes slipped it down. Her undergarments became a lacy froth at her ankles as he released them with trembling hands. Remaining on his knee, Wes stared up at Honesty's naked splendor, his throat tight. She was so perfect in every detail, each curve and fragile hollow a mystery he needed desperately to explore.

Almost beside himself with longing, Wes sought her gaze.

"Honesty . . ."

His ragged whisper drew Honesty's eyes to his. Seeing in their glowing depths a passion that matched his own, knowing he must make her intimately his before another moment passed, Wes cupped her buttocks with his palms and drew her toward him. Slowly, deliberately separating her thighs with his lips, he pressed his mouth to the warm delta awaiting his kiss.

The first taste of her, honeyed and hot, sent Wes's senses reeling. Pressing intimately into the moist crevice awaiting him, Wes plundered it with his kiss, drawing, indulging. Glorying in Honesty's struggle to restrain her gasps, exalting as her thighs separated more fully to allow him greater access, he stroked her with his tongue. Discovering the sweet bud of her passion, he fondled it with growing abandon, a lightning jolt of pleasure stealing his breath as Honesty groaned aloud.

Looking up at her, Wes revelled in the flush of rapture that colored her exquisite features, urging in a throbbing whisper, "Talk to me, Honesty. Tell me what you want. Tell me, darlin'."

Honesty shook her head, her expression growing strained as she whispered, "Wes . . . please . . ."

"Tell me." Wes fought to control his shuddering. "Do you want me to love you, darlin'?"

Honesty took a quaking breath.

"Do you want me to love you like no man's ever loved you before? Do you want me to make you feel good . . . so good that you'll never want me to let you go?"

Honesty was shuddering almost out of control, and Wes felt a new joy rising.

"Give to me, darlin'." His voice heavy with emotion, Wes rasped, "Give to me, and I'll make it all worthwhile."

Not waiting for her response, Wes pressed his mouth flush against the waiting font of Honesty's passion. Her ecstatic gasps rang in his ears as he drew from her with new fervor, as he fondled the moist slit, making it his own, as he breathed in all that was Honesty, knowing only the moment and the woman in his arms.

Devouring, consuming, Wes pursued his sweet quest. His ministrations pressed deeper. His kisses searched wider. His loving thrall expanded. He felt the wonder of Honesty . . . the beauty . . . the heat.

Suddenly alert as a new shuddering began within Honesty, Wes drew intimately from her sweetness. He held the bud of her passion the prisoner of his seeking kiss until her body convulsed with a sudden, spontaneous spasm, then quaked again and again. Accepting the sweet reward of her passion, Wes took it deep inside him, knowing no satiation until Honesty's soft gasp and sagging limbs signaled that she could take no more.

Sweeping Honesty up into his arms, Wes carried her to the satin-draped bed nearby. His heart pounded as he laid her on its surface. The gold locket at her throat glinted in the meager light as he stood above her for long moments, feasting his gaze on her naked splendor. Her dark hair was spread across the pillow, her exquisite features colored with passion. Like a man dying of thirst, he drank in the matchless glory of her luminous gaze . . . a gaze that was totally yielding . . .

Wes stood above her, his chest heaving, his enigmatic gaze intent. Unmindful of her nakedness, held in the thrall of ecstatic passion so recently spent, Honesty allowed Wes's silent perusal. She had never felt the way Wes made her feel. His touch, so new, was yet familiar. He had touched her as no man had ever touched her, and he had loved her in a way she had never dreamed of being loved, yet all had seemed so right.

Her heart began a new pounding as the heat in Wes's gaze burned brighter and he lay down beside her. Honesty trembled anew. She moved into his embrace as his palms smoothed her skin, as his hands stroked her intimately. The musky, male scent of him filled her nostrils as he bathed her flesh anew with his kiss, as he sought and found hidden points of pleasure of which she was not aware, as he touched and petted, restoring the need within her to a heated pitch.

A spontaneous protest escaped her lips when Wes drew back from her unexpectedly. She attempted to clutch him close, but he resisted, maintaining the distance between them as he linked her gaze with his. When he spoke at last, his voice was a throbbing thread of sound.

"Do you want me, Honesty? Tell me you do."

Uncertain whether she could speak past the rapid pounding of her heart, Honesty chose to demonstrate instead. She raised a tentative hand to his cheek. His skin was warm and taut. Longing to taste it, she drew him toward her, pressing her lips to the skin there, trailing her mouth to his where she licked gently at his lips before covering them with her mouth. She was drowning in the moist wonder of his kiss when Wes drew back abruptly.

"Tell me you want me, Honesty. I want to hear you say the words."

Honesty remained breathlessly silent.

"Say it."

"Wes, please . . ."

"The words, Honesty. I want to hear the words."

Striving for control, Honesty whispered, "I want you."

Silence.

"Wes?"

"I didn't hear you. Say it again."

"I want you, Wes. You know I do."

He kissed her again then . . . and again, each kiss more powerful, each kiss more searching, each kiss more demanding. Her excitement raised to a fever pitch, Honesty returned kiss for kiss, caress for caress, seeking his flesh, working at the buttons of his shirt, aching to feel his skin warm against her.

Her heart was pounding with her need when Wes went unexpectedly still. She felt the change in him the moment before he drew back abruptly. A chill engulfed her when she saw that his flush of passion had changed to cold sobriety. Slow reality began dawning when he spoke at last, his voice as glacial as his eyes.

"Am I borin' you now, Honesty?"

Honesty could not respond.

"I asked you a question, Honesty. Isn't that what you told me downstairs, earlier . . . that I bore you?"

Refusing to react, unwilling to believe what she knew was all too real, Honesty remained motionless as Wes continued, "Maybe you aren't bored now, *dar-*

lin', but I am. I've gotten just about everythin' I came for, so I'll be sayin' good night."

An aching reality spread through Honesty's veins as Wes drew himself to his feet beside the bed. She made no sound at all as he reached for his hat on the chair nearby, lingering only long enough to put it on and touch the brim with a polite salute.

"Thank you, ma'am."

Silent, unmoving, Honesty watched as Wes pulled the door closed behind him.

The music of the saloon below engulfed Wes as he stepped out into the hallway and drew Honesty's door closed behind him. He hesitated, listening. All was silent within.

He took a stabilizing breath, his expression resolute as he stretched his taut frame to its full height, then started in the direction of the stairs.

He had come close . . . very close. Instinct—and a last, fleeting spark of sanity—had been all that saved him from the moment of final consummation. In that moment of sanity, he had seen all too clearly that to claim Honesty would have been to surrender.

She would never know how close he had come to proving that everything she had said was right. But he'd be damned before he would give her the chance to laugh in his face again!

Wes's step faltered.

But Honesty hadn't been laughing.

He remembered how she had looked.

And he wondered if his payback had been worth the price.

The lamp had sputtered and died, casting the room into darkness. The strip of light from the hallway beyond was the only illumination in the darkness of her room. Honesty stared at it, seeing instead Wes's emotionless expression as he had tipped his hat and walked away.

A slow trembling began inside her. Honesty reached for the coverlet at the foot of the bed and drew it up over herself. She was cold, both inside and out. She had been chilled by a gaze as frigid as the cruel words he'd spoken. Sharper than blades, the words had been slivers of ice that had slashed and left her bleeding.

Honesty closed her eyes to shut away the pain.

She had been a fool.

She had learned a fool's lesson.

She would not forget it.

Chapter Four

A relentless morning sun beat down on Jeremy's pounding head, beading his brow with perspiration as his horse picked its way along the rough trail. Lifting his hat, Jeremy ran a shaky hand through his moist blond hair and wiped his sleeve across his forehead. He replaced his hat and spurred his mount to a faster pace, wincing as the jolting quickly became more than he could bear.

Forced to rein the animal back to a modest gait, Jeremy cursed aloud. He had been on the trail since sun-up. Hardly able to raise his head, he had forced himself into the saddle and headed out of town, determined. In the time since, he had kept to a northerly direction despite a deepening physical distress compounded by the increasing heat, persistent insects, and the knowledge that he must go on despite his misery.

But, damn it all, this whole mess wasn't his fault! If Bitters had shown up in town as expected the previous evening, everything would be settled by now. Instead, one drink had become two until he had spent the night drowning his uncertainties in the bottle.

Jeremy reached for his canteen. His tongue was like cotton, his throat was dry, and the drumming in his head wouldn't quit . . . but through it all, the images that haunted him remained painfully clear.

Honesty standing in the curve of Wes Howell's arm . . . Howell whispering to Honesty, their lips only inches apart . . . Honesty's expression so intent on Howell's that she saw no one or nothing but him . . .

Jeremy raised his canteen to his lips, grimacing as the warm liquid slipped down his throat. He wasn't certain what he had intended when he approached them where they stood at the bar, but he had known instantly that he had made a mistake. Howell, the arrogant bastard that he was, had talked to him like he was dirt! He had seen the look on Honesty's face then. For a moment, she had looked at him through Howell's eyes, and she had not liked what she saw. Unable to bear that realization, he had turned away, vowing to erase that look from Honesty's eyes forever.

He knew what he had to do.

But first he had to find Bitters.

The problem was that no one really knew where Bitters was living. The frequency with which Bitters visited Caldwell indicated that he was staying in the vicinity. Rumor had it that Riggs, Gant, and Bitters had taken over an abandoned cabin north of Caldwell. If those rumors were correct, Jeremy knew there were only two places where that cabin could be. He also knew there could be only one reason for the mystery the three men maintained about themselves. He intended to solve that mystery today, once and for all.

His rambling thoughts abruptly curtailed by his stomach's queasy roll, Jeremy closed his eyes. His senses reeled and he snapped his eyes open, realizing that the situation was again dire. Drawing his horse to an abrupt halt, he dismounted in a rush. Within a few steps, he was brought to his knees by more of the violent, heaving spasms that had plagued him all morning long.

Taking a few minutes to catch his breath, Jeremy then drew himself to his feet and remounted. He looked up at the sun as he spurred his horse forward, again cursing. His mind was weary and his body ached. He felt damned sick. All he wanted to do was to lie down somewhere and sleep, but he had no time for that indulgence.

His throat suddenly tight as Honesty's face flashed before him, Jeremy took a steadying breath. It was now or never. He had already waited too long.

With that thought uppermost in his mind, Jeremy attempted to dismiss the churning in his stomach and urged his horse on. So great was his misery that he was uncertain how much time had elapsed before he saw the first of them.

Cattle. Scores of them grazing peacefully as one herd while others bawled in a makeshift corral. The number in itself had no true significance, but the brands . . .

Jeremy almost laughed aloud. The Circle R. The Double Bar D. The S M S. All were brands he recognized—just as he recognized the reason for the branding irons heating in the fire nearby.

He should have known.

* * *

Bed linens were piled on the floor, with washcloths and discarded nightclothes lying in a heap beside them.

Honesty turned to look around her. Her face was pale and her expression sober. She had been working since dawn to erase every trace of Wes Howell's presence in her room, but it hadn't been easy.

Honesty fought to control her emotions as she recalled the sleepless night past. The first light of dawn had found her still attempting to escape the memory of mesmerizing dark eyes filled with a passion that had lied.

Realization had come slowly, with embarrassment and shame. She was still uncertain how Wes had struck the chord inside her that had left her so vulnerable to his ardent assault. But there was no doubt in her mind that she had correctly recognized him as the man in her dream. Her mistake had been in interpreting the message the dream conveyed, a meaning that should have been clear when Wes's shadowy image moved into view to replace Chastity's red-haired figure with his own.

Only now did she realize that the dream had been a warning.

Only now did she understand that the determination, the anger, the danger that she had sensed in his advance had been all too real.

Finally despairing, she had arisen from bed and slipped down to the kitchen where she had heated water and then carried it up to her room so she might scrub every inch of her body free of Wes's spell. But memories had proved as inescapable as the sensitivity of intimate flesh that had known his touch alone.

Standing fully clothed at last in a pale cotton gown, her freshly washed hair hanging unbound down her back, she had seen in the mirror haunted eyes reflecting the knowledge that there was not a part of her that had not been touched by Wes in some way.

And in that moment of total acknowledgement had come fury.

She had damned Wes then, for the bastard that he was! She had damned him for the tremors that had shaken his voice when he rasped his hunger for her. She had damned him for the gentleness with which he had stroked her tender flesh. She had damned him for the patience, for the loving, for the wonder with which he had raised her, step by step, to the aching, throbbing pinnacle of desire, only to dash her so cruelly back to reality when he had snatched it all away.

She had damned him for making her *believe.*

She had sworn not to forget.

And then she had cast thoughts of him aside.

Forcing aside her trembling as well, Honesty glanced around the room once more before sweeping up the soiled linens and turning toward the door. She was on the street minutes later, the linens left behind in the laundry where they belonged, with her regrets carefully discarded beside them.

With the morning sun warm on her skin and its golden glow enveloping her, Honesty forced a smile. She was Honesty Buchanan. She had been fooled, but she was not a fool. She would teach Wes Howell . . . and anyone else who cared to learn . . . where the difference lay.

That thought sustaining her, Honesty started across Main Street, which was coming to life with the new day. She saw Willard Grimes as he opened the door to his general store, broom in hand. She acknowledged the rotund businessman's appreciative leer with a wave, noting that he would never change. She crossed the street, exchanging words briefly with three drovers on horseback who greeted her warmly, somehow grateful for their open admiration. She fluttered her lashes at Elizabeth Dooley, the maiden aunt of a visiting preacher who had made her the subject of several heated sermons, thereby acknowledging, as she always did, the woman's contribution to the vehemence of her nephew's diatribe. She walked between the inanimate and human litter that covered the boardwalk, carefully avoiding the sidestreet where Charles maintained his residence, knowing she was not up to the possibility of meeting Jewel.

When she arrived at the door of Jeremy's shack, Honesty felt a premonition rising. The hour was early, but she somehow knew before she knocked that there would be no answer, just as she knew when she pushed the door open that she would find a freshly emptied bottle of red-eye on the unkempt cot.

Out on the street again, she turned hopefully toward the holding pens, walking briskly. Her agitation was barely under control when she walked back down the street minutes later. Jeremy had not reported for work. Nor was he in Birdie Cotter's restaurant or any of his other usual haunts.

The absurdity of her panic suddenly struck her, and Honesty forced herself to take a steadying breath. Jeremy had been hurt and angry the previous night, but he would do nothing desperate without speaking to her first. That was his way. She knew it was.

Finding herself again in front of Jeremy's shack, Honesty pushed open the door and entered. She'd wait for him. It would please Jeremy to find her waiting. It would restore his confidence and make him smile. She'd explain about Wes. She'd tell Jeremy that Wes Howell had been testing her, and she had been testing him in return. She would not tell Jeremy what had later come to pass, or that the lesson she had been taught was one of the most difficult she had ever learned. She would apologize for the way Wes had spoken to him, and she would promise Jeremy that she would never give Wes the opportunity to act that way again.

Honesty's eyes suddenly filled. She would hug Jeremy then, and he would hug her back. She'd enjoy the warmth of his embrace and the strength of his arms around her, knowing that Jeremy and she were *family*, and as such, they would always be there for each other.

Suddenly more tired than she could ever remember being, Honesty smoothed the rumpled bed linens on Jeremy's cot and lay down. She'd close her eyes for a little while, and she'd wait.

"What in hell are you doin' here?"

The snarled question came from behind Jeremy. It rent the silence of the hot morning air, snapping his head around with a quickness that set it to throbbing as Riggs stepped into sight from behind a tree. His stubbled jaw tight, his shirt ringed with perspiration, Riggs made no attempt to hide his feelings as he continued, "You ain't got no business here, so get movin'—now!

Incensed by Riggs's greeting and infused with a sense of purpose he had not known before, Jeremy hissed, "I'm not goin' anywhere! Besides, whatever made you think you got the right to talk for Bitters? He's the man who makes the decisions."

"Bitters might be the man who does all the talkin'"—Riggs took a threatening step forward, his hand clenched tightly around the handle of the branding iron he carried—"but I'm the one who does everythin' else. You get my message?"

Jeremy paused, his head pounding. He didn't feel well, and Riggs wasn't making him feel any better. Besides, he didn't like Riggs. He didn't trust him. There wasn't a single time when he and Bitters were talking when Riggs didn't stand to the side, sneering. As if he had anything to sneer about.

Jeremy's temper flared. "Yeah, I get your message. Now I'm goin' to give you mine." He glanced toward the cabin hidden in a bank of trees in the distance. "Bitters is in that cabin, isn't he? I'm goin' to ride over there to talk to him. I've got somethin' to tell him that I think he'll be real interested to hear. You just keep at your work"—It was Jeremy's turn to sneer—"*enlargin'* the herd and doin' what Bitters tells you. Like you said, you're better off workin' than thinkin' anytime."

Not bothering with a backward glance, Jeremy spurred his horse on toward the cabin. He did not see Riggs's hand snake toward the gun at his hip. Nor did he see the struggle in the fellow's black expression before he dropped his hand back to his side and threw the branding iron back in the fire.

Dismounting a few minutes later, Jeremy approached the cabin. His heart was pounding. His mouth was dry. He could have used a drink to steady himself, but he knew this wasn't the time. He had the feeling that despite all the bottles they had shared, Bitters and his crew were a little wary of his drinking, what with everybody harping on it all the time. He could have a drink later.

"What are you doin' here, Sills?"

Jeremy turned his head toward the sound of Gant's voice as the fellow stepped into sight. He turned back toward the cabin as Bitters appeared in the doorway and asked, "How in hell did you find this place, Sills?"

Jeremy smiled. "I know this country real well . . . better than most. I figured you'd be here." At Bitters's obvious discomfort, he added, "I used to go huntin' out here for my ma when I was a kid. Nobody else knows about this place but me."

Bitters nodded. He motioned with his chin toward the herd grazing peacefully nearby. "I told you I was gettin' a herd ready to take up to the Blackfoot Agency in Montana. I've been puttin' it together with the boys."

Jeremy smiled. "Yeah. I saw." His smile was knowing. "That's the way I like to collect a herd."

Bitters's tone tightened. "You sayin' that me and the boys are doin' somethin' illegal here?"

Jeremy's smile faded. He saw from the corner of his eye that Riggs had joined them, adding to the hostility of the moment. Things were not going as he had planned.

Suddenly angry, Jeremy addressed Bitters directly. "What's all this about? I thought we were friends. We had some good times together. I figured this was as good a time as any to show you I could do you some good if you decided to let me in on your next business deal."

"Business deal . . ." Bitters laughed, his swarthy coloring deepening. "Yeah, well, you see it. We're collectin' cattle and we don't need your help."

"That isn't all you're doin'. You know it, and I know it." Jeremy was beginning to feel sick again, and he was past patience. He took a hard step forward. "You aren't foolin' me. You're waitin' to find out if those rumors about the big shipments of cash that are supposed to start comin' into Caldwell soon are true. Well, I'm here to tell you that they are."

"Really?" Bitters's small eyes narrowed. "How do you know that? And even if you do, what makes you think I need you to tell me?"

"Let's put our cards on the table, Bitters." Jeremy could feel it all slipping away from him. Desperation twinging, he pressed, "Everythin's out in the open, now that Wes Howell arrived in town yesterday."

"Wes Howell—the Texas Ranger?" Bitters' expression stiffened. "What in hell is he doin' in Kansas?"

"He isn't a ranger anymore. That Eastern syndicate hired him to protect their cash while it's in Caldwell." Jeremy straightened up, restraining a smile. He had Bitters interested now. "Howell arrived yesterday mornin' . . . just in time to stop a holdup at the bank and shoot the two fellas who tried it."

Bitters nodded, hatred flashing in his eyes. "He did, huh?"

"The town's been buzzin' ever since about the shipments that are supposed to start arrivin' soon."

"How soon?" Bitters's tight gaze pinned him.

Jeremy felt a flush of triumph, realizing he had captured Bitters' full attention at last. "Nobody's sure about the timin', but I could find out."

"You could."

"You know I could!" Jeremy gave a short laugh. "You've been in Caldwell enough to know how things stand, so I'm not tellin' you anythin' you don't know when I say I've got a way to get you all the information you need about the shipments—when they're comin' and how they're goin' to be guarded."

"Don't listen to him, boss!" Riggs shot Jeremy a scathing glance. "Look at him! He's comin' off another drunk! He's shakin' so bad, he can hardly stand, and he's tellin' you he's goin' to get you information that you're supposed to bet your life on!"

"Shut up, Riggs!"

"But—"

Livid, Bitters snapped, "I told you to shut up! I'm the boss here, and I decide who's dependable or not."

Turning back to Jeremy, Bitters hissed, "You'd better not be tryin' to fool me, boy. . . ."

"Why would I do that?" Jeremy attempted to straighten his shoulders, but the pain in his stomach was growing. He was going to have to settle everything quickly before he made a fool of himself. He couldn't afford to do that—not now. He pressed, "You know what I want. I want to be a part of the deal."

"How much of a part?"

"A fair share."

"How do we know you're not settin' a trap?"

"A trap?"

Jeremy shook his head, disconcerted, and Gant laughed. "Hell, this kid don't know that Howell's an old friend of yours, boss!"

Jeremy looked at Bitters. Realization dawned. "So, Howell knows you! He probably knows Gant and Riggs are travelin' with you, too. It would be too dangerous for any of you to come to town to get information for yourselves, now that he's here . . . so it looks like you need me more than I thought."

Jeremy was unprepared for Bitters' sudden advance toward him, for the menace that shone in his eyes as he halted so close that the bitter smell of his breath set Jeremy's stomach to churning. "Need you? I suppose you could say we do, so this is the deal. You give us the information about when the first shipment is supposed to arrive . . . and the second and the third."

"The second and the third?"

"*I'll* pick the shipment we're goin' to take!"

"It's a mistake to wait!" Jeremy's protest was spontaneous. "Somebody will beat us to it!"

"We sure as hell ain't goin' after the first shipment! There'll be all kinds of precautions taken then. But the second shipment . . . well . . . or maybe the third . . ."

"But—"

"That's the way it's goin' to be! Take it or leave it!"

Bitters' heated response left no room for argument. Jeremy nodded reluctantly. "I'll get the information on any shipment you want."

"You're sure you can manage it?"

"Yeah."

"How're you goin' to get this information?" Bitters's smile was mocking. "You goin' to go and ask Charles Webster himself?"

"That's my business."

"No, it ain't. Not with my life on the line."

"My life will be on the line, too!"

"Let's get somethin' straight!" Bitters pressed closer. "It ain't *your* life I care about. So, how are you goin' to get this information?"

"Look—" Jeremy had had enough. Knowing he couldn't hold out much longer against the queasiness in his gut, he hissed, "Do you want the deal, or not, because I'll be damned if I'll tell you anythin' else—even if I have to end up gettin' that cash by myself!"

Bitters sneered. "You're hot to get the job done, ain't you, boy?"

"Don't call me boy!"

Bitters laughed. "All right. You get the information and we'll cut you in for a fair share." Bitters sobered. "But you're goin' to be right by my side when we do it . . . just to make sure."

Jeremy nodded.

Bitters paused. "Since me and the boys won't be comin' into Caldwell no more, we'll be expectin' you to keep in touch."

"I'll get back to you in a couple of days."

Jeremy turned to leave when Bitters gripped his arm, staying him. Bitters's sudden smile was coy. "What do you say we seal the deal with a drink?"

"No."

"What? You're turnin' me down?" Bitters raised his hairy brows. "That ain't friendly."

Jeremy shook his arm loose. "I have to be goin' before somebody starts lookin' for me."

Bitters cocked his head. "Now, who in the world would do that?"

Jeremy did not bother to respond. Covering the short distance to his horse in record time, he spurred his mount into motion and rode off.

His queasiness almost beyond control, Jeremy jerked his horse to an abrupt halt as soon as he was out of sight of the cabin. He leaped from the saddle, unable to take more than a few steps before the spasms began again. Breathless and weak from the heaving that continued long after his stomach was emptied, Jeremy sat back on his heels and attempted to catch his breath. Damn, he was sick! But he had done what he came for, anyway. He had made the deal that would change his life forever. Everything would soon be well.

And when it was over and done, Honesty would forgive him . . . for everything . . . because he would have proved that he could accomplish something at last.

And because she loved him.

Forcing himself back on his feet, Jeremy remounted, anxious to leave the area and Bitters behind. It occurred to him that Honesty had been right. Bitters wasn't his friend. It was his thought that Bitters had been planning to use him all along.

But that was all right.

Two could play at that game.

His smile weak, Jeremy spurred his horse on.

Watching until Sills disappeared from sight behind a rise, Gant turned toward Bitters, breaking the tense silence that had lingered.

"Well, he's gone."

"Sure he's gone. He couldn't wait to get away." Bitters gave a scoffing grunt. "Riggs is right. Sills could hardly stand. He's probably on his knees right now, pukin' up whatever's left in his stomach." Bitters appeared amused. "That boy's got a drinkin' problem, but he'll do for what we need him for."

"Do we need him? I ain't so sure."

Riggs's interjection turned Bitters toward him with a viciousness that set the shorter man a step backward as he spat, "What's the matter, are you deaf? You heard what Sills said. Wes Howell's in Caldwell—of all the damn luck! We're just lucky that Sills took it into his head to come out here to find us. I ain't about to guess what happened to make him do that, but at least I got the sense to be glad he did! Hell, we could've ridden into town and right into Howell's arms!"

"I ain't afraid of Howell!"

Bitters' face flushed hot. "Are you sayin' I am?"

"All I'm sayin' is that you're sure enough goin' out of your way to avoid him."

"That's because I've got more sense than you!" Bitters strove visibly to draw his anger under control. He walked toward the cabin door, then turned back abruptly. "There's one thing I know, and know for sure. Things are goin' to go much easier for us if Howell don't know I'm around. He's been after me for a long time, and he don't give up. It'll only complicate things if he gets wind of me bein' anywheres near here."

"So, you're tellin' me you think Sills can handle things just like he said . . . gettin' us all the information we need?"

Bitters sneered. "You saw his face. Somethin' happened and he's runnin' scared to get some cash. For a minute there I thought he was goin' to get down on his knees and beg to be let in on this job."

"You think he'll be able to follow through with all his promises?"

"He'll get what he needs."

Riggs's jowled face drew into downward lines. "I ain't as sure of that as you."

"Doubt it, do you?" Bitters's small eyes narrowed into an assessing squint. "All right, so I'll make both you boys a promise. If Sills don't come through with what he promised, I'll make sure he never promises nobody nothin' again."

Gant's bony face broke into an unexpected grin. "You know, I almost hope he don't, just so's we'd be rid of him."

"Do you?" Bitters gave a harsh laugh. "You know somethin'? So do I."

His laughter ceasing as unexpectedly as it had begun, Bitters instructed his men tightly, "We've got two or three weeks left here at most. We ain't got no time to waste. We ain't goin' to be able to sell that herd if all them beeves aren't wearin' the same brand."

Riggs shook his head. "We're cuttin' things mighty close, wouldn't you say?"

"No, I wouldn't." Bitters's expression hardened.

"Just grab them brandin' irons and get to work!"

Bitters saw the resentment that flashed briefly in Riggs's eyes the moment before he turned back toward the herd with Gant following close behind. Thoughtful, Bitters stared after them. He was getting sick of Riggs and his complaints. It looked like it might be time for a parting of the ways after this job was done. He'd think it over and he'd decide then if a larger share of the loot looked better to him than Riggs ever did.

Yeah, he'd decide later.

Honesty awakened slowly. Momentarily disoriented, she looked around her, seeing the battered table and chairs on which a dirty cup rested, the potbellied stove sporting its blackened coffee pot, the corner cabinet revealingly empty of food, and hooks on the wall hung with familiar clothing that had not seen the washtub for more time than she dared estimate—as she dared not estimate the number of empty bottles that she knew had been carelessly discarded beneath the cot on which she lay.

She was in Jeremy's cabin.

Oh, yes, she remembered now. She must have fallen asleep.

But she remembered better times as well, when her visits to Jeremy were to a cabin on the outskirts of town that was spotlessly clean. Mother Sills had been alive then, and Honesty had always been welcome. She realized now that she had been too young to notice the gradual worsening of the illness that had eventually overwhelmed that gentle woman, but she had never been too young to realize that Mother Sills was one of the kindest women she had ever known.

Strangely, Mother Sills's death had increased Honesty's love for Jeremy. But the bond that had been forged between them when Mother Sills died now chafed sorely, and her concern for Jeremy was slowly escalating to fear.

Where was he? What had driven him from his bed so early in the morning?

Honesty drew herself to her feet and walked to the window. The morning sun had risen and Caldwell had awakened to the new day. She must have been sleeping for an hour or more, but Jeremy still had not returned. And the truth was that she had no way of knowing when he would.

Glimpsing her reflection in the glass as she turned away, Honesty groaned. All trace of her stringent attempts at grooming earlier that morning had been erased by her restless nap. Her hair was disheveled and her gown wrinkled. Were it any other day, were her spirits not so low, she supposed she would not venture out on the street looking as she did, but somehow it didn't matter much now.

A dark-eyed gaze flashed suddenly before her, but Honesty thrust it from her mind, refusing to submit. The night past had been a mistake. She would allow herself neither to dwell on it . . . nor to repeat it.

Drawing the cabin door ajar moments later, Honesty stood briefly in the opening. She looked back at the disorder behind her, acutely aware that the sad scene reflected the downward spiral of Jeremy's life. She needed to help him reverse that spiral before it was too late, because she knew with innate certainty that if she could not, he was lost.

Submitting to impulse as she prepared to leave, Honesty spoke earnestly into the silence.

"It's time to come home, Jeremy. I'm waiting for you, you hear?"

Surprising even herself, Honesty blew a kiss into

the empty room—a kiss for Jeremy who needed her loving support so badly. Did he feel it and her love—wherever he was?

Hoping he did, Honesty drew the door closed behind her and walked out onto the street.

Standing in the doorway of Birdie Cotter's place, Wes was hardly aware of the clatter of dishes behind him. He had had a poor night's sleep at the Night's Rest Hotel, and he had eaten breakfast without tasting it at all.

Suddenly aware that he was staring at the entrance to the Texas Jewel a short distance down the street, he glanced away. He stretched tight muscles and flexed broad shoulders that were unnaturally stiff after his restless night. The problem was that his hotel room had been too small for the images that had crowded it through the long, dark hours—images of glorious eyes incandescent with passion, of white skin brushed to a rosy hue with his kiss, of warm lips . . . sweet lips . . . lips that in seeking to deny him, had offered him all instead. His room had been too small for the sound of the ecstatic gasps that had rebounded over and again in his mind.

Wes scowled, annoyed at his straying thoughts. He had better things to do than to relive the night past.

I want you, Wes . . . you know I do.

Wes's stomach squeezed tight. Damn it, would Honesty's words forever haunt him? How different was her breathless whisper from the words another young woman had uttered to him years earlier in the same impassioned tone?

Wes forced himself to remember.

Dolores had not been as beautiful as Honesty, but she had been just as popular in the saloon where she worked. He supposed he should have been warned by the convincing tone of Dolores's declarations of love . . . so practiced . . . so perfect. But he had believed her, and he had gone against all manner of sage advice, including his father's, until the day when he had returned with the memory of his father's dying words still fresh in his ears and found her with another man.

I love you, Wes. I just get so lonesome . . .

He had made sure that Dolores never needed to make excuses to him again.

I want you, Wes . . . you know I do.

Honesty . . .

He wondered what excuse she would give her young lover this time.

And he wondered why he cared.

"Good mornin', Wes!" Wes turned sharply toward the voice that broke into his painful thoughts, greeting John Henry Brown with a frown as the dauntless deputy continued, "It's pretty early, but the marshal's been up for hours, and he's not one to waste time. He wanted me to tell you he'd like to meet with you this mornin', if you had a mind."

"The marshal wants to meet, huh?"

"Yes, sir—him and Mr. Webster, at the bank."

Wes's attention was suddenly acute. "When?"

"Now's a good time, since they're already waitin' for you."

So, the marshal wanted to see him.

Wes fell into step beside John Henry as they walked out onto the boardwalk. He was about to comment on the marshal's invitation when movement at the doorway of Sills's shack caught his eye.

A slender figure emerged.

Wes's stomach knotted tightly as Honesty paused briefly in the doorway, turning back to speak a few words to someone behind her before throwing a kiss and closing the door. Watching as she walked back toward the Texas Jewel, he saw that her hair was disheveled and her gown was in disarray. He wished it wasn't so obvious that she had just awakened and was making her way back to her room, just as she had done the previous morning. And he wished it wasn't so clear that Honesty would have no need to make excuses to her lover, because she had spent the night in his arms.

John Henry followed his line of vision. "That Honesty Buchanan sure is good-lookin', ain't she? It's no wonder to me that she manages the fellas so easily." He paused. "Of course, I wouldn't say nothin' about that in front of Mr. Webster, because like I told you yesterday, he wouldn't take it kindly."

"So you said."

"That's right. Honesty's a favorite of his." John Henry shrugged. "And since Miss Jewel don't seem to mind all the attention he gives her, well, I expect nobody can blame the man."

Suddenly unwilling to hear more, Wes lengthened his step, forcing the shorter man to comment, "There ain't no rush. The marshal will wait. He's got all the time in the world."

Honesty turned into the entrance of the Texas Jewel without seeing him. As he glimpsed her face more clearly, Wes was struck by the thought that she appeared somehow sad.

Sad . . .

He must be crazy!

Wes continued on down the street.

"The wire came first thing this morning."

His refined features composed, his dark suit immaculate, Charles maintained a sober facade that gave no indication of the difficult night past. He waited for Wes Howell to close the office door behind him and Deputy Brown. He hadn't needed to ask Marshal Carr what he thought of the former ranger when Carr personally delivered the telegram to him a short time earlier. It had been written all over the fellow's face when he mentioned Howell's name.

Charles strove to maintain a neutral mask. He wasn't up to this. Jewel has stayed with him through the night, something she rarely did. Attuned to his feelings as she so often proved to be, she had offered him the compassion of her presence and the love she refused to put into words. Strangely, he truly believed that Jewel suffered as much as he at the thought that Emily was dying. Even more strange, considering the disparity between Emily's background and Jewel's, was his conviction that had things been different, Emily and Jewel could have been friends.

But as things stood, he would never know. Nor did he believe he would ever again see Emily's smile or hear her sweet voice speak his name. Most devastating of all was the thought that he might not have the chance to say good-bye.

That thought did not lose its impact as the morning hours dawned. And then he had not been in his office more than a few minutes when Marshal Carr brought him the telegram.

Intensely aware that the harsh feelings between the marshal and Howell were mutual, Charles handed Howell the printed wire. He watched carefully as Howell read it, noting the almost indistinguishable twitch in the former ranger's cheek the moment before Howell looked up with those black eyes that were as frigid as ice.

"So, the first shipment arrives next week. You say you'll be ready for it?"

"I had the safe moved up front this morning."

Howell turned toward the marshal. The smaller man stared at him without warmth. "Are we goin' to work together on this, marshal, or are we goin' to get in each other's way?"

"I'd say that's up to you."

"No, I don't think so." Howell's strong features hardened. "It's up to you. I can do this job with you, or without you, but I don't want any blame bein' placed on me if somebody gets caught in the crossfire."

"You're so sure there's goin' to be trouble, are you?"

Howell tapped the printed message in his hand. "Somebody at Slater Enterprises isn't too bright. Everythin's spelled out in this message—the amount they're shippin' in, the route, the estimated time of arrival, and the number of men they're goin' to have guardin' the shipment."

"Damned right! Eight men with a lot of firepower! There ain't many who'll take a chance against them odds!"

"There'll be eight men guardin' the shipment until it gets to Caldwell. There'll only be one after it gets here. It's up to you, marshal, if you want to make it three."

Charles silently observed the conflict between the two men. Marshal Carr was a hardheaded lawman determined to handle all aspects of his job his own way, but he doubted Carr was any match for the formidable Wes Howell. He didn't think there were many who were.

Marshal Carr's wiry mustache twitched. "From my viewpoint, the numbers are different—more like *two* men guardin' the shipment after it gets to town, and *three* if you've a mind to help."

"Look, marshal," Howell took an aggressive step forward, his features darkening. Charles recognized the courage it took for the marshal to stand his ground as Howell continued, his patience obviously at low ebb, "Slater Enterprises hired me to protect the shipments they'll be sendin'. To my mind, that gives me responsibility for them. I don't really care if you agree. If you called me to this meeting just so we can argue, you're goin' to be mighty disappointed. I'm not goin' to play that game."

Marshal Carr's lined face tightened. "I ain't the one who called you here. That was Webster's idea."

Charles felt the full impact of Howell's stare as the former ranger turned back abruptly toward him. The enmity that flashed briefly in his gaze startled him into momentary speechlessness when Howell stated flatly, "Then I suppose we'd better get on with it." Addressing the two lawmen again, Howell added, "Stay or go, whatever you want to do, but I tell you now, I haven't any time for bickerin'."

His face flushing a bright red, Marshal Carr growled, "Well, I guess you're on your own, then."

Suddenly annoyed, Charles interrupted, "It seems to me this shouldn't be a battle of wills! You're all lawmen and—"

"That's where you're wrong!" Marshal Carr's small eyes snapped. "*I'm* the law here, not this puffed up *former* lawman who thinks he's goin' to order me around!"

"I'd watch what I said, if I were you."

"Yeah, but you ain't me, or you'd know that I ain't takin' orders from nobody, much less you!"

Howell's expression remained unchanged. "Then

there's nothin' left for me to say but good-bye, marshal."

His anger obviously under tenuous control, Marshal Carr turned abruptly toward Charles. "Is this the way you want it, Webster? Just say the word and I'll throw this fella out of your office and out of town! For all his reputation, he probably ain't worth a damn anyhow!"

Charles felt Howell's control slipping. He saw it in the almost imperceptible stiffening of his features, in the twitch of his hand, and he heard it in the depth of his tone as Howell addressed him softly, "There's no need for you to answer the marshal's question, because the fact is that I was hired to do a job, and I intend to do it. I'll study this schedule that was wired in, and I'll let you know what I'm goin' to set up. Is that all right with you?"

Howell's eyes were so intent that they seemed to bore right through him.

Charles turned to face the marshal. "I'm sorry, marshal, but my orders come straight from back East. Howell's in charge of security at the bank."

Marshal Carr was almost twitching. "You just remember you said that." He turned toward the silent deputy behind him. "Let's go."

The marshal's booted steps were still ringing on the boardwalk outside the door when Howell turned to address Charles curtly.

"I've got a lot of questions about your procedures here."

Questions.

Charles asked a question of his own.

"You don't like me much, do you?"

His mouth a hard, straight line, Howell did not respond.

* * *

A loud chorus of laughter burst from the saloon below, momentarily overwhelming the other sounds of frivolity that had been growing as the hour wore on. The gay echoes rebounded dully within Honesty's mind as she dressed. She glanced at the window, noting that dusk had turned to evening. She was late. She would have been downstairs at her usual table an hour earlier if this had been a normal evening.

But it was not.

Aware that her hand trembled, Honesty tucked an ebony curl into the gleaming mass gathered artfully atop her head. She had taken great pains with her hair, securing it with pins decorated with glittering silver stars that matched the trim on her gown, a special touch that was somehow necessary in her present state of mind. She studied her face, unconsciously noting that the tension tightening her stomach into painful knots and draining the color from her cheeks was not visible there—a tribute to her skill with the brush, a talent she had absorbed through the years of watching a master of the art.

Not that she had applied color with Jewel's liberal hand. No, never. She admired some of Jewel's qualities and even sought to emulate a few, but the vision of her mother's natural beauty, however blurred it had become over the years, had remained an example ever before her as she had grown.

But this night was different. She had wanted the touch of kohl that darkened her lashes and brightened her eyes. She had been desperate for the dusting of color she had applied to her pale cheeks. And she had needed the balm applied to her lips . . . lips sensitized by kisses that had both bemused and betrayed her.

Her anxiety, however, was not solely due to the

stirring memories of the night past. Jeremy had not yet returned.

She dared not count the number of times she had gone back to Jeremy's shack to see if he was there. As darkness began to fall, she had listed the variety of excuses she had concocted in her mind for Jeremy's unexplained absence.

Jeremy was out hunting. He liked to hunt.

Jeremy had visited one of the other saloons, where one of the girls taken with his blond good looks had taken him home for the night.

Jeremy had joined some drovers returning to Texas for another drive.

Jeremy had taken himself off prospecting for gold as he so often threatened.

Or . . . Jeremy had ridden off with a bottle, had fallen from his horse, and was lying dead in a ditch somewhere, *like his father before him.*

No!

Honesty attempted to still the trembling that began within her. She would not let herself believe that. Jeremy was somewhere close, and he would return.

Not up to Jewel's keen-eyed assessment, Honesty had avoided her the entire day. Strangely, it was not condemnation that she feared. Rather, she could not bear to see the affirmation of her own pain in Jewel's eyes.

Taking a firm grip on her emotions, Honesty retreated a few steps from the full-length, gilt-framed wall mirror that had been a gift from Charles when she turned sixteen. Charles had had it shipped from the East as a special surprise for her. He had winked, saying she should be able to get as much pleasure from looking at herself as everybody else got from looking at her. She had been flattered because she admired Charles. The reasons for her admiration were many—because he had traveled across the ocean and had been places and seen things that she had not, and because he shared his knowledge with generosity and with an affection that she knew was true—because the wealthy, privileged life he had once lived was as foreign to hers as a fairy tale, but the silent torment she sensed within him was similar to her own, and because without asking anything in return, he cared enough to attempt to fill a void in her life that no one truly understood, even herself.

And she admired Charles because, unlike any man before him, he made Jewel happy.

Her feelings for Charles had endured the test of years, as had the love Jewel and he seemed to share. As for the mirror . . .

Honesty assessed her reflection with a peculiar detachment, acknowledging that she had achieved the effect she sought. Her gown was extravagantly beautiful. The black satin enhanced the glimmering sheen of her hair, and the lace insets studded with silver beads complemented her delicate features. She had had the gown copied by the town seamstress from a photograph she had seen in a ladies' journal a year earlier, and she had been insistent that the garment be tailored perfectly. She had near to driven Mattie Clark mad by demanding that the neckline hug her shoulders in a way that allowed the gleaming beads to highlight her smooth flesh, and that the silver beads on the skirt be sewn to resemble stars, thereby creating an illusion of shimmering fantasy as she moved. Mattie had surpassed herself, and the result was a garment that Honesty had decided was too lovely to waste on an ordinary night in the Texas Jewel. She had saved it for a special circumstance. She had believed she would first wear this gown on a happy occasion, but she was presently in more desperate need of the reassurance it gave her than she had ever dreamed she could be.

Honesty surveyed her reflection again, head to toe. Her locket, resting just below the hollow at the base of her neck, was a solitary touch of gold amidst glittering silver. Sparkling in the light, it seemed to wink at her, helping to alleviate her distress and bolster her badly flagging confidence. She forced a smile. Yes, she looked beautiful . . . and when she smiled there was no trace of the anxiety within.

She was ready.

Head high, smile firmly fixed, Honesty walked down the hallway minutes later. She steadied herself, then turned into view of the floor below as she descended the staircase. She felt the startled stillness and spontaneous gasps that accompanied her appearance, then heard shouted greetings rise over the din.

"You're beautiful, Honesty!"

"You're the woman of my dreams, darlin'!"

"Over here, Honesty—come sit by me so my old eyes can drink their fill, and I can die content!"

That last from Pete Tubbs, a graying drover with a lopsided smile, brought true laughter to her lips. She scanned the room, the laughter fading as an enigmatic, dark-eyed gaze met and held hers.

Bastard.

Just as she expected. He had come to gloat.

Pride forced Honesty to hold Wes's gaze boldly as cruel words returned to wound once more.

Am I boring you now, Honesty?

Honesty maintained his gaze as she descended to within a few steps of the floor, then looked away abruptly to smile at a virile young drover who made no effort to control his infatuation as he approached her.

"Honesty, darlin'." Josh Parker grinned boyishly. "You're so beautiful that you make me want to cry."

"That wasn't my intention, Josh." Submitting to impulse, Honesty raised herself on tiptoe to brush his lips with hers. "Now, does that make you feel better?" She laughed aloud at the howls and calls that came from the tables surrounding her. Careful to leave Josh beaming in her wake, she made her way through the maze of tables toward her usual spot, where a final round of cards was being dealt. She nodded a greeting to Jewel and Charles, who were seated a short distance away, acknowledging friendly faces and speaking warmly to customers as she passed—even as the heat of that relentless, scorching gaze continued.

Bastard! Had he no conscience at all?

Fury suddenly suffusing her, Honesty turned deliberately toward the bar where Wes stood, noting as she approached that despite her earlier denials, he looked almost demonically handsome in the black shirt and trousers he had chosen to wear. It occurred to her as she drew nearer that the guns on his hips glinted with the same hard glow that shone from his eyes. Both were weapons that he employed with callous skill. And both were deadly.

Deliberately switching her course at the last second, Honesty glided past Wes to slide her hand onto the arm of a fellow almost hidden in the crush nearby. She spoke to him with true warmth.

"Ethan Hackett . . . when did you hit town? I haven't seen you in over a year."

The smiling cattleman's reply was a step forward to enclose her in a crushing hug and a moist kiss pressed squarely on the lips before he whispered, "I was beginnin' to think that you might've forgotten me . . . even though I knew I could never forget you,

Honesty, darlin'. I got here this afternoon, turned my cattle out to graze with a few men watchin' them, and I've been waitin' to see you walk down them stairs ever since, the way I've been dreamin' you would for the last two hundred miles. And you didn't disappoint me. You're still the most beautiful woman I've ever seen, just like I remembered. Let me buy you a drink."

Hardly able to concentrate on the fellow's earnest chatter, so aware was she of Wes' presence nearby, Honesty waited until her drink was poured before raising it with a flirtacious wink. "Here's to the handsome fellas who follow the cattle trail north . . . and all they bring with them."

Excusing herself when her glass was emptied, despite Ethan's protests, Honesty turned back toward the card table where her chair awaited her. She did not bother to spare Wes a glance as she passed. She had no need. The heat of his gaze lingered.

Jewel watched Honesty as she made her way toward the table awaiting her. It occurred to her in that moment how deceiving appearances were. Anyone looking at Charles and her as they sat together would probably see nothing unusual. No one would guess how greatly her life had changed in the last twenty-four hours, most especially in the few that she had spent in Charles's bed, lying in his arms.

But it had.

She knew she would never forget the moment when Charles turned toward her with Emily's letter in his hand, his anguish clearly visible. She supposed it was strange that there had been no jealousy in her realization that his love for his dying wife was still as strong as it had been the day Charles and she first met. Stranger still, she supposed, was the reality that she felt no relief that the impediment to a permanent commitment between Charles and her might soon be eliminated. Instead, she had felt only sorrow at the potential demise of a woman who was so loved—and pain for the man who would mourn her.

And she had felt *fear*.

Thrusting that last thought aside, Jewel recalled that she had urged Charles to visit his wife before it was too late. She still could not understand his refusal, his need to remain in Caldwell simply because of Howell's arrival and the shipments that would soon begin.

Watching as Honesty was finally seated at the table, Jewel glanced back at the bar. She gave a scoffing laugh before turning back to Charles.

"Well, Wes Howell might be all he's talked up to be, but he's no different from any other man where Honesty's concerned. He can't take his eyes off her."

Jewel's comment did not get the reaction she expected. Instead of amusement, she saw lines of concern tighten around Charles's lips. "Honesty made a mistake playing up to him at the bar last night. Everybody's talking about it. She's dealing with the wrong man this time. That fellow is as cold as ice, and he is not about to let anyone put anything over on him."

"He doesn't look so cold now—not when he looks at Honesty."

"Don't be misled, Jewel!" The harshness in Charles's tone rang a warning bell in Jewel's mind as he continued, "He's a lawman to the core. Word must've gotten back to Slater Enterprises about what happened at my father's bank back East. They probably sent him to make sure what happened there isn't going to happen again."

"That was years ago, Charles, and you had nothing to do with it!"

"Webster Banking and Trust—I was a part of it by virtue of my name and the fact that I refused to acknowledge what was happening until it was too late."

"Your father was in debt. He never intended to run away with that money. He intended to pay it back. He *did* pay it back."

"Not until he was caught and everything the family owned was sold off to do it. Knowing he was totally without funds and facing a future in jail killed him as surely as that heart attack did."

"You didn't have anythin' to do with it. It's all over and done. Why can't you forget about it? Everybody else has!"

"If that was true, Howell wouldn't be here now."

"You're imaginin' things."

Charles shook his head. "I saw the way he looked at me in my office this morning."

"And I see the look in his eyes right now." Suddenly angry, Jewel continued, "I'm tellin' you, that man hasn't got a thought in his head for anythin' else right now but Honesty!"

"Honesty should stay clear of him."

"Well, if you want her to do that, don't go sayin' anythin' to her about it. You know how damned mulish she is. She's liable to do the opposite, just to prove she's got her own mind."

Charles's response was a nod. "I know Honesty as well as you, and you're right."

Jewel looked back at Honesty, anxiety niggling. But did Charles know her well enough to see that she was *too* beautiful tonight—unnaturally so—and too gay? Did he see that she was trying too hard? Did Charles know Honesty well enough to see something was wrong—something that probably had to do with that little scene Charles had referred to and with the fact that Jeremy hadn't been seen around town all day? In addition to that, did he realize that Honesty was avoiding her—which was the surest sign that something was amiss?

Jewel's voice was suddenly gruff. "How long did you say Howell was goin' to be in Caldwell?"

"Until fall, or until Slater's shipments stop."

"When do the shipments start?"

"Next week. They should start arriving on Monday."

"How many shipments are there goin' to be?"

"I don't know, yet. Slater's trying to keep things quiet." Charles's short laugh was devoid of amusement. "It seems like those executives back East don't realize how fast things get out in a town like Caldwell—especially with Joe Pierce at the telegraph."

Jewel looked at Honesty, then glanced back at Wes Howell where he stood at the bar. Howell wasn't looking at Honesty directly, but his eyes were glued to her reflection in the mirror. She had tried to deny it to herself and to Charles, but she didn't like the way things looked, either.

A chill ran down Jewel's spine at the thought of what Howell's unrelenting stare was doing to Honesty. She didn't like this . . . not at all.

Would he never learn?

Wes dropped his gaze from the mirror and downed his drink. The wounded look in Honesty's incredible eyes when he walked out on her the previous night had haunted him. As the long hours of the day passed, he had even searched his mind for an innocent explanation for Honesty's emergence from her lover's cabin that morning. Only now did he realize how great a fool he had been.

Wes sipped at his refilled glass. He glanced at the fellow who had met Honesty at the foot of the steps, the one she had kissed, the one now seated at a table a distance away. The fierceness of his reaction when Honesty kissed the fellow had startled him. One look at Honesty afterward had revealed that the kiss meant nothing to her at all, but the burning in his gut had not ceased.

As for the trail boss, the one still standing at the bar a few feet away, whom Honesty had greeted so effusively, it was obvious that his kiss had meant no more to Honesty than the other.

Wes's smoldering gaze grew more heated. Honesty enjoyed toying with men—but he had taught her to face the consequences when she toyed with him.

The question remained.

Had the payback been worth the price?

That question lingered, even as Wes's gaze again strayed to Honesty's reflection in the mirror. Neither her smile nor her flirting manner at the table faltered. She had not spared him even a fleeting glance, but the frequency with which she looked toward the door was increasing. She was waiting for someone.

Honesty looked up again, as she seemed to do each time the saloon doors swung open. Wes saw her spontaneous intake of breath when her lover walked in the door. He saw her rise from her chair, then turn as if in afterthought to summon a replacement dealer, appearing not to hear the protests of the men around the table as she started toward Jeremy Sills.

That was the name of Honesty's lover—Jeremy Sills. He had learned the fellow's name easily enough, and a lot of other things about him, too.

Watching openly as Honesty wound her way across the floor, Wes saw the moment when she caught her lover's gaze. He saw her eyes fill as she slid both her arms around Sills's waist and whispered up into his face.

The burning in Wes's gut squeezed into a painful ache. Damned, conniving little witch, going from man to man . . .

He wondered if Sills knew that Honesty had gone to his shack the previous night directly from a bed she had briefly and willingly shared with another man.

He wondered if Sills cared.

And he wondered why it made any difference to him at all.

Somehow unable to tear his eyes away, Wes watched as Honesty drew Sills toward the end of the bar. She began talking earnestly, turning in a way that made her face no longer visible. But he saw Sills. He saw Sills touch Honesty's cheek. He saw Sills place his hand on her shoulder to caress it gently. There was familiarity in the gesture. There was . . . love.

The damned young idiot! Didn't he know she was making a fool of him!

Finding it increasingly difficult to maintain an unaffected facade, Wes realized his emotions were rapidly slipping out of control. Still unwilling to ask himself the reason for his agitation when he had so effectively settled his score with Honesty the previous night, he reached for his drink and downed it in a gulp. The resulting heat did nothing to calm the fire within.

Turning her back deliberately so her face could not be seen by anyone nearby, Honesty battled relieved tears. She saw Jeremy's confused smile as he touched her cheek, and she realized that he had no idea at all of the day-long torment she had suffered because of him. That thought abruptly brought anger to replace the tears as Honesty demanded, "Where were you all day?"

Jeremy's bemused smile stretched a little wider. "Why? Were you lookin' for me?"

"You know damned well I was looking for you!"

Jeremy's smile faltered. "Do I?"

"Well, you should!" Honesty scanned Jeremy's face. He was pale, with dark circles under his eyes, and he appeared almost gaunt. She recognized the look, and her anger wavered. "Are you feeling all right?"

"I'm fine. I . . . I went hunting today. I guess I forgot to mention it."

"You forgot to mention it at the stockyard, too. They're angry. You'll be lucky if you have a job when you go back."

Jeremy's expression took on a belligerent look. "Maybe I don't care."

"You don't mean that, Jeremy."

Wariness flashed briefly before Jeremy's belligerence dropped away to be replaced by a smile. "Maybe I don't. Don't worry about it. I'll take care of it. The truth is, I wasn't feelin' so good, so I went for a ride."

"Went for a ride . . . when you weren't feeling well?"

"I had a lot to think about."

"Jeremy . . ." The heat of tears Honesty refused to shed returned. "I'm sorry about last night."

Jeremy shrugged. "What about last night?"

"Don't pretend with me, Jeremy. The way Wes Howell spoke to you was unforgivable, and it was my fault."

"Oh, that. I forgot about it."

He was lying. Jeremy seldom lied to her. Was it his pride?

She was still uncertain when Jeremy placed his hand on her shoulder and caressed it with a familiar gesture that warmed her to the heart. He whispered, "Look, let's forget about it."

Honesty managed a smile. "I waited for you in your cabin this morning. It's a mess."

"Yeah, well, I wasn't thinkin' much about cleanin' it when I left."

"Are you waiting for me to clean it?"

"What makes you think that?"

"Because I always end up cleaning after you."

Jeremy's smile spread into a grin that almost broke her heart. She remembered a time when that grin was frequent and the anger was rare. It seemed lately that the reverse was true, despite her greatest efforts to change things.

"You know why you do that for me?"

Jeremy's grin forced her to play the game as she responded, "No, why?"

"Because you'll do anythin' for me."

"True."

"Just like I'll do anythin' for you."

"Right."

"Because you love me."

Honesty nodded. "I do."

Unprepared for the deep voice that sounded unexpectedly behind her, Honesty jumped, turning as Wes Howell interjected, "I suggest you don't take what she says too much to heart, partner. She said the same thing to me last night . . . or words to the effect."

Hardly conscious of the shudder that went through Jeremy the moment before his hand dropped from her shoulder, Honesty turned to link Wes Howell's cold gaze with hers.

"Bastard . . ."

"That isn't what you called me last night, *darlin'*."

"Oh, no, that *is* what I called you last night."

"Only because you were angry that I left."

"You flatter yourself."

"No, I don't think so."

"Then you're wrong. But the truth is, I don't really care what you think. You have no place in this conversation."

"I'll be happy to leave, but I wanted your boyfriend here to know that he isn't your only *friend*."

Jeremy interrupted their exchange, his voice low with anger. "You've said enough."

Honesty looked at Jeremy. His face was flushed. His lips had that quiver that revealed he was losing control, and his gun hand was twitching as he continued, "Honesty doesn't want to talk to you."

"She did last night."

"She doesn't want to talk to you now!"

The brief silence tightened in the long moments before Wes responded, "That's fine with me. I was just passin' the time."

His smile deliberate, Wes touched two fingers to his temple in an informal salute as he whispered directly into Honesty's eyes, "And thanks again, ma'am."

Fury blurred Honesty's vision as Wes strode away. She barely managed through stiff lips, "I'm sorry, Jeremy. He *is* a bastard."

"Don't apologize for him. He's the one who should be doin' the apologizin'. And when I'm done with him, he will."

"No." Honesty shook her head. "I'll take care of him myself . . . in my own way."

Looking into Jeremy's eyes a little longer, seeing the question there that he dared not ask, she whispered, "He lied, you know. I never said I loved him.

I've never said those words to any man, much less him." She gave a short laugh. "I doubt if he'd know the meaning of the word."

"You said them to me."

"Yes, but that's different."

Cognizant of the danger that still prevailed, Honesty tugged at Jeremy's arm. "You don't look well, Jeremy. Why don't you go home and get a good night's sleep? I'll come tomorrow morning and help you clean up your cabin a bit before you go to work."

Jeremy did not respond.

"Jeremy . . . please. I have to go back to the table and deal now. That's what Jewel pays me for, you know."

Jeremy's hand was still twitching. "I'd like to wipe the smirk from that bastard's face."

Honesty felt a familiar desperation surge. "Jewel doesn't like fights, and neither do I. Besides, I can take care of myself."

"But he—"

"Go home. Do it for me."

Silence.

"Please."

Honesty saw the myriad emotions that flickered across Jeremy's face the moment before he nodded. "All right. I'll see you tomorrow."

Remaining at the bar until Jeremy disappeared out onto the street, Honesty then walked directly back to her table and resumed her seat. Laughing and joking moments later, despite her inner turmoil, she felt Wes's gaze on her again.

The despicable bastard . . .

She continued smiling.

She'd get her chance.

* * *

Jeremy strode down the street, blind with fury. He felt sick—sicker than he had that morning when he had finally fallen from his horse and had been too weak to remount. The hours had stretched damned long after that, while he had barely managed to pull his blanket from his saddle and cover himself against the shaking that had beset him despite the heat of the day.

Drawing himself under the protection of a tree, he had dozed fitfully as the bouts of shaking continued, as his stomach cramped and convulsed, and he had been certain he was spending his last hours on earth. He had finally fallen asleep, and he had dreamed of Honesty. When he awakened, he was strong enough to ride, but only barely. He had arrived back in town at twilight knowing that he dared not show himself to Honesty in the condition in which he had returned.

He had visited the bath. He had shaved the stubble from his chin, and he had bought a new shirt because he hadn't had a clean one to his name. A new shirt was a luxury he couldn't afford, but he knew that he would soon have all the money he needed . . . and he knew that Honesty was waiting.

Fury flared anew.

Damn that Howell to hell! If he hadn't known that to start anything with him now might upset his plans . . . if he didn't need to prove to Bitters that he could be depended upon not to draw attention to himself so he could get the information he needed . . .

Jeremy accepted a truth that had not been denied. Howell had been in Honesty's room last night. Something had gone wrong. He couldn't be certain what, but the animosity between them was too strong for it not to have resulted from some kind of intimate exchange.

Oh, God . . .

Jeremy clenched his teeth tightly against the pain of it. Had Howell made love to Honesty the way he had always wanted to make love to her? Had he held her in his arms, flesh against flesh, breathing in the sweet scent that was Honesty's alone? Had he touched her . . . tasted her skin . . . made her his, even if only for a little while?

No, damn it! No! Honesty wouldn't do that! She had indulged brief flings before, but she had never given herself to any man. He knew that was true. He was positive of it, because Honesty had always told him that she valued herself too highly to casually give herself away!

Jeremy struggled to draw his emotions under control. That was the reason Honesty gave for not giving herself to any man. She believed it was true, but he knew the *real* reason.

A smile touched Jeremy's tight lips as he nodded in silent confirmation. Whether Honesty realized it or not, she was saving herself for him.

That thought allowed Jeremy only momentary satisfaction as Wes Howell's image returned again to taunt him. His hands balling into fists, Jeremy walked only a few more steps along the boardwalk before thrusting open the nearest swinging doors and striding inside. He pushed his way toward the bar, frustration soaring. He had left the Texas Jewel because he had known that if he stayed, he would have finished things with Howell then and there. He needed to be patient, to wait.

He'd get his chance.

But waiting was hard. He needed a drink to make it easier. Just one.

* * *

Wes stood at the bar, glass in hand, incredulous at what he had done.

He glanced up into the mirror to see that Sills had left the saloon. Honesty had managed to get rid of her lover before trouble started. A part of him was almost sorry that she had. He saw that Honesty had returned to her table and was considering her cards as if nothing had happened at all.

Well, what *had* happened? What had possessed him to approach Honesty and Sills while they were conversing intimately? The unprincipled witch that she was, Honesty had been right when she said that he had no right to interfere with their conversation. He had sacrificed that right—or any he might have earned—the previous night when he had tipped his hat and walked away.

What had prompted his subtle viciousness? Had it been the way Honesty had made his heart pound when she walked down that staircase, knowing she was so damned beautiful that the sight of her would somehow slash his innards like a knife? Had it been because she had raised his anticipation to the brim when she had walked directly toward him where he stood at the bar, only to slide past to welcome another man? Was that when it had all snapped inside him? Or had it been when Honesty looked up at the young pup, Jeremy Sills, as if he were the only man in the world, and Sills then touched her, allowing his hand to rest so familiarly on the bare skin of her shoulder, which his own lips had tasted so passionately the night before?

Or was it when he overheard the words they whispered to each other as he approached.

. . . because you love me.

And Honesty's nod. *I do.*

Damn her for how easily she had said those words!

Damn her for lingering so vividly in his mind!

And damn his own unexplained weakness for her! He had taught Honesty Buchanan a lesson last night, but he had taught himself one as well. For the truth was that no matter what Honesty was, no matter what she said or did, he wanted her.

Wes struggled to subdue the emotions that admission evoked. He'd get his chance again because Honesty knew as well as he that all was not finished between them. And the next time, he wouldn't walk away.

"It ain't goin' to happen, fella."

Wes turned toward the unexpected gravelly voice at his elbow. The old fellow standing there pinned him with a peculiarly piercing stare, continuing, "What you're thinkin' . . . it ain't goin' to happen."

"I don't know what you're talkin' about, old man."

"Sure you do."

Crazy old rooster.

Wes turned away, only to hear a new note of warning enter the old fellow's raspy tone.

"It ain't polite to turn your back on a man when he's talkin' to you. I wouldn't like havin' to teach you some manners, but I always do what I have to, you know."

Wes turned back toward the old man, almost amused at the open threat in his voice. The fellow's uneven hair was grayed with age, and the lines on his grizzled countenance attested that the color was not premature. Even standing as stiffly erect as he did, the fellow reached no farther than his shoulder, and from the look of him, he didn't weigh more than a hundred pounds. But his hands did not tremble . . . callused, knobby hands that clenched into fists as they hovered near the gunbelt he wore. Neither did the look in the beady eyes falter.

Feisty old boy.

"Sorry." Wes owed him that. "What's on your mind?"

"I think the point is more like, what's on yours?"

"I don't know what you're talkin' about."

"You know as well as I do what I'm talkin' about. But if you want me to spell it out for you, here goes." The old fellow's gaze sharpened. "I saw you talkin' to Honesty before . . ."

Wes stiffened.

"And I'm thinkin' you wasn't too polite there, neither, judgin' from the way she had to send Jeremy packin' to keep him out of trouble. But Honesty can take care of herself. I wouldn't be sayin' nothin' right now if it wasn't for that look in your eye."

"The look in my eye . . ."

"That's right! The look in your eye! And don't you try makin' out that you don't know what I mean! Hell, I ain't that old that I can't recognize it!"

Wes surveyed the old man's face. Who in hell was he, and what was his relationship to Honesty?

"Wonderin' who I am, are you?"

Wes did not reply.

"My name's Sam Potts. No need to tell me yours. I already know it and your reputation, which don't impress me worth a damn. No, I ain't Honesty's pa or her grandpa, neither, so you can get that out of your head. I'm just somebody who's droppin' a word of warnin', that's all. And the word is this. If you expect to last long enough to do the job you came here for, you'd best mend your ways."

"Or what?"

"I could spell that out for you too, if you've a need."

Wes was no longer amused. "Do you think you're big enough to run me out of town?"

"It wasn't runnin' you out of town that I was thinkin' of."

Wes was astounded. The old fellow *was* crazy! Disregarding the fact that he was outmatched in every way, the old boy was actually threatening him—obviously meaning every word he said.

Well, he meant what he said, too.

"Mind your own business, old man."

"I told you, my name's Sam."

"Mind your own business, Sam."

Sam smiled for the first time, a gap-toothed smile that bore no hint of warmth. "My advice to you would be to do the same. And stay away from Honesty. That way, things'll work out just fine."

Allowing a moment longer for his warning to linger, Sam started to walk away. He looked back unexpectedly, his lined face sober. "You remember what I said, you hear?"

Wes did not bother to respond. He turned back to the bar and watched in the mirror as the old fellow's bowed legs carried him directly to Honesty's side.

"Honesty, darlin' . . ."

Honesty looked up at the sound of Sam's familiar voice. The sight of his homely old face stirred the first genuine smile of the evening.

"Sam, you handsome old dog . . ."

"Yeah, I am that, ain't I?"

But Sam's eyes remained sober. "You got time to talk for a minute, darlin'?"

"Hey, Honesty, what's goin' on tonight? Are you goin' to deal or not?"

Honesty turned toward the big drover who addressed her. She responded with a single word.

"Not."

Signaling the replacement dealer amidst a chorus

of groans from around the table, Honesty eased the frowns with a few softly spoken words, then allowed Sam to take her arm. He led her to a corner a few steps away, where he suddenly smiled truely.

"You look mighty beautiful tonight, darlin'."

"Don't I usually look beautiful? You always tell me I do."

Sam gave an unexpected sigh. "I suppose that's the trouble, ain't it?"

A premonition growing, Honesty barely resisted the desire to glance toward the bar. "What trouble?"

"You always was the prettiest girl any man ever saw, and now that you're a woman, it all got to be too much to resist."

"Sam . . ."

"Stay away from him, Honesty." Sam's expression was suddenly intense. "He ain't like other men. You can't play with him like you do with them." At her sober glance he said, "You know who I'm talkin' about."

Honesty did not bother to pretend ignorance. "Don't worry about me."

"I ain't goin' to worry."

Something about Sam's tone frightened her. "What are you saying, Sam?"

"I'm sayin' that I looked into Wes Howell's eyes after he looked at you, and I saw trouble. So I'm tellin' you this. I've been watchin' after you all my life, and the truth is, I ain't goin' to stop now, no matter what you say. I already warned him—"

"You *warned* him?" She shook her head in disbelief. "What did you say to him?"

"Nothin' much. I just told him to watch himself . . . just like I'm tellin' you."

"I'm not afraid of Wes Howell or any man!"

"Now don't go gettin' all hot under the collar!" Sam

shook his head when her lips tightened. "And don't go gettin' mad at me, neither."

"I'm not mad."

"You are, too."

Honesty considered the thought. Yes, she was mad.

"Yes, I am mad! I'm a big girl now, Sam! I've been making my own decisions and my own way for a long time, and I don't need anybody to fight my battles for me!"

Taking hold of her emotions when Sam made no response, Honesty raised a conciliatory hand to stroke his stubbled cheek. She continued in a softened tone, "I know you mean well, and I appreciate everything you've done for me, but you don't have to watch out for me now."

Sam returned her stare with his small, unblinking eyes.

"I'm not that little lost girl you found by the river anymore, Sam."

Sam's eyes grew unexpectedly moist. "Yes you are, darlin'."

Her own eyes suddenly as moist as his, Honesty gave a short, hoarse laugh. She had no response, either to the warmth in his eyes or the warmth in her heart.

"You old rascal!" Honesty forced away the thickness in her throat. "All right. You told me and I've listened. Don't worry anymore." Honesty stepped back. "I have to go. The boys at the table are getting angry, and Jewel's watching me like a hawk."

"Oh, that woman . . ." The benign conflict between her two saviors reared its head again as Sam grumbled, "She's the stubbornist woman I ever did know . . . and the bossiest. She'd try tellin' the sun how to shine if she thought she could get away with it. But don't you go worryin' about her. She's as tough as nails and twice as sharp, but she won't do nothin'. She's too used to havin' you around." Sam winked unexpectedly. "Besides, you got me to stick up for you."

Honesty was grateful to see the plucky Sam she knew so well return as he added, "And if you need me, all you got to do is call."

"I'm all right, Sam." Honesty forced a smile. "If you had taken the time to shave today, I would plant a kiss on that cheek of yours right now."

"Yeah, well, I told you, I'm too old for that silly stuff. You get back to your table, or somethin' tells me I'll have to set Jewel straight before I leave."

Seated at her table minutes later, Honesty watched Sam's scrawny figure slip through the crowd and out the entrance to the street beyond. She wondered, as she had many times before, if the old man was sometimes actually able to read her mind.

"You goin' to deal, Honesty?"

Honesty snapped back to the present. A teasing smile ready, she whispered to the tall cowboy across from her, "Anything for you, Buck."

She wasn't sure what made her look up then—just in time to see Wes Howell weave his way purposefully across the floor toward the door. He slipped from sight without a backward look, and Honesty returned to the cards, strangely at a loss.

"All right, tell me about Honesty Buchanan. Everything you know."

Catching up with Deputy John Henry Brown on the street only minutes after leaving the Texas Jewel, Wes could not believe his luck. It occurred to him that of all the people he had met since arriving in

Caldwell, the pleasant former Texan was the only one he felt he could trust.

It hadn't taken him long to talk John Henry into accompanying him to Birdie Cotter's Place so they might talk. The deputy's weakness for Birdie's doughnuts made that place the logical choice. He also knew that given his own present state of agitation and the fact that he had already had more to drink than was prudent, he was safer with a coffee cup in his hand than he was with red-eye in his glass.

Birdie's ample form waddled back toward the restaurant kitchen as Wes gave the room a cursory glance. They were the only customers. Birdie would soon be shutting her doors for the night. He turned back to John Henry, waiting for his reply.

The soft-spoken deputy appeared surprised. "There ain't much more to say about Honesty. I've only been in town a couple of years, and I told you just about all I know. She ain't got much of a history, you know."

Wes strained for patience. "No, I don't know. You told me as much as I guessed by lookin' at her—that she handles cards and men easily."

"She sure enough does. Hell, I'd never play with her. Them long, slim fingers are quicker than the eye."

Those long, slim fingers. Wes remembered them, all right.

. . . long, slim fingers, moving warmly against his back . . .

. . . long, slim fingers that trembled as they worked at the buttons of his shirt . . .

Struggling to dismiss the familiar heat stirring to life, Wes responded, "Yeah, I've seen her at work. But

I need to know more. Where does she come from? What's her background?"

"Oh, well, nobody seems to know for sure. Some say that Honesty ain't sure herself."

"What are you sayin'?"

"There's a couple of stories circulatin'. Jewel came to town with Honesty in tow some years back. Some said she had owned a place in Abilene, and when things dropped off, she sold it and came to Caldwell. She's a smart businesswoman, that Jewel. A real tough lady, but accommodatin' to her customers."

"About Honesty . . ."

"Well, some say she's Jewel's daughter, and that Honesty was never sure who her father was. And then there's that other story."

"What other story?"

"Some say Jewel found her."

"*Found* her?"

"When she was a little gal . . . beside a river."

Wes remained silent.

"I know, don't sound right, does it? I mean, even if a wagon did get swamped and a little gal got washed downstream, somebody'd be out lookin' for her, wouldn't they? Especially if there was more than one little gal involved?"

"More than one?"

"Yeah. Talk is that a fella came to town some years back and said he knew about Honesty from Abilene. He said Honesty had two sisters in that wagon and she ain't seen hide nor hair of her parents or her sisters since that day. He said when Honesty was little, she used to go around askin' everybody new who came into Abilene if they had seen her sisters. He said it used to make Jewel real mad. I guess that's why she stopped doin' it—at least that's what that fella said."

"So Jewel raised her."

"Seems like. Of course, there was Sam Potts hangin' over her all the while."

Potts . . .

"Some say he was with Jewel when Jewel found her."

So, that explained it.

"What about her and Charles Webster?"

"I ain't quite figured that one out." John Henry shrugged, his angular face disturbed. "Like I told you, Jewel, Webster, and Honesty are thick as thieves. Webster's always hangin' around one of them women or the other. Everybody says Jewel's his woman, that she's been his woman for years."

"For years . . ."

"Yeah, but the way I figure it, Honesty was nothin' but a little gal when he first took up with Jewel. But Honesty ain't little no more, and he's always given' her presents and such."

"Presents?"

"Yeah, pretty good ones, too." John Henry's face registered momentary grievance. "As a matter of fact, he bought a horse I wanted right out from under my nose—a real pretty roan mare—and gave it to Honesty for her birthday, saddle and all."

"A horse? What does somebody like Honesty want with a horse?"

John Henry's sudden grin was unexpected. "I guess you ain't never seen her ride then." He chortled, raising Wes's annoyance up a level before continuing, "She goes ridin' out mid-mornin' sometimes. She wears britches when she rides, real slim ones, and ain't that a sight to make a grown man cry."

A sharp pang of an emotion he dared not identify twinged within Wes as he responded more sharply than intended, "All right. So Webster likes dance hall women."

"No. He ain't never given any of the other girls a second look as far as I know. As a matter of fact, some was thinkin' that he might marry Jewel for a while, but then when somebody found out he was already married—"

"He's married?"

"Yeah, his wife's sick . . . in some kind of hospital back East . . . so he took up with Jewel and Honesty."

Wes nodded. "And Jeremy Sills?"

"I already told you about him. His pa was the town drunk, and Sills is on the way to followin' in his footsteps. He's always messin' up, but he's harmless enough to everybody but himself."

Wes swallowed, the words more difficult than he expected as he asked, "What do you know about Honesty and Sills?"

John Henry shrugged.

"Well?"

"They're real close, and real secretive. Tell you one thing. If there's somethin' between them, that Sills has a real strong hide, 'cause Honesty flaunts herself with every man who walks through them saloon doors." John Henry gave a short laugh. "Come to think of it, maybe that's why the poor fella drinks!"

Wes winced at the memory of the glasses he had emptied just that night.

John Henry had finished his doughnut between sentences and was busy licking his fingers as Wes questioned, "What do you hear people sayin' about the shipments due to arrive soon at the bank?"

John Henry looked up and gave a short laugh. "It's the talk of the town."

"How does the marshal feel about that?"

"Whatever he's thinkin', he ain't tellin' me."

"Well, I'll tell you what I'm thinkin'." Wes held the former Texan's gaze intently. "I'm thinkin' that I'm goin' to be raisin' some men to guard that bank. I'd like your help."

"I work for the marshal."

"That doesn't mean you can't help me."

"I don't know . . ."

Wes did not smile. "It's called cooperation—somethin' your marshal refuses to extend. That's his problem. I don't want it to become mine. Your help would make my job much easier—and safer for everybody concerned, includin' you and the marshal."

John Henry remained silent.

"Slater Enterprises is payin' me for the work I'm doin'. They'll pay you for helpin'."

"Helpin' to do what?"

"I need a few men who can be trusted. Slater Enterprises has already spoken about bonuses if none of their money is lost. Since you know this town better than I do, you can give me some names."

John Henry nodded, his expression sobering. "I can tell you a few who might be interested right off the top of my head, but the truth is, I'd like to talk to them first, if that's all right with you."

"I'll need to know soon. The first shipment's scheduled to arrive on Monday."

"I know. So does the whole town."

Wes restrained the comment that rose to his lips as Birdie waddled back toward them, her round face weary. "I'm closin' up, boys."

Leaving his coin on the table with a nod, Wes waited until John Henry stood up and turned toward the door. Out on the street, he extended his hand toward the former Texan. "I'll be pleased to have you with me, John Henry."

"Likewise." John Henry's pleasant smile flashed. "I'll get back to you tomorrow about the others."

Watching as the deputy strode away, Wes turned spontaneously to look back at the entrance to the Texas Jewel.

. . . those long, slim fingers . . .

A chill ran down Wes's spine.

She was a witch.

She had to be.

Sam kept his mount to a steady pace as he moved along the trail. The familiar fragrance of the land filled his nostrils as the night sounds swelled around him. The air was cool, and above him the black velvet sky was littered with stars. The full moon lit the rolling landscape with a silver incandescence that was almost as bright as day. He had depended on that light to make his way—so he might get a head start on what he had to do.

Sam grumbled, his lined face twitching with distaste as he recalled the scene he had witnessed in the Texas Jewel earlier. He had known immediately that something was wrong when Honesty walked down those stairs to the saloon below. For a fleeting second, he had glimpsed again, too clearly for comfort, the frightened, fevered child who had escaped a flooding river only to find herself alone in an unfamiliar world. That child had looked from Honesty's glorious eyes, and when those eyes had locked with Wes Howell's, Sam knew what the problem was.

He'd always told Honesty she was heading for trouble with her teasing ways! Sam's jaw locked tightly. She had played with the wrong man. He knew relentless determination when he saw it, and Howell had it written all over him. Written all over Howell, too, was the fact that he wanted Honesty.

Sam adjusted his seat in the saddle, his agitation growing. He knew why all this was happening. It was because Honesty was still unsettled, as she had been all her life. She was waiting . . . waiting for something that would never come, for the day she would miraculously meet the sisters separated from her by the muddy waters that had almost taken her life. She was angry because no one believed her sisters and she would meet again. And she was afraid, because as the years had passed, a seed of doubt had crept into her own mind.

Sam angrily brushed the moistness from his eyes. Honesty was frustrated. She misbehaved, as if challenging the same fate that was denying her what she wanted most. She was suffering, and when Honesty suffered, Sam suffered, too.

Sam's throat tightened. He was no stranger to Honesty's kind of torment. His own darling little daughter had slipped away from him when she was no older than Honesty had been when they found her. The smallpox had already taken her mama, and when she died from another outbreak of the same disease a year later, he had been left in a daze. He had spent years in that daze, trying so hard to forget that he would not even speak her name. He had believed the pain would never end. Then he had seen that beautiful little angel lying limply on the riverbank, and when she opened her eyes and reached toward him for comfort, well . . .

Sam took another steadying breath. He had never told anyone, not even Honesty, about his daughter. He knew Honesty now thought he had made up all that stuff about a little girl of his own when Jewel and he first found her, just so she would listen to him and take her medicine. But the truth was that he understood Honesty better than anybody did. Honesty had spent half her lifetime angry, simultaneously mourning and seeking her sisters, just as he had wasted countless years mourning the loss of his daughter while simultaneously seeking to deny that she was gone from him forever. He knew Honesty felt she could never rest until she knew for certain her sisters' fate. He knew she believed that they were out there somewhere, silently calling for her, feeling as incomplete as she.

He wished with all his heart that he could help. The truth was that he'd give his life if it would make a difference. That was just the way it was.

As for Wes Howell . . .

Sam's expression darkened. The man was no fool. Howell knew Sam had meant every word he said to him. The only problem was that he doubted his warning would make a difference.

Howell would do what he must.

And so would he.

That thought lingering, Sam raised a knobby hand to rub his neck. Hell, things were getting too complicated! It was as if Honesty was caught in a whirlpool of everything that was happening around her and was being dragged ever downward—while he stood there at the water's edge, wondering which way to jump!

Well, he had made his move with Howell. He would have to wait to see what came afterward.

Now it was time to look into the rest.

Sam glanced up at the night sky. He'd ride a little longer, and then he'd bed down for the night. And in the morning, he'd go on.

Sam unconsciously nodded. Yes, trouble was coming, and the worst thing was, as hard as he was trying to stop it, he had a slowly creeping fear that all his effort wouldn't be worth a damn.

* * *

The sounds of revelry on Caldwell's main street accelerated as Wes continued determinedly down the boardwalk. His talk with John Henry a few hours earlier had accomplished little, except to bring more strongly into focus the fact that he had much to do and little time in which to accomplish it.

Wes strode on toward the next set of swinging doors as he made his way systematically along the street. His patience was ebbing. Strangely, the background work that was so much a part of his job had never seemed so tedious before. To the contrary, he had always found that entering a new town was akin to separating the pieces of a puzzle that he would later assemble so he might finally view the total picture clearly. He knew a clear picture was essential. Such clarity had saved his life on numerous occasions. As for the information John Henry had provided . . .

. . . *those long, slim fingers* . . .

Wes' thoughts came to a jarring halt as that image displaced all else in his mind. Anger soared. Distracted—that's what he was! And he knew the reason. His groin was overpowering his brain—a dangerous situation, and one which he had not anticipated. If he thought it would do him any good, he would accept the invitation of the next whore who approached him on the street, but he knew instinctively that it was not just any warm, willing, female body that he wanted.

Once a man gets a taste of me, he won't want to let me go.

The sudden bark of gunshots wiped all other thought from his mind as Wes snapped around toward the sound. He whipped his gun from his hip even as the crowd parted to reveal a cowboy with a lopsided grin standing in the middle of the street, his weapon raised to the sky. The fellow fired off another shot, then dropped his gun back into his holster, draped his arm around the brightly painted woman at his side, and staggered on.

Wes slapped his own gun back in his holster, aware that the gunshots had stirred no more than a moment's interest on the street. The danger here was obvious. He would need reliable men and all his wits about him if he were to protect Slater Enterprises' money in a town like this.

Holding that thought foremost, Wes thrust open the swinging doors nearby. A few steps inside, he halted, assessing the crowd. How many saloons had he already visited? Five? Six? He was beginning to lose track. With few exceptions, they were identical—the same loud music, the same boisterous conversation and bursts of laughter, the same gaming tables draped in clouds of blue tobacco smoke, the faces of the saloon women and drovers blending until they were hardly distinguishable from those he had seen in the previous saloon.

Struggling to keep his attention acute, Wes continued his perusal of the patrons around him. He had learned from long practice that wanted men often believed they could find anonymity in a crowd such as this. What they did not know was that they couldn't hide from him.

Wes's gaze stopped cold at the sight of the familiar figure who stood unsteadily at the bar. It was Jeremy Sills, with his glass half empty and a saloon woman pressed tightly to his side.

So, Sills played that game as well as Honesty did.

Wes walked directly toward Sills, disgust tugging at his lips when he realized that Sills was too drunk to be aware of his approach. He stopped a few feet away, slipped into the crush at the bar, and ordered a drink. He was close enough to hear the saloon girl as she spoke softly to Sills.

"You sure are a handsome fella, Jeremy. I always had a weakness for you. I wouldn't mind takin' you upstairs with me right now, if you had a mind."

Jeremy gave a wobbly laugh. Millie was a pretty little thing. Her blond hair was just a shade darker than his, and her brown eyes were earnest. She was a year or so younger than he was. He knew because he talked to her often, when Honesty was too busy for him, and when he needed somebody to make him feel like a man. Millie did that. The trouble was that making a man feel like a man was Millie's job.

He responded, "You know your boss doesn't want his girls off the floor so early in the evenin'."

"He'd make an exception, if I asked."

Sills leaned closer to the young woman's youthful, painted face. "You'd do that for me, Millie?"

"Sure would."

"Even if every cent I've got to my name is lyin' on the bar right now?"

She nodded.

"That doesn't make much sense, does it? There're plenty of fellas here who can make your time more worthwhile than I can."

"Maybe. But then, there ain't many fellas here who could make me feel the way you could make me feel."

Jeremy smiled. "You sure do know the right things to say to make a fella feel good."

"Maybe." Millie's smile faltered. "And maybe it just sounds right cause it comes from the heart."

Jeremy was touched. "Are you sayin' you have a place in your heart for me, Millie?"

Millie pressed closer. "Why don't you give me a

chance to show you? It could be real good between us, you know. You've always been special to me."

Jeremy studied Millie a silent moment longer. A few weeks ago, he would have been tempted. It would have meant nothing at all to him to sate his bodily needs at a willing invitation. No matter whose female flesh warmed his, it was always Honesty's face that he saw. But not now, not when things were going to be settled so soon. He could wait. He needed to wait. To do otherwise would somehow seem a betrayal of his love for Honesty.

Jeremy touched Millie's cheek. Her lips parted and he felt a pang of genuine regret. "I wish I could, Millie, but I can't."

Millie's eyes unexpectedly filled. "Why can't you?"

"Because of somebody else."

"Oh, *her* . . . I know about her." Millie's thin lips tightened. "That Honesty Buchanan's got a lot of fellas, not just you."

Jeremy stiffened. "That's where you're wrong, Millie. You don't know anythin' at all!"

Emptying his glass, Jeremy turned to leave, only to feel Millie's small hand stay him.

"Don't go, Jeremy. I'm sorry."

Jeremy shook his arm free, suddenly aware that he was unsteady on his feet. He was glad Honesty couldn't see him now. He took an uncertain step.

"Jeremy, please, don't be mad."

Something in the tone of Millie's voice turned Jeremy back toward her. Her small face was tight with contrition, and her eyes were full. His heart melted at the realization that her feelings were sincere. He knew how Millie felt. It was hard when you cared for somebody and things just didn't seem to be working out.

He attempted a smile. "I'm not mad. I have to go home."

"Not yet . . . please."

Jeremy shrugged. "Just like I told you, all my money's lyin' right there on that bar. There isn't any more."

"I have money."

Reaching into the neckline of her dress, Millie produced some folding money and placed it on the bar. "Stay a while longer, so I know you ain't mad."

Jeremy considered the invitation and the pleading look on Millie's face that accompanied it. He nodded. "Just one more."

Allowing Millie to draw him back to the bar, Jeremy leaned heavily against it, grateful for its support. He waited until his glass was refilled and smiled when Millie stood unexpectedly on tiptoe to brush his lips with a kiss. She was a nice girl, Millie was.

But she wasn't Honesty.

And it was Honesty he loved . . . with all his heart.

Jeremy picked up his drink.

Wes did not smile. He had heard all of the conversation between Sills and the saloon girl that he had needed to hear. Sills was a fool for turning down what the little tart offered him.

Or was he?

Unwanted images rose again in Wes's mind.

He saw Sills holding Honesty in his arms, as he had held her.

He saw Sills tasting Honesty's mouth, as he had tasted it.

He saw Sills sinking himself deep inside Honesty, claiming her as he had *not*.

A flush of heat suffusing him, Wes turned abruptly toward the door.

* * *

"This is the last hand, fellas."

"Come on, Honesty!"

"That ain't fair, Honesty!"

"You can't do that to us!"

Honesty could not help smiling. "Oh, yes, I can."

Struggling to hide the weariness that had beset her in the last hour, Honesty dealt cards around the table. She responded by rote to the usual comments, then picked up her cards. Her luck had been phenomenal ever since she had looked up a few hours earlier and had seen Wes disappear out onto the street. She wondered if that was some kind of sign, then decided that even if it was, she had neither the time nor the inclination to try to decipher it. She was intensely aware that those few fellows who had stayed with the game the entire evening now had empty pockets, or nearly so, which accounted for the protests.

Honesty checked her cards.

Four queens.

Oh, well . . .

Honesty stood beside the table minutes later, amidst grumbles all around. She smiled at the somber faces. "Tough night, boys. Better luck tomorrow."

Jack Hardesty shook his shaggy head. "Ain't never seen such luck! There ain't goin' to be a tomorrow for me—not at this table anyhow. I ain't even got enough change left to buy myself a drink!"

"Well, we can't let that happen, can we?" Honesty turned toward the bar. The early morning hour had already thinned the crowd, allowing her voice to be heard as she called out, "Set up drinks all around for these fellas from my table, Henry. And leave the bottle. They've earned it."

"Mighty nice of you, Honesty!"

"Yeah!"

"Always did know you was a lady!"

The scramble toward the bar precluded any further responses. Honesty started toward the saloon doors, only to halt at the sound of Jewel's husky voice behind her.

"Now that was a waste of money."

Honesty turned to Jewel's assessing gaze. Standing beside her, Charles admonished, "Leave her alone, Jewel. Honesty's smart. She saved you a lot of complaints and made sure those fellas would be back as soon as they could fill their pockets again."

"That's fine with me." Turning her disapproval on Charles, Jewel continued, "I'll just tell Henry to charge that bottle to you."

"You can tell Henry to charge that bottle to me, if that's what's bothering you." Not in the mood to face another of Jewel's lectures, Honesty continued, "Do whatever you want. I'm tired. I'm going out for some air before I go to bed."

"I don't know if that's a good idea, Honesty." Charles glanced out toward the street. "It's been pretty lively out there tonight. Some of Mitch Powell's wranglers are still in town, and they're a wild bunch."

"I can take care of myself, Charles."

"But—"

"You heard her, Charles." Jewel's expression tightened. "Honesty doesn't take advice. When she says she needs some air, she needs some air. When she says she can take care of herself, she means that, too."

Honesty recognized the tone of Jewel's voice. She was angry again. Jewel was always angry when Honesty resisted her authority. It had been that way since she was a child. And she knew there was more behind Jewel's mood than a complimentary bottle for a few cowpokes.

Charles's lips had tightened, and his handsome face was drawn into a frown. Honesty knew what was coming. He would stand up for her, and the loving truce that had existed between Jewel and him would dissolve into an argument. Again. Because of her. She didn't want to be responsible for that, but it seemed she always was.

Honesty forced a smile for Charles's benefit. "I'm not going far. Don't worry."

"You can be sure *I* won't."

That last from Jewel dragged the warmth from Honesty's smile as she turned determinedly toward the door. Jewel knew something was amiss. She was using her usual tactics to try to anger Honesty into revealing what it was. Well, this time it wasn't going to work.

Outside on the street moments later, Honesty took a deep breath. She needed to clear her lungs and her head. She needed to stretch her stiff muscles and allow the blood to flow. She needed . . .

Wes Howell's dark, almost demonic image appeared again before her mind. Honesty felt the knot within her tighten as the question loomed. Yes, what did she need?

Honesty walked along the boardwalk, nodding at familiar faces in passing. Charles was right. The mixed crowd of drovers and itinerant cowboys now lingering on the street was not entirely reliable. But the question returned. What did she need?

Honesty briefly closed her eyes. She snapped them open again, unwilling to face the images that had flashed across her mind. Despite herself, the sound of Wes Howell's deep voice resounded again in her ears, repeating the hungry words of loving desire that he had whispered against her lips. She remembered the warmth of his mouth against her flesh. She recalled the quaking of his powerful body as his passion had grown. She remembered that she had sensed in his loving assault his surrender to the powerful emotions that had encompassed them both, destroying her resistance. She recalled so vividly that it had all seemed so *right* . . . before it had all gone so wrong.

Am I borin' you now, Honesty?

Thank you again, ma'am.

How could she have made such a mistake? How could she have allowed herself to be so misled? She had always been so proud of her ability to maintain control over any situation . . . yet when Wes's arms had held her close . . . when she had heard the tremor in his voice . . . when he had . . .

No, damn it! She wouldn't allow herself to relive her mistakes over and over again! She would do what she always did. She would learn from them. Then she would cast the memory aside.

Suddenly aware that her feet had taken her on a familiar path to the door of Jeremy's shack, Honesty hesitated. Set back from the street, the doorway was cast in shadow. The interior was in total darkness, and her heart fell. Jeremy left the lamp burning when he slept. He had done that ever since she could remember. The only time the cabin was dark was when he didn't have the money to buy fuel, or when he wasn't home.

If he wasn't home, there was only one place he would be.

She placed her hand on the door latch. She wanted Jeremy to be there. She wanted him to be sober and repentant, ready to reclaim both his job and his life when morning came. She wanted to know that when all else seemed to be going so badly, this one, important thing was going right.

She lifted the latch.

"Don't bother goin' inside. He isn't there."

Starting, Honesty drew back as a shadow materialized out of the darkness to take on a familiar form. She fought to subdue the wild pounding of her heart as Wes Howell approached, halting so close to her that she could feel his breath on her lips as he spoke.

"He's in the Longhorn, propped up against the bar."

"How do you know where Jeremy is? Were you spying on him?"

"That would be a waste of my time. I saw him there earlier." He paused as if intending to continue, then concluded abruptly, "I don't expect he'll be comin' home too soon."

"I don't really care what you expect or don't expect. What Jeremy or I do is none of your business."

Wes's short laugh was unexpected. "You're the second person who's told me that tonight."

Sam . . .

Honesty grated through clenched teeth, "So it looks like you hear well enough. You just don't listen."

"No, I don't."

Gathering her strength, Honesty attempted to turn away, only to have Wes grip her arms to hold her fast. She saw the muscle that ticked in his jaw as his dark eyes swept her face.

"You're tremblin', Honesty."

Honesty did not respond.

Holding her mesmerized with his gaze as his chest began a slow heaving, Wes stroked her cheek. His callused fingertips slipped up to rest against the wildly throbbing pulse in her temple as he whispered, "And your heart is poundin'. Why?"

Honesty attempted to jerk herself free of Wes's grip. Her effort failed as he slipped his arm around her, tangling his hand in her hair to hold her fast. "Tell me why you're tremblin', Honesty," he whispered. "Is it because you've been thinkin' about last night? Is it because you've been wonderin' what it would've been like if I—"

"If you hadn't been *bored?*"

Realizing her presence of mind was rapidly slipping, Honesty fought to ignore the sensation of Wes's heart pounding against her own, of the growing raspiness in his voice as he whispered, "Did I say I was bored?"

"You said you had gotten everything you came for."

"Not everythin'."

"What do you want?"

"Don't you know?"

Not waiting for her response, Wes lowered his mouth to hers. Honesty steeled herself against the persuasive caress of his lips, silently cursing the perverse part of her that longed to melt in his arms, the part of her that longed to separate her lips and welcome his kiss.

But she did not.

Drawing back when Honesty kept her lips locked tight, Wes brushed her cheek, her forehead, her trembling eyelids with his kiss. She felt his passion swell hard against her as he grated, "Open your mouth for me, Honesty. Let me in. There'll be no backin' off . . . not this time. You know you want it. And I know damned well I do."

"You want me, Wes?" Honesty's trembling had turned to shuddering. She ached inside. She longed with a yearning so deep that it was shattering to feel Wes tight against her, to know that he shared the emotions that turned her blood to fire as it coursed through her veins. She felt the sweet warmth of his tongue as it licked at her lips. She groaned as he caught her bottom lip in his teeth, suddenly nipping so hard that she gasped in protest.

Grasping the opportunity he sought, Wes cupped her head with his palm, holding her fast as he pressed his kiss with new fervor. He swept the sweet hollows of her mouth. He sought her reticent tongue with his, caressing it gently with his own. Pressing her back against the wall of the shack, he kissed her harder, longer, drawing hotly from her. She was unconscious of Wes's hand as it slid her gown from her shoulder, as he freed a warm, rounded breast and dropped his mouth to its crest. She heard his groan as he laved it with his tongue, then covered it with his mouth. She was beside herself with longing when he grasped the hand she raised in feeble resistance and pinned it behind her, then pushed her gown to her waist to indulge himself in the heated womanly flesh.

Honesty caught her breath. She was lost in the wonder of the emotions Wes stirred to life, yet somehow conscious of the exact moment when his trembling became shudders that matched her own, when his coaxing words became driving yearning. She saw the hunger in his eyes when he drew back, staring down at her for endless seconds before covering her mouth again with his.

Random laughter echoed distantly from the street behind them, and Wes tore his mouth from hers. Adjusting his broad frame to ensure that she was totally shielded from view, he pushed her deeper into the shadows. The laughter faded, but the passion that throbbed in Wes's tone did not as he whispered, "Let's get away from here, where we can be alone. Come with me, Honesty. Come with me now. You won't regret it. I'll make it better for you than you've ever known. There'll be no pullin' back—not this time. I promise you that. I couldn't do that again, darlin'. I wouldn't be able. Darlin' . . ."

He meant it, every word—Honesty knew that for sure. And she knew she had never—never—wanted anything as much as she wanted this now.

Honesty's breath came in short rasps as she stared at the shadowed face above hers. The darkness could not hide the heat of his desire, the need, the hunger that she somehow knew was for her alone. Those thoughts rebounded in her mind, even as she heard herself whisper, as if from a distance, words that rose unbidden to her lips.

"Are you *bored* now, Wes?"

Silence. No trace of movement.

"I asked you a question."

The muscular wall of Wes's body, pressed so tightly to hers, reacted with growing tension. She felt the power building as he responded.

"No, I'm not bored."

"Well . . ." The inevitable words followed. "I *am*."

"Honesty."

"Let me go."

Wes did not release her.

"I said . . . let me go!"

Wes's hands dropped to his sides. He stepped back. The shadows did not hide the burning heat of his gaze. It scorched her as he watched her raise her bodice to cover herself, as she moved around him and started toward the street.

Behind her, his whisper was more a statement than a threat.

"You'll regret walkin' away from me now, Honesty. I'm tellin' you, because I know. You'll regret it."

Would she?

Honesty stepped out onto the street.

Chapter Five

Pain penetrated Jeremy's numbed mind, and he groaned aloud. He attempted to open his eyes, and a brilliant light pierced his pounding head like a knife. He squinted, then released a disgusted breath as he identified the source of his torment.

It was the sun.

Shielding his eyes from the brilliant rays shining through the window of his shack, Jeremy turned his face to the wall. He stiffened, suddenly aware that he was not alone on his cot as a naked female form lying beside him turned into his embrace.

Oh . . . no.

"Good mornin', Jeremy." Millie pressed warm lips against his. She rubbed her naked breasts against his chest and laughed. "You feel real good, do you know that?"

"Millie, how did you get here?"

"You and me walked together, holdin' each other up." She laughed again. "You was so nice that I couldn't resist you."

"Millie . . ." Jeremy shook his head. He was hurting, and it wasn't just his head. "You shouldn't be here."

"That isn't what you said last night."

"I don't know what I said last night."

"Sure you do." Millie's eyes misted. "You said you thought I was real nice. You kissed me and I liked it. I liked it a lot."

"I shouldn't have done that, Millie." Jeremy pushed himself to the side of the bed. "Hell, I was drunk."

"But that didn't stop you from doin' what came naturally." Millie raised herself to a sitting position. The coverlet dropped away, exposing her small, firm breasts as she continued, "I'm sorry you can't remember, but you did real good. I can't remember it ever bein' that good for me."

Jeremy stood up and reached for his pants. He fastened them and turned back. Millie had not moved. Her blond hair was half unpinned and hanging limply on her bare shoulders, and her face paint was almost comically smeared. But there was an air about her that was strangely innocent . . . and there was a plea in her eyes. He couldn't submit to that plea, no matter how fervently he wished he could.

Besides, he felt so damned sick.

"I don't feel too good, Millie. Maybe you'd better go home."

"I'll stay a while. I can fix you somethin' that'll help."

"No. I have to go to work."

"But you're sick."

"I have to go to work."

"But—"

Jeremy's head began a new and vicious pounding and his patience snapped. "Go home, Millie!"

Regretting his outburst as soon as the words had emerged, Jeremy attempted a smile. "Please. I . . . I'll see you tonight."

"No, you won't. You won't come to see me."

Millie threw back the coverlet. Unmindful of her slender nakedness, she stood up and reached for her dress. She pulled it down over her head, then faced him soberly. "You won't come to see me because you can't get that *other one* out of your mind."

"I'm sorry, Millie."

"Yeah, well, I ain't—not for all of it." Millie's brown eyes again misted. "You'll get tired of waitin' for her, and when you do, you know where to find me." She attempted a smile. "I ain't proud, you know. I'll be at the Longhorn, like I always am. I ain't got no place else to go."

Taking a moment to scoop up her underclothes, Millie walked toward the door. Her hand on the latch, she turned back. "You remember what I said, you hear?"

"I'll remember."

The door had hardly closed behind Millie before Jeremy rushed to the bucket in the corner. His stomach empty moments later, he forced himself upright and reached for his clothes. He was already late for work. He was going to have to do a lot of explaining if he wanted to keep his job.

Jeremy fumbled at the buttons on his shirt. He needed to keep his job. He had promised Honesty that he would fix things up there. Besides, he needed everything to seem as normal as possible so he could get the information Bitters wanted without causing suspicion.

Fully dressed at last, Jeremy took only a moment to dispose of the bucket, then ran a hand through his hair and reached for his hat. He felt bad about Millie. He hadn't wanted to hurt her. He knew she'd get over it, but this whole thing had taught him a lesson. No more drinking. As much as he disliked admitting it, he wasn't reliable anymore when he drank. If he was, he would've awakened alone.

Agitated, uncertain, Honesty covered her eyes with her hand in an effort to avoid the sunlight streaming through her bedroom window. Morning had finally come after a horrendous night of twisting and turning, followed by disturbing dreams that she could not seem to comprehend. All anxious dreams, they had paraded across her mind in an endless stream. They had left her tired and filled with uneasiness.

What did they mean?

She had seen Purity again, only this time Purity's face was clearer than she had ever seen it before. She had suffered a silent torment at Purity's uncanny resemblance to her dear mother with her pale golden hair, light eyes, and delicately sculpted face—and with the gold locket that glinted at her throat. But that stubborn chin had been Purity's own. Honesty almost laughed at the sudden certainty that although Purity had grown up, she hadn't changed at all.

Honesty's desire to laugh soon faded. Purity had looked disturbed—far more disturbed than she had ever seen her—and when a male shadow had loomed behind her, a shadow that appeared somehow savage, she could tell Purity felt angry, threatened. She could feel that Purity needed her.

Honesty threw back the coverlet and stood up abruptly. She did not want to relive the dreams that followed—fragmented dreams filled with the image of Wes Howell. The man was a villain, a devil incarnate, who brought out the worst in her!

You'll regret walking away from me now. I'm telling you, because I know. You'll regret it.

Did she regret leaving Wes behind in the shadows?

Yes.

No!

Suddenly furious, Honesty stripped off her nightgown and reached for her dress. On impulse, she threw it back on the chair and pulled a worn pair of pants and a shirt from the closet. She dressed quickly, finishing with boots and an old hat before turning toward the door.

In the hallway, Honesty glanced toward Jewel's room, then walked quickly toward the stairs. She breathed a deep sigh of relief when out on the street at last. Something was bothering Jewel, something more than the complimentary bottle she had ordered for those cowpokes the night before, and she had neither the time nor the patience to find out what she had done this time to annoy her.

Honesty paused at Jeremy's door minutes later. Struggling to retain control of her emotions, she realized that although a brilliant morning sun eliminated the previous night's shadows, the memory of all that had transpired in the darkness remained.

Determined that she would allow that memory to taunt her no longer, Honesty looked up at the sky. It was barely past mid-morning, but she knew that if all was well with Jeremy, he would already be at work. She hoped he was. So intense was the hope that she would not find him in the same condition she had found him so many times before, she unconsciously held her breath as she raised her hand to knock.

Honesty rapped once . . . twice. When there was

no response, she pushed the door open. She scanned the familiar disorder of Jeremy's room, relieved to see that Jeremy's cot was empty. The rest would be easy. Bud Harper had known Jeremy since he was a boy. He liked Jeremy and he would allow Jeremy to talk him into giving him another chance at his job because he also knew that Jeremy was a conscientious worker when he was sober.

When he was sober . . .

Honesty looked around her. She shook her head. How Jeremy could live in such a mess when he had been brought up in Mother Sills's meticulously kept cabin, she would never understand.

Moving efficiently around the small room with the aid of long practice, Honesty swept the table and floor clear of debris, pulled the soiled clothing from the wall hooks and piled it in the corner to remove later, then turned her attention to the rumpled cot nearby. She pulled the coverlet up and smoothed the surface with her hand, jumping as a sharp object stabbed her palm.

A hairpin . . .

The sudden realization that Jeremy had not slept alone in his bed the previous night was somehow startling.

Honesty stared down at the hairpin caught in the folds of the coverlet. She knew Jeremy was not adverse to using the services of Maude's House of Pleasure when he felt the need. She knew the girls liked him, but she also knew that he had never brought a woman back to his shack before this. This woman, whoever she was, must have been special to him.

Honesty's throat was suddenly tight. Dear Jeremy. Maybe that was the key. Maybe the love and attention she gave him was not enough. Maybe he needed more—the love of someone who would love him in a way she never could. She hoped this woman, whoever she was, was the one.

Honesty placed the hairpin carefully on the nightstand and continued her work.

Out on the street a short time later, Honesty left Jeremy's soiled clothing at the laundry and strode on, ignoring the appreciative stares and comments that followed her as she made her way toward the livery stable. Somehow now, more than ever, she needed to get away, to leave the aching present behind her in the rush of the wind and the freedom she felt only on horseback. As for the unconventional clothes she wore—Honesty tugged at the pants Jeremy had outgrown a year earlier—they were tight, but they suited her purpose and she didn't care what people thought or said about them.

Mounted, Honesty guided her mare through the morning traffic toward the outskirts of town. Drawing back on the reins as she passed the holding pens, she slowed her horse's pace, straining to penetrate with her gaze the grainy dust rapidly proliferating as the cattle were prodded and pushed from pens through a maze of gates, runways, and chutes toward the railcars awaiting them. Her stomach tightened until she spotted Jeremy in their midst.

Relief flooding her eyes with unexpected moistness, Honesty urged her horse on. Jeremy was working. He would make it. He would be all right.

Digging her heels into her mount's sides as soon as Caldwell's main street was behind her, Honesty headed out into open country.

Strangely, she had never felt more alone.

Seated in his office, the door closed against the buzz of activity beyond that signified another busy day had begun, Charles stroked Emily's letter with his fingertips as it lay on the desk in front of him. He read again the carefully written lines. The unfamiliar script did not weaken the impact of Emily's words. They tore at his heart as they had throughout the day and night past, stirring emotions too myriad to be recounted.

The familiar, almost debilitating wave of love could no longer be denied as Charles gathered his courage, picked up his pen, and began writing.

Emily, my dearest love,

Your letter means so much to me. I wish with all my heart that I could be at your side right now so you might read in my eyes confirmation of my words when I tell you how much I miss you. I miss your smile and your gentle ways. I miss the touch of your hand and the warmth of you close beside me. There is not a day that goes by that I do not think of all we were to each other when we were young and carefree, and of all you came to mean to me when the carefree years were gone and only our love remained. You were my rock. You saved me from a desolation so black that I might never have survived had I not your loving heart to turn to. The most difficult day of my life was the day I was forced to leave you behind.

You write that you are comfortable, my darling. I take solace in those words. I would fear that you only write them to provide me peace of mind were I not certain that you are incapable of deceit even in an effort to be kind. You are my angel. You are the joy of my life. And you are my torment, for as much as I wish it was not so, I must write that I cannot come to you now. You see, the past has reared its ugly head, and I must stay to face it so that it will not further threaten our already tenuous future.

I would ask you to understand, my dearest, but I know you already understand. I would ask you to forgive, but I know you feel no need to forgive. I would ask for your love forever, but I know it is mine until the day when the light passes from both our eyes. I know all of this, not because I am so worthy of your love, but because you are my dearest Emily.

Please thank the young woman who penned your letter to me and tell her that I shall be forever grateful for her consideration of you. If the generous God above will spare us, I will see you again in the fall and I will thank your friend personally for all she has done to ease your days.

I ask you to remember always that you are my life and my love, my darling. You are the dearest part of me. You are the only true worth in all that is past, and you are the light that guides me on. You wished me joy. You wished me consolation. Please know that you are those things to me even though we are apart. You are the breath of my soul, the sacred part of me that will never die. You are forever with me, and I will always love you.

Your Charles.

Hardly conscious of the dampness that stained his cheeks, Charles lowered his pen to his desk. He covered his eyes briefly, the pain within momentarily more than he could bear.

Continuing to ignore the business of the morning, which progressed in the tellers' cages beyond his office door, Charles reached into his pocket to withdraw another letter, one which he had previously crushed in anger. He unfolded the wrinkled sheet and reread Mary's uneven scrawl. So involved was he that he did not hear the step outside his door until a sharp knock sounded, jarring him from his darkening mood. Slipping the letters into his desk drawer, Charles responded, standing as the door opened to reveal Wes Howell. He did not bother to smile.

"Bob Blackwell. Jason Storms. Herb Walters. John Agree. Mike Leach. Nate Wilson . . . Do you know these men?"

Wes watched Charles Webster's reaction as he recited the names John Henry had given him only a few minutes earlier. Webster's usual conciliatory manner was markedly absent, and he appeared somehow disturbed. He did not immediately respond, providing Wes the excuse needed to further scrutinize the man.

Physically, Webster looked the same. Standing a few inches shorter than he, Webster was impeccably clothed and groomed. His fair skin, even features, and comportment marked him as an educated man of affluent background as clearly as he knew his own intimidating stature and unyielding demeanor implied threat in the eyes of others. To his credit, Webster looked him directly in the eye, although his gaze was guarded. He wondered if that direct gaze was due to early training or to the integrity of the man behind it.

And he wondered if it was that aura of old money that drew Honesty to the man.

He did not need to question what it was that drew Webster to her.

That thought rankled more than Wes cared to admit as he awaited Webster's response. Tired, out of sorts, and short on patience, he prodded, "Well?"

"Yes, I know those men." Webster frowned. "What do you want to know about them?"

"Are they reliable? Would you feel safe putting Slater Enterprises' money under their protection?"

Webster paused. "It was my understanding that Slater's money would be under *your* protection."

Wes almost smiled. "It will be. You haven't answered my question."

Webster shrugged. "I don't know them well, but they're as reliable as any other men in town, I suppose."

"You have no objections to them?"

Webster stiffened. "I don't know what you're trying to get me to say. I've already told you that I don't know these men well enough to indicate objection or approval."

"What are you afraid of, Webster?"

"Look . . ." Surprising him, Webster abandoned all pretense at civility. "I've tried to be cooperative, but I'm getting tired of your games. If you have something to say, say it. As far as I'm concerned, the job of protecting Slater's money is yours. I want nothing to do with it. If there's something else you want to know, ask. Otherwise, I'm a busy man."

Satisfaction loomed inside Wes. Another side of Webster was gradually emerging. He goaded, "For a man who's so careful about what he says, you're not so careful about what you do."

"Meaning?"

"Meaning the intimate company you keep isn't exactly respectable."

"That's none of your concern."

"It is if it interferes with the conduct of your job."

"It doesn't."

"I'm not so sure."

"Look, Howell, let's put our cards on the table. The truth is, for whatever reason, you don't like me. That's all right, because I don't like you, either. But we both have a job to do. I know where my responsibilities begin and end. We'll get along fine if you'll try remembering the boundaries of yours."

"That's exactly what I'm doing. To my mind, Slater Enterprises would be very interested in some of the friends of the man they've entrusted with their money."

"My friends?"

"Friends like a dancehall woman with a shady past."

"Leave Jewel out of this!"

"And another woman . . ."

A sudden flush colored Webster's face. "That's what all this is about, isn't it? Honesty. I don't know what you're thinking, but she has nothing to do with the job you were sent here to do, and you'd damned well better not cause her any trouble!"

"Is that a threat?"

"It's anything you want it to be."

"Seems to me Honesty can take care of herself."

"I don't intend arguing with you, Howell. I've said all I have to say about it, and you'd be wise to remember it."

"And if I don't?"

Webster did not back down. "Then you'll get what you've got coming."

"Another threat?"

"That's up to you."

Wes studied Webster more closely. It was obvious that the fellow had already been agitated when he entered, which accounted for the lapse of his customary control. He had come to Webster's office for the specific purpose of rattling him—but he didn't like being threatened.

"I don't take threats lightly, Webster."

"Neither do I."

On the boardwalk outside the bank minutes later, Wes paused, automatically scanning the street as his thoughts ran rampant. He had been right from the beginning. Webster was hiding something. Whether that something had to do with an incident in his past or with something planned for the future, he was not yet certain. But he would find out. That was his job and his mission. And if the path to that discovery was tied to a sultry, blue-eyed witch who would not yield her place in his mind, well, all the better. He—

A slim figure emerged onto the street in the distance, and Wes's thoughts stopped cold. Honesty, dressed in the informal riding gear that John Henry had described so appreciatively. But John Henry had not detailed the way in which the long, graceful length of Honesty's legs would be so clearly outlined in the faded pants, or that her gently curved bottom would be so sweet to behold. Nor had he detailed the way the light breeze would mould the thin cotton shirt she wore against her breasts as they bobbed with her rapid step. He remembered the taste of that warm flesh and the sweet scent of her that had filled his senses, a memory that even now set his heart to pounding.

The peculiar knot Wes had come to know so well constricted in his stomach.

Watching as Honesty slipped out of sight into the livery stable, Wes started in its direction. He paused partway down the street, waiting until Honesty emerged mounted a few minutes later and headed out of town.

Where was she going?

Why did he care?

His gaze lingering for long moments in the direction in which Honesty had disappeared, Wes turned abruptly and started back down the walk.

Damned if the dust wasn't choking him!

Standing back as the last freight car door was slammed closed amidst a chorus of bovine protests from within, Jeremy coughed. He wiped his handkerchief across his forehead, immune to the grimy residue that scratched his skin as he looked up at the clouds rapidly accumulating overhead. The day that had started out in almost blinding sunlight was turning dark, but the stock would be well on their way before the storm broke.

Jeremy shrugged. At least that had gone right.

Glancing back at the train, Jeremy saw Bud Harper squinting in his direction. Good old Bud, who had given him a damned hard time when he showed up for work a few hours earlier. Not that he had expected much else. Every time Bud took him back, it was the *last* time. But the truth was that the old bachelor had a soft spot in his heart for the son of the woman he had once asked to be his wife.

Jeremy studied Bud Harper as he approached, wondering what it would have been like to have that gruff old man for a father instead of the staggering drunk who filled his memories. It occurred to him that he would probably be in a different position now . . . not dirty and hot, with his empty stomach churning . . . not without a cent in his pocket and scrambling to find a way to earn the respect of the woman he loved before it was too late. Bud drew closer and Jeremy saw the almost imperceptible shake of the old fellow's head as he fixed him with a discerning eye.

"You don't look so good."

"I'm all right."

"Yeah, well, I'm thinkin' it's just about sappin' the last of your energy to stand there the way you are."

"What are you tryin' to say, Bud?" Jeremy was annoyed. It seemed as if everybody felt free to either comment on his appearance or give him advice. He was sick of it. "You got any complaints about the way I did my job this mornin'?"

"No."

"Well?"

"Kinda pickin' a bad time to get so testy with the boss, ain't you?"

"Maybe."

Bud nodded. "Get out of here."

"What?"

"Go get somethin' to eat. Whether you know it or not, you're green around the gills, which tells me that if I want to get a full day's work out of you, you'd better get somethin' in your stomach right quick."

"I told you, I'm all right."

"Listen, boy!" Bud took a step closer, frowning so hard that his hairy brows all but hid the small light eyes beneath as he continued, "Don't push me too far! You did a fair mornin's work and you need somethin' to eat. Take advantage of it, 'cause I'm tellin' you now, I'm expectin' a full afternoon's work from you, too. And I don't mind tellin' you, there's a lot of fellas ready to step into your job if you're not up to doin' it!"

Cranky old coot . . .

"You hear me, boy?"

"Don't call me boy."

Bud Harper paused. "I asked you if you heard what I said."

"I heard you."

"Then git! And come back with a better attitude, or don't come back at all!"

Not choosing to respond, Jeremy left the old man mumbling in his wake, even as he silently cursed all the way to Birdie Cotter's place. The fragrance wafting through the doorway as he neared set his stomach to gurgling and his hand to searching his pockets for the necessary coins. He breathed a silent sigh of relief to find a few that had previously escaped his notice. About to sit at the counter, he noticed a familiar bald head at the opposite end. Not quite believing his good fortune, he made directly toward it, extending his hand with a grin as he approached.

"Well, if it isn't Joe Pierce! How's that old telegraph key treatin' you?"

Jeremy's grin broadened as Joe shook his hand. He sat down next to the smiling telegrapher, thinking it might be his lucky day after all.

Emerging from Birdie's a half hour later, Jeremy stretched up to his full height, extremely pleased with himself. Glancing down the street as Charles Webster emerged from the bank and started in his direction, Jeremy turned automatically toward the holding pens. He felt too good to spoil it all by running into Webster now. His stomach was full and settled. His headache was gone, and things were looking up. All because he had spent the last half hour at Birdie's counter with Joe Pierce.

Friendly Joe.

Talkative Joe.

Yeah.

He'd ride out to see Bitters tonight.

Jewel paused on the boardwalk outside the Texas Jewel, looking up at the bank of clouds rolling in overhead. She hadn't seen storm clouds that black and threatening in a dog's age.

Judging that the approaching storm was not an immediate threat, she started down the street. She was, after all, wearing a special dress, one Charles had picked out for her himself. She didn't want it spoiled. The cool blue batiste decorated sparingly with a dainty white lace that had particularly impressed Charles was not exactly her taste. It was too pale, too insignificant when compared to the glowing satins in vivid colors she usually wore. And the neckline was too modest, unlike the deeply slashed bodices she preferred, which displayed to full advantage her greatest asset.

Jewel knew she would never forget the look in Charles's eye when she wore the dress for the first time. Charles had stared at her so intently as to raise a flush to her cheek and had whispered with a particular catch in his voice that she had never looked more beautiful.

Strangely, she had not worn the gown again after that day. In looking back, she had the feeling that Charles had glimpsed in her at that moment the woman she could have been . . . the woman that time and circumstance had removed forever beyond her reach. She did not want to be reminded of that woman . . . nor did she want Charles to want her.

Jewel blinked the moistness from her eyes. But today she would be that woman, if only for a little while. She would do that for Charles, to atone for her shrewishness the previous evening when she had disturbed him by attacking Honesty for a generous act that had promoted good will where resentment could have festered. She had realized her mistake immediately. But she had been too proud to admit, even to herself, that she had again allowed her frustration at Honesty's stubbornness to set into motion a vicious circle appearing to have no end, one which inevitably ended with another confrontation with Charles and further alienation from Honesty.

It had been her fault that Charles had left the Texas Jewel early, without joining her in her room. She had regretted her actions, realizing that with Emily failing and with all the uncertainties sure to follow, her timing had been exceedingly poor. The blue batiste she wore and her unusual visit to the bank with an invitation to share an afternoon meal was her apology.

Jewel straightened her spine and turned down the street, her step brisk. She smiled into the familiar faces she passed, taking the time for a flirtatious wink for favored customers. Her smile briefly faltered at the disapproving glances of a pair of stern-faced matrons as she approached Charles's bank. At such times she was self-consciously aware of the chasm that truly existed between the disreputable saloon woman and the respectable banker who would soon be free to choose any woman he might desire.

Forcing that thought from her mind, Jewel entered the bank with her head high. She ignored the surprised glances of tellers and customers alike as she walked directly toward Charles's office. She knocked once and boldly entered. To her disappointment, the office was empty.

Her smile stiff, Jewel turned in the doorway as the teller offered, "Mr. Webster stepped out, ma'am."

Realizing that the respect with which she was addressed was more closely related to the sizable deposits regularly made in her name than it was to her stature in the community, Jewel inquired in as level a voice as she could manage, "Do you expect him back soon?"

"Yes, ma'am."

"I'll wait."

The speculative glances and buzzing that ensued touched off a familiar irritation as Jewel entered the office and closed the door behind her. She walked to the window behind Charles's desk and stared out for long moments, seeing little and cursing her impulsiveness. Charles had very carefully kept his professional life separate from the personal life he'd shared with her over the years. She should have respected that wish. She had made a mistake in coming and had succeeded only in providing grist for the gossip mill.

Jewel considered that thought a moment longer, her agitation growing. She would stay only a few minutes and then she would leave. No. She would leave *now*.

The small purse dangling from her arm swung out as Jewel turned abruptly toward the door. It caught the corner of the pen still resting in the open inkwell on Charles's desk. She gasped aloud as the inkwell tipped, splashing its contents across the polished surface.

Infuriated by her own clumsiness, Jewel attempted to blot up the stain with her handkerchief. Immediately aware that the fragile scrap of fabric was inadequate for the task, she felt a moment's panic. Jerking open the desk drawer in search of a better device, she went stock still at first sight of the letter written in Charles's distinctive hand. The letter began, "Emily, my dearest love . . ."

Without conscious intent, Jewel read on, unable to look up from the sheet until the last word was read.

Tears streaked Jewel's cheeks. The closing words of Charles's love letter to his dying wife echoed in her mind. The sob that escaped her lips grated harshly on the silence as Jewel closed her eyes. She knew Charles's words were sincere. They spoke directly to the heart of the woman he loved . . . the *only* woman he loved. Suddenly clear was the realization that what Charles felt for her was only a pale shadow of the powerful emotion that would forever be Emily's alone.

What was it like to be loved as Emily was loved?

Jewel reached a trembling hand toward the carefully scripted sheet and picked it up. Only then did she notice the letter beneath, written in a careless, feminine scrawl that began:

"Dear Charles . . ."

She read the three short lines.

. . . If you don't come to see us, the children and I will come to see you . . .

She stared at the signature.

The woman's name was Mary.

Motionless for long moments as powerful, bittersweet emotions stirred only moments earlier were dispatched by those few words, Jewel took a halting breath. She had suspected something all along, hadn't she? She had known there was someone else, someone Charles secretly visited every few months when he was supposedly out of town on business. She had known because one of her customers had inadvertently informed her . . . and because she had seen the guilt reflected in Charles's eyes each time he returned. But she had denied it and told herself there was an honest explanation, one that she had no right to demand from Charles.

. . . the children and I will come . . .

. . . the children . . .

Fool that she was!

Jewel slammed the desk drawer shut. The gallant Charles who was so kind and loving to his dying wife was the same Charles who professed his love for her while neglecting the woman who had borne his children—children who were his own flesh and blood!

Feeling cheap and used as she had never felt before, Jewel took a deep breath, wiped away her tears, and turned to the door.

The wind was getting stronger. Grasping her hat as an unexpectedly strong gust lifted it from her head, Honesty looked up at the sky. A bank of dark clouds was rapidly closing in overhead, clouds that were heavily laden.

How long had she been riding?

Truly uncertain, Honesty looked at the landscape around her, recalling that she had set Ginger to a gallop for what seemed an endless time as soon as she reached open country. The young mare had seemed to enjoy the run as much as she, and there had been little time to think with the world rushing past her in a blur. It was only when she had drawn back on the reins in order to allow her laboring mount respite that unwanted thoughts had again begun parading across her mind.

Forbidding them access, she had again spurred her mount into a gallop, finally slowing her pace when neither her mount nor she could maintain it any longer.

The solitude surrounding her had been the perfect spot to indulge distant recollections that soothed her troubled spirits, and she had allowed them full rein.

Those recollections again returning, Honesty smiled. The gleaming color of the sorrel on which she had been mounted when she shared the saddle with Purity that day so long ago was vividly clear in memory. She recalled that she had been desperate to experience the thrill of flying across the flat Texas plains as she had seen her father ride so many times, and she had deliberately disobeyed her mother by kicking their mount into a full gallop. She remembered the warm wind in her face and the pale strands of Purity's hair flying wildly as her sister's screeches of delight echoed her own. She recalled that she had never felt so free, and that she had never felt closer to Purity than at that moment when her sister and she shared the excitement of their wild ride.

And she remembered Papa's anger when he caught up with them and brought them back to face the punishment awaiting them. Her backside had throbbed for hours—but it had all been worth it. Purity and she had secretly relived that moment over and again in the weeks that followed, while poor Chastity, too young to have been included, had listened with wistful yearning. She remembered promising Chastity that she would take her on their next ride—as soon as they reached their new home and Mama and Papa weren't so worried all the time. The glow in Chastity's eyes had assured her that her baby sister would not forget that promise.

But their time together had proved too short for her to keep it.

Nor had she kept the promise she had made to her father . . . the father whose reprimand on the day of their wild ride had been laced with silent pride at his daughter's daring.

She had refused to surrender her love of riding, despite Jewel's protests when she was younger. Tolerant drovers had indulged her, going so far as to allow "Jewel's wild little girl" to ride their horses while they amused themselves with all that Abilene had to offer. None were aware of the hours she spent stubbornly searching the empty countryside for her sisters, calling out their names as she rode until she was so hoarse she couldn't speak. Years passed, and she stopped calling. But she never stopped looking.

But as stubborn and wild as she had been as a child, she had never abused either the horses or the drovers' kindness. She had had a soft spot for soft-hearted, fun-hungry cattle drovers ever since.

Strangely, she had never owned a horse of her own until Charles presented her with Ginger. She considered the gift proof of Charles's innate sensitivity to her feelings.

Dark eyes unexpectedly intruded into her thoughts, but Honesty pushed them aside. She needed time before she could again face them and the torment they raised.

The rumble of thunder sounded.

How long *had* she been riding? One hour? Two? Judging from the growling of her stomach and the position of the sun when it had last been visible, she had ridden out farther than was wise.

That thought prompted a fleeting smile. Honesty Buchanan had been accused of many things over the years, but no one had ever accused her of being *wise*.

A vicious blast of wind and Ginger's frightened whinny raised Honesty's gaze to the sudden swirling of clouds overhead as a peculiar darkness began closing around her. Jumping as an unexpected crack of lightning lit the sky, Honesty tightened her grip on the reins. The deafening boom of thunder that followed shook the ground and set Ginger to prancing nervously.

"That's all right, girl." Honesty patted Ginger's neck, noting that the animal's eyes were bulging with fright as she attempted to turn her back in the direction of town.

Ginger whinnied again as the first drops of rain fell. The simultaneous crack of lightning and deafening roll of thunder that followed as the sky opened up with a sudden, torrential downpour was more than the terrified mare could bear.

Honesty was almost unseated as the animal suddenly reared, and she struggled to retain her composure. The huge pellets of rain pounded like miniature hammers against her skin, rain that was colder than any she had ever experienced. Drenched to the skin in a moment, but refusing to admit she was fast losing the battle, she fought to draw the panicked mare under control. She would not be thrown! She was too good a rider. She was too proud. And she would not return to town in a condition that allowed anyone to say I told you so!

Ginger reared again, and Honesty gasped aloud as her grip began slipping on the water-soaked reins. She was a second from panic when another rider appeared suddenly beside her in the deluge. His strong hand closed tightly over hers, allowing her to regain her grip as he held the animal under tight control.

Not Wes Howell, damn it! She didn't want his help!

"Let go!" Honesty shouted over the roar of the rain. "I can handle her."

Wes's hand remained fixed on the reins. "Don't be a fool!"

"I said, let go!"

Thrusting off his hand, Honesty jerked back on the reins and turned her mare just as lightning again split the sky and a deafening roar of sound exploded above them. Ginger reared again. In a second of fragmented reality, Honesty realized that all of Ginger's hooves were off the ground as the animal suddenly whirled in a dizzying gyration that jerked the reins from her hands and sent her flying into the air.

The resounding crack as she hit the muddy earth reverberated in Honesty's ears in the few seconds before the world went dark.

Fear unlike any Wes had ever known shot through his veins as he knelt beside Honesty on the soggy ground. Hardly able to see through the unrelenting deluge, he touched Honesty's cheek. She was breathing, but he knew it was useless to speak to her. She was unconscious.

Resisting the panic rapidly invading his mind, Wes blocked out the battering furor of the storm, forcing himself to be calm as he examined Honesty with trembling hands. Finding the long length of Honesty's legs undamaged, he moved systematically to her arms, her shoulders, her delicate collar bone, her neck. All seemed well except for the ugly bump he felt on the back of her head.

"Honesty . . . can you hear me?"

Wes stroked a wet strand of hair from Honesty's cheek.

No response.

Wes took a shuddering breath. He was wasting valuable time. He needed to find help . . . shelter.

Wes glanced around him, frustration soaring. Damn her! Why did she choose today to ride out into this godforsaken desolation? There wasn't a house, a shack, anything that could provide them even temporary protection from the storm!

The rain was growing more frigid, its pounding force more painful, and Wes realized with growing dismay that the rain had turned to hail. Large, damaging balls of ice were striking Honesty's limp, unshielded form.

No, damn it! No!

On his feet in a moment, Wes turned to the gelding

that had remained at his side despite the furor enveloping them. Stripping off the pack strapped to his saddle, he shook out the large oilskin sheet that had served him well many times on the trail. He wrapped it loosely around himself, then leaned down to scoop Honesty up into his arms.

She was cold . . . too cold.

Honesty's fragile weight was no test for his strength as Wes strained to penetrate the icy deluge with his gaze. Hope surged as he spotted a boulder in the distance. He raced toward it. Breathing heavily when he arrived, he pressed his back against the flattest part of the stone, grateful for the slight overhang as he slid slowly to the ground with Honesty still in his arms. Adjusting Honesty between his thighs, he propped her back against his chest, allowing her head to rest against his throat as he reached down to raise her knees against her chest and clamp his legs against hers to hold them securely there. His breath coming in gulping gasps, he held Honesty steady as he pulled the oilskin up and over them both, wrapping them in its folds to effectively seal them in against the storm.

Limp, Honesty did not move as Wes curled his arms more tightly around her. Her breathing was shallow. Her warm breath against his neck was his only reassurance as he drew her closer. The heavy hammering of hail gradually returned to pounding rain as he rested his lips against Honesty's wet brow, cursing himself for waiting so long before riding out after her. His own shuddering gradually lessened as the heat in their moist cocoon increased. Before long he felt the slow warming of Honesty's skin, skin with the sweet fragrance that had haunted him.

Wes closed his eyes as sudden realization touched his mind. This was the way it was meant to be—

Honesty and him together. However poor the timing and circumstance, she was the woman who was made for his arms. He had somehow known that from the beginning, hadn't he?

"Honesty . . ." Wes whispered against Honesty's rain-soaked hair. "Open your eyes. You're cold and you're wet, but you're safe with me, now. Open your eyes . . . please, darlin'."

Honesty shivered. She groaned. She ached, but the pleasant warmth enclosing her was comforting. She felt a gentle pressure against her throbbing head—like the touch of butterfly wings. She heard someone speak, words she could not quite comprehend because of the strange buzzing in her ears. She opened her eyes, but it was dark.

Panic suddenly invading her mind, Honesty attempted to move, only to feel the pleasant warmth close more tightly around her.

"Honesty . . . don't be afraid, darlin'. It's all right. Don't try to move."

Wes.

"How do you feel?"

Honesty attempted to clear her vision. She realized that she was lying with her back against the wall of Wes's chest, shielded against the furor of the elements that still raged outside their strange haven.

"It's all right. You were thrown. You hit your head."

Honesty struggled to identify the strange shell wrapped around them.

"This oilskin's the best I could do, darlin'. It'll keep the rain off us for a while."

Her mind still unclear, Honesty stared up at Wes. She was wet and cold, her head hurt and her thinking was fuzzy, but she knew one thing for sure. She liked having Wes's arms wrapped around her. She liked being closed in with him against the storm. But she was tired. Her eyes drooped closed.

"No, don't sleep." Wes shook her lightly, his eyes darkening with concern. "You hit your head hard. It isn't good to sleep."

"I'm tired."

"No, you're not."

"D . . . don't tell me I'm not tired." Honesty's words emerged weakly. "I want to sleep."

"No, Honesty . . . please don't."

He had said *please.*

Honesty felt the smile that somehow did not reach her lips. "My lips are cold. I . . . it's hard to talk."

Wes searched Honesty's face for long moments, then whispered, "Let me warm them for you, darlin'."

Lowering his mouth to hers, Wes kissed her lightly, then drew back. She heard the groan that sounded low in his throat the moment before he kissed her again. His second kiss lingered as Honesty separated her lips under his, allowing him to drink deeply from her mouth. She felt his reluctance when he tore his lips from hers. She shared it, wondering if the trembling that had beset them both was due to the misery of the storm or to the growing heat within their makeshift shelter. She raised her hand to stroke his cheek, remembering that she had touched it once before in such a way before Wes had turned his back on her and walked away. She was about to draw back when Wes slid her hand to his mouth to press his lips to her palm.

She heard the longing in Wes's voice when he whispered, "I wish—" He halted, then questioned hoarsely, "How does your head feel, darlin'?"

"It hurts."

"Are you feelin' sick to your stomach?"

"No. I'm tired."

"You can't sleep, not yet. Talk to me, darlin', so you'll stay awake."

"I can't."

"Talk to me, Honesty."

"I don't want to."

"Tell me about yourself."

Honesty closed her eyes, only to have Wes insistently urge them open. She felt so strange. Her thoughts were unclear, but the rest of her felt so right in Wes's arms.

"Honesty." The note of alarm in Wes's voice caught Honesty's attention. "Please, darlin'."

Please.

Honesty took a breath. He wanted her to talk . . . to tell him about herself.

Honesty's voice emerged in a broken croak she hardly recognized as her own. "All right. I . . . I'll tell you about Honesty, Purity, and Chastity."

Honesty felt Wes stiffen. She saw the alarm that registered in his eyes, and she would've laughed if she could. "My sisters and me." Her trembling fingers moved with unconscious will toward the locket at her throat. Her voice gained strength. "My sisters are waiting for me to find them. Papa said that when we grew up, we'd be three dangerous virtues. Mama said he was wrong."

"Tell me about your sisters, Honesty. Start from the beginnin'."

Honesty struggled against the heavy weight of her eyelids. It occurred to her that the rain was still pounding as she began slowly. "We came from Texas, you know . . ."

Feeling strangely comforted as Wes drew her

closer, as he rested his lips against her cheek, Honesty continued.

"Where in hell is she?"

Jewel looked out the window of her room, her jaw tight. The rain continued battering the muddied ruts in the street beyond. It was mid-afternoon. It had been raining for hours, and Honesty had not been seen since morning. Jewel supposed she should not be concerned. Honesty was a grown woman and her time was her own, but she had a feeling something was wrong.

Jewel turned back to face Sam's grizzled countenance. "You're tellin' me that you looked all over town for her?"

"I looked ever'where."

"You looked in Jeremy's cabin?"

"I told you, I looked *ever'where!*"

Jewel struggled to retain her composure. She had had a difficult day since she had walked into Charles's office that morning and left a different woman minutes later. She had not stopped at Honesty's door on her return. She had had no intention of telling Honesty about the letters she had found. She supposed she never would. She could not account, however, for the strange uneasiness that had driven her to Honesty's door a short time later, or the anxiety with which she had continued to wait for Honesty's return as the hours slipped past. Sam's appearance at her door and his inquiry as to Honesty's whereabouts had somehow brought her apprehension to the surface.

"Did you talk to Jeremy?"

"Bud said Jeremy headed out of town when he was done workin', just before the storm broke. You know

Jeremy. There's no tellin' where he went or when he's comin' back."

"He was alone?"

"Damn it, woman! Don't you think that's the first question I asked Bud? I ain't no fool, you know!"

"Don't you yell at me!"

"I'll yell all I damned well please! This is still a free country, you know! And don't you go gettin' my dander up when I'm needin' all my concentratin'."

Jewel took a stabilizing breath. As much as she hated to admit it, she wasn't helping matters. Her state of mind had not been conducive to rational thought since it had occurred to her that the second of the two people closest to her in the world might have also slipped suddenly beyond her reach.

Jewel had a thought. "Did you check the livery stable?"

"I did. Hiram Winters wasn't no place around."

"What about Honesty's horse?"

"The mare wasn't there."

"She wasn't?"

"But that don't mean nothin'. Hiram's been rentin' that animal out without Honesty's knowin'. I know, 'cause I already called him down about it. He promised he wouldn't do it no more, but that old fella's a snake, you know."

"Still—"

"Give Honesty more credit than that, will you? She wouldn't go ridin' out with this kind of storm brewin'! And even if she did, she'd head back when she saw them clouds comin' in."

"You give Honesty too much credit sometimes."

"And you don't give her enough!"

"I don't want to argue with you, Sam."

"You don't? Funny, it sure seems to me like you do!"

"All right, Sam. You win. Now you tell me where Honesty is."

"I'll tell you one thing." Sam paused, his small eyes narrowing. "I'll tell you that maybe it ain't any business of ours where she is."

Sam's expression stopped the rapid progression of Jewel's thoughts. "What are you tryin' to say?"

Sam shrugged. "I'm sayin' just what I said! Maybe it ain't no business of ours where she is. Maybe she's taken herself off someplace for some privacy."

Jewel stiffened. "Spit it out, Sam!"

Surprising her, Sam flushed a hot red. "That Wes Howell ain't nowhere around neither."

Sam's response left Jewel momentarily without response. Not *that* man. Honesty knew he was trouble.

"You're right!" Sam's ability to read her mind was uncanny. "That fella's trouble. The only thing is, Honesty ain't backed away from trouble not once in her whole life!"

Sam turned toward the door, putting an abrupt end to their conversation as he snapped over his shoulder, "I'm goin'. I'll talk to you later."

Jewel's response died on her lips as Sam pulled the door open and she caught sight of Charles standing in the hallway. Uncertain if she had indeed invited him in, Jewel watched as Charles entered the room and closed the door behind him. Charles . . . handsome as ever, his brown eyes sincere as he surveyed the tension on her face.

"Is something wrong, Jewel?"

Jewel did not immediately respond. Instead, she drew herself up to her full, impressive height, secure in the brilliant gold satin dress she wore, which bore no resemblance to the pale garment she had worn earlier and which now lay discarded on her wardrobe floor. She stared coldly into Charles' sincere gaze.

"Jewel?"

"I visited you earlier in the day."

"I know. I thought you'd come back. I came by as soon as I could. Did you want something?"

"I spilled the ink on your desk."

"I hope you weren't concerned about that. I cleaned it up." Charles smiled and walked closer.

"I opened your desk drawer to find somethin' to mop it up, and I read your letter."

"Oh." Charles had the grace to look disturbed. "I'm sorry, Jewel, but you know that Emily—"

"Who's Mary?"

Charles blanched.

"You bastard."

"Jewel, please try to understand."

"Understand? I want to understand, Charles, so tell me, who is Mary? And the children . . ."

No response.

"I'll ask you again, Charles. Who's Mary?"

Charles's voice was a soft plea. "You know I love you, Jewel."

"Who's Mary?"

"Jewel . . ."

"Get out."

"But—"

"Get out!"

Charles was so still that it seemed he had turned to stone. "I love you, Jewel."

Bastard . . . bastard . . .

The word echoed in Jewel's mind as the sound of Charles's retreating footsteps faded.

* * *

Jeremy shook off his oilskins and slammed the cabin door, shutting out the rain behind him. The water ran in rivulets from the broad brim of his hat, and he was soaked to the skin despite the protective clothing he had worn as he rode through the storm. But the whole miserable trip was worth it just to see Bitters' anticipation as his swarthy face grew florid and he grated, "Well, what's the news?"

"Monday. The first shipment's comin' in Monday mornin' on the six-thirty train."

Bitters shot Riggs a glance and Jeremy felt triumph surge. Riggs had no doubt been trying to talk him down, trying to say he'd never come through with the information he had promised. Well, he had shown that pouchy-faced lizard how wrong he was!

Jeremy continued, "Eight men are goin' to be guardin' the money all the way until it reaches the Caldwell Bank. Then Howell's goin' to take over."

"That's no news!" Riggs interjected with a scowl. "And we ain't interested in the first shipment, anyway."

Jeremy stripped off his oilskins. He looked up with true pleasure to add, "And if everythin' goes right with the first shipment, the second shipment's goin' to follow a week later—same time, same set-up."

"Hell, that can't be right! It's too easy!"

"Easy?" Bitters turned toward Riggs with a snarl. "Eight men guardin' that damned money's goin' to be easy?"

"We ain't goin' after it while it's on the train, anyway. You said so yourself!" Riggs did not back down. "And Howell ain't goin' to hire no eight men to guard that money day and night."

"How in hell do you know?"

"*I* know." Jeremy wiped the rain from his face and pushed back his rain-soaked hair as all heads snapped in his direction. He was chilled to the bone, but his physical discomfort was the farthest thing from his mind as he continued casually, "Howell already had Deputy Brown talk to six men who're goin' to work with him."

"Six . . ."

"Do you want their names?"

"I don't give a damn what their names are! How's Howell goin' to set everythin' up?"

"Round-the-clock protection, I hear."

Bitters nodded as Jeremy walked toward him. "Has he set up anythin' yet?"

"Not yet, as far as I can tell, but it won't be a problem findin' out once he does."

Bitters nodded again. His thick lips stretched into a smile. "You done good, Sills. It's good to know you're a fella we can count on."

Riggs made a scoffing sound that snapped Bitters back toward him. "You got somethin' to say? If you do, spit it out!"

Riggs did not respond, and Jeremy's satisfaction soared. He glanced at Gant where the fellow remained silent near the fireplace. Gant's expression was blank, and the thought struck him that he had left the fella speechless. Hell, things couldn't be much better than that!

Rubbing his cramped hands in an attempt to restore their circulation after his long ride, Jeremy looked at the pot that was bubbling on the fire and the coffee pot hanging beside it. "I'm kinda hungry. Think that pot there'll stretch to feed four?"

Bitters's smile returned. "Help yourself. You earned it."

Jeremy approached the fire, plate in hand. He helped himself liberally and turned back to the table. He dug into the stew with relish, knowing Riggs was seething and Bitters was looking at him in a way he never had before.

Jeremy watched as Bitters picked up a bottle on the mantle. He saw Bitters' smile gain a new quality as he offered, "You look cold. How about a drink to warm you up?"

Jeremy's hand froze midway to his mouth. The amber liquid drew his eye. He *was* cold. A drink would warm him up fine . . . faster than the food he was eating, that was for sure. His mouth watered in a familiar way.

Jeremy swallowed, then returned with as casual a manner as he was able, "No. I'm not in the mood. Anyway, I want to start back in a little while, before anybody gets to wonderin' where I went."

Bitters was obviously surprised at his response. Jeremy dug into the stew with his spoon, suddenly realizing that he was, too.

Yeah, things couldn't be much better . . . not at this stage of the game.

Jeremy's thoughts grew actually rosy. Just two more weeks . . . no longer. He'd be his own man then, and at last he'd have the right to tell Honesty he loved her.

Two more weeks . . .

Sam crossed the virtually deserted street, realizing that it would normally be filled with noisy cowpokes gearing up for a night on the town were it not for the relentless downpour. He cursed the rain that battered the wilting brim of his hat and the mud that sucked at his boots as he trudged determinedly toward the livery stable. He didn't bother to try to escape the rain. What was the use? He couldn't get much wetter than he was.

Sam's scowl deepened. The truth was that his conversation with Jewel a few minutes earlier had upset him more than he had let on, because he was more worried than he had let on. It wasn't like Honesty to disappear for any length of time without letting somebody know where she was heading. Hell, even if she was always in silent battle with Jewel, she knew how *he* felt about her, that he was always looking out for her. She wouldn't take off with Wes Howell without letting somebody know.

Would she?

As for Howell, there was no way of knowing which way that fellow was going to jump . . . even if the look in his eye when he watched Honesty said it all.

Stomping up onto the boardwalk and under the protection of the overhang extending out from the general store, Sam paused to scan the street again.

"Hello, Sam." Sam turned toward the high-pitched tones of Willard Grimes, grimacing. It never ceased to amaze him that a man as big and round as an elephant could have a voice that squeaked like a mouse. And damned if that voice didn't hurt his ears as the storekeeper continued, "Looks like you finally got enough sense to get in out of the rain."

Sam did not judge the comment worthy of response. He turned toward the livery stable as Grimes spoke again, more softly than before. "You were askin' about Honesty Buchanan earlier, askin' if I saw her today."

Sam turned back, squinting at Grimes's sweaty face. "Yeah. You said you didn't."

"Well, my wife was standin' right next to me."

"So what're you sayin'? You did see her?"

"Sure did."

"When?"

"This mornin', real early. She was walkin' down

the street toward the other end of town . . . and a sight it was to see, too."

"Meanin'?"

"Honesty was wearin' those pants she wears when she goes out ridin'—you know, those tight ones."

Honesty was wearing her riding clothes. Sam's temper flared. "Damned fool! Why didn't you tell me that before?"

"I told you why. My wife was standin' right by me!"

"You overgrown barrel of blubber!" Sam's knobby hands balled into fists. "I got half a mind to teach you a lesson and go right inside now to tell that wife of yours—"

"You wouldn't do that, would you, Sam?" Grimes's sweaty face began to glisten. "After I did you a favor, and all?"

"Yeah . . ."

In the livery stable minutes later, Sam pinned Hiram Winters with a beady eye. "You say she rode out this mornin'?"

"She ain't back yet, huh?" Winters shook his head. "I suppose she got caught in the storm. It was right sunny when she started. Wasn't nobody expectin' things to turn like they did, not even me." He shrugged. "Wasn't nobody fool enough to start out of this stable after them clouds started rollin' in, neither, except for that Howell fella. You'd think he'd have better sense, but he came barrelin' in here when that sky started lookin' nasty, and he took off pushin' his horse to the limit."

"Howell."

"Yeah."

"Where'd you put my horse?"

"In the back stall." Winters was incredulous. "You ain't goin' out in this? This rain ain't goin' to let up for hours!"

Sam strode toward the rear stall.

"You're too old to go ridin' out in this kind of weather!"

Sam grabbed his saddle.

Wes awoke slowly. He was stiff and cramped, and the air was hot and sticky. He attempted to move when the warm weight lying in his arms brought him abruptly to full realization. Damn it all, he had fallen asleep!

The brush of Honesty's breath against his throat allowed Wes a moment's respite from his panic as he drew back to study her more clearly. She was sleeping. Her face was motionless, the long length of her lashes dark against smooth cheeks that were unnaturally pale. Her hair curled in damp tendrils at her temples, framing the exquisite sculpting of small features that seemed too perfect to be real. She frowned in her sleep, and her lips parted with a soft groan. Her eyes flickered slowly open.

"You fell asleep." Wes held Honesty's disoriented gaze. "So did I. How are you feelin'?"

"M . . . my head hurts."

Honesty was looking at him strangely. He adjusted her position against him. "Do you remember, darlin'? Your horse threw you. You hit your head."

"And we couldn't get out of the rain."

"Right."

Honesty's eyes flickered closed again, and Wes allowed her the moments she needed to draw her confused thoughts together, silently admitting that he needed those moments as well. At his urging, Honesty had talked in an almost automatic monologue until they fell asleep, revealing a part of herself that he was sure was known to few others.

Lowering his head, Wes brushed Honesty's lips

lightly with his—a kiss for the child who had lost everyone she loved at so young an age, and who stubbornly refused to accept her sisters' deaths. He kissed her lips again, this time more warmly, for the woman that little girl had grown to be, who stubbornly maintained her belief that her sisters were somewhere out there, waiting for her to reunite them again.

It had occurred to him, as Honesty's halting words continued, that her quest was not unlike his own. She responded with silent determination to a tragedy that was long past, a tragedy that haunted her, one that she was unable to abandon and that she needed to bring to a satisfactory conclusion, at least in her mind.

It had not escaped his notice, however, that Honesty had told him little about the life she now led, about her friends . . . or about those who were *more* than friends. The idea occurred to him that Honesty had not thought it to be his concern.

She was wrong.

Forcing that thought aside in favor of the more pressing situation at hand, Wes was suddenly aware that the relentless rain appeared to have stopped. Strangely reluctant to end their intimate interlude, he separated the oilskin shielding them, noting as he did that the sky directly above them was clearing, although the sun was still concealed behind the remaining clouds. A temporary break in a storm that would soon continue? He could not be sure.

Intensely aware that Honesty had resumed her shuddering the moment she was exposed to the brisk breeze, Wes looked around him. He was relieved to see his gelding had not strayed far from the spot where he had dismounted. Closer scrutiny of the countryside revealed that Honesty's mare was nowhere to be seen.

His choice suddenly made, Wes urged gently, "Open your eyes, Honesty." Anxiety surged as Honesty responded with a weak flutter of her eyelids. "We're goin' to have to start back before the weather turns again. Do you think you can stand?"

Honesty opened her eyes. "I can stand."

Wes's jaw clamped tight as Honesty made an attempt to pull herself to a seated position. He saw her frustration as the effort failed, and his concern deepened.

Slipping himself out from behind her, Wes allowed her to lean back against the boulder that had supported them through the storm. He instructed, "Wait here, darlin'. I'll be back in a minute."

Covering the soggy distance in long strides, Wes stood beside his horse minutes later. He grasped the reins with a few soothing words for the sturdy animal and turned back toward Honesty, his breath catching in his throat when he saw her standing in the spot where he had left her. She was swaying, her balance so tenuous that his heart all but stopped for the few moments until he reached her side and slipped a supportive arm around her.

Anxiety forced an unintended harshness to Wes's voice.

"I told you to wait! You shouldn't have stood up, damn it! You could have fallen and hurt yourself!"

"I told you, I can stand."

Honesty met his anger with a steady stare. But she was trembling, from weakness or cold, he could not be sure. That uncertainty tempered his response as he scooped her up into his arms and stated flatly, "I don't have time to argue."

Lifting her up onto his saddle, Wes mounted behind her and wrapped his arms around her. He drew her back against him, intensely aware of the inadequacy of the protection he afforded her from the chill following the storm. He dug his heels into his mount's sides and started off.

They had not ridden far when Honesty spoke unexpectedly.

"I'm cold."

"I know."

Honesty burrowed back tighter against him as her shuddering increased. Swept with a devastating feeling of helplessness, Wes curled his arms more tightly around her.

Her words broken by the uncontrollable chattering of her teeth, Honesty whispered, "Talk to me, Wes. Tell me about yourself."

Yes, he would. He wanted to.

A hint of a smile touched Wes's lips as he started, "I come from Texas, you know . . ."

Damned if his old bones didn't ache . . .

Sam squinted up at the sky and snorted. There wasn't any way of telling for sure, but it looked as if the rain had stopped for a while. And it was about time! He didn't think he'd ever been as cold and uncomfortable as he had been since he rode out of Hiram Winters' livery stable with that old goat's warning echoing in his ears and the wind blowing ice-cold rain in his face.

. . . *You're too old to go ridin' out in this kind of weather* . . .

Damned right he was! But what Hiram Winters didn't know was that it didn't make no nevermind to him how hard it was raining or how wet he would get when Honesty's safety was threatened. Because the truth was that if Honesty was still out there for some reason, she was as cold and as wet as he was, and that was a thought he couldn't abide.

As for that Wes Howell riding out at full gallop . . . well, it might be coincidence. But if it wasn't . . .

Sam swore and reached down to adjust the gun in his holster. He might be old, but his hand was steady, his aim was still true, and he had no hesitation about using his gun if the situation demanded.

Movement in the distance caught Sam's eye, interrupting his thoughts. He squinted against the glare, holding his breath as a rider appeared on the horizon. It was a man . . . a big man, riding toward him at a steady pace. But there was something strange about the way he was riding, almost as if—

Sam's short intake of breath at the moment of realization preceded his savage kick to his mount's sides and his sudden spurt forward at a gallop.

The silence of his empty room reverberated with the sound of his own breathing as Charles stood looking down at the wrinkled sheet on his desk. He glanced up at the window, suddenly aware that it was not yet dark, although the day had seemed incredibly long.

So much had happened.

He had openly challenged Wes Howell, a mistake he would have believed himself incapable of making only a week earlier, considering the consequences that he might reap.

And, incredibly, he had allowed the unceremonious termination of the relationship that had brought love back into his life when he believed the mistakes of the past had removed it forever beyond his reach.

The letter lying on the desk in front of him seemed to glow with an energy all its own as Charles looked back down at the carelessly scrawled words.

Mary.

He had erred in becoming involved with her. And he had paid for his error in the most costly of ways.

The image of Jewel's stiff expression returned, tightening the knot in his throat. He had hurt her. Jewel deserved better. He wished with all his heart that he could be the man for her.

But there was Mary.

The chestnut gelding pounded down the muddy trail toward them as Wes held his mount to its steady pace. Honesty was sleeping. In response to her request, he had maintained a monologue not unlike Honesty's a few hours earlier, in which he had told her about his youth in Texas. He had known as she slowly slipped into an uneasy sleep, however, that it had not been the soft tone of his voice that lulled her. Her body had gotten hotter with every mile they traveled as he remained helpless to combat her rising temperature.

Unable to identify the rider fast approaching, Wes slipped his hand to the gun at his hip, loosening it in its holster. His jaw tightened as he recognized the old man who was riding toward them at breakneck speed.

Sam Potts's horse drew to a laboring halt beside them. The old man looked at Honesty, his face reddening as he demanded, "What did you do to her?"

"Don't waste my time with stupid questions, old man!" Wes's face flushed angrily as well. "Do you have a blanket—anythin' that's dry to wrap around her?"

Allowing his piercing gaze to linger a moment longer, Sam reached behind him toward the roll on his saddle. Wes accepted the oilskin-wrapped blanket Sam handed him and draped it around Honesty, tucking it across her shoulders and around her legs where they rested against his. She did not stir, raising his uneasiness a notch as he turned back to Sam's intense perusal.

"Her horse threw her. She hit her head. She needs a doctor."

Sam's scrutiny intensified. "Honesty's mare's as gentle as a kitten—and Honesty's too good a rider to get thrown."

"She may be a good rider, but her horse threw her." Wes's patience was waning. "She needs a doctor, and that's where I'm takin' her, so get out of my way."

"Hand her over to me. I'll take her."

"No."

Sam's knobby hand moved toward his gun. "I said, hand her over to me."

Honesty groaned. Her body twitched, then stirred. He felt her moment of recognition as she rasped, "Sam . . . what are you doing here?"

The old man's face softened almost comically as Honesty spoke, but Wes felt no inclination to smile as Sam responded, "I came out to find you, little darlin'. This fella here says you got throwed."

"The lightning scared Ginger. She bucked." Honesty raised a shaky hand to her head, then looked up at Wes. Her eyes were bright with fever as she rasped, "Are we almost home, Wes? I'm so tired."

"It's just a little way farther." Wes stroked her arm. "Sam was worried about you. He brought you a blanket."

Wes felt her effort at a smile as she turned back to the old man's scrutiny. "I'm all right, Sam. I just want to go home."

Sam swung his horse abruptly. "Let's get goin' then!"

They were moving steadily onward when Honesty shifted her weight. Wes looked down, his gaze meeting the startling blue of her eyes as she whispered, "So, you came from Texas . . ."

"Henry, get the doctor!"

Jewel's face was pale under the color she had so carefully applied. She looked up at the tall Texan who had entered town with Honesty riding in front of him—a weak and limp Honesty who reminded her vividly of the child she had found beside the river those long years ago. Howell's expression was sober, unaffected, but she saw the proprietary manner with which he shunned help, refusing to allow anyone to touch Honesty as he lifted her from his saddle and carried her into the saloon.

Jewel forced a calm she did not feel as Howell reached the second floor and turned toward Honesty's bedroom door without direction, a frowning Sam following close behind. She watched the Texan's face as he reached Honesty's bed and lowered her carefully onto it. She saw the change in those impassive dark eyes as he crouched beside Honesty, speaking words obviously meant for her ears alone.

"What's he sayin' to her?" Sam's grating tone turned Jewel toward him with a frown as he continued, "I don't trust that fella. I don't like the way he's lookin' at Honesty."

"Is that it, Sam? Or maybe the truth is that you don't like the way Honesty's lookin' at Howell? Actually, I don't give a damn how anybody's lookin' at anybody. All I know is that Honesty has to get out of those wet clothes—now." Jewel took a steadying breath, then spoke out authoritatively. "All right! I want everybody out of this room!"

Howell looked up. His gaze whipped her as he

spoke in a voice so cold that it sent a chill crawling up her spine.

"I'm not goin' anywhere."

Jewel's face flamed. She had taken all she could stand for one day, and she'd be damned if she'd take any more!

She snapped, "Well, you're not stayin' here! Honesty has to get those wet clothes off her. If you don't get out, I'll get somebody to throw you out!"

"Wes, please . . ."

Honesty's whisper turned Wes back toward her. Jewel saw their gazes meet. She saw Howell's hard features twitch the moment before he leaned down to whisper something to Honesty. Startled, she saw him brush Honesty's lips with his before he rose and silently headed for the door.

So, that was the way it was.

"I don't like this." Sam's voice grated again in her ear. "Somethin's goin' on."

"That right?" Jewel pinned Sam with her gaze. "Whatever it is, I don't have time to talk about it. Get out, Sam."

Waiting only until the door closed behind the two men, Jewel approached Honesty's bedside, forcing as normal a tone as she could muster.

"So, you got yourself in trouble ridin' out when you shouldn't. I can't say I'm surprised." She paused. "The doctor's on his way. Can you sit up? I'll help you get those damp clothes off."

"I can sit up." Jewel saw the effort Honesty expended as she added, "And I can undress myself."

"No, you can't."

"Yes, I can."

Honesty attempted to sit up. She was still struggling when Jewel's guard crumbled and she spoke from the heart.

"Let me help you, Honesty. I want to."

Silent for a long moment, Honesty responded, "This *is* a day of surprises."

The ache within Jewel lessened as Honesty took her hand.

Wes stood in the hallway outside Honesty's room as sounds of frivolity from the saloon below grew gradually louder. He unconsciously stretched broad shoulders and tight muscles that were stiff and aching from the ordeal recently past, but his mind was far from his own physical discomfort. The doctor had entered Honesty's room minutes earlier, and Wes had thought of little else since.

"Why don't you take yourself down and get yourself a drink?" Wes turned to Sam as the old man added, "Them clothes of yours are still damp. You could probably use somethin' to warm you up. Just tell them it's on the house. Jewel's real generous with them that does her a favor."

"I didn't do Jewel a favor."

"You helped Honesty, didn't you? You did both Jewel and me a favor takin' care of her like you did."

"I didn't do either of you a favor."

"Meanin'?"

"Let's get somethin' straight, old man."

"My name's Sam."

"Let's get somethin' straight. What happens between Honesty and me is our business, and nobody else's."

"Think so, huh?" Sam's small eyes narrowed into intense slits. "Well, let me tell *you* somethin'. I don't know what happened between Honesty and you out there, but this is fact. There ain't nothin' that affects Honesty that don't affect me as well. And I'll tell you somethin' else, too. I don't like you . . ."

"I don't give a damn what you like."

"I'd say the feelin's mutual, except that you seem to be thinkin' you've got a right to somethin' that ain't yours!"

"I told you before—"

Wes's words came to an abrupt halt as Honesty's door opened unexpectedly and Doc Carter emerged out into the hallway, bag in hand.

"How is she, doc?"

The bearded doctor responded with a shrug to Sam's anxious question. "She's all right. She hit her head pretty hard, and she's goin' to have to take it easy for a day or two."

Wes pressed, "What about the fever?"

"I gave her a powder. It's already goin' down." Doc Carter paused. "Your name's Howell, isn't it? She asked to see you. You may as well go inside now if you want to see her before she falls asleep. But don't excite her. She needs to rest."

Wes nodded. Sam cursed under his breath and turned to accompany the doctor back down the hallway as he pushed open Honesty's door. Annoyed to see Jewel standing like an armed sentry beside the bed as he strode toward it, he stared pointedly in her direction.

Jewel sneered. "All right, I can take a hint."

Wes crouched beside Honesty, assessing her silently as the door closed behind Jewel. Dressed in her nightclothes, Honesty was exceedingly pale, and her eyes were heavy-lidded. The dark length of hair spread across her pillow made a sharp contrast with her white skin and the gleaming blue of eyes she struggled to keep open. The gold locket at her throat winked in the dim light as he moved closer and cupped her cheek with his palm. Contact with the smooth, flawless skin stirred a hunger within him so deep that it shook him to the core as he whispered, "The doctor says you're all right. You'll just have to rest for a few days."

"I . . . I'll be all right tomorrow."

"A few days, Honesty."

Honesty's eyes held his. "I'll be better tomorrow."

Stubborn . . .

"Is Sam outside?"

Wes stiffened.

"Tell him I'm all right."

He didn't want to talk about Sam!

Wes paused in an effort to rein in emotions rapidly slipping out of control. He had made a startling discovery in the last few hours. He was uncertain if Honesty was ready for what he had to say, but his need to voice the words would not be denied as he whispered, "Everythin's changed now—you know that, don't you, darlin'? Everythin' that happened between us before today was all just a game."

"A game?"

"A game we were both playin' without realizin' it at all. But the time for games is over now."

Honesty was silent.

"Things are goin' to be different from the way they were before."

Honesty's eyes flickered closed.

"Honesty . . ."

Honesty did not respond, and Wes's frustration surged. He had waited most of his adult life to say words that now must wait for yet another day. But even unsaid, the thoughts were clear in his mind. He didn't care what had happened before. Honesty belonged to him now, to him alone. She had opened her heart to him in those few hours she had lain in his arms. In doing so, she had allowed him into her life. He would not yield his place there to any man.

That thought lingering, Wes stroked a wisp of hair from Honesty's cheek. He ran his callused fingertips along the edge of her jaw, then followed the same path with his lips until his mouth rested lightly against hers. Intimate, yet chaste, the contact provided him consolation as he held stronger feelings cautiously in check. The locket at her throat glinted again and Wes stroked it lightly. He knew the significance of that locket now. It was Honesty's bond to the sisters she had lost, just as the badge he carried was his bond to the father he had yet to avenge. Looking at Honesty for several moments longer, Wes drew himself to his feet. He glanced at the window. The gray afternoon was rapidly fading into evening. The hours would stretch long and empty until Honesty and he could speak.

A sudden commotion in the hallway, voices raised in anger, drew Wes's attention the moment before the door was thrust open and Jeremy Sills burst inside. Sills's youthful face was white, his expression anxious, but the flash of pure hatred in his eyes when they briefly met his was vividly clear as he strode toward Honesty's bedside.

Catching his arm, Wes whirled the fellow toward him. "Honesty needs rest. She shouldn't be disturbed."

"Says who?" Sills's expression grew vicious. "You?"

Sills attempted to shake off his grip, but Wes's hand tightened. "I'm askin' you to leave . . . now."

"Take your hand off me."

"I'll tell you one more time . . ."

"All right, that's enough!" Insinuating herself between the two men, Jewel hissed, "You're actin' like two dogs fightin' over a bone! Get out, both of you, or I'll be damned if I won't throw you both out myself!"

Sills turned to Jewel, his expression stiff. "I found Ginger wanderin' outside town, and I rode hell-for-leather back in. I'm not leavin' until I talk to Honesty."

"You can't talk to her." Jewel's stubborn jaw rose a notch higher. "The doctor gave her somethin' to make her sleep."

"I don't give a damn what the doctor gave her!"

Wes attempted to stop Jeremy as he turned toward Honesty's bedside, but Jewel thwarted his grip, ordering, "Leave him be! If Honesty was awake, she'd want him here."

Jealousy cut like a knife as Wes spat, "Not anymore, she wouldn't."

Surprising him, Jewel gave a sharp laugh. "You've got a rude awakenin' comin', big fella. Honesty will always have time for Jeremy."

Jewel's words rang in Wes's ears, sending a flush of heat to his face as Jeremy leaned over Honesty, speaking softly. His sudden step toward them was halted by the cold barrel of the gun Jewel pressed to his side as she hissed, "That's far enough! I've used this gun before for less reason than I have right now. You're makin' a mistake if you think I won't use it again if you take one more step!"

Wes looked back at Jewel, his chest heaving, his fists clenched.

Jewel spoke again, her painted face cold. "Get out. Get out of this room and out of this saloon. And don't come back unless Honesty sends for you."

Wes hesitated.

Jewel cocked her gun.

Wes glanced back toward Honesty's bed. His powerful frame twitched as Sills leaned close to Honesty.

Jewel's gun jammed sharply into his side. "One last time . . . *walk* out, or you'll get *carried* out."

His jaw tight, Wes turned abruptly toward the door. Outside in the hallway, he stopped to rein his emotions under control. He couldn't afford the type of scene he had almost allowed to happen inside. He had worked too hard and waited too long for the opportunity that would soon present itself.

Holding that thought foremost in his mind, Wes strode down the steps and across the crowded saloon floor. He did not stop until he emerged into the twilight of the street beyond.

Chapter Six

Honesty tried again, her frustration growing. She had difficulty remembering. She had awakened minutes earlier to the silence of her sunny room with her head aching dully in a way that confused her thoughts. She recalled riding out the previous day, and she remembered being thrown from her horse at the onset of the storm.

And she remembered Wes.

A familiar warmth again surged. Had she really lain for long hours in Wes's arms? Had he really protected her from the storm, holding her close, whispering encouragement against her cheek in a voice that throbbed with emotion as the rain drummed against their oilskin shield? Had he really delivered her back to the safety of her room and left, but not before speaking words so tender that her heart had been hopelessly stirred?

Or had it been a dream?

Honesty raised her hand to her head in an attempt to clear her foggy thoughts. She needed to get up and wash her face so she could think more clearly.

Throwing back the coverlet, Honesty slid her legs over the side of the bed. When her first attempt at standing was a failure, she tried again. Gaining her feet and managing to negotiate the distance to the washstand, she groaned aloud as she glimpsed her reflection in the mirror. She was wearing her old cotton nightdress. Her hair hung in a tangled mass on her shoulders, her face was devoid of color, and dark circles shadowed her eyes, making them appear even larger and bluer. She raised a hand to the back of her head, gasping as she discovered the painful bump there. She attempted to pour water into the washbowl, only to succeed in spilling most of it.

She stood momentarily still, suddenly aware that she was all but incapacitated.

And she was dizzy.

Honesty dipped her hand into the washbowl and patted the cold water on her face. No help. A debilitating darkness gradually encroached, and she took a deep breath. She heard a rapping sound in the distance and attempted to respond, but was uncertain if she did. She was swaying, the floor rapidly rising to meet her, when she was swept suddenly from her feet.

Strong arms, familiar arms, carried her back toward her bed as the light returned to her vision and she looked up into Wes's concerned expression. His arms felt so good around her. She didn't want him to let her go. For that very reason, she spoke sharply as he attempted to place her back on her bed.

"No, I don't want to lie down."

"The doctor said—"

"I don't care."

"You can't stand up. You're too weak."

"I don't want to lie down."

"Damn it, don't fight me, Honesty!"

Honesty's response came without conscious volition. "I don't want to fight you anymore, Wes . . . and I don't want to fight the way you make me feel."

Wes's reaction to her soft reply was immediate. She felt the words ripple through him, lending new heat to the darkness of his eyes, tightening the sharp planes of his face, and tensing the muscular expanse of his chest as he whispered in return, "Don't play with me, darlin'. You're not in condition to handle what might come of it."

"You think so?"

Honesty's response was an honest question that hung on the air between them. She felt more than heard Wes's sigh . . . or was it her own? . . . as he replied, "Yeah, I think so." He paused, his gaze holding hers. "We're goin' to have to talk, Honesty." Wes slid her to her feet, clasping her tightly against the rock-hard wall of his body as he whispered, "We have to set the rules for this game."

Honesty rasped, "I thought you said the game was over."

"So you do remember. I wasn't sure." He searched her face, drawing her closer. "Are you feelin' better now, darlin'?"

Honesty's response tumbled from her lips, truths she was somehow unable to withhold, as she whispered, "My head hurts and I'm dizzy. But I don't want you to go."

"You have to lie down and rest."

"I want you to stay."

Wes demanded softly, "Honesty, look at me and think. You don't know what you're sayin' right now."

"I do."

"No, you don't." Wes's jaw tightened. "But I do. And I know I can't stand here holdin' you the way I am now, with you lookin' up at me that way you are, without doin' somethin' I'll be sorry for later."

"Tell me how you feel about me, Wes."

"Honesty . . ."

Wes's strained reply faded into silence as he looked longingly down at her mouth, his heart pounding against her breast. A strange giddiness assailed her as his hands moved caressingly against her back. She remembered the touch of those hands. She knew what they could do. She whispered, "Show me how you feel."

Cursing, Wes swept her abruptly from her feet and deposited her on the bed. He crouched beside her, a muscle ticking in his cheek as he grated, "It's not goin' to be this way. When I make love to you, darlin', when I *really* make love to you, I want you to be able to love me back with every ounce of strength you have in you. And I want you to be able to remember every minute." He paused to take a ragged breath. "Do you understand?"

"But—"

"No buts, damn it! No buts!"

Standing suddenly, his features tightly drawn, Wes strode toward the door and disappeared into the hallway. From a distance, Honesty heard a sharp rap, the sound of a door opening, and mumbled voices seconds before footsteps returned back down the hallway. Wes entered, followed by Jewel. Jewel—a wrapper tied hastily around her waist and her hair uncombed—stopped a few feet away as Wes continued toward her bed.

Wes crouched again beside her. "Jewel's goin' to stay with you for a while. I'll be back later on to make sure you're all right. And you'd better remember what you said to me just now, because I'm goin' to remind you, darlin'. I'm goin' to make sure you remember every word."

His gaze lingered a moment longer, and then Wes strode from the room and snapped the door closed behind him.

Honesty was still staring after him when Jewel snapped, "What in hell did you do to that fella?"

Honesty closed her eyes. Wes had promised to return. That was all she needed to know.

Jeremy sat unmoving at the edge of his cot, his fist clenched around the thin metal article in his hand. The previous day's rainstorm was past. A bright sun had risen, and the only trace remaining of the deluge that had continued through the long afternoon was the deep, muddy furrows in the street outside his shack. The world appeared so bright, yet everything that had seemed to be going so right was now going wrong.

Jeremy again pondered the events of the previous day. He had impressed Bitters favorably with his report and temporarily silenced Riggs's objections to him. His plans had started falling into place and he had anticipated a near future when he would no longer be Honesty's penniless friend, but the man who would finally have the right to claim her love.

And then he had returned to town to find Ginger wandering on the outskirts, fully saddled with reins dangling.

The rest was a blur in his mind . . . his race to the Texas Jewel to find Honesty injured and unable to talk to him . . . Howell somehow claiming a place at her side. Jewel's explanations had told him little. Enraged, he had been left to wonder how it had all come about.

Finally satisfying himself that Honesty's injuries were not serious, he had returned to his room to find that Honesty had cleaned and put his shack to right, no doubt before she had set out that morning. But it had not been until he awakened and dressed a few minutes earlier that a shaft of sunlight shining through the window had brought to his attention the article placed carefully on the nightstand beside his cot.

Jeremy unclenched his fist to look again at the hairpin in his hand. He knew where Honesty had found it.

Helpless rage suddenly overwhelming him, Jeremy threw the hairpin across the room and covered his face with his hands. Was Honesty angry with him? Would she forgive him? Would she ever be able to love him with confidence now?

As for Howell . . .

His fair skin flushing with a new surge of volatile emotions, Jeremy snapped to his feet and strode toward the bottle on the table nearby. He filled a glass with the amber liquid and raised it to his lips, only to halt abruptly. No. He had made that mistake too many times before.

His jaw set, Jeremy lowered the glass back to the table. It wouldn't be much longer. He needed to maintain his composure. Whatever hold Howell believed he had over Honesty would be cast aside when Jeremy told Honesty that he loved her, and she finally came to realize that they were meant to be together.

With that thought as his only consolation, Jeremy turned toward the door.

* * *

Wes strode onto the boardwalk outside the Texas Jewel and halted abruptly for a steadying breath. His heart was pounding and his control was so tenuous that he was not quite certain that he could make himself take another step. Walking away from Honesty had been the hardest thing he had ever done.

But he didn't want it that way! He didn't want to make love to Honesty when she was fragile and weak, when she was so confused that she could not think clearly!

A figure moved abruptly into sight farther down the street, and Wes's thoughts froze. Sills.

. . . *Honesty will always have time for Jeremy* . . .

No, Jewel was wrong. Honesty would have time for no other man but him.

That thought turned Wes toward the bank, where the day's business had already begun. Charles Webster, another of Honesty's devoted admirers, was doubtless at his desk now. His own purpose in coming to Caldwell was clearly defined. He could not allow anyone or anything to distract him from that purpose—not even Honesty.

The shipments would start soon. It wouldn't be much longer.

"I want to know everythin' you know about Wes Howell."

Sam's grizzled countenance was stiff as he faced Charles in his small office. It occurred to him that Charles was looking poorly, that he'd never seen him looking as bad as he did that morning. He would have told Charles so, but he didn't have the time. He had more important things on his mind.

Instead, Sam pressed, "Well, why are you standin' there lookin' at me like that? I asked you a question."

"What's the matter, Sam? Why are you so agitated?"

"Agitated? Is that what I am?" Sam gave a short laugh. "I thought I was just hot under the collar! And you would be, too, if you saw the attitude that Howell fella's takin' with Honesty."

"What are you talking about? Is something wrong with Honesty?"

"Where in hell have you been?" Sam raised his hairy brows. "You mean to tell me that Jewel didn't tell you nothin' about Honesty bein' thrown from her horse in that storm yesterday and hittin' her head, and Howell bringin' her back to town all shook up?"

Charles avoided his eye. "I didn't know. Is she all right?"

"I suppose. The doc says she just needs to rest—as if Honesty ever listened to anythin' anybody told her she should do."

Charles started toward the door, but Sam grasped his arm, staying him. "There ain't no need to go hot-footin' it over there right now. Jewel's got everythin' under control. You know how she is. If anybody can make Honesty toe the mark, it's her."

Charles did not respond.

"Well?"

Charles returned his stare.

"What do you know about Wes Howell, damn it!"

Charles shook his head. "Nothing that everybody else doesn't know. Except that he's hard to get along with and that he's not making himself any friends in Caldwell."

Sam gave a low snort. "Oh, yes, he is."

"Who's that?"

"Honesty."

Charles paled. "Howell's trouble. I thought she knew better. I told Jewel—"

"Maybe that was your first mistake. You know Honesty don't listen to a word of Jewel's advice."

Charles appeared strangely shaken. "I'll talk to Honesty."

"You're wastin' your breath. Honesty won't listen to you no more than she listens to nobody else. And I wouldn't care, neither, if I didn't have a sneakin' suspicion that there's more to that Howell fella than meets the eye."

"What are you trying to tell me, Sam?"

"What am I tryin' to tell you? I came in here lookin' for information, not tryin' to give it! Oh, hell . . ." Sam turned with a disgusted wave of his knobby hand. "You ain't no help at all. Looks like if I want to find somethin' out, I'm goin' to have to do it myself."

Turning without another word, Sam stomped toward the door. It had barely closed behind him before Charles grabbed his hat and followed.

Purity's pale, unbound hair floated on the warm breeze, and her fine features were sober. She rode her powerfully muscled horse easily, advancing toward Honesty in a rapid, zigzagging pattern across the flat, sun-swept land.

Honesty's heart began pounding. Purity was getting close . . . so close.

Purity reached for the rope on her saddle. She swung it into the air and watched as it looped out, only to fall short of a mark beyond Honesty's range of vision. Purity's frown was sudden and harsh, and Honesty frowned as well as Purity turned her mount in the opposite direction.

No, Purity! Come back!

But Purity did not heed her call. Instead, she rode on, drawing her horse to an abrupt halt only when a familiar figure rode into her path.

Honesty recognized Wes's muscular, broad-shouldered form as he blocked Purity, forcing her to turn around. Purity rode back toward her. She was traveling faster, driving her horse harder. She was suddenly near, so close that Honesty could see the sun-touched color of her sister's cheeks, the firm line of her lips, and the anger in her eyes. The locket at Purity's throat caught the rays of the sun unexpectedly, abruptly obliterating the scene before her eyes, and Honesty gasped aloud with the pain of it.

Purity was gone with the flash of glittering gold—but Honesty's pain remained.

The pain dulled to a familiar ache that was forever with her.

The ache dissolved into useless tears.

So near and yet so far.

Honesty opened her eyes, the devastation of loss renewed. She heard mumbled voices outside her door. The male voice was deep, insistent. The woman's voice was angry. Was it Wes? Had he brought an angry Purity back to her?

Honesty waited . . . breathless.

Lines of strain marked Charles's sober face. "I want to see her, Jewel."

"Honesty's sleepin'. The doctor says that's the best thing for her. She hit her head hard when she fell."

"I know. Sam told me."

Jewel make a small, scoffing sound. "That old man always was better than a newspaper at spreadin' the news."

Charles did not immediately respond. It occurred to him as they stood in the hallway outside Honesty's room that Jewel showed no ill effects from the abrupt ending of their loving arrangement. Dressed in a yellow gown, her makeup artfully applied in the usual manner and her bright hair piled high on her head, she looked little different from the woman who had appealled to him so strongly years ago.

She was all warm color . . . all woman.

But she was no longer *his* woman.

Charles repeated, "I want to see her, Jewel."

Charles saw the flicker of malice in Jewel's eyes the moment before she nodded unexpectedly. "All right. Just a few minutes. After that you'll have to wait until Honesty's up on her feet again, like everybody else."

It occurred to Charles that he shouldn't have expected more.

Charles entered Honesty's room, with Jewel following. He noted Honesty's surprise at seeing him, but her words halted him in his steps as she rasped, "I . . . I thought it was Purity."

Charles sensed rather than felt the startled intake of Jewel's breath that was simultaneous with his own. He approached Honesty and took her hand. His voice sounded strange even to his own ears as it rang in the anxious stillness of the room.

"How are you, dear?"

"I'm all right, Charles. At least I will be when my head stops hurting."

Charles dragged a nearby chair to Honesty's bed and sat beside her. His throat tightened at her fragile appearance as she spoke again.

"Ginger threw me."

"I'm sorry. I thought she was entirely dependable. I wouldn't have bought her for you if I thought—"

"It's not your fault, Charles." Honesty winced, pressing a hand to her temple before continuing, "Don't blame yourself. It's nobody's fault but my own." She took a short breath. "Wes came after me.

He helped me. I couldn't have made it back without him."

"Honesty . . . dear . . ." Charles hesitated, attempting to draw his growing anxiety under control, "I can understand that you'd feel indebted to Wes Howell, but you must try to see this situation clearly. You mustn't let gratitude color your thinking. You mustn't make a hero out of Wes Howell in your mind. He's a lawman. You know his reputation. He lives and breathes for the administering of justice. That's all he really cares about."

Honesty's eyelids were suddenly heavy, her focus uncertain. She was drifting off as she whispered, "You don't understand, Charles. I just saw it all. He's going to help me find Purity."

"Honesty . . ." Consternation flushed Charles's face a hot red. He repeated, "Honesty . . ."

But Honesty's eyes had closed.

Shaken, Charles nervously watched the steady rise and fall of Honesty's chest for long moments. Temporarily reassured, he then stood and turned abruptly toward Jewel.

"Does Doc Carter know she's hallucinating?"

"I'll take care of it."

"Jewel, please . . ."

"I said, I'll take care of it!"

Beside Jewel in a few quick strides, Charles grasped her shoulders. He whispered, "You know how I feel about Honesty. She's like a daughter to me. I'm losing Emily and I've lost you. I can't lose Honesty as well."

Her eyes sudden pools of ice, Jewel responded, "But there's always Mary . . ."

Charles dropped his hands to his sides.

Within minutes he was back out on the street.

* * *

Sam slowed his rapid step as the boardwalk that stretched along Caldwell's main street dwindled to an uneven dirt walk, only to resume again a few yards farther down. He had long since stopped wondering why the walk had been allowed to deteriorate into its present seesaw condition. He supposed it could be because more people rode than walked in Caldwell . . . or because cattle had somehow become more important than people to the town. Or maybe it was because nobody really cared.

Whatever the reason, the slowing of his step allowed him precious moments to think ahead as he left Charles Webster's bank in the distance behind him and neared the marshal's office. He considered the approach he would take in talking to Marshal Carr. His first inclination was to be forthright and honest in his own blunt way, but he reconsidered, deciding on caution. Nobody had to remind him that the marshal was a stubborn, single-minded fellow.

Taking the final step that brought him into the doorway of the marshal's office, Sam saw that the lawman was sitting at his desk, writing. Sam shook his head. That was a fine place for him to be when his should be out making himself visible to those rowdy Holmes drovers who were still in town and aching for trouble.

Marshal Carr looked up and Sam nodded a greeting, managing to keep disapproval out of his voice as he offered, "How's things, marshal?"

Marshal Carr's wiry mustache twitched. "What do you want, Sam?"

"Well, how do you like that? Can't a man even pay a friendly visit without somebody askin' him what he wants?"

"Sure he can. Just the same, what do you want?"

"Well, if that's all you got to say . . ." Sam walked

into the office and closed the door behind him. Marshal Carr stood up, his expression growing wary.

"Hell, what's wrong with you? You ain't got no cause to look at me like that! I ain't never robbed no bank or killed nobody, you know! I'm just a harmless old man who stopped by to pass the time of day!"

"Sure, you're harmless—like an old rattlesnake, and everybody knows an old rattlesnake's bite is just as deadly as a young one's."

Sam's sudden smile was sincere. "You know somethin', marshal. I think I'm flattered." His smile dropping away, Sam added, "Well, since you ain't in the mood for chit-chat, I guess I'll have to come right out with what's on my mind."

"That's fine with me."

"It's that fella Wes Howell."

The marshal's face reddened. Sam was unprepared for the sudden string of cuss words that emerged from the man's lips as he pounded his hand on the desk, then demanded, "Did that fella send you here—is that it?"

Sam shook his head. "No, that man ain't no friend of mine."

"It's a good thing, because if he were, you'd be out of here so fast that your head would spin!"

"I don't like the fella." Sam hesitated. "As a matter of fact, I don't trust him, neither."

"So what's that got to do with me?"

Sam hesitated, then decided on a half truth. "Well, he's been tryin' to get a friend of mine to work with him protectin' that money that's supposed to be comin' into town on the Monday mornin' train."

The marshal stared. "Isn't there anybody in this town who *doesn't* know when that money's due in?"

"Don't think so, marshal."

"Well, that's good!" Marshal Carr's flush deepened.

"Howell's been takin' over the town as it is, with those six fellas he hired to protect the bank and with him goin' up and down the street askin' questions and nosin' around like *he's* the marshal. Let him work for his money! I'm sure as hell not goin' to help him. I got my hands full just with keepin' liquored-up drovers in line!"

"I suppose a man with Howell's reputation can handle it."

"His reputation? I suppose it sounds good to some to hear a man's relentless in trailin' criminals, but that doesn't speak for the man himself. I've looked into things since Howell came to town, and Howell isn't just a dedicated lawman. He's driven, he's vicious, and he's done a lot of killin' that might've been handled in other ways."

"That right?"

"Yeah! And maybe Howell isn't all he's cracked up to be, either. His father was a ranger who died in his arms—shot in the back while he was right beside him. He didn't do so good a job of protectin' his own, did he? As for him bein' so dedicated to the law, talk is that it's not the law Howell's so dedicated to, that he's really just dedicated to trackin' down the gang responsible for his father's death, and that every bank robber he's shot and killed durin' that time is just standin' in for them."

"He didn't find any of them?"

"Talk is that he got all but one, and that the last one's been leadin' him a hard chase."

"That right?" Sam paused at that thought. "You think Howell trailed his father's killer to Caldwell?"

"I didn't say that, and it doesn't make any difference to my mind anyhow! The truth is that Howell's nothin' more right now than a killer with a badge. If he can't find the man he's lookin' for, anybody else'll do till he does!"

"So, you're sayin' Howell's dangerous."

"As dangerous as hell! He's cold as ice and he never looks back when he leaves a dead man behind him. He proved that the day he came to town."

"Doesn't sound like a man who has much time for women."

"Women?" Marshal Carr gave a harsh laugh. "That man has only one use for them."

"You sure do seem to know a lot about Howell."

Marshal Carr slapped the flat of his hand against the desk again. "I made it my business to find out! He's not any more liked by the law officers in the towns he's been through than he is here. And I'm tellin' you now, I'm watchin' him. One false move and he won't get any more leeway than any other killer gets in this town!" Carr paused, then added, "And you can tell him that, too, if you have a mind."

Sam took a slow breath. "I told you, marshal, I ain't no friend of Wes Howell. Everythin' you said just tells me my instincts was right when I met him. Just so I make myself clear, I'm tellin' you now that I may be an old rattlesnake, but I look out for my friends. And you can take that any way you like."

Marshal Carr remained silent as Sam tipped his hat. "I appreciate the information, marshal. I figured I couldn't go to a better source to find out what I wanted to know."

Out on the street again, Sam walked slowly back in the direction he had come.

So, it looked as though he had been right from the beginning. There was more to Wes Howell than met the eye.

* * *

Doc Carter stepped out into the hallway and pulled Honesty's bedroom door closed behind him. Sounds of early evening drifted up from the saloon below as he addressed Jewel with open annoyance.

"Honesty's all right, I tell you! She might talk a little strange for a day or so, but it'll pass. You're acting like an old mother hen!"

"Mother hen!" Jewel felt the blood rush to her face. Damned old fool! Jewel spat, "Are you tryin' to tell me it's normal for a girl to be talkin' to a sister who's been dead for fifteen years!"

"In this case, it is." Doc Carter made a visible effort to retain his patience. "You're forgetting that I've known Honesty for years. I know how she feels about her sisters."

"They're dead."

"She doesn't accept that."

"They're dead anyway."

"She's injured. Her mind is wandering. She's finding consolation where she can. The memory of her sisters provides it."

"They're dead."

"That attitude won't help Honesty, Jewel! Persist and you'll irritate her condition. She shouldn't be excited. Just the reverse is true. Anything that makes her feel calm and peaceful is to be tolerated—*no matter how difficult it is for you to accept right now.* Do you understand?"

Jewel frowned. She didn't like this. She had listened to Honesty's ramblings most of the day, and it went against her grain to let the girl continue without trying to set things straight.

"Jewel . . . do you understand?"

"I understand!"

Jewel glanced back at Honesty's door as sounds of activity in the saloon below grew louder. Making an abrupt decision, she turned toward the staircase with Doc Carter. She had had enough for a while. She needed to get away for a few minutes so she could clear her mind. The day had been endless, with Honesty sleeping fitfully and mumbling incoherently in her sleep. Most disturbing to Jewel was the fact that Honesty had mentioned Wes Howell's name over and again. She didn't like that at all.

Nor could she count the times during the day when Charles had returned to her mind, when she had longed to share her concerns about Honesty with him . . . or when she had just hungered for the warmth of his arms around her. She hated herself for the realization that she felt somehow incomplete without him. She despised that weakness, almost as much as she despised the realization that no matter how Charles had betrayed her, she still loved him.

Jewel's step came to an abrupt halt on the staircase as Wes Howell came into view, striding across the saloon floor below. It occurred to her that she couldn't miss him if she tried. He stood a head above the crowd and walked with an almost deadly focus, those damned eyes looking right through a person with an expression that dared anybody to get in his way. She couldn't be sure what it was about the man that had made her certain from the beginning that Charles was right, that Honesty had made a mistake getting involved with him.

Jewel steeled herself as Howell started up the stairs toward them. His expression betrayed no emotion as he spoke.

"How's Honesty?"

Doc Carter responded in her stead. "She's coming along. She's sleeping off and on."

Jewel added coldly, "If you're thinkin' of goin' up, think again. She shouldn't be disturbed."

"On the contrary." Doc Carter turned toward Jewel with a raised brow. "Honesty's been asking for Mr. Howell. I think it would do her good to see him."

"She hasn't been asking for him. She's been ramblin'. There's a difference."

"Not in my mind, there isn't." Doc Carter addressed Howell directly. "Go up if you like."

"This is my place, Doc!" Hot color rose to Jewel's cheeks. "I do the talkin' here!"

"Honesty's my patient."

"I'm goin' up." His low-voiced statement allowing no further room for discussion, Howell moved past the quarreling pair and continued up the stairs. It occurred to Jewel as she glared after him that it was senseless to argue any further. The look in his eye said there was no way Howell would be stopped this time. And the truth was that whether he was good for her or not, Honesty wanted to see him.

And Honesty usually got what she wanted. That was just the way it was.

Jewel continued down the stairs.

Wes paused in front of Honesty's door, aware that he had spent the entire day trying to avoid thinking of the moments now approaching. Actually, he had employed his time well. He had met with the six men he had hired, and Deputy Brown and he had worked out a schedule of round-the-clock protection for the Caldwell Bank for as long as it would be needed. He had sent a wire confirming his plans to Slater Enterprises and had requested confirmation of the delivery dates. He had also impressed on the gregarious telegrapher, as firmly as the law allowed, the importance of confidentiality.

And all the while, foremost on his mind had been Honesty.

Powerless to resist the thought of her any longer as evening approached, he had followed his heart through the front doors of the Texas Jewel and up the staircase toward Honesty's room, knowing that no one and nothing could keep him from her.

His heart pounding, Wes knocked on the door. He waited impatiently for a response, then pushed the door open when he received none. The room was dimly lit as he approached the bed. Asleep, Honesty turned restlessly toward him, her total vulnerability eliciting an unexpected wave of tenderness that brought Wes to his knees beside her. She was still so pale, so fragile, so *needy*—the reverse of the woman who had approached him so boldly that first night, which now seemed so long ago. Yet, he knew this part of Honesty had not emerged as a result of her injury alone, that it was an equally true part of her that she allowed few people to see. In opening her heart to him, Honesty had struck a chord that still reverberated within him. He needed to protect this Honesty. He needed to cherish this Honesty. He needed to help this Honesty realize her dreams.

And he needed to love her.

Honesty . . . Wes stroked a lustrous strand of her hair. He touched a curling tendril at her hairline. Her pale skin summoned his kiss, and he pressed his mouth against her temple, enjoying its warmth and the throbbing of life pulsing there—knowing with unalterable certainty that Honesty's life pulsed as surely through his veins as through her own.

Because she had become part of him.

That thought lingered, and Wes pressed his lips against her eyelids as they fluttered gently, against her cheek as it twitched with a muttered word, against her sweet lips as they parted with an incoherent phrase. Drawing back from Honesty's mouth,

Wes saw that her eyes were open but were still clouded with confusion, and tenderness surged once more. He whispered, "How are you, darlin'?"

Honesty attempted a smile. "I'm tired."

"I should go so you can rest."

"No."

Honesty raised her mouth again to his, an invitation that Wes could not refuse. He cupped her face with his hands and held her fast under his kiss, experiencing the taste of her . . . the bliss of holding her close . . . the feeling that this was right . . . so right . . .

No, he wouldn't leave. Not this time.

Wes drew back with the sudden realization that he could not make himself leave, even if he tried.

Drawing himself to his feet, Wes took a moment to turn the lock on the door before returning to the bed. Stripping down to his smallclothes so he could hold Honesty as close as he dared, he slipped under the coverlet and took her into his arms. The supreme beauty of the moment was made bittersweet by the determination that he would ask little more than to hold her.

Honesty settled against him. The innate fragrance of Honesty, the velvet texture of her skin, the joy lying just beyond his reach—all were wonders he had tasted only briefly, and all were torments assaulting him. Honesty's hand moved against the bare flesh of his chest as she whispered, "I was waiting for you to come back."

"I'm here now, darlin'. You don't have to worry about anythin' anymore. I'll take care of you."

With those words of commitment, Wes watched as Honesty's eyes gradually drifted closed and she went limp against him.

* * *

Twilight closed over the crowded street behind him as Jeremy pushed open the saloon doors and looked toward Honesty's gaming table. Sykes was seated in her chair, dealing to dour-faced men who would doubtless have been smiling had it been Honesty handling the cards instead. Jeremy's disquiet grew. He had had a frustrating day at the holding pens with one problem after another extending his hours there. The facade of normalcy he was forced to maintain had been oppressive. If he had not known how important it was to keep up appearances until he and Honesty could put Caldwell forever behind them, he would have walked away from the baking sun, endless dust, and bawling cattle and never looked back. But he had stayed, the hours stretching ever longer as the day wore on. Determined, he had even forced himself to take time for another visit to Joe Pierce at the telegraph office at the end of the day, but that hadn't gone well. The usually talkative Joe had been unusually cautious. It had taken him an hour to soften the fellow up to the point where Joe had finally confided that Howell had sent a wire outlining his plans to Slater Enterprises, and that Slater's confirmation of the shipping particulars would soon follow.

Jeremy started toward the staircase to the second floor. He had also taken the time for a few personal matters, which included scrubbing off the dirt of the day and shaving hardly existent blond stubble from his fair skin. He had picked up the freshly laundered shirts that Honesty had dropped off for him and had donned the better one, spending an inordinate amount of time slicking back his hair afterward. The time had seemed endless before he finally made his way down the street to the door of the Texas Jewel, but he had known how important it was for him to impress Honesty favorably this night. He needed to prove to her that he was sober and in control, so she could feel good about him again . . . so she could push the memory of the hairpin she had found in his bed to the back of her mind.

He had already decided that he would explain how that all came about someday, after Honesty was his wife and he had proved his devotion to her. He knew he would never be able to rest without dismissing every last doubt from her mind. For the truth was that he needed Honesty to love him totally, without reservation, the way he loved her.

And she would someday. He knew she would if—

Jeremy's foot was on the first step of the staircase to the second floor when a hand closed over his arm, halting him. He turned toward Jewel as she addressed him soberly.

"I wouldn't go up there now, if I were you."

Jeremy glanced up toward Honesty's door. "Why not?"

"Honesty has company."

Jeremy hesitated, his stomach slowly knotting. "Company?"

"Wes Howell's with her."

Jeremy ripped his arm from Jewel's grasp and turned back to the stairs, only to have Jewel grasp his arm more strongly than before. "Don't be a fool, Jeremy! Howell's there because Honesty wants him to be there."

"No, you're wrong!" Jeremy's heart was pounding, his stomach suddenly sick. "Honesty's confused—you said so yourself! She couldn't even talk straight yesterday when I was with her. She's grateful to Howell because he helped her, that's all." He paused, suddenly angry.

"You don't want me to see her. You never approved

of me. You're just like all the others, thinkin' Honesty's too good for me. Well, maybe you're right and maybe you're not, but what you think doesn't mean a hill of beans to Honesty or me."

"Listen to me, Jeremy!" Jewel glanced around them, obviously relieved to see that their conversation was not attracting undue attention. "Whether you believe it or not, if I had my way, Howell wouldn't be up there with Honesty any more than you would be. But I didn't have any choice. Doc Carter sent him up because Honesty was askin' to see him. If you go up there now, there's going to be trouble, and the excitement might be bad for Honesty."

"You're just makin' excuses!"

"No, I'm not!" Jewel's eyes pinned him with malevolent heat. "You're not goin' up there now, understand? You're goin' to wait until Howell comes back down and is out of the way before you put one foot back on those stairs." Jewel's heavily rouged lips compressed into a hard line as she gritted through her teeth, "Because if you do, I'll see to it that you never walk up those steps again."

Jeremy's mind was racing. Howell with Honesty in her room. He was touching her . . . caressing her.

No!

Jeremy advanced another step, his hand moving to the gun at his hip.

Jewel's low hiss was an angry accusation. "And you think you love her . . ."

Jeremy turned sharply back toward her. "I do love Honesty!"

"I don't believe you! If you loved her like you say you do, you'd think of Honesty's welfare before your own feelings. You'd listen to what the doc said—that if anyone upsets Honesty now, it could be bad for her."

Jeremy took a shuddering breath. He did love Honesty. He had never loved anyone the way he loved her. If something happened to her now . . . because of him . . .

Damn that Howell!

Jeremy shook his arm free of Jewel's grip. He saw hope flash in her eye as she asked, "Are you leavin'?"

He saw the gleam fade with his succinct reply. "No."

Jewel was still standing at the foot of the staircase when Jeremy positioned himself against the bar and reviewed the situation again in his mind. It would do him no good in Honesty's eyes if he burst into her room now. She'd consider it just another example of his lack of control, and he didn't want that. He'd wait. And when Howell left, he'd go up to talk to Honesty. She'd listen to him. She always did. He'd turn it all around again.

That determination strong, Jeremy trained his gaze on the second floor.

Honesty stirred. A heated warmth enclosed her—a powerful warmth, a comforting warmth.

She opened her eyes to a darkness alleviated only by the sputtering flame of her bedroom lamp.

She awoke to the reality that she was lying in Wes's arms.

Sounds of an evening in full play trailed into the room from the floor below as Honesty turned to the sight of Wes sleeping beside her. His face was only inches from hers, his strong features so like the figure in her dreams that she questioned the reality of the moment.

Uncertain, Honesty touched Wes's cheek. It was warm and firm. She inched closer and felt the brush of his breath, satisfying herself that he was not a figment of her wandering mind. She pressed her mouth to his, a sense of wonder growing as Wes's lips moved under hers. A languorous warmth slid over her as Wes drew her closer, as his hands smoothed the curve of her back. She welcomed the fluid heat that moved through her veins as their lips clung, as she slid her hands into his hair, allowing them to wander along his neck and the broad expanse of his shoulders. His skin felt so good under her palms. She had never felt anything like its firm texture or the hunger it stirred.

Gentle kisses deepened . . . tongues met in sensuous play . . . caress followed caress, and the wonder grew . . .

Uncertain when Wes's mouth left hers, Honesty did not protest as he slid back the coverlet and slipped her gown from her shoulders, baring her flesh. She was breathless at the first touch of his lips, incapable of any response but a gasp of spontaneous joy as his mouth closed over her breast. The elation growing, Honesty cupped Wes's head with her palms, holding him tight against her as he laved her warm flesh with his tongue, as he suckled and teased, drawing from the engorged crests with sensuous ardor.

Trembling . . . needing . . . wanting . . . Honesty knew only the touch of Wes's lips, the heat of his passion. The hunger within her rose to aching yearning. She trembled with expectancy as Wes slipped off her gown, welcoming his naked length upon her. She felt his heat hard against the warm delta awaiting him.

"Honesty . . ."

The consternation in Wes's voice opened Honesty's eyes. His expression was tormented as he rasped, "I didn't intend . . ." He took a shuddering breath, and his next words emerged in a throbbing whisper, "I need you, darlin'."

He waited.

Feelings too myriad to be defined rushed through Honesty at the realization that Wes awaited her response—that however strong his need, he awaited her word to fully consummate the emotion between them. She whispered those words willingly, lovingly.

"I need you, too, Wes."

He entered her then, in a swift hard thrust of fleeting pain and simultaneous joy that stole her breath.

Halting abruptly, Wes searched her face. She saw his expression flicker, then tighten as he began moving slowly within her. She heard the tremor in his voice as he spoke low words of encouragement, gradually accelerating his thrusts. She sensed his elation as her thighs separated of their own accord, as she welcomed him fully, as she, too, experienced the mounting tumult of the rhythm of love.

And she felt the moment approaching. Lost in Wes's arms, her heart had never pounded harder. Her joy had never been brighter. Her sense of wonder had never been more keen. She was floating on the wings of supreme joy, soaring ever higher in a world of color that bore only Wes's name as a throbbing began inside her. She heard Wes's hoarse rasp in her ear.

"Honesty, my darlin' . . ."

His words were swallowed by the mutual cataclysm of emotion that burst within them at Wes's final thrust. Gasping aloud, wishing the glory would never end, Honesty clasped Wes close as ultimate ecstasy overwhelmed them.

The heat of their joining still warming their flesh, Honesty opened her eyes moments later to Wes's intense scrutiny. There was something about the way he stroked her hair, his fingers curling in its length, about the way his dark eyes linked with hers, that tightened a knot in her throat. Yet, she was unprepared for the throbbing emotion in his voice as he whispered, "You're mine, Honesty. You're mine."

The evening was on the wane. The boisterous tone of celebration on the saloon floor had dulled to a steady rumble punctuated only occasionally by shouts of laughter. The crowded dance floor had thinned. The call of keno numbers from the balcony had been suspended for the night, and only a determined few remained at the green gaming tables scattered around the floor.

At the corner of the bar where he had stood unmoving all evening, Jeremy looked up again toward the second floor. The ache within him tightened. He was a fool for tormenting himself. Neither Honesty nor Howell had appeared all evening. Howell was still inside her bedroom, and he was not going to leave.

His throat tight, Jeremy ran his hand through his hair, uncaring that the strands he had so carefully slicked for Honesty's benefit returned to their normal, fair-haired disorder. It was his own fault! He should have ignored Jewel's warnings. He should have charged up the stairs to Honesty's room and thrown Howell out as he had originally intended. Howell would not be in there now if he had!

No. That would have been a mistake. Honesty would have been the one to suffer.

Then he should have sent someone up to tell Honesty that he was waiting to see her. Honesty wanted to see him. He knew she did!

No. Jewel had kept a strict eye on the staircase all evening. No one could've gotten past her.

He should have done something, somehow—anything, rather than just wait!

But the truth was that he had never for a moment considered that Howell might stay.

Should have . . . could have . . .

Jeremy closed his eyes, swallowing hard. Whatever he should have done, it was too late.

No, it wasn't too late. Jeremy opened his eyes. Honesty had been disappointed in him because of Millie. That damned hairpin . . . But she'd forgive him. And he'd forgive her, because the truth was that he had no choice. Honesty was all he had ever wanted. She was the reason that the glass in front of him had sat in the same spot on the bar all evening, despite his desire to empty it. She was the reason he still aligned himself with Bitters even though he now knew the man couldn't be trusted. He'd do anything that was necessary to earn Honesty's respect again—*anything.*

Jeremy straightened up and picked his hat up from the bar. Honesty loved him, even if Howell was with her now. She would always love him. His day was coming.

Fixing his thoughts on the future even as the pain of the present slashed deeply through him, Jeremy walked toward the door.

The flame of the bedside lamp had sputtered and died, leaving only the silver moonlight streaming through the window to light Honesty's room. The incandescent glow illuminated Honesty's matchless features as she slept, and Wes allowed his gaze to linger. Her naked flesh was warm against him, her breasts pressed to his chest. The wonder of the moment when he had finally claimed her as his own was still fresh in his mind, as was his incredulity.

A virgin . . .

But why had he chosen to believe otherwise? Had he used that misconception as a shield against the emotions that assaulted him the first moment he saw Honesty?

Honesty stirred, and Wes drew her closer. The scent of her filled his nostrils, stirring a heat he dared not indulge again.

He kissed her lips.

Her eyes drifted open, eyes that were gloriously blue even in the pale light of the room. But uncertainty was reflected there as Honesty searched his face, then reached up to touch his lips. Reassured, she smiled.

"I wasn't sure it was you."

Wes stiffened. "Who did you think it was?"

"I thought it might be a dream, like the other times."

"The other times?"

"With Purity."

Her sister.

A sense of familiarity returned as the locket at Honesty's throat glinted in the pale light. He had seen it somewhere before.

Honesty moved against him, interrupting that thought and stirring another as Wes whispered, "Am I the only man you dream about, darlin'?"

Honesty nestled her cheek against his chest. He felt the warm brush of her breath with her spontaneous response, "Sometimes I dream about Jeremy."

Wes stilled, then pressed softly, "Tell me about Jeremy."

"I worry about him." Honesty rambled on. "His drinking . . . and that man. He's bad for Jeremy."

"What man?"

"Bitters . . ."

Wes caught his breath.

"I don't like him or those two fellas he travels with."

"Tom Bitters?"

Honesty opened her eyes and looked up at him. She nodded, her disquiet obviously growing. He felt her heart begin a slow, agitated pounding as she continued, "I told him to stay away from Bitters, but Jeremy's stubborn. He's going to get into trouble."

Honesty's hand trembled as she raised it to her head. He saw her wince with pain as she mumbled, "I can't seem to make him realize . . ."

"That's enough . . . don't think about it now." Wes stroked her cheek. "Go to sleep, darlin'. You can think about it tomorrow, when you feel better."

Honesty slowly closed her eyes. He drew her closer, softly whispering words that sprang from a warmth deep inside him that was for Honesty alone. Relaxing as her breathing gradually returned to normal, as her body grew lax and she drifted off to sleep, Wes felt his love for her swell even as dark reality intruded.

Jeremy had never been Honesty's lover. He was her friend.

And then there was Bitters.

Wes's thoughts went cold at what was to come.

Chapter Seven

"It's now or never, Bitters!"

Ignoring the flush that heated Bitters's swarthy complexion, Jeremy entered the secluded cabin and slammed the door behind him. This time, he wasn't worried about Bitters's reaction to what he said. Nor did he spare a glance for Riggs' scowl or Gant's cautious expression.

Three long weeks had passed since the first shipment of Slater Enterprises' money had reached Caldwell. He had struck up a chummy relationship with Joe Pierce despite his distaste for it, thereby learning everything he needed to know without the need for wheedling the information from Honesty as he had originally thought would be necessary. He had watched the manner in which the money was transported from the railroad to the bank. He had spent endless, boring hours watching the bank so he could establish the guards' daily routine. He had waited expectantly for Bitters's reaction each time he had made the long ride to deliver the details, and each time Bitters had said nothing at all!

And all the while Honesty and Howell . . .

The golden light of late afternoon slanted through the cracked windowpanes as Jeremy swallowed the bile that thought again raised. He advanced aggressively into the room, continuing, "I'm tellin' you that I'm gettin' tired of ridin' out here and givin' you the information I pull out of Joe Pierce word by word, only to have you nod your head and go on like I said nothin' at all."

"You're gettin' kind of big for your britches, ain't you?" Bitters' expression grew deadly. "I don't like fellas who think they can give me orders."

Jeremy stared at Bitters, his eyes hard. It was strange how different Bitters looked to him without a full belly of red-eye to influence his judgment. But those days were behind him. He hadn't had a drink since that night with Millie. Not that he hadn't wanted to, but he had seen himself too clearly the next morning, and the outcome of that night had been too hard to bear.

It occurred to him that Honesty had been right all along. Bitters was a snake.

That thought was fresh in Jeremy's mind as Bitters pressed, "Well, did you come here today to complain, or do you have somethin' to say?"

"You already heard part of what I got to say." Jeremy refused to back down. "And now I'm goin' to say the rest."

Jeremy felt Riggs's subtle movement and halted abruptly, dropping his hand toward the gun at his hip.

Bitters turned sharply toward the men behind

him. "Relax! I want to hear what this fella's got on his mind."

Jeremy's gun hand remained ready, even as he continued, "The next shipment's set to come in tomorrow."

"That's unusual, ain't it? The others were set a week apart."

"That was Howell's idea—to break the pattern. Besides, Joe Pierce said this shipment's goin' to be a special one. They aren't schedulin' another one for ten days or more."

"Why's that?"

"I don't know, and I don't care." Jeremy squared his stance, desperation forcing new courage as he continued, "The fact is, if you don't intend goin' after this shipment, I'm goin' after it myself."

The spontaneous burst of laughter his statement evoked from the two standing behind Bitters trailed away as Jeremy growled, "I'm a damned good shot. If you want me to prove it to you right now, I will."

"What's got into you?" Bitters's small eyes narrowed into assessing slits. "What's the rush?"

Jeremy did not respond.

"It's that woman, ain't it? That Honesty Buchanan you was always moonin' after."

"That's none of your business!"

"What happened, boy? She get an eye for somebody else and set you to scramblin' for some foldin' money to impress her?"

"I told you—"

"Hell!" Bitters gave a short laugh. "That I can understand. I was startin' to get worried, what with you cleanin' yourself up and all, and pushin' us here to ride into town after that money. I was startin' to think maybe you was workin' with Howell."

The surge of heat that colored Jeremy's face at the

mention of Howell's name widened Bitters's eyes. "Wait a minute . . . it's Howell, ain't it? That Honesty woman's taken up with the Texas Ranger. She took a shine to him that first night and now she left you high and dry. Well, I'll be damned."

Jeremy's aggressive step forward was halted by Bitters's low-pitched hiss. "Save it, boy! Don't go wastin' none of your energy here, where you're among friends. You are, you know . . ." Bitters' thick wet lips stretched into a sudden smile. "I'm a better friend than you ever thought I could be, 'cause we're goin' to town to get that money, just like you want. And after we do, there ain't goin' to be no Wes Howell no more."

Jeremy went suddenly still.

"That's right." Bitters smile slipped into a sneer. "I'm done with havin' to look over my shoulder for Howell to be ridin' up behind me everywhere I go. So you can count on it that your lady friend's goin' to be turnin' to you for comfort soon, 'cause her boyfriend's goin' to be lyin' six feet under." Bitters paused, his smile returning. "Now tell me, ain't that music to your ears?"

Jeremy paused to consider.

Howell out of the way for good.

Himself with more money than he had ever dreamed.

Honesty turning to him for comfort.

Jeremy's face creased into a smile. The music was already beginning.

Where was he?

Honesty stood in the doorway of Jeremy's cabin, frustration a tight knot inside her. She glanced around, her discomfort growing. The cabin was swept, the table was clean, and the coverlet was smoothed carefully over the bed. Even the clothes on the wall hooks were freshly laundered. She unconsciously shook her head.

Under any other circumstances, she supposed she would have been glad to see this new side of Jeremy emerge the way it had. She had been stunned at the suddenness with which Jeremy had stopped drinking. She believed it had something to do with her accident. She recalled that Jeremy had visited her a day or so after her accident. Alone with her, he had told her that he felt he had failed her, that it should have been he who had come after her the day of the storm. She had been unable to convince him otherwise.

Jeremy hadn't been himself in the time since. It wasn't like him to be so distracted. It wasn't like him to loiter on the street for long hours, speaking to no one. It wasn't like him to keep to a steady, lifeless routine of rising in the morning, reporting for work, and visiting her afterward only until Wes walked through the doors, when he left abruptly.

It wasn't like him to have lost his smile.

She had never discussed Wes with Jeremy. It was obvious that the antagonism between them was mutual and that Jeremy disapproved of her closeness with Wes. Jeremy would not allow her to tell him that she had discovered an inner man in Wes, who emerged for her alone—all tenderness, all warmth—that she had spent hours talking with this man as they had lain in each other's arms, and that although there was a part of Wes that still remained carefully guarded, she had sensed that guard faltering. Jeremy would not let her relate her certainty that Wes would help her settle the uncertainties of her past after his own obligations in Caldwell were fulfilled. Nor would he listen when she tried to explain that she had discovered a new part of herself as well, and the hopes and dreams that before had seemed hopeless took on new life when she was in Wes's arms. And Jeremy would not allow her to express her fervent wish that he would find someone who could add all these new, brilliant facets to his life.

But the truth was that she and Jeremy no longer discussed much at all. And she missed their talks. She missed leaning against him and sharing her thoughts with him. She missed the casual warmth that came to life inside her when his freckled face crinkled into a smile that was just for her. She missed laughing with him. She missed knowing that Jeremy and she were parts of each other's lives in a way no one else could ever be.

Honesty approached Jeremy's cot. She leaned down to smooth its surface, recalling the hairpin she had found there. Whoever the woman was, Jeremy had apparently let her slip out of his life as well. For all intents and purposes, Jeremy now was totally alone.

Where was he? The anxiety within Honesty grew. She had checked all over town for him. She didn't like this new silence about him, this new secrecy. She didn't like his new practice of disappearing from town for regular, extended intervals without reasonable explanation.

Intuition nagged. She hoped . . . so desperately . . . that her suspicions were wrong.

Honesty straightened up with new resolution. She'd talk to Jeremy today . . . tonight. She could not bear her steadily growing fear that to wait longer might be too late.

Charles stood up abruptly, kicking his desk chair back against the wall with a loud thud before striding to the window of his office to stare blindly out the mottled pane. He glanced back at the surface of his desk, where the letter written in a familiar, careless hand lay. He had received it an hour earlier, this one as brief as the first. He had read it so often that the words were imprinted on his mind.

Dear Charles,
We can't wait much longer to see you. The children and I are nearing desperation. If you don't come to us, we will come to you.
Mary

Charles ran a hand through heavy brown hair already showing the effects of several previous rakings, then covered his eyes. It was all coming apart. Emily was failing, and Jewel had cast him aside. He had known she would some day . . . when she found out. Despite her own checkered past, Jewel was too decent a woman to tolerate a man who had made such grievous mistakes.

Charles dropped his hand back to his side, his handsome face sagging with despair. It had all seemed harmless enough when it had first come about, but everything had progressed so quickly and was ending so badly.

Charles gave a short laugh. But the truth was that it hadn't really ended at all.

It occurred to him that his problems had begun when Howell came to Caldwell, bringing suspicion and tension with him. With Howell's men now guarding the bank day and night, with Howell coming and going as the fancy struck him, there was no peace for him. Nor was there an opportunity to leave and satisfy Mary's demands. Fall, and the cessation of Slater's shipments, was the only bright light on the horizon. The first thing he would do would be to visit Emily. He hoped he would not be too late.

As for Mary . . .

The heaviness in Charles's chest grew wearying.

A knock on the door raised Charles's head. His response opened it to reveal Honesty's concerned expression. The concern deepened when she looked at him, and within moments she was slipping her arms comfortingly around him.

"Charles, I'm so sorry." Honesty attempted a smile. "I tried to talk to Jewel, but you know she never listens to me."

A smile tugged at Charles's lips. "She says the same thing about you."

Honesty shrugged. "I guess you can say there's truth in both viewpoints."

"It isn't Jewel's fault anyway." It was Charles's turn to shrug. "It's mine."

To her credit, Honesty did not press him for explanations. Instead, she looked up at him, the incredible blue of her eyes fastened on his face as she whispered, "You were always so good to me, Charles. I always knew that whatever problems I had, you would be understanding. Whatever happens between you and Jewel, I hope you know that my feelings for you will never change."

Supremely grateful for those words, Charles slipped his arms around Honesty and hugged her tightly. His throat squeezed with pain as Honesty whispered, "I know Jewel loves you."

Charles responded hoarsely, "Jewel was never quite sure of that, you know."

"Yes, she was."

Charles drew back. He struggled for control. "I suppose I'll never be certain."

"Oh, Charles . . ."

Honesty pressed her cheek against his, and Charles closed his eyes. This beautiful woman he held so close had secured a place in his heart that was forever hers. He only wished—

A sharp knock shattered the silence of the small office. Charles did not have time for a response before the door was thrust suddenly open. Motionless, Charles was sure that he had never seen eyes that glared virulence more bitterly than Wes Howell's as he stood silently in the doorway.

Honesty in Charles Webster's embrace.

A cold rage suffused Wes as the bright light of midafternoon streamed through the window behind them, holding their silhouettes in dark relief—two silhouettes blended intimately into one.

Knowing he dared not take another step, Wes spoke in a tone that was low and lethal.

"Take your hands off her."

Honesty gasped, and Webster dropped his hands.

"Wes! What's the matter with you?"

Ignoring Honesty's shocked reaction, Wes addressed Webster again. "You're a damned fool if you think this is goin' to get you anywhere!"

"Wait a minute!" Webster's face hardened with unexpected anger. "Whatever you're thinking, you're all wrong here. Honesty and I—"

"There is no 'Honesty and I' as far as you're concerned!" Wes shifted his gaze. "Get away from him, Honesty."

"Wes, you—"

"I said, get away from him!"

Honesty's stunned expression turned to anger. "I don't take orders from you or anyone else!" Honesty's face flushed, and her breast began an agitated heaving. The locket that lay at the hollow of her throat glinted in the light as she turned back to Webster, her expression contrite. "I'm sorry for exposing you to this."

"Don't apologize to Webster for me."

Honesty turned back toward Wes, ire and incredulity exploding into a stunned question. "What makes you think you have the right to tell me what to say or do?" Honesty paused, continuing, "You're wrong if you think you do—just as wrong as you are in thinking that I was doing anything other than spending time with a friend when you came in this office!"

"Charles Webster is not your friend."

Honesty stilled. Wes saw her expression flicker, and he saw the extreme control she exerted as she rasped, "Charles *is* my friend. You're the one who is suddenly a stranger—one I don't care to know." Honesty turned back toward Webster. "I'm sorry, Charles. I'll see you later."

Striding past him without another word, Honesty jerked open the door. Wes followed her progress across the outer office with his gaze, then turned back to Webster with a low-voiced warning.

"Don't try gettin' to me through Honesty, Webster. It won't work—and it might get real dangerous to try."

Out on the boardwalk behind Honesty moments later, Wes grasped her arm. Refusing to allow her to jerk her arm free, he turned her toward him.

"You don't realize—"

"Let me go!"

"Listen to me, Honesty!"

"I said, let me go!"

Honesty's chest was heaving and her face was flushed. Looking up at him with her eyes sparking azure fire, she had never looked more beautiful—or more furious.

Honesty wrested her arm from his grip. She managed only a single step away from him before Wes grasped it again. Frustration thrusting him past rationality, Wes ignored the curious stares their hissed conversation had stirred and dragged her into the alleyway behind them.

Honesty's protests turned into physical attack as he drew her deeper into the shadowed corridor. Grasping her flying fists, he pinned her against the building behind her with the weight of his body, regret replacing his former anger as he rasped, "Stop, Honesty. Stop . . . please."

The growing ache inside him expanded as Honesty's struggles gradually slowed. Her breasts heaved against his chest as he spoke again in a ragged whisper.

"I'm sorry. I wasn't tryin' to make you angry."

Honesty made an obvious effort to draw her emotions under control. "You know Charles and I are friends."

"He isn't anybody's friend."

Honesty's face flamed. "You don't know what you're talking about! You don't know Charles at all! I've looked into his heart and I *do* know him! I won't listen to any more of this! Let me go!"

The futility of further argument clear, Wes whispered, "I won't let you go, Honesty." His voice dropped a pained note lower as he continued with words that came directly from the heart. "It's too late for that, now. I couldn't let you go, even if I tried."

Honesty turned away as he attempted to press his mouth to hers. Wes rested his cheek against hers, his lips touching her ear as he whispered, "You're angry.

I don't blame you. I can see you're tellin' the truth as you see it."

"It is the truth!"

"No, let me finish. I look at the truth through different eyes. I suppose that's somethin' that just is, but there is one truth that can't be denied. I can't see you without wantin' to touch you, Honesty. I can't touch you without wantin' to love you. And I can't abide the sight of another man's arms around you."

The pounding of Honesty's heart accelerated as she turned slowly back to face him. But her expression remained stiff. "Charles is my friend."

Obstinate. She did not understand.

But Honesty's body was warm against his, and the erratic beating of her heart echoed his own. He saw the conflicting emotions raging behind the glorious orbs fixed so intently on his, even as she refused to relent.

How could he reach her? How could he make her understand?

Wes raised his hand to stroke a silken wisp back from her cheek. He curled his fingers in her hair as words drifted across his mind, seeming to come from an unknown part of him as they emerged from his lips without conscious volition.

"Hair as black as the devil's heart and eyes as blue as the heavens . . ."

Honesty's eyes widened with incredulity at the words Wes had spoken. They were cherished words from her childhood, the same words that her father had spoken, words that had gone straight to her heart to become a symbol of love . . .

Now they were Wes's words as well!

It was suddenly all so clear. Joy replacing anger, Honesty recognized love in the intense lines of Wes's strong features. She discerned regret at their harsh exchange. She saw commitment in his eyes—a bridge that would carry her from her lost past to the future.

Beyond words, her heart filled to bursting, Honesty offered Wes her lips.

Wild, whooping sounds and the thunder of horses' hooves pounding down Caldwell's main street overwhelmed the bawdy music of evening, turning Jeremy to face the commotion. He watched as celebrating drovers skidded their horses to the drunken finish of their race, setting observers and pedestrians alike into a chaotic scramble to escape them. Tumbling from their horses, the drovers wove an unsteady path toward the swinging doors of the Longhorn Saloon a few feet away, their shouts of laughter and the promise of ready coin bringing brightly painted ladies to the doors in welcome.

Jeremy observed their reckless frolic in detached silence. Efrim Parker's herd had reached the outskirts of town at mid-day and Tod Butler's herd had arrived the night before. With three other trail herds already in town, Caldwell was bound for a few days of raucous celebration.

Perfect timing.

Jeremy straightened his shoulders, his hand following his thoughts to the gun at his hip. It would be a long wait until tomorrow night, when he would be his own man at last. He had no doubt that Bitters would follow through as they had planned. It would not be much longer.

"Well, stranger . . ." Jeremy turned at the sound of the familiar feminine voice. Millie's ready smile flashed as she pushed open the doors of the Longhorn and took his arm. "I figured if I waited long enough and watched hard enough, I'd catch you walkin' by one night."

"Nice to see you, Millie." Jeremy managed a smile.

Millie inched closer. She spoke as softly as the surrounding din allowed, the smile on her lips not quite reaching her eyes. "I missed you. I heard you've been behavin' yourself real well of late, breakin' all us ladies' hearts by keepin' out of the saloons at night."

Jeremy was immediately alert. "Where'd you hear that?"

"Oh, you know this town. People do a lot of talkin'."

Jeremy searched Millie's small, painted features. "What else are people sayin'?"

"They say you're like a different fella, that you're walkin' a real straight path these days." Millie gave a short laugh. "But I was kinda hopin' they was wrong. I liked you the way you was . . . and I figured you wouldn't like me no more if you turned into this straight-up fella they was talkin' about."

Jeremy's gaze lingered. He saw a sadness behind Millie's small brown eyes that was not betrayed by her words. He knew what it was to feel the way Millie was feeling. Something inside him softened. His smile was gentle. "I like you the way you are too, Millie."

Millie's eyes brightened. "You feel like comin' in for a while? You don't have to drink or nothin', not if you don't want to. The boss won't mind. I'll make it up to him."

Jeremy shook his head. "No, I don't think so, Millie."

The brightness in Millie's eyes faded. An underlying anxiety shone through as she squeezed his arm and her voice dropped a note softer. "She's got herself somebody else now, Jeremy. I saw them together this afternoon. That Howell fella ain't about to let her go . . . not the way he was lookin' at her. You're only goin' to break your heart if you keep on waitin'."

Heat flushed Jeremy's face. "That's my business!"

"Oh, don't go gettin' mad at me!" Millie's smile became a silent plea. "I was just tryin' to help."

Jeremy nodded. He knew she was. Millie couldn't possibly understand how he felt. She didn't know that Honesty was his life, that if he really believed Howell had taken her away from him for good, he'd have nothing left at all.

"I have to go now."

"You ain't mad?"

How could he be? "No."

"You'll come back to see me sometime?"

"I don't think so, Millie. I—" He hesitated, deciding on caution. "I'm goin' to have things that will be takin' up all my time soon."

Millie dropped her hand. She took a step back. "All right. I just thought I'd ask."

Millie was about to turn away when Jeremy took her thin arm and stayed her. He regretted the hope that sprang into her eyes the moment before he whispered, "I'm sorry, Millie. I wish it could be different."

Millie gently dislodged his grip. Her smile was tremulous as she pushed a wayward blond strand back from her face. "Me, too."

Slipping into the crowded interior of the Longhorn seconds later, Millie disappeared from Jeremy's sight. She slipped from his mind just as quickly as he walked on, his eye fixed on the Texas Jewel.

Squaring his shoulders, Jeremy paused just outside the swinging doors. He lifted his hat and patted his carefully slicked hair, then adjusted the fresh bandanna around his neck. The purchase, as small as it was, had been another drain on his diminishing funds, but he hadn't cared. He knew he'd soon have all the money he needed. Honesty would see a sober, dependable Jeremy tonight. She would remember him this way when it was all over tomorrow. He was counting on her remembering.

Two steps inside and Jeremy saw her. Honesty was dealing the cards with a look in her eyes that said the players at the table wouldn't be getting a winning hand this round. He smiled. Honesty hadn't really changed at all. She looked up, catching his eye. She smiled, and the glow of that smile lit his heart.

His Honesty. She would always be his. He'd let no one take her from him.

She had never been so glad to see anyone in her life.

Signaling Sykes to replace her, Honesty stood up and started toward Jeremy, her heart warming in a way it did for no other. She took his arm, leaning companionably against his side as she steered him past the bar to a corner of privacy. She turned to face him with a teasing smile.

"Jeremy, you devil. You look downright handsome tonight." She tugged at his new bandanna. She winked. "Real nice."

Jeremy's face crinkled into the smile she had so missed as he responded, "I thought you might like it."

Honesty's smile faltered as she continued, "I was looking for you this afternoon. You weren't anywhere to be found."

"I had some things to do."

"Things? What things?"

"Nothin' important . . ."

"What did you have to do, Jeremy?" Honesty's expression sobered. "Please tell me." And when he stared at her in response, "I know something's wrong. I can feel it."

"Nothin's wrong."

Honesty searched Jeremy's face. She saw the blond, wiry brows and the earnest brown eyes underneath. She saw the sun-reddened skin and the line of freckles across his short nose. She saw the familiar smile now seeking to reassure her . . . all making up a face that was so dear to her that she ached inside . . . ached because she didn't believe him at all.

Honesty paused, then pressed, "You're not bothering with Bitters, are you, Jeremy?"

Jeremy stilled.

"Jeremy?"

"Bitters hasn't been around town for weeks."

"I know."

"So?"

"That doesn't mean he isn't still in the area and that you don't know where he is."

"I don't know what you're talkin' about."

"You've changed so much in the past few weeks, Jeremy."

"I thought you'd be happy about the change. You were always tellin' me—"

"I don't mean that. I'm proud of the way you've taken your life in hand. It's just that I'm worried."

"About what?"

"Jeremy, please . . ."

He should have expected it.

Jeremy stared into Honesty's glorious eyes. Honesty and he had always been so close that they practically knew each other's thoughts. It was a special bond between them . . . a bond that was threatening him now, for all the love it conveyed.

Jeremy took Honesty's hands in his. Her hands were small . . . so delicate. He wanted to raise them to his lips to kiss every finger. He dreamed of the day when those hands would caress him as he would caress her. He dreamed of the day when her hands would seek his with love. He wanted it so badly that he was almost sick with the wanting.

"Jeremy . . ." Honesty's eyes implored him. "Tell me you're not letting Bitters lead you into doing something you shouldn't."

Jeremy swallowed the tight lump in his throat and again spoke the necessary lie. "I told you, I don't know what you're talkin' about."

"Don't do anything you shouldn't. Not now. Everything is going so well. You're doing so fine. I've never seen you looking so good. Mother Sills would be so proud."

"What about you, Honesty? Are you proud?"

"Yes, I am." Tears sparkled in Honesty's eyes. "I've always been proud of you."

"No, you haven't."

"Oh, Jeremy . . ." Honesty's smile trembled. "I wasn't always proud of what you did, but I was always proud of who you are."

Jeremy took a steadying breath. He was so close to taking her into his arms right out in the open, without caring what anybody said or saw. He was so close to telling her that he loved her, that she was all he ever wanted. He was so close to saying—

Movement in the doorway behind Honesty caught Jeremy's eye, and his thoughts froze. It was Howell standing there, his damned broad shoulders seeming to fill the opening, that damned, dark stare of his so cold that it chilled Jeremy to the bone.

Howell started in their direction.

The bastard.

Honesty turned to follow his gaze. She saw Howell approaching, and the look in her eyes was more than Jeremy could bear. Honesty relinquished his hands as Howell slid his arm around her waist. Jeremy turned away.

"Jeremy . . ." The plea in Honesty's voice stayed him as she pressed, "Can't we *all* be friends?"

No, damn it! No!

"Jeremy . . ." Honesty's voice could hardly be heard over the growing din around them. "It's going to happen, you know. It's going to be just like we dreamed when we were younger . . . you, me, Purity, and Chastity, all together. Wes is going to help us find them."

Jeremy glanced up to see Howell's eyes boring into his. He read the truth there. Howell knew the way he felt about Honesty. He'd never let it happen. It could never be—not while Howell was able to prevent it. He had no choice in what he must do.

"I have to go, Honesty." Jeremy did not bother to speak to Howell. As far as he was concerned, everything had been said.

Jeremy walked directly toward the door. He turned back in time to see Honesty look up at Howell. And he saw the look in her eyes . . . the moment before she took Howell's hand the way he had always wanted her to take his.

Jewel stood at the bottom of the staircase, suddenly unable to move. Her blood went cold at the look in Jeremy's eyes as he stood in the saloon entrance looking back at Honesty and Howell.

Hatred. Deadly malevolence. She had not dreamed Jeremy capable of such savage emotions.

No, it wasn't true. Jeremy couldn't feel anything other than love for Honesty. She was certain of that.

Honesty was perfection in his eyes. He excused her failings and saw her faults as virtues. Jewel knew instinctively that he blamed himself for Honesty's turning to Howell. That reality had been painfully evident during the past few weeks, while he had struggled to change himself into the man Honesty had always wanted him to be.

Poor Jeremy.

It was too late.

Jewel stared at Wes Howell's composed features. He allowed no one close enough to get to know him, except Honesty, but Jewel knew the *kind* of man he was. Howell had laid claim to Honesty, and he would allow nothing short of death to separate them.

That last thought sent a tremor down Jewel's spine as Jeremy strode abruptly out onto the street and disappeared from sight.

Jewel struggled for breath, her full breasts heaving under the purple bodice of her gown. Honesty and Howell were talking softly. Honesty was listening to Howell's reply with rapt attention, oblivious of Jeremy's rancor. She wished she could warn Honesty. She wished Honesty would listen to her the way she was now listening to Howell—just once. How could she make Honesty realize that the future she had dreamed of, the life that now seemed within her reach in the person of Wes Howell, might be in danger from the person she loved as a brother?

Jewel's throat was tight. She could not swallow. She clutched the staircase rail. . . .

"Jewel, are you all right?"

Charles's arm slipped around her waist as Jewel turned toward him. She felt his anxiety as he drew her against him, supporting her with his strength. She did not protest.

"Jewel . . ."

The sound of Charles's voice fortified her. The look in his eyes restored her hope. Perhaps together they could do something.

Her voice unnaturally breathless, Jewel did not bother to smile as she questioned abruptly, "Do you love me, Charles?"

Jewel felt the shock of her question reverberate through Charles. She saw his sudden flush of color. She read the truth in his eyes as he responded with a single word.

"Yes."

"I love you, too."

Jewel saw incredulous joy flash in Charles's eyes. She regretted her next words with all her heart as she continued, "But I don't love you enough to share you with Mary."

The joy faded. Determined to continue, the words more difficult than she had ever imagined they could be, she whispered, "But . . . I need your friendship."

Jewel waited. She saw the tight working of Charles's throat as he strove to form his reply. When it came, the words were simple and spoken with love.

"Whatever you want from me is yours."

Allowing Charles to lead her to a nearby table, Jewel waited until he sat beside her. Her expression solemn, she took his hand.

"You can't help him, Honesty."

Honesty recognized the uncompromising lines in Wes's tense features. A familiar agitation soared. She wanted to tell him about her fears. She wanted to confide her suspicion that Jeremy was planning something, and that she feared Bitters was involved, but she could not. The betrayal would be too complete. Jeremy needed her.

"Jeremy needs me."

"You're only making matters worse."

"Jeremy depends on me."

"You're making a mistake. Leave him alone."

"He needs me, especially now."

"You don't really see it, do you?" Wes's eyes raked her face. "How can you be so blind?"

"What are you talking about?"

"He's jealous!"

Jealous.

"Of you and me."

The thought struck Honesty cold. Dear Jeremy . . . the brother she had never had . . . the boy who had willingly shared her childhood dreams . . .

Honesty shook her head. A supreme sadness overwhelmed her.

"Why, Wes? First Charles . . . now Jeremy. Who's next? Sam?"

"Open your eyes, Honesty."

"Stop it."

"You don't see what you don't want to see."

"Stop it!"

Her outburst caught the attention of men at surrounding tables, and Honesty was suddenly incensed. Seesawing passions . . . unreasonable demands . . . Her head was spinning. She had had enough.

"I've had enough."

Wes's jaw clenched tight.

Honesty turned back toward her table. She had taken no more than two steps when she realized her hands were shaking and she was almost past control.

Damn him!

Honesty strode toward the staircase to the second floor as her head began pounding. The pain she had suffered after her injury resumed with unexpected intensity. She pressed her palm against the pulsing distress in her temple. She needed to be alone . . . to be able to think.

Honesty glanced in the wall mirror. Wes stood where she had left him, his expression rigid.

Damn him!

Behind the bar, Henry looked at her as she passed. She paused.

"I don't want anyone to follow me upstairs, Henry."

Henry nodded.

Honesty did not look back as she continued up the stairs.

His hands balled into fists, Jeremy strode rapidly down the narrow boardwalk, unmindful of the continuing bedlam of evening around him as he left the Texas Jewel behind.

One more day. He could not afford to let Howell distract him. Tonight was important. He needed to watch and make sure the guards' routines did not change. It was important . . . important.

Jeremy approached the bank, his heart aching at the images still vivid in his mind.

Howell's arm around Honesty, as if he owned her . . .

Honesty looking up at Howell and taking his hand . . .

No, he would not think about it anymore!

Jeremy forced his mind clear as he drew closer to the bank. He slipped into the shadows nearby where he had spent many previous watchful hours.

He waited.

Herb Walters and Jason Storms approached, conversing casually. They were right on schedule. Storms walked around to the rear of the bank as Walters engaged John Agree in short conversation in front. Agree waited a few minutes, until Mike Leach sauntered around from the back of the building. The changing of the guard was completed.

Jeremy's jaw hardened. Tomorrow night would work out fine.

Sam shifted, then drew back into the alleyway opposite the bank. He could barely see Jeremy in the shadows across the street, but he knew he was there.

Another night of watching and waiting.

His bones creaking in protest, Sam propped himself against the nearby wall. He was getting too old for this. The only trouble was that he had to be sure.

Sighing, Sam drew back farther into the darkness.

Wes strode across the saloon as Honesty stepped out of sight on the second floor.

She was angry.

No, she was incensed.

Honesty truly believed he had fabricated everything he had said in order to turn her against a friend. The problem was that Honesty did not realize how much she was loved.

His foot was on the staircase when he heard Henry's voice beside him.

"You're not wanted up there, Mr. Howell."

Wes's eyes narrowed as he looked at the sober-faced bartender.

"Says who?"

"Honesty."

Wes did not smile. "I'm goin' up."

"No, you're not."

About to respond, Wes felt the barrel of a gun tight against his side.

Henry's eyes did not flicker.

Neither did Wes's.

"You're going to have to pull that trigger if you want to stop me, because I'm goin' up."

"I'm warnin' you . . ."

Wes started up the stairs. The click of the hammer on Henry's gun did not affect his pace. He did not look back to see Henry turn abruptly to make a path straight to Jewel's table. Nor did he see Jewel look up toward the second floor after Henry finished speaking, considering her reply for long moments before she sent him back to the bar.

Instead, Wes halted in the hallway outside Honesty's door, his eye caught by a glittering object on the floor. Honesty's locket . . . He picked it up, smoothing the delicate heart with his thumb as he held it. Still warm from Honesty's skin, it glinted in the light of the flickering hall lamps. He had seen it shine in just that way so many times as Honesty had lain in his arms, and each time he had felt that same sense of familiarity. . . .

Wes caught his breath as a dormant memory returned with sudden and unexpected clarity.

It had been a few years earlier, when he was after the Sommers gang. He and another ranger were tight on the gang's trail when they ran across a huge herd being driven to a nearby railhead. He remembered that the trail boss had struck him as strange—tall, with a build that was slender beyond the norm, and with a voice that turned his drovers on the dime despite its high-pitched quality. He had watched the fellow work the herd for a few minutes, realizing that he had never seen a man ride harder or rope better than that fellow did, despite his lean frame. He recalled the unexpected glimmer of pride with which a nearby drover had grumbled that their outfit had the toughest trail boss in Texas. He had been stunned when the trail boss had suddenly ridden directly toward him in pursuit of a maverick steer, and *the heart-shaped locket had become visible, glinting in the sun.*

The trail boss had been a young woman—a young woman who had spared no time to speak to him, but who had been close to Honesty's age.

The young woman's face flashed vividly before Wes's mind. Her hair had been blond under the worn, oversized hat she wore. Her complexion had been fair where it was not reddened by the sun, with a line of freckles stretching across the bridge of her nose. And her eyes had been pale and hard.

She had borne not even the slightest resemblance to Honesty.

But the locket was the same.

Wes closed his hand tightly around the locket. He knocked on Honesty's door. There was no response, and Wes knocked again, then pushed the door open.

Wes paused in the doorway, glancing around as his eyes became adjusted to the dim light of the room. Honesty was lying unmoving on the bed, her hand pressed to her temple, and Wes's heart began hammering. Beside her in a moment, he crouched by the bed.

"Your head hurts again, doesn't it?"

"Please leave, Wes."

"No."

Wes saw the pain in Honesty's eyes as she turned toward him, and he cursed the jealousy that had forced their heated exchange. He held out his hand and opened it slowly.

"I found your locket."

Honesty's hand flew to her neck. He saw her relief as she took it from him.

"It was your mother's . . ."

"No, I told you . . . my father gave it to me. He gave

us all lockets that matched my mother's . . . Purity and Chastity, too."

"His three, beautiful, dark-haired daughters . . ."

Honesty clenched the locket tight in her hand as she looked up at him. Her question was abrupt . . . unexpected.

"What do you want from me, Wes?"

Filled with regret, Wes took the fist Honesty had closed around her locket and raised it to his lips. He kissed each knuckle in turn before whispering, "I want you to believe me when I say I'm sorry. I didn't mean to upset you, darlin'."

Honesty searched his face. Her eyelids were growing heavy. "I took one of the powders Doc Carter gave me and I'm tired. I don't want to talk anymore."

"I'll stay until you fall asleep."

"No, I don't want you to."

"I want to stay."

"No."

"I love you, Honesty."

Honesty's brilliant gaze flickered. She did not respond. Nor did she protest as he slid himself onto the bed beside her and drew her close.

"Close your eyes, darlin'."

Honesty closed her eyes. Her head drooped against him, and the knot within Wes gradually loosened. Honesty was comfortable in his arms. He would see to it that she always stayed there.

Honesty muttered softly against his chest, as if in afterthought.

"I told you . . . Chastity's hair is red . . . like my father's. Purity is a blonde."

Blonde . . .

Wes drew Honesty closer.

* * *

Activity on the street continued as Jeremy shifted his position, his gaze remaining fixed on the bank as it had been since the guard had changed. He withdrew his watch from his pocket and checked it again, squinting in the darkness. A full hour had passed since he left the Texas Jewel.

Jeremy muttered a low curse. Howell was late on his rounds. He should've been here five minutes ago. It would be just like the bastard to change things now and complicate matters.

Glancing up, Jeremy saw a familiar figure emerge from the doorway of the Texas Jewel. Howell's size made him unmistakable in the crowd as he worked his way along the boardwalk. He watched as Howell approached Herb Walters where the fellow stood guard in front of the building, conversing for a few minutes before walking around to the rear.

Same routine.

Perfect.

Jeremy smiled.

A bright light blinded her despite the grainy mist engulfing her, and Honesty shielded her eyes with her hand. Where was that light coming from? She separated her fingers and peeked through.

Someone was riding toward her—tall and slender, dressed in male clothing. But the figure wasn't male. The brilliant light again flashed, hurting her eyes, but Honesty recognized its origin this time. It was the reflection of the sun on the glittering gold locket the figure wore.

Honesty gasped as the figure rode closer.

Purity.

But Purity was angry. She didn't smile. She had a gun in her hand.

A shaft of sunlight pierced the mist, allowing a

glimpse of red hair in the distance, and Honesty's throat choked tight.

Chastity . . . always so far away.

Honesty strained to see Chastity's face.

She implored Purity to help her, but the words did not emerge from her lips.

She struggled to speak, but she could not.

Honesty awakened abruptly. She looked around her. She was alone. Disoriented, she attempted to clear her mind. How much of what had happened had been a dream, and how much had been real? Had Wes really been with her? Had he really said he loved her? She felt oddly lost.

A sound in the hallway.

A shaft of light as the door opened.

A tall figure standing there.

Wes.

Beside her in a moment, Wes searched her face. "I had to leave for a little while, but I won't be leavin' again."

Honesty watched as Wes stripped off his clothes. Taut skin stretched smoothly over powerful muscles as he slipped under the coverlet beside her. The bed creaked under their combined weight as Wes drew her against him. The warmth of him . . . the strength . . .

Honesty's heavy eyelids drooped closed. She felt Wes's mouth brush hers and uncertainties drifted away.

Chapter Eight

Secrets.

He had so many of them.

Silver slivers of dawn peeked through the window shades of Honesty's room, penetrating the somber darkness. Raising himself on his elbow, Wes frowned down at Honesty. She was lying with her face turned to his chest, her lips so close that he could feel the brush of her breath against his skin. The unbound length of her dark hair was stretched across the pillow, her lashes resting against her smooth cheeks, her lips lightly parted. She was so beautiful that it hurt to look at her. It hurt because she was sleeping. He didn't want to awaken her . . . and he ached to make love to her.

But he needed this time, these few, short minutes while she lay silently against him. He needed that reassurance—especially today. He needed to feel that all obstacles between them were temporarily dismissed by the warm press of their flesh.

Honesty's hand lay lax against his chest and he curled his palm around it, raising it to his lips. He lightly kissed the long, slender fingers that so flagrantly manipulated cards, making a mockery of Honesty's name. He had warned her of the dangers there, but she had chosen to ignore him. She did not need to tell him that it was her retaliation against the fate that had turned her life upside down so long ago and left her dangling, because he knew.

Wes's frown tightened as he glanced at the locket lying on the nightstand beside the bed. He had found the key to turning Honesty's life right side up again, but he wasn't ready to surrender it. Too many uncertainties stood in the way. He couldn't afford the possibility that Honesty would run off without him in search of the woman he had seen that day. Nor could he afford to offer Sills the opportunity to take his place.

Sills and Bitters . . . Honesty didn't realize the significance of the comment she had made that day. Bitters would show up sooner or later. He had no doubt about that. The Caldwell Bank was now too great a temptation for a man like him to ignore. As for Sills, if he was connected to Bitters in any way, he had already sealed his fate.

And then there was Charles Webster.

Wes faced a tormenting reality. He loved Honesty. He had spoken the words earnestly, from the bottom of his heart, but Honesty had not said she loved him. He knew she wanted to . . . but he also knew that too many impediments stood in her way.

A gradual desperation overtaking him, Wes lowered his mouth to Honesty's lips. He tasted them lightly, the contact bittersweet. He had staked his claim on Honesty with love, but it wasn't enough. He needed to make Honesty want him the way he wanted her. He needed to impress his passion so deeply into her heart and mind that she would have no room there for any other man. He needed her to need him as much as he had grown to need her . . . or he would lose her.

Those thoughts never stronger, Wes tasted Honesty's mouth once more.

Jeremy stepped out onto the early-morning street and looked around him. The sun shed its golden rays onto the discarded remnants of the previous night's celebration as the town slumbered.

Just another morning. Just another day.

No.

A nervous smile flickered at Jeremy's lips. He took a steadying breath before turning in the direction of the holding pens. The sound of his booted steps echoed hollowly against the boardwalk as he continued past Birdie Cotter's place without a break in stride. He knew he couldn't eat. He'd never be able to hold the food down. And he knew the day would stretch long and endless until nightfall, when it would all be over and done at last.

"Get them cattle movin'!"

The bright morning sun had become intense midday heat that increased Bitters' discomfort as he wiped the perspiration from his face with his stained bandanna. The grainy dust enveloping him caught in his throat and he coughed, then coughed again. Cursing, he glanced around him at the bawling cattle traveling at a leisurely pace along the trail. He was never more keenly aware of the reason he had traded his lariat for a gun so many years ago than he was as he shouted again toward the two men riding alongside the herd a short distance away.

"You heard what I said, you two! We ain't got all day to get rid of these damned critters!"

Gant looked up, his lean frame stiffening the moment before he swung his rope against the hide of the nearest animal in halfhearted compliance. Bitters saw the glance Gant slanted at Riggs as Riggs spurred his horse toward him. He was prepared as Riggs jerked his mount to a halt. He did not react as the fellow growled without preamble, "You're crazy, you know that! It ain't worth it, I tell you! We're takin' a chance ridin' up so close to Caldwell while it's still daylight, just so's we can sell these damned beeves off to that Parker herd outside town! Don't you think that Parker fella's goin' to be suspicious of where we got them?"

"He don't care! It's all set. We're sellin' them to him at half the price he's goin' to get for them when he runs his herd into the holdin' pens. You know how it works. All herds pick up strays along the trail. Nobody'll give these beeves a second glance once they're mixed in with Parker's herd, and he knows it."

"What if he realizes we're sellin' some of his own stock back to him?"

"Don't be a damned fool! One longhorn looks like another."

"What do we need the money for, anyway? After tonight we're goin' to have all the money we need!"

"Yeah, well, I ain't about to throw away the three weeks' work we sank into them brands."

"We?" Riggs gave a short laugh.

Bitters eyes narrowed. "You got any complaints?"

"I got plenty!"

"That so?" Bitters felt the hair on the back of his

neck stiffen. He was getting sick and tired of this no-account he had picked up along the way trying to tell him what to do. He snarled, "Spit it out, then!"

"You're lettin' this old business with Howell get out of hand! If you was usin' your head, you'd realize we should've taken that bank before Howell had a chance to get himself situated in town."

Bitters stared coldly. "That's all water under the bridge now, ain't it?"

"You still ain't thinkin' clear! All you're thinkin' about is puttin' a bullet through Howell so you can get him out of your hair once and for all!"

"What else is there to think about?"

"Gettin' out of Caldwell alive, that's what!"

"You are a stupid bastard, ain't you, Riggs?" Bitters ignored the flush that colored Riggs's face as he pressed, "You're so damned stupid that you can't see what's in front of your eyes."

"What are you talkin' about?"

"We ain't never had a better setup than we got this time. That Sills is so hot to get a piece of that money so he can look good to his girlfriend that he's willin' to do anythin'. If I told him to go in, guns blazin', he'd do it without a second thought. But that ain't the way it's goin' to be. You heard what Sills said. Howell checks that bank every night at twelve o'clock. He's as regular as clockwork. The town'll be in full swing by then, the street crowded with drunks and with cowboys ridin' haywire around town. Hell, somebody could shoot off a cannon on Main Street, and nobody'd pay it no mind! When Howell comes to make his rounds, the fellas at the bank will be expectin' him. With a gun in his back, Howell will take us right up to them guards, easy as pie, and we'll take care of them without a shot bein' fired. It'll go real smooth from there."

"What about the marshal?"

"Him? Hell, Sills says he ain't gone nowheres near the bank since Howell got into town. They got a war goin' between them, that Howell and the marshal. That marshal even reeled in his deputy so's the fella can't lift a finger to help Howell."

"You're goin' to get rid of Howell . . ."

"I sure am."

"What about Sills?"

Bitters stilled. "I ain't decided."

"I thought you said—"

"He ain't the same fella he was before. If things go right, he just might take a likin' to the kind of work we do. People trust that baby face. They enjoy talkin' to him. He could make things easy for us on the next job, too."

"I don't like him!"

"I don't care what you like!"

Riggs's jowled face tightened, and Bitters pressed, "Now that you got that straight once and for all, I'm tellin' you what we're goin' to do. We're goin' to run these beeves right into Parker's herd, just like I said. We're goin' to collect our money, and then we're goin' to find ourselves a nice, shady tree somewhere and sleep the afternoon away so we'll be nice and rested for our little party tonight."

Riggs muttered under his breath.

"Did you say somethin'?"

"I didn't say nothin'."

"Good. Then get them cattle movin'! We ain't got all day."

Riggs spurred his horse roughly. The animal reacted with a nervous jump and a whinny that scattered the surrounding beeves and startled the others into a sudden spurt forward.

Bitters smiled, the heat of the day suddenly more

bearable. He had put a bee in Riggs's bonnet, and it had felt damned good. And when he put a bullet in Howell, it was goin' to feel even better.

He was lookin' forward to it.

"Where are you goin', Honesty?"

Honesty stepped out into the hall, turning toward Jewel as she pulled her bedroom door closed behind her. Jewel's expression halted the spontaneous rejoinder that rose to her lips. The tight line of Jewel's lips . . . was it anger? No. Concern? Could it possibly have been *fear* that flashed so briefly in Jewel's eyes?

Honesty canceled that thought. Not Jewel. Jewel wouldn't allow so weak an emotion any place in her life. Yet, there had been something.

"What do you want, Jewel?"

Jewel's hesitation in responding was uncharacteristic, as was the way she glanced away, avoiding Honesty's eye as she motioned with her chin toward her room at the rear of the hall. "I want to talk to you."

Honesty straightened, suddenly wary. "You can talk to me here."

"No, I can't." Jewel's expression turned stony. "What I've got to say has to be said in private."

Honesty's stomach clenched tightly. She wasn't up to another of Jewel's tirades. Her conflict with Wes yesterday had been difficult enough. Had it not been for the night that followed, she would have been uncertain where they stood right now. But the truth was that despite Wes's unexpected apologies, despite his tender attention when she had briefly relapsed into another of the almost paralyzing headaches that had followed her injury, and despite the gentle passion to which Wes had awakened her and the loving hour that had followed, nothing had truly been settled between them.

Wes had said he loved her. But he disapproved of her life. He disapproved of everyone *in* her life. She knew that he occasionally even disapproved of her.

She recalled Wes's expression the last time she had deliberately "adjusted" the cards she was dealing while he was standing nearby. His jaw had locked so tightly that she had thought his teeth might shatter. She had almost been able to feel the Texas Ranger badge he still carried in his pocket singe his skin. How she had enjoyed that moment!

Jewel's expression twitched. "Well, are you comin'?"

Jewel turned abruptly toward her room, the brilliant green of her gown sweeping out behind her. Falling in behind her, Honesty waited only until the door of Jewel's room clicked closed before demanding, "All right, what is it now?"

Startling her, Jewel's voice softened. "You're not going to like this, Honesty."

Honesty raised her chin against the strange tension suddenly besetting her. "What is it, Jewel?"

"You're heading for trouble . . ."

Not again.

"Don't look at me that way, damn it!" Jewel's face was suddenly a hot red. "You're so stubborn! The trouble is that you think you live a charmed life! You think you can do anythin' you want and it'll always turn out right in the end."

"That isn't true."

About to speak again, Jewel halted. Her full breasts were heaving against the deep neckline of her gown as she rasped, "I'm not goin' over that again. If it wasn't that—" Jewel hesitated. "Damn that Charles! He was supposed to be here with me now, but he's stuck at the bank."

"Charles?"

Jewel read the immediate thought that had jumped into Honesty's mind. "No, Charles and I aren't gettin' back together. Everythin's gone too far for that. But I knew you'd react just the way you are now when I started talkin', and I figured you'd listen better if Charles backed me up."

Honesty was suddenly past patience. "Say what you have to say and get it over with, Jewel! I have things to do."

Jewel's small eyes widened with anger. "Do you have anythin' to do that's more important than savin' somebody's life?"

Jewel's raised tone was still rebounding in the room when she continued more softly, "Don't you see what's happenin'? Don't you spare even a minute to wonder what's goin' on with Jeremy?"

"Jeremy?"

"You know Jeremy better than anybody else does. You know what frustration does to him. You know how he can twist things in his mind—like thinkin' everybody's against him when it was just himself that was goin' all wrong. You know he acts before he thinks—and he sometimes doesn't think at all when things get bad enough."

Honesty remained silent. Everything Jewel had said was true.

"And you know he'd reach for a gun just as easily as he'd swing his fist if the situation pressed him hard enough."

A chill crawled up Honesty's spine. "What are you trying to say?"

"I'm sayin' that Jeremy's almost at that point, and you're goin' to have to watch it or you're goin' to push him over."

Honesty was incredulous. "Why would I do that? *How* would I do that?"

Jewel stared at her. "Didn't you ever . . . *ever* see the look in his eye when you're with Wes Howell?"

"He doesn't like Wes. I know that." Honesty fought a slowly encroaching trepidation. "You don't like Wes either. Neither does Charles, but that doesn't mean—"

"Jeremy's *jealous,* Honesty."

No.

"He doesn't want anyone to have you but him."

"Jeremy knows I'd do anything for him. He knows he'll always be my friend."

"It isn't *friendship* that he wants."

"You don't know what you're talking about!"

"Don't I?"

"I don't want to discuss this any more."

"You can't run away from this! I saw Jeremy's face last night when you were with Howell. Somethin' bad's goin' to happen. Even Charles agrees."

"I don't believe it!"

"Ask Charles yourself, if you think I'm lyin'!"

Jewel's shoulders were suddenly stiffly erect. Honesty knew the signs. She was nearing the end of her tether. Suddenly realizing that she was nearing that point herself, Honesty answered with forced restraint.

"I *will* ask him!"

Out on the street moments later, Honesty struggled against the trembling that had beset her limbs as she started toward the bank. Her rapid step halted abruptly when she saw Wes approaching it from the other direction. Drawing back so she would not be seen, she waited, frustration soaring as Wes halted outside the doorway, then assumed a watchful posture beside the guard there.

No. She couldn't talk to Charles while Wes was there. She needed to talk to him alone. Charles would tell her the truth. He'd tell her that it was all a misunderstanding, that Jewel was wrong about Jeremy . . .

. . . just as Wes had been wrong?

That question rebounded in Honesty's mind, stirring a familiar discomfort. Discomfort rapidly increased to pain, and Honesty's stomach began churning. A sense of helplessness overwhelmed her as the familiar debility returned. Honesty turned unsteadily back in the direction from which she had come. Damn this lingering weakness she could not seem to shake! It was incapacitating her.

Minutes later, pressing her hand tightly to the pulsing pain in her temple, Honesty closed her bedroom door behind her.

Exasperated, Charles glanced up from the papers spread across the desk to see that twilight had faded into night on the street beyond his office window. He had removed his jacket hours earlier, unbuttoned his shirt to mid-chest, and rolled his sleeves up to his elbows as the stuffiness of the room grew increasingly greater, but he knew his discomfort was not entirely physical.

He had received the telegram that afternoon. Joe Pierce—damn his pleased smile—had delivered it to him personally. Slater Enterprises had been granted permission to review the paperwork for the business they had funneled through his bank. They would be conducting an audit of the books if they deemed it necessary. They were sending someone to "handle it within a few days."

The past had returned to haunt him, and the chill that had run down his spine still lingered. He knew there were no discrepancies, but he had immediately called for the accounts of Slater activity since the beginning of the year. He had been poring over them ever since.

Charles slipped a weary hand over his eyes. It was not going well. The figures were not balancing—due to his own agitation, he was certain—but he needed to be sure. He could not afford a problem now, not while the expenses incurred by Emily's illness were at their highest and while Mary was pressing him so relentlessly.

Charles dropped his hand back to his desk. It was getting late. He had promised Jewel he would talk to Honesty about Jeremy tonight. It was important that he did.

Charles glanced at his watch. Eleven o'clock. He had time to work the columns a little while longer.

The bark of gunfire on the street.

Wes's hand snaked toward his hip, barely touching the handle of his gun before the crowd separated to reveal a reeling drover standing in the middle of the street, waving his gun at the sky. The fellow jammed his smoking weapon back into his holster and staggered toward the next set of swinging doors.

But he never made it. To his credit, Marshal Carr and John Henry were a step ahead of him. Taking the protesting drover in tow, they headed toward the jail, making it a total of three locked up for the same offense that evening.

Wes turned at the sound of pounding hooves behind him, frowning at the pair of howling cowboys racing down the center of the street, oblivious to the danger to those in their path. This particular competition seemed to have become a nightly occurrence. With spectators cheering them on, the cowboys reined their horses to a breakneck finish in front of the Longhorn Saloon a short distance away. He watched their unsteady dismounts and their equally unsteady progress back into the bar.

Gunfire barked again, whirling Wes toward the sound as the grinning fellow responsible slipped into the crowd, unidentified and totally ignored by merrymakers roaming the street around him.

Wes withdrew his watch.

Eleven o'clock.

It was going to be a long night.

Jeremy moved nervously as gunshots echoed again on the street. Hidden in the shadows of the holding pens, he strained to see into the darkness at the entrance to town.

Where in hell were they?

Jeremy did not have to check the time to know it was getting late, that if Bitters didn't show up soon, the plan would start falling apart. It was a good plan. Howell would get them into the bank without any trouble, and each man would carry a separate portion of the money when they made their getaway.

That last had been a necessary insurance, since they would all separate to ride in different directions, with a plan to meet later. As for himself, Jeremy had decided simply to sneak back to his shack in the commotion. He would change out of the old clothes he had picked up as a disguise, putting them, the bandanna he used to mask his face, and his portion of the loot into a well he had dug under the floor. He would then slip back out into the street in the confusion that would prevail and become part of the curious crowd.

An unconscious smile touched Jeremy's lips. He expected that Honesty would be upset when they found Howell, but he would be there to console her. He would tell her that he would always be there for her, as he always had been. He would tell her to forget everything except the future they had always talked about, and he would eventually convince her that he was all the future she would ever need.

After that, he would gradually introduce the money into his life. And when that was done, Honesty's and his future would be secure.

Yes, it was a very good plan.

Jeremy glanced again toward the center of town, where bright lights blazed, where the street was even more crowded than usual with carousing drovers, reeling drunks, and painted ladies actively plying their trade.

Gunshots sounded, barking once, then twice more. The loud reports hardly raised the heads of passersby. This was not the first gunfire of the evening. The marshal had already marched three drunks off to jail, and he was sporting a black eye from one of them, which would keep him close to his office the rest of the night.

Things couldn't be better.

But where was Bitters?

"Lookin' for us?"

Jeremy started at the unexpected voice in the darkness behind him, turning as Bitters and two others became visible in the shadows.

Jeremy took an unsteady breath. "What in hell kept you?"

"We've got plenty of time. I wanted to make sure our horses would be real handy when we needed them. What's the problem?" Bitters raised his thick brows. "You ain't gettin' cold feet, are you?"

Jeremy stiffened. "Don't worry about me doin' my part."

"I ain't." Bitters did not smile. "Let's get goin'."

Jeremy led the way.

Fully recovered from her earlier physical discomfort, Honesty looked up from the cards in her hand to glance again at the clock on the saloon wall. It was after eleven, but the gaiety of the evening had already far exceeded its usual level. Cowboys were stacked three deep at the bar, and two deep behind every player at her table. There was money to be made tonight, a fact that normally raised her spirits, but her spirits were anything but high.

Honesty glanced behind her. Jewel had decided to add a monte table on the floor and was dealing herself in order to accommodate the unusual demand, but the sparkle that increased profits usually added to her eye was missing. Jewel's brightly painted face showed the effects of strain, which Honesty knew was due to the tension that had existed between them since their discussion that morning.

It startled her to realize that Jewel was deeply concerned. Somehow, as much as she knew Jewel's affection for her was true, she had always believed that Jewel was able to shut her out of her thoughts at will, and that she would not allow herself such discomfort. Jewel had said as much to her countless times—and Honesty had believed her.

As if seeing Jewel for the first time, Honesty realized she had been wrong.

Had she been wrong about Jeremy, too?

That thought almost more than she could bear, Honesty looked again toward the door. Where was Charles? She needed to talk to him before Wes returned. Charles would tell her the truth.

"Are you goin' to deal or not, Honesty?"

Honesty snapped her attention back to the table to find herself the focus of all eyes. She forced a teasing smile, responding automatically.

"I was daydreaming, fellas. Now, tell me, which one of you do you think I was daydreaming about?"

Old Harry Black winked. "Me, of course."

Joe Mitchell smiled. "Tell me it was me, darlin'."

Honesty's candid, flirting reply did not betray the continuing ache within as she replied, "Truth is, you fellas will never know."

"Webster's in his office!" Observing the bank from the shadows, Riggs looked at Jeremy, his voice accusing. "You said the office would be empty!"

"How was I supposed to know he'd pick tonight to work late?" Jeremy's jaw twitched. "He's usually at the Texas Jewel by ten every night!"

"We wasn't expectin' this! If things start goin' wrong because of you—"

"Shut up, Riggs!" Bitters' voice was a low snarl. "You don't know a good break when you see one! We was goin' to have to blow that safe, but we won't, now, 'cause Webster can open it for us."

Jeremy scowled. "What if he won't?"

"Did you ever see somebody say no when he's lookin' down the barrel of a gun?"

Jeremy did not reply.

"All right . . ." Bitters held the eye of each man in turn. "This is the way it's goin' to be. I'll take care of gettin' Howell to the bank. I ain't afraid to let him see my face on the street. He ain't goin' to be able to do nothin' with a gun pokin' in his ribs. Riggs and Gant will take care of the guard. Sills will wait in front until I show up with Howell—just in case. Once we're in, Riggs and Gant can follow. Webster won't be expectin' nothin' if he sees Howell first. The rest will be easy."

Jeremy nodded. His heart was pounding.

Bitters' glance was sly. "Enjoyin' yourself, boy?"

Anticipation growing, Jeremy watched as Bitters slipped off into the crowded street without waiting for his reply. At a word from Riggs, Jeremy turned toward the bank.

Gunshots . . . again.

Wes turned toward the sound, suddenly realizing that aside from the puff of gunpowder that hung temporarily on the night air, it was impossible to identify the exact location where the shots were fired. And nobody seemed to care. The crowd on the narrow boardwalk had thickened to such an extent that drovers bumped and shoved in order to make their way, with one person hardly discernable from another amidst the sea of faces extending unbroken from saloon to saloon.

Wes gave the street another cursory glance. He didn't like this. The situation was growing increasingly uncontrollable. Too many people . . . too many opportunities. He withdrew his watch from his pocket. It was almost twelve.

"Goin' someplace, Howell?"

Wes grunted as the barrel of a gun was jammed into his side. He recognized Tom Bitters' deadly rasp. He'd never forget it.

"No, don't turn around!" Bitters' tone deepened with malice as he slipped the gun from Wes's holster and jammed it into his own belt. "I bet you wasn't expectin' to hear my voice tonight. And you wasn't expectin' to feel my gun in your ribs, neither, but that was just the way I wanted it. You was goin' to take a stroll to the bank, like you do every night at twelve o'clock, wasn't you?" Bitters snickered. "That's right . . . I know your routine real well, and I figured I'd come into town to keep you company tonight." Bitters paused, his voice dropping to a new level of threat as he ordered, "So start walkin'!"

The hidden gun barrel prodded, forcing his step as Wes looked around him. Laughing faces, uninterested glances—no one aware of what was taking place as he stepped onto the street and started toward the bank. His mind was racing.

"Don't go gettin' any ideas, Howell." Bitters gave a low snort. "I wouldn't mind pullin' this trigger. If you don't care about your own hide, you might think about all them innocent fellas around you who could end up stoppin' a bullet because they got in the way. An upstandin' lawman like you wouldn't like that, would you?"

"You won't get away with this, Bitters."

"Yes, I will. As a matter of fact, things are lookin' better by the minute."

"Slater Enterprises won't stand for it. They went to great expense to protect these shipments."

"Yeah . . . and look what it got them."

"They won't spare any expense to find the man who got their money, either."

"I'm shakin' in my boots."

Wes's anger flushed hotly. "You won't live to spend a penny of that money!"

"Just like I didn't live to spend the money from that other bank job you was chasin' me for?"

Wes' stomach knotted tight. "Bastard . . ."

"Shut up!" Bitters cocked his gun. "No, I ain't goin' to shoot you—not yet. That's just a warnin'. We're gettin' close to the bank and we're goin' to walk up to that guard *smilin'*, just like we was old friends. If that guard gets suspicious 'cause you're not smilin', he won't live to find out if he was right or wrong—and neither will you." Bitters gave a short laugh. "Chances are nobody'll even turn around to see where the shots came from with all the carryin' on in the street tonight."

The gun in Wes's ribs poked harder. "Smile, Howell . . ."

Wes forced a smile.

Honesty glanced up at the clock on the saloon wall. It was almost twelve.

Honesty looked toward Jewel's table. Jewel was frowning, no doubt for the same reason as she. Charles still hadn't come. Was he still working? She needed to talk to him, to straighten everything out in her mind.

Honesty halted in mid-deal. She had lost count. She glanced at the men around the table, suddenly confused.

"Are you all right, Honesty?" Harry Black's hairy brows knit in a frown. "You're lookin' a little peaked, darlin'."

No, she wasn't all right.

Honesty stood up abruptly. "No, I'm not all right. Sorry, boys." Motioning Sykes to the table, Honesty handed over her cards.

Beside Jewel in a moment, Honesty stated flatly, "I'm going to see Charles."

Jewel's small eyes locked with hers the moment before Honesty turned toward the door.

Crouched in the shadows, Jeremy watched as Howell and Bitters approached. Elation flushed through his veins at the flash of metal jammed against Howell's back. Bitters had done it! He had shown Howell up to be nothin' but a reputation with no substance at all! He had known it all along, hadn't he? He had known Howell wasn't the man for Honesty. Now all he had to do was prove to Honesty that *he* was.

Jeremy's heart was hammering. Jamming his hat down on his forehead, he pulled his bandanna up over the lower half of his face. He turned at a rustle behind him to see that Riggs and Gant were approaching in the shadows, their bandannas drawn up to conceal their faces as well. They crouched behind him. The guard addressed Howell as he approached.

"Sure is a noisy night, ain't it, Mr. Howell? Everybody's havin' too much fun to suit me. I'm thinkin' maybe I'll join them just as soon as Leach can take my place here. Hell, it ain't no fun at all just watchin'."

When Howell did not respond, the fellow studied Bitters more closely. "Who's that with you, Mr. Howell?"

From his angle of view, the nudge that Bitters gave Howell with his gun was clearly visible. Howell grunted, "He's a friend."

Jeremy held his breath as Howell and Bitters stepped up onto the boardwalk. He saw Bitters move closer to the guard, his gun still jammed into Howell's side. He saw Bitters's lips moving. The guard glanced up at Howell, hesitating only a moment before lowering his shotgun to the chair behind him.

Jeremy snapped into motion, hardly aware of the men behind him as he leaped up into the shadows of the bank entrance and snatched up the shotgun, noting that Bitters pulled up his bandanna as he pushed the door open. Jeremy closed the door quietly behind them just as Riggs struck the guard on the back of the head with his gun. The fellow fell to the floor with a thud.

Charles Webster's voice rang out in the silence from behind his closed office door. "Who's there?"

Bitters nudged Howell again.

"It's me . . . Howell."

Gant slipped up to the closed door, concealing himself against the wall as it opened. Charles emerged. Jeremy heard his gasp as Gant pressed the barrel of his gun against him.

Webster's startled expression said it all.

Uncertain whether he was relieved or disappointed to discover Webster was not a party to the robbery, Wes saw the gunman push Webster toward the safe. Using the moments while Webster was the focus of attention, he studied the gunmen more closely. One fellow, the one with his gun on Webster, was of medium height, bony, stoop-shouldered. The second gunman, the one who had struck the guard with his gun, was shorter, heavier, with small eyes and wiry brows visible over the bandanna he wore. The third . . . Wes glanced back at the doorway where the last fellow stood guard. The dim lighting shadowed his masked face, but his carriage, the way he moved . . . He was obviously younger and making an effort to draw as little attention to himself as possible.

Bitters muttered instructions to his men, his voice muffled through the bandanna he had slipped up to conceal his face—an action that had been chillingly revealing. Bitters had made no attempt to hide his face until he entered the bank. The guard didn't know Bitters, so there was no problem there.

The conclusion was obvious. He was the only person who would be able to make a positive identification of Bitters, and Bitters did not intend to let him live to do it.

That thought registered sharply in Wes's mind as Bitters motioned Webster closer to the safe, speaking in a tone that conveyed clear threat despite its muffled quality.

"Open the safe!"

His expression unrevealing, Webster made no move to comply.

"Do it now! I ain't waitin' for you to make up your mind." Bitters' words were venomous. "I'd just as soon blow the safe as stand here waitin', but if I do, there ain't a one of you who'll get out alive."

Webster glanced at Wes, then moved toward the safe. He kneeled beside it. His hands trembled as he worked the combination. His expression tight, he made the final twist of the dial and stepped back from the door.

Bitters turned the handle and the safe snapped open. The gunmen moved toward it in a rush that was halted abruptly by Bitters' angry growl.

"Stay where you are, damn it! You'll all get your chance!" He turned, commanding, "Howell, get over here, by Webster." He pointed to the young fellow at the door who held the shotgun steadily trained on Webster. "You watch them both while we get started." He pointed to his other two men. "Start emptyin' the safe."

Wes glanced around him, realizing that time was growing short. He needed a chance . . . just a minute of distraction.

The younger gunman moved closer, and Wes turned toward him. The fellow dipped his head, keeping his eyes in the shadow of his hat's brim, but the hand that held the gun did not waver.

The hand was light-skinned and *freckled*. . . .

Wes snapped his gaze back up toward the fellow's face just as Bitters pushed the first two gunmen away from the safe. "That's enough. Watch over those two so we can pack up the rest."

Wes saw Charles glance at him out of the corner of his eye as both men turned their guns toward them. The look said that Webster was waiting for a chance to make a move as intently as he. He was waiting for Wes's signal.

Moving quickly, the younger gunman withdrew a sack from his jacket and kneeled beside the safe as he and Bitters removed the last of the cash. He stood when he was done. He glanced nervously at Bitters as Bitters turned his gun toward Wes.

Wes's blood grew hot. The young bastard knew what was coming. They all knew.

The sound of a step on the walk outside the door jerked everyone's eyes toward it the moment before a knock sounded.

"Charles, are you in there?"

Honesty!

The younger gunman dashed toward the door. Wes took a step in pursuit, only to hear Bitters hiss, "Stay where you are."

Honesty called again. "Charles, are you in there?"

The doorknob turned, and the door was pushed open. Standing in the doorway, Honesty went stock still.

Honesty gasped.

Men with bandannas over their faces were holding Wes and Charles at gunpoint!

The safe was standing open and empty!

Fear crawled up Honesty's spine. She took a spontaneous step toward Wes, only to have another masked fellow step into view behind her.

"Get her over here, beside these two!"

The voice of the gunman in command was muffled, but it sounded vaguely familiar. Honesty attempted to follow his instructions, only to have the fellow behind her grasp her arm, staying her.

"Let her go. I want her over here!"

The gunman did not release her. Honesty glanced between the two as the leader growled, "Get her over by these two, damn it! You're wastin' time!"

The grip on Honesty's arm tightened to the point of pain. Honesty struggled to escape it. She was still struggling when a startling sense of familiarity brought her to an abrupt halt. She looked at the hand holding her captive. She looked up.

Old, oversized clothes.

A worn hat and bandanna.

But the eyes . . .

No . . .

"Jeremy?"

Honesty's whisper snapped Jeremy's eyes to hers. Startled by the look there, she caught her breath just as the leader commanded again, "Get her over there, I said!"

Tearing her arm from Jeremy's grasp, Honesty ran to Wes's side. She leaned against him, only to be startled when Wes pushed her away.

"Stay away from me."

She moved back toward him, and Wes snapped, "Stay away!"

"Why?"

"Just do it!"

Suddenly at her side, Jeremy grasped her arm and attempted to pull her back. She fought his grip, turning suddenly toward him. "What's happening? Tell me, Jeremy!"

The leader of the gang laughed. "So, she recognized you!" He pulled down his bandanna and Honesty gasped at the sight of Bitters' vicious smile as he continued, "That's too bad. But first things first."

Bitters turned his gun abruptly toward Wes and fired. Wes dropped to the floor and Honesty screamed. Her rush toward him was halted as gunshots again sounded and the door burst open with a crash of splintering wood. Thrust suddenly from her feet by the weight of Charles's body, Honesty looked up to see Jeremy swing his shotgun toward the men in the doorway. She called out in horror as his finger clenched on the trigger—the moment before Jeremy's body jerked suddenly upright with the force of the bullet that struck him. His shot fired wildly into the air as he pitched to the floor. The room exploded into action as Honesty's head snapped in the direction of the shot that had felled Jeremy to see Wes crouched with a smoking derringer in hand.

Shouted commands!

Gunshots ricocheting!

Shuffling feet!

Thudding fists!

Grunts of pain!

Silence.

Sullen gray clouds blocked out the sun as the funeral procession moved slowly toward the hillside. The wind whipped in sudden assault, raising a cloud of dust from the road to abrade the mourners as they walked behind the wagon bedecked in black.

Honesty brushed back the strands of hair that lashed her face, as unconscious of nature's abuse as she was of those walking beside her. Inescapable images paraded before her mind.

Gunfire, rapid and deafening. Then silence.

She remembered that she was dazed but aware, as Charles raised her to her feet, that he had shielded her against the ricocheting gunfire with his body, protecting her life at the risk of his own.

She recalled the activity around her vaguely—Wes standing with the derringer still in his hand, Marshal Carr assuming control, Sam calling for a doctor—but all faded from her consciousness as she dropped to her knees beside Jeremy and heard his labored breaths.

Strangely, some things remained so vividly clear—the glint of Jeremy's gold hair in the dim light, freckles that had seemed to darken against the ashen pallor of his skin, his struggle to breathe as blood pumped from the ragged hole in his chest with every beat of his heart.

His hand was cold when she took it in hers. She remembered that Jeremy's gaze had been clear, despite his physical distress, and that she had seen torment mixed with pain in his eyes as he struggled to speak. She had not been conscious of her tears until she heard his ragged whisper.

"D . . . don't cry, Honesty. I never wanted to make you sad."

"Jeremy . . ."

"Don't be mad at me . . . please. I'm sorry."

She had collapsed upon him then, hugging him close, her cheek pressed tightly to his. She had known that she would never love anyone the way she loved Jeremy, and she had whispered those words into his ear, begging him not to leave her. But he had gone still beneath her and breathed no more.

She recalled that it was Wes who drew her to her feet from beside Jeremy's still form, appealing to her as she shrank back from him. He had continued speaking, his deep voice earnest, but she had not listened, knowing there were no words that could wash Jeremy's blood from his hands.

She had glanced around her then, seeing Bitters lying dead, with Riggs a few feet away and Gant in the marshal's custody. She had realized belatedly that it was the marshal, his deputy, and Sam who had burst through the doors at that crucial moment, turning the tide of the robbery.

The wind gusted more strongly, knocking Honesty back a step as a strong arm slipped around her. She looked up at Charles, seeing Jewel walking somberly beside him. She remembered that Jewel had been shaken when she arrived at the bank shortly after the attempted robbery. Her skin pale under her bright face paint, Jewel had hugged her with trembling arms, forever dismissing the distance between them with that open display of love. And Jewel's tears had flowed as freely as her own as Jeremy was carried away.

The wagon drew to a halt beside the gaping hole in the ground that awaited the silent entourage. Honesty watched as Jeremy's simple wooden coffin was lowered into it. The preacher's words rumbled unintelligibly across her mind as she heard instead the echo of a gay exchange so sweet that she ached with the joy of it.

You'll do anythin' for me, Honesty.

True.

Just like I'll do anythin' for you.

Right.

Because you love me.

I do.

The first shovel of dirt that fell on the coffin rebounded strangely in Honesty's ears. The second and the third were the drumbeats to which the mourners turned and started back down the hill. The sound of the scraping spade reverberated as she walked past the spot where Wes stood silently apart from the sober group—as she walked on as if she had not seen him at all.

Chapter Nine

The leaden gray of the sky hung in a visible pall over the mourners as their wagon returned to town. Watching as the solemn group alighted at the livery stable, Wes dismounted as well. He kept pace with them, walking on the opposite side of the street, keenly aware that the distance between Honesty and him stretched far wider than that short expanse.

Suffering his impotence against Honesty's grief, Wes watched as Sam slid his bony arm around Honesty's shoulders. The old man's eyes were reddened from tears he had not been able to withhold, honest tears he knew were shed as much for the young woman he held in the curve of his arm as for the young man they had buried that morning. Jewel walked behind them with Charles Webster. Solicitous of both women, Webster had handled all the arrangements for Jeremy's funeral, stirring Wes's gratitude despite his remaining hostile feelings.

Wes looked back at Honesty, the deadening ache within expanding to the point of pain. He wanted so much to hold her, to console her for the tears she had shed. He wanted to tell her that he felt no remorse at all for the first bullet he had fired from the derringer concealed in his boot, the one that had brought Bitters down, but that he knew he would always regret the second. He had gone over that moment a thousand times in his mind—the split second between when he had seen Jeremy raise his gun toward the men in the doorway and when he realized that Jeremy was going to fire. He had searched for the vaguest indication that he had been wrong, that his actions had been influenced by his negative feelings for Jeremy, but the conclusion was always the same. He had had no choice.

But Honesty didn't care about motivation. She cared only that Jeremy was dead, and that his bullet was responsible.

Tormenting Wes even more deeply was his realization that the anguish he would deal Honesty wasn't yet over.

His gaze narrowing, Wes halted as Honesty reached the entrance of the Texas Jewel. He watched as she conversed with Sam in low tones. He saw her kiss Sam's cheek. He saw that Webster was watching Honesty, too, and that he had taken Jewel's hand.

A wagon that rattled to a halt beside the solemn group momentarily obstructed Wes's view. Annoyed, he glanced at the driver.

The driver was a woman.

Incredulity struck Wes momentarily motionless at the realization of who she was.

Unable to take his eyes from the woman's face as

the full significance of the moment suddenly loomed, Wes prepared himself for what was about to unfold.

His heart heavy, Charles watched as Sam and Honesty conversed. Her eyes were red, her face puffy from tears shed, but she was all the more beautiful in her sorrow as she spoke softly to Sam, struggling for words. Sam was similarly affected, and the lump in Charles's throat thickened. He clenched Jewel's hand tighter. He was grateful beyond measure that Jewel allowed his consolation and his friendship. He had needed it as much as she through the ordeal recently past.

The rattle of a wagon drawing up alongside the walk interrupted Charles's thoughts. He turned instinctively toward the sound, his blood going cold at first sight of the woman driving.

Charles glanced across the street to see Wes Howell observing the scene. He saw the tight lock of Howell's jaw and the deadly chill in his eyes, and he knew it was over. He turned back to Jewel, realizing that the moment had not escaped her. He released her hand.

Charles stepped down into the street and approached the woman and two children seated in the wagon. Solemnly, he accepted the inevitable finale of years of torment with two, simple words.

"Hello, Mary."

Charles heard Wes's heavy strides approaching. He turned as they stopped beside him. His shoulders were squared, ready when Wes spoke in a low voice devoid of emotion.

"You're under citizen's arrest, Webster, for complicity in the robbery of the Citizens First Bank of Texas, and in the murders of Joshua Martin, Isabel

Farr, and Captain William Bennett Howell of the Texas Rangers."

Charles heard Jewel's soft protest.

He heard Honesty gasp.

And he saw Honesty's gaze lock with Wes's the moment before she slid limply to the ground.

Honesty opened her eyes slowly. She was in her satin-draped bedroom, and Doc Carter was leaning over her. His lean face was drawn into familiar lines of concern.

"This kind of excitement isn't good for you, you know. It takes considerable time to heal after the kind of head injury you had. You're lucky Mr. Howell caught you before you hit your head again."

Doc Carter picked up a glass from the bedside table. "I want you to take this powder right now."

"No."

"Honesty . . ."

"I want to see Charles." Honesty raised a hand to her spinning head. She was confused. Wes could not have said—

Honesty took a gulping breath and repeated, "I want to see Charles."

When the doctor did not react, Honesty threw back the coverlet in an attempt to stand.

"All right." Doc Carter drew the coverlet back over her. "He's outside . . . with the others."

"The others?"

"With Jewel, Sam . . . and Wes Howell."

"I want to see Charles."

Doc Carter walked to the door and called Charles's name. She heard Charles respond, "I'd like all of us to come in. It'll be easier that way."

Honesty held her breath.

* * *

Charles followed Doc Carter into Honesty's room, deep sadness overwhelming him. The daughter he would never have, as sweet to him as any child of his own could ever be . . .

Charles crouched beside Honesty and took her hand. His handsome face was earnest as he said, "I'm so sorry, Honesty. I never considered how you might be affected when this day came." He paused. "I suppose that was the flaw in my thinking, my inability to look past the present to consider the repercussions of my actions."

Honesty glanced past Charles to see Wes watching. She whispered to Charles, "What are you saying?" Her glorious eyes implored him. "You couldn't have done those things Wes accused you of!"

"Honesty, dear . . . let me try to explain." Charles's gaze grew pained. "You know the story of my past . . . my wealthy beginnings back East, the family scandal that drove me West, my wife's illness. What you don't know was that I was destitute and just short of panic when I finally found a banking position in Texas. I was certain all would go well from that point on, but it didn't. A year passed, then six months more, and the doctors told me that Emily was failing. They said she'd die within the year if she wasn't removed to an environment more advantageous to her condition. They said there was only one hospital—back East—that might be able to help her. I was desperate to get the money to take her there. I had known Emily since childhood, and I loved her. I couldn't let her die."

Emotion almost overwhelming him, Charles paused to regain control. He continued hoarsely, "I recognized a known bank robber on the street from a wanted poster I had seen. His name was Pete Barton. I was so desperate that I was grasping at straws.

I convinced myself it was an omen that I had recognized him when no one else did. I took a chance and approached him with a plan. It didn't seem so wrong at the time. I didn't think anyone would get hurt. The plan was simple enough. He would rob the bank I managed during the night when no one was there. I would set everything up for him, take my portion of the proceeds out in advance, and leave the vault open before I left at night, with the provision that he would make it look as if it had been broken into to cover up my participation in the robbery. Barton agreed, but nothing went as planned. I didn't take into account the fact that Barton was a killer, that he wouldn't hesitate to use his gun. When it was all over, two innocent bystanders lay dead."

Charles felt Howell's gaze burning him as he continued more softly, "Captain Howell and his partner were sent to investigate. They made short work of running down the first few members of the gang, but the case lingered on. In the meantime, I used the money I had stolen to take Emily back East to the hospital. I eventually put her into a sanitarium there. The sum quickly dwindled, and when I couldn't find a position back East that would support the continuing expenses of Emily's care, I was forced to return to Texas. But I felt it was too dangerous to remain. I found my present position here in Caldwell shortly afterward. Then I learned that Barton had ambushed Captain Howell and shot him in the back. What Barton didn't anticipate was that Howell's son would pursue his father's murderer to the end."

Charles continued, "I thought I was safely out of it after Barton was tracked down and killed . . . until Mary Barton made her first contact. I hadn't taken into account that her husband had told her about my part in the robbery. She said she didn't want much, that she'd keep quiet about what she knew if I supplied her with enough money to support herself and her children." Charles sighed. "With Emily's bills mounting, and with the realization that the sanitarium was her only hope, I had no choice but to comply."

A smile flicked briefly across Charles's even features. "I was at an all-time low in my life when I met Jewel and you for the first time. My life became tolerable because of you and Jewel. Seven years passed, and I actually convinced myself all would turn out well in the end."

Charles continued more softly, "It wasn't my intention to deceive either you or Jewel, but I couldn't tell you the truth for fear of involving you . . . and because I was ashamed. I realized it was all coming to an end the day Wes Howell walked into my office, yet I still hoped . . ."

Charles sighed. "I had no idea Howell had discovered that Barton had had help with the robbery. Nor did I know he'd found out by happenstance, years after the robbery, that Barton was married, and that his wife had an unknown means of support. As for the rest . . ."

Charles's voice dropped a note lower. "I'm not the person you thought I was, Honesty." He paused as his voice broke, and then added hoarsely, "But I wish with all my heart that I was."

Tears flowed freely from Honesty's eyes, and Charles brushed them away with his palm, realizing that she was beyond verbal response. He kissed her damp cheek and stood up, unable to bear her distress any longer. He walked out into the hallway with Jewel beside him. As Sam continued toward the staircase with an expression of abject sadness, Charles realized that Wes had remained behind in

Honesty's room. But that thought was swept from his mind as Jewel turned to face him. The sorrow in her eyes matched his own as she rasped, "Why didn't you tell me?"

"How could I involve you in such a sordid affair? Bank robbery, two deaths, and then a deliberate murder! I was ashamed of my part in it." Charles took a steadying breath, "I knew if you discovered what I had done, you—"

Sliding her hand over his lips to halt his words, Jewel whispered, "Do you love me, Charles?"

Charles's response came from the bottom of his heart. "I've loved you from the first day I saw you."

Pressing her womanly warmth against him, Jewel whispered, "That's all that really matters."

Jewel slid her arms around his neck and Charles clutched her close. He felt her love and knew he had never loved her more.

Honesty leaned against Doc Carter's supporting arm and drank steadily until the glass was empty. The gritty residue of the powder remained on her tongue as she closed her eyes and leaned back against the pillow.

Jeremy was gone. She would never again see his smile . . . hear his laughter . . . feel his love. And now Charles.

Wes . . .

She had believed him when he said he loved her.

But he had taken away those she loved.

Sleep.

Escape from torment.

Oblivion.

Honesty's breathing became slow and rhythmic. Doc Carter gripped Wes's arm, staying him as he moved out of the corner of the room where he had concealed himself from Honesty's view.

"You shouldn't be here."

Silence.

"She doesn't want you here."

Wes returned Doc Carter's scrutinizing stare. How could he explain that he needed to be near Honesty while he attempted to sort out the feelings running riot within him—while he tried to understand why the successful conclusion of a search to which he had dedicated seven long years of his life had fallen so flat.

He responded, "I'll only stay a little while."

"All right, but don't wake her."

The door closed behind the bearded doctor as Wes crouched beside Honesty's bed and took her hand.

Honesty woke abruptly to the semi-darkness of her room. She looked at the window, seeing the gray glare of afternoon against her drawn window shade.

Reality returned with painful suddenness.

Her room suddenly felt stifling. Honesty threw back her coverlet and drew herself to her feet. Ignoring her momentary dizziness, she stripped away her somber dark dress with distaste. Jeremy would have disliked it. He had loved bright colors, just as he had loved life.

That thought twisting the knife of pain within her, Honesty succumbed to impulse and reached to the back of her wardrobe for her riding gear.

Jeremy's cast-off clothes . . .

Bittersweet recollection turned to ire. She wanted no more tears and sadness! She wanted no more solemn faces and gentle voices! She wanted to fight back! She wanted to go somewhere—do something—anything that would overcome the feeling of helplessness that compounded her grief.

Moving quickly down the back staircase, Honesty emerged into the alleyway and started toward the rear of the livery stable. The damp breeze buffeted her as she mounted her horse minutes later and rode out of town.

Caldwell was far behind her. Ahead were gray clouds, a moist breeze, an endless wilderness devoid of human habitation.

Mindless fury suddenly overwhelmed her, and Honesty dug her heels into her mount's sides. She gripped her reins tightly, leaning low over the saddle as her mare spurted forward with a sudden thrust. Abandoning herself to the heavy air that battered her, to the land passing in a blurred rush, to moments forced free of thought as her horse pounded across the terrain, Honesty allowed the animal full rein. She rode faster, harder, uncaring as Ginger stumbled, barely managing to right herself before plunging on.

Caught up in her frenzied chase, Honesty momentarily ignored the hoofbeats thundering behind her. Driving on, she knew only the need to escape, to retain the solitude that freed her mind from its torment. She turned with bitterness toward the horseman who gradually drew up alongside, to the big man who reached for her reins, his dark eyes hot with an anger that matched her own as he attempted to wrest them from her grasp.

"Let go!" Honesty shouted in protest. "Leave me alone!"

Ripping the reins from her hands, Wes pulled them back, drawing her mount to a shuddering halt as he turned to her with fierce intensity.

"What were you tryin' to do?"

Honesty's fury turned savage. "What makes you think you have the right to ask me questions? You're nothing to me!"

"That's not true."

"No, it isn't, is it?" Rigid, Honesty spat, "You're the man who came to Caldwell on false pretenses. You're the man who insinuated himself into my life, using me as I *allowed* myself to be used. You're the man who killed Jeremy, the same man who is punishing Charles for trying to save someone he loves!"

"Tryin' to save someone at the expense of the lives of others—you're forgettin' that!"

"Charles didn't think—"

"Charles didn't *care*."

"It's so easy for you to judge, isn't it?" Honesty's gaze bore hotly into his. "Charles was losing his wife—the woman he loved. He was powerless to help her. He knew money could save her life, money that was within his daily reach. He loved her too much to let her die! What would *you* have done?"

Wes did not reply, and Honesty grabbed for her horse's reins. Enraged when Wes refused to surrender them, she snapped, "All right, the horse is yours!"

Dismounting, Honesty turned back in the direction from which she had come. She was walking with long, rapid strides when she heard Wes's heavy steps behind her. His face was stiff with anger as he turned her roughly toward him.

"You asked me what I would've done if I had been Charles, but you didn't wait for my answer."

"I know what your answer is!"

"No, you don't, damn it!" Wes' gaze pinned her. "You don't know because I don't know what I would've done." Wes paused, his hard features taut. "If you had asked me that same question two months ago, the answer would've been easy. I would've told you that nothin' could ever force me into doin' what Charles did . . . but now I'm not so sure, because now I know what he felt at the thought of losin' the woman he loved. He was dyin' a little more with each passin' minute, sufferin' more than she was because he was unable to change things. I know because I feel that same way at the thought of losin' you."

Honesty steeled herself against the dark eyes that seared her, allowing only bitterness as she spat, "Words—with nothing behind them. Your only love is the law!"

"Honesty . . ."

"You used me! I told you about my fears for Jeremy. I told you about Bitters, and you used my confidences against Jeremy!"

"Bitters was a murderer with a long record behind him in Texas! He had killed before, and he was willin' to kill again! You saw that for yourself!"

"Jeremy was desperate. I didn't know how desperate. If I did—" Honesty took a breath against the pain slicing within.

"You can't blame yourself. Lovin' someone doesn't mean you can control their lives."

"I should've—"

"No, there was nothin' you could do . . . nothin' either one of us could do."

Honesty shook her head, refusing to listen. "Jeremy's dead! You killed him . . . and I helped you."

Filled with anguish, Honesty attempted to jerk herself free of Wes's grip as he grated, "Stop this, Honesty! You know you can't walk back to town."

"Can't I?"

"No. I won't let you!"

"You can't stop me!"

"Yes, I can."

Wes's dark eyes bore hotly down into hers the moment before his anger visibly drained and he whispered simply, "Honesty . . . I don't want it to be this way between us."

Honesty fought the sudden surge of tears that Wes's unexpected gentleness evoked.

"Don't cry, darlin'. I never wanted to make you sad."

The blood drained from Honesty's face. "Don't you dare say that! Those are Jeremy's words—the last words he spoke to me! I won't let you demean them!"

"Jeremy's words?" Wes shook his head. "Maybe they are, but they're mine, too, because they're the words of a man who loves you."

"Don't you dare speak of love!"

"Why?" Wes's expression hardened. "Look at me, Honesty. Do you really believe I wanted to kill Jeremy? Think back and remember what happened. Bitters turned his gun on me, and I knew he was goin' to shoot. I dropped to the floor just in time to avoid his bullet and fire one of my own. You know what happened then. The door burst open and Jeremy swung his gun toward it. He was goin' to fire."

"No, he wasn't! He wouldn't do that!"

"Honesty, listen to me. Do you think I enjoy seein' you lookin' at me the way you are now? Don't you think I've gone over those few seconds again and again in my mind? But the truth is that I didn't fire the shot that killed Jeremy. *Jeremy* did . . . because he left me no choice!"

"No!"

"Honesty . . ." Wes drew her closer. His voice was broken with emotion, "I'm sorry, darlin'. I'm so sorry. If there was any way I could've changed things so they'd turn out right for you, I would have."

Honesty took a shuddering breath. "You came to Caldwell with a lie!"

"I came to Caldwell because I needed proof that Charles Webster was involved in the robbery that cost my father his life."

"I trusted you! I hid nothing from you, not my past, not my hopes for the future. And all the while you hid secrets that you knew could change my life forever!"

"I had no choice."

"The same excuse! The truth is that you knew what Jeremy and Charles were to me, but it meant nothing to you at all!"

"I didn't plan it the way it turned out. I tried to stay away from you." Wes's jaw hardened. "Do you remember what you said to me that first night? You said that once a man gets a taste of you, he doesn't want to let you go. You were right, Honesty. I saw the complications that were in store. I tried to tell myself I didn't want you, but it didn't work. I couldn't do it then, and I can't do it now."

"No."

"I love you, Honesty."

"You don't love me! You don't know what it means to love!"

Wes's fingers cut into her shoulders. "I know what it means to love . . . because you taught me. Let me prove it to you, darlin'."

Honesty shook her head. There were no words . . . nothing that could heal the ragged wounds within.

Wes continued hoarsely, "I sat by your bed this mornin' when you were sleepin', wonderin' how and why this whole thing had come about . . . wonderin' why we should have met like we did only to have everythin' go wrong. There was only one answer. You were meant to be mine, darlin'. Somehow, somewhere, that truth was set in stone long before we met, and nothin' that happened along the way had the power to change it."

Honesty's heart was sore. No matter how sincere, his words of love were all too late! Jeremy was dead, and the deceits could not be wiped away.

As if in tune with her thoughts, Wes whispered, "Jeremy loved you. He wanted to make you happy. I want to make you happy, too, darlin'. I want to love you and take care of you. I want to help you leave all the sadness behind." Wes stroked the locket at her throat. She felt the warmth of his callused fingertips as he rasped, "I want to make the good things come true . . . for both of us. Let me do that, darlin'."

Honesty searched Wes's impassioned expression. The love in his eyes was plainly visible, but it left her aching.

Jeremy had asked for forgiveness. Her forgiveness had always been his, because she loved him. Why hadn't he known?

Wes had said they were meant to be together, but so much had happened to put distance between them. Had that distance stretched a step too far?

The wind gusted, whipping loosened strands of Honesty's hair against her face as the first oversized drops of rain struck the ground around them. Wes stroked back the strands as the soft, pattering sounds increased, resting his palm against the flying wisps as he whispered, "Hair as black as the devil's heart . . ."

Honesty closed her eyes at the bittersweet joy of the familiar words. She heard in them the echo of another voice from long ago. That voice had been filled with love . . . the same love that now sounded so clearly in Wes's rasping tones.

Oh, yes . . . love.

Honesty opened her eyes again as the rain fell in earnest. She saw in the heavy drops tears of forgiveness that washed away the anguish of the past . . . tears that purged the bitterness as they soaked her skin, setting her free.

A shaft of sunlight glittered briefly through the rain.

Jeremy's smile.

Honesty's heart filled to bursting.

She felt the strength of Wes's emotion as his powerful arms enclosed her. She offered him her lips. She surrendered her heart. She slid her arms around his neck, completing the circle of love as the past and the future melded into one.

Epilogue

"Mr. Charles Webster
Caldwell Bank,
Caldwell, Kansas
Dear Mr. Webster,

By now you have received the telegram informing you that Emily Webster, your dear wife, has passed on. I was privileged to pen Emily's last letter to you and to be at her side during her final hours. We were friends, and she spoke of you so often and with such love that I felt I must write.

I knew you would want to know that Emily's last days were peaceful. They were filled with her love for you and her compassion for all you suffered in loving her. With her final words, she asked me to tell you that should the Almighty accept her into the heavenly kingdom, she would implore Him to smooth your way on earth and grant you the joy that your love provided her all her life. She asked that you not grieve, but celebrate that He has called her home at last.

Most of all, I wanted to thank you for giving me the opportunity to know dear Emily. My life has been greatly enriched because of her. I will be forever grateful.

Your friend,
C. Lawrence."

The young woman blotted the letter, then folded it carefully and slipped it into the envelope. She reached for her handkerchief and wiped away a tear. She was nineteen years old and now totally alone. The spinster sisters who had raised her with rigid but loving care had died within months of each other. They had always been so close, she supposed she shouldn't have expected anything else.

Aunt Penelope, the older of the sisters, had encouraged her to accept the proposal of the local minister who had recently left for missionary work in Africa.

Aunt Harriet, who was more progressive, had urged her to retain her independence and volunteer her services to the Bowery poor.

But she had cherished another dream.

Emily had shared it. Emily had advised her to contact Mr. Webster when she decided to go West and pursue her dream. She had insisted that all she would have to do was tell Mr. Webster her name and he would do everything in his power to help her.

C. Lawrence raised her hand to the locket at her throat. It was a very special locket.

C. Lawrence smoothed a wisp of hair back into its

tight bun. The strand was a vibrant red.
C. Lawrence stood up abruptly, her decision made.

"Damn that maverick!"
Tall, whip-cord slim, and dressed in drover's gear, Boots Corrigan drew her mount up sharply, ignoring its snort of protest as she scanned the brush for a sign of the longhorn that had again eluded her. She cursed under her breath. She had been chasing the oversized brute for longer than she cared to admit as it zigzagged across the sun-swept landscape. Crafty and belligerent, it had run her a merry chase until she was now separated from the main portion of the herd and left to wallow in the trailing cloud of red dust that presently hid the animal from view.
There it was!
Her teeth clamped tight with determination, Boots dug her heels into her mount's sides, her blood rushing as the steer spotted her and resumed its race across the wild terrain. Spurring her horse to life-threatening speed, Boots leaned low over the saddle, a sense of victory surging as she gained steadily on the obstinate beast.
Finally within range, Boots swung her rope over her head and threw the loop.
Missed again!
Still riding hard and cursing her luck, Boots gasped as a rope looped unexpectedly around her own shoulders. She was too late to avoid the sudden tightening of the coil that jerked her from her saddle to hit the ground with a stunning crack! She was still disoriented when a buckskin-clad male form fell suddenly upon her, knocking the breath from her lungs. She looked up to gasp a single word.
"Kiowa!"
With a knife pressed tight to her throat, Boots was

unable to move. She felt the tightly muscled length of the savage tense the moment before he ripped her hat from her head, spilling out the pale mass of unbound hair beneath. She gasped again as he twisted his hand tight in her hair and grunted, "A woman!"

But the voice held none of the guttural tones of the Kiowa. Instead, it sounded almost—

On his feet in a flash of movement, the Indian dragged her upright, grasping her by the shirtfront to hold her fast as he pressed the knife to her stomach and hissed, "Tell me what you did with him!"

Boots stared into the face of her attacker. Sun-reddened skin . . . sharply chiseled features . . . black, shoulder-length hair secured by a headband . . . but *green* eyes . . .

"Tell me!"

"I . . . I don't know what you're talkin' about!"

The tip of the knife pierced Boots' shirt. She felt her blood trickling. She heard the grated warning.

"I'll ask you one more time . . ."

She heard the shot! She saw the Indian's body jerk with the impact of the bullet that struck him. And she saw the look in his eyes, a promise that sent shudders down her spine as he fell to the ground at her feet.

And she knew she would never forget the chilling warning he rasped the second before his eyes closed: "I will remember. . . ."

The golden sunlight of late afternoon shone against the drawn shade of the small hotel room, casting its glowing warmth over the narrow bed and the couple lying lovingly entwined on it. Wes's lips trailed the warm curve of Honesty's breast, and her lips separated with a sigh. Flesh to flesh, heart to heart, they had spent long hours in lovemaking that grew deeper and more profound with each passing day. They were making their way back to San Antonio, their progress slowed by a hunger not easily satiated when two hearts beat as one.

They had exchanged their vows a week earlier. Wes would have it no other way.

Freshly bathed and shaven, Sam had stood proudly as best man. She had never loved that old man more than when he had hugged her with quaking arms and then looked up at Wes, his beady eyes intent as he congratulated and cautioned him in the same breath, telling Wes what he might expect from an angry old rattlesnake if he did not treat Honesty the way he should.

Her emotions under tight control, Jewel had stood supportively beside her through the ceremony as she had for so many years. And if they had disagreed on the gown Honesty had chosen to wear, on the way she had arranged her hair, and on a hundred other details that were of no consequence at all, and if she was still convinced that Jewel was the bossiest woman she had ever known, Honesty had finally accepted the fact that everything Jewel said and did—no matter how annoying—was motivated by love.

Dignified and handsome as only he could be, Charles had stood proudly at Jewel's side.

Yes, *Charles*.

Honesty knew she would never forget the moment when Wes announced with a solemnity bespeaking the depth of his soul-searching that he had decided the evidence linking Charles to the bank robbery years earlier was too weak, and the interval of time between was too long to warrant taking him back to Texas. But Honesty knew otherwise. And she knew she would never need greater proof of his love.

There were no secrets between Wes and her now.

Wes had told her about the young woman he had seen sometime earlier, the trail boss who rode and roped better than any man he had ever seen—the *blond* young woman who wore a locket similar to hers. They were determined to find her . . . together.

Wes shifted, raising himself on his elbow to look soberly down into her face. Black eyes formerly as hard as onyx were now a dark, loving velvet. Strong features, formerly harshly composed, were softened with a love reserved for her alone as he spoke.

"Honesty Howell . . . that's a right nice name."

Honesty raised her slender brows. "Honesty *Buchanan* Howell . . ."

Dipping his head to trace the line of her jaw with his lips, Wes whispered, "Tell me you love me, Honesty."

The words came easily. "I love you."

His gaze flickered as he touched his mouth to hers. "Tell me you need me, darlin'."

Those words were easy as well. "I need you."

Appearing momentarily uncomfortable, Wes whispered against her lips, "When we first met, I never thought I'd see the day I'd think your name suits you, darlin', but the truth is that you taught me some things about honesty that I never considered before. So, there's somethin' I have to say."

He continued with soft determination, his gaze linked with hers, "I don't know how all this is goin' to come out—this searchin' for your sisters. Everythin' I told you about the young woman I saw that day aside, I don't know that I've got the confidence you have that we'll ever find them. But I'm promisin' you this. We won't stop searchin' until *you're* ready to stop searchin'. The reason is simple. You've fulfilled my dreams, darlin'—every last one of them—just by lyin' here now in my arms, and there's nothin' or no one who will ever stop me from tryin' to fulfill yours."

"Wes . . ."

"I love you, darlin'."

She knew that.

"I'll never stop lovin' you."

She knew that, too.

Honesty wanted to tell Wes that the promise had not been necessary, that she was now certain their meeting was somehow bound as much by the past as by the future. She wanted to say that she was more sure now than ever before that she would find her sisters again—sometime, somewhere.

And those beliefs aside, she wanted to tell him that she was never happier than when she was lying in his arms.

But her thoughts were broken by Wes's caress.

Her words were swallowed by Wes's kiss.

And then there was time only for each other.

Brokenhearted and bitter, Shadoe Sinclair vows that he will never return to Oregon, never look back on the past that has destroyed his hopes and dreams, and never think about Lilly McFall, the woman he truly loves. Loving Lilly means facing the truth, and Shadoe fears the truth will destroy her.

When Shadoe returns home to bury his father, Lilly knows she should ignore the handsome rogue who hurt her once before. But while his secrets are dark and dangerous, in his arms she finds an ecstasy like none she has ever imagined. Their passion is a temptation Lilly cannot deny, and this time around she is determined to do whatever it takes to satisfy their forbidden desire.

_51906-2 $4.99 US/$5.99 CAN

"Patricia Gaffney is one of the finest writers to come along in recent years!"

—Romantic Times

She arrives at Darkstone Manor without friends or fortune, welcomed only by the hiss of the sea in the midnight hush. Lily Trehearne was born a lady, but now she has resigned herself to a life of backbreaking drudgery, inescapable poverty...and unquestioning obedience to the lord of the manor.

Tormented and brooding, Devon Darkwell threatens Lily's safety almost as much as he thrills her senses. From the moment he catches her swimming nude in the moonlight, his compelling masculinity holds her spellbound. But each step he takes toward claiming her body brings him closer to learning the terrible secrets of her soul. In his arms she will know tempestuous passion, bitter despair, and a soaring joy that will humble them both before the power of love.

_3946-X $5.99 US/$7.99 CAN

Dorchester Publishing Co., Inc.
65 Commerce Road
Stamford, CT 06902

Please add $1.75 for shipping and handling for the first book and $.50 for each book thereafter. NY, NYC, PA and CT residents, please add appropriate sales tax. No cash, stamps, or C.O.D.s. All orders shipped within 6 weeks via postal service book rate. Canadian orders require $2.00 extra postage and must be paid in U.S. dollars through a U.S. banking facility.

Name ____

Address ____

City ____________________________ State ______ Zip ______

I have enclosed $______ in payment for the checked book(s).

Payment must accompany all orders. ☐ Please send a free catalog.